W9-COW-394

Her mind wouldn't let go of the memory of that moment before Christmas when she'd fallen in love . . . or lust . . . or whatever this hideous inconvenience was . . . with Cato, Marquis of Granville.

She'd watched him ride into the yard on his bay charger—something she'd seen many times. He was bareheaded and Phoebe had noticed how in the sunlight his dark brown hair had a flicker of gold running through it. He'd moved a gauntleted hand in a gesture, and Phoebe's heart had seemed to turn over. This kind of thing happened in poetry all the time. But, poet though she was, Phoebe was rarely plagued by an excess of sentiment and she had never imagined that verse was a veritable expression of reality.

And yet she'd sat in the apple loft, her quill dripping ink on her precious vellum, her apple halfway to her mouth, while the entire surface of her skin had grown hotter and hotter.

He'd dismounted and she'd gazed, transfixed, at the power behind his agile movements. She'd gazed at his profile, noticing for the first time the slight bump at the bridge of his nose, the square jut of his chin, the fine, straight line of his mouth. It should have been a moment of angelic lunacy.

But it hadn't gone away. . . .

JANE FEATHER

The ACCIDENTAL BRIDE

BANTAM BOOKS

New York   Toronto   London   Sydney   Auckland

THE ACCIDENTAL BRIDE
A Bantam Book / July 1999

All rights reserved.
Copyright © 1999 by Jane Feather.
Cover art copyright © 1999 by Alan Ayers.

No part of this book may be reproduced or transmitted in any form
or by any means, electronic or mechanical, including photocopying,
recording, or by any information storage and retrieval system,
without permission in writing from the publisher.
For information address: Bantam Books.

ISBN 0–7394–0500–4

Bantam Books are published by Bantam Books, a division of Ran-
dom House, Inc. Its trademark, consisting of the words "Bantam
Books" and the portrayal of a rooster, is Registered in U.S. Patent
and Trademark Office and in other countries. Marca Registrada.
Bantam Books, 1540 Broadway, New York, New York 10036.

PRINTED IN THE UNITED STATES OF AMERICA

Preface to The Brides Trilogy

LONDON, MAY 11, 1641

Phoebe swiped one hand across her eyes as she felt for her handkerchief with the other. The handkerchief was nowhere to be found, but that didn't surprise her. She'd lost more handkerchiefs in her thirteen years than she'd had hot dinners. With a vigorous and efficacious sniff, she crept around the hedge of clipped laurel out of sight of the clacking, laughing crowd of wedding guests. The high-pitched cacophony of their merrymaking mingled oddly with the persistent, raucous screams of a mob in full cry gusting across the river from Tower Hill.

She glanced over her shoulder at the graceful half-timbered house that was her home. It stood on a slight rise on the south bank of the river Thames, commanding a view over London and the surrounding countryside. Windows winked in the afternoon sunlight and she could hear the plaintive plucking of a harp persistent beneath the surge and ebb of the party.

No one was looking for her. Why should they? She was of no interest to anyone. Diana had banished her from her presence after the accident. Phoebe cringed at the memory. She could never understand how it happened that her body seemed to get away from her, to have a life of its own, creating a wake of chaos and destruction that followed her wherever she went.

But she was safe for a while. Her step quickened as she made for the old boathouse, her own private

sanctuary. When her father had moved the mansion's water gate so that it faced the water steps at Wapping, the old boathouse had fallen into disrepair. Now it nestled in a tangle of tall reeds at the water's edge, its roof sagging, its timbers bared to the bone by the damp salt air and the wind.

But it was the one place where Phoebe could lick her wounds in private. She wasn't sure whether anyone else in the household knew it still existed, but as she approached she saw that the door was not firmly closed.

Her first reaction was anger. Someone had been trespassing in the one place she could call her own. Her second was a swift pattering of fear. The world was full of beasts, both human and animal, and anyone could have penetrated this clearly deserted structure. Anyone or anything could be lying in wait within. She hesitated, staring at the dark crack between door and frame, almost as if the tiny crack could open to reveal the dim, dusty interior for her from a safe distance. Then her anger reasserted itself. The boathouse belonged to *her*. And if anyone was in there, she would send them off.

She turned into the rushes, looking for a thick piece of driftwood, and found an old spar, rusty nails sticking out in a most satisfactory fashion. Thus armed, she approached the boathouse, her heart still pattering, but her face set. She kicked the door open, flooding the dark mildewed corners with light.

"Who are you?" she demanded of the occupant, who, startled, blinked but didn't move from her perch on a rickety three-legged stool by the unglazed window where the light fell on the page of her book.

Phoebe entered the shed, dropping her weapon. "Oh," she said. "I know who you are. You're Lord Granville's daughter. What are you doing here? Why

aren't you at the wedding? I thought you were sup-posed to carry my sister's train."

The dark-haired girl carefully closed her book over her finger. "Yes, I'm Olivia," she said after a minute. "And I d-d-didn't want to b-be in the wedding. My fa-ther said I d-didn't have to b-be if I d-didn't want to." She let out a slow breath at the end of the little speech, which had clearly cost her some effort.

Phoebe looked at the girl curiously. She was younger than Phoebe, although she was as tall, and en-viably slim to the eyes of one who constantly lamented her own intractable roundness. "This is my special place," Phoebe said, but without rancor, sitting on a fallen beam and drawing a wrapped packet from her pocket. "And I don't blame you for not wanting to be in the wedding. I was supposed to attend my sister, but I knocked over the perfume bottle and then trod on Di-ana's flounce."

She unwrapped the packet, taking a bite of the gingerbread it contained before holding out the of-fering to Olivia, who shook her head.

"Diana cursed me up hill and down dale and said she never wanted to lay eyes on me again," Phoebe continued. "Which she probably won't, since she's going to be in Yorkshire, miles and miles away from here. And I have to say, if I never lay eyes on her again, I won't be sorry." She looked defiantly upward as if braving heavenly wrath with such an undutiful statement.

"I d-don't like her," Olivia confided.

"I wouldn't like her for a stepmother either. . . . She'll be absolutely horrible! Oh, I'm sorry. I always say the wrong thing," Phoebe exclaimed crossly. "I always say whatever comes into my head."

"It's the t-truth, anyway," the other girl muttered. She opened up her book again and began to read.

Phoebe frowned. Her stepniece, as she supposed she now was, was not the friendliest of creatures. "Do you always stammer?"

Olivia blushed crimson. "I c-c-can't help it."

"No, of course you can't," Phoebe said hastily. "I was just curious." In the absence of a response from her companion, she moved on to the second piece of gingerbread, idly brushing at a collection of tiny grease spots that seemed to have gathered upon her pink silk gown. A gown specially made for her sister's wedding. It was supposed to complement Diana's pearl-encrusted ivory damask, but somehow on Phoebe the effect didn't quite work, as Diana had pointed out with her usual asperity.

There was a sudden whirlwind rush from the door that banged shut, enclosing the girls in semi-darkness again. "God's bones, but if this isn't the peskiest wedding!" a voice declared vigorously. The newcomer leaned against the closed door. She was breathing fast and dashed a hand across her brow to wipe away the dew of perspiration. Her bright green eyes fell upon the boathouse's other occupants.

"I didn't think anyone knew this place was here. I slept here last night. It was the only way I could get away from those pawing beasts. And now they're at it again. I came here for some peace and quiet."

"It's my special place," Phoebe said, standing up. "And you're trespassing." The newcomer didn't look in the least like a wedding guest. Her hair was a tangled mass of bright red curls that didn't look as if they had seen a brush in a month. Her face looked dirty in the gloom, although it was hard to tell among the freckles what was dirt and what wasn't. Her dress was made of dull coarse holland, the hem dipping in the middle, the perfunctory ruffles on the sleeves torn and grubby.

"Oho, no I'm not," the girl crowed, perching on the upturned holey hull of an abandoned rowboat. "I'm invited to the wedding. Or at least," she added with scrupulous honesty, "my father is. And where Jack goes, I go. No choice."

"I know who you are." Olivia looked up from her book for the first time since the girl had burst in upon them. "You're my father's half b-brother's natural child."

"Portia," the girl said cheerfully. "Jack Worth's bastard. And so you must be Olivia. Jack was talking about you. And I suppose, if you live here, you're the bride's sister. Phoebe, isn't it?"

Phoebe sat down again. "You seem to know a great deal about us."

Portia shrugged. "I keep my ears open . . . and my eyes. Close either one of 'em for half a second and the devils'll get you."

"What devils?"

"Men," Portia declared. "You wouldn't think it to look at me, would you?" She chuckled. "Scrawny as a scarecrow. But they'll take anything they can get so long as it's free."

"I loathe men!" The fierce and perfectly clear statement came from Olivia.

"Me too," Portia agreed, then added with all the loftiness of her fourteen years, "But you're a little young, duckie, to have made such a decision. How old are you?"

"Eleven."

"Oh, you'll change your mind," Portia said knowledgeably.

"I won't. I'm never going to marry." Olivia's brown eyes threw daggers beneath their thick black eyebrows.

"Neither am I," Phoebe said. "Now that my father

has managed to make such a splendid match for Diana, he'll leave me alone, I'm sure."

"Why don't you want to marry?" Portia asked with interest. "It's your destiny to marry. There's nothing else for someone as wellborn as you to do."

Phoebe shook her head. "No one would want to marry me. Nothing ever fits me, and I'm always dropping things and saying just what comes into my head. Diana and my father say I'm a liability. I can't do anything right. So I'm going to be a poet and do good works instead."

"Of course someone will want to marry you," Portia stated. "You're lovely and curvy and womanly. I'm the one no one's going to marry. Look at me." She stood up and gestured to herself with a flourish. "I'm straight up and down like a ruler. I'm a bastard. I have no money, no property. I'm a hopeless prospect." She sat down again, smiling cheerfully as if the prophecy were not in the least disheartening.

Phoebe considered. "I see what you mean," she said. "It would be difficult for you to find a husband. So what will you do?"

"I'd like to be a soldier. I wish I'd been born a boy. I'm sure I was supposed to be, but something went wrong."

"I'm going to b-be a scholar," Olivia declared. "I'm going to ask my father to get me a t-tutor when I'm older, and I want to live in Oxford and study there."

"Women don't study at the university," Phoebe pointed out.

"I shall," Olivia stated stubbornly.

"Lord, a soldier, a poet, and a scholar! What a trio of female misfits!" Portia went into a peal of laughter.

Phoebe laughed with her, feeling a delicious and hitherto unknown warmth in her belly. She wanted

to sing, get to her feet and dance with her companions. Even Olivia was smiling, the defensive fierceness momentarily gone from her eyes.

"We must have a pact to support each other if we're ever tempted to fall by the wayside and become ordinary." Portia jumped to her feet. "Olivia, have you some scissors in that little bag?"

Olivia opened the drawstrings of the little lace-trimmed bag she wore at her waist. She took out a tiny pair of scissors, handing them to Portia, who very carefully cut three red curls from the unruly halo surrounding her freckled face.

"Now, Phoebe, let me have three of those pretty fair locks, and then three of Olivia's black ones." She suited action to words, the little scissors snipping away. "Now watch."

As the other two gazed, wide-eyed with curiosity, Portia's long, thin fingers with their grubby broken nails nimbly braided the different strands into three tricolored rings. "There, we have one each. Mine is the one with the red on the outside, Phoebe's has the fair, and Olivia's the black." She handed them over. "Now, whenever you feel like forgetting your ambition, just look at your ring. . . . Oh, and we must mingle blood." Her green eyes, slanted slightly like a cat's, glinted with enthusiasm and fun.

She turned her wrist up and nicked the skin, squeezing out a drop of blood. "Now you, Phoebe." She held out the scissors.

Phoebe shook her fair head. "I can't. But you do it." Closing her eyes tightly, she extended her arm, wrist uppermost. Portia nicked the skin, then turned to Olivia, who was already extending her wrist.

"There. Now we rub our wrists together to mingle the blood. That way we cement our vow to support each other through thick and thin."

It was clear to Olivia that Portia was playing a game, and yet Olivia, as her skin touched the others, felt a strange tremor of connection that seemed much more serious than mere play. But she was not a fanciful child and sternly dismissed such whimsy.

"If one of us is ever in trouble, then we can send our ring to one of the others and be sure of getting help," Phoebe said enthusiastically.

"That's very silly and romantical," Olivia declared with a scorn that she knew sprang from her own fancy.

"What's wrong with being romantic?" Portia said with a shrug, and Phoebe gave her a quick, grateful smile.

"Scholars aren't romantic," Olivia said. She frowned fiercely, her black eyebrows almost meeting over her deep-set dark eyes. Then she sighed. "I'd b-better go back to the wedding." She slipped her braided ring into the little bag at her waist. With a little reflective gesture, as if to give herself courage, she touched her wrist, thinly smeared with their shared blood, then went to the door.

As she opened it, the clamor from the city across the river swelled into the dim seclusion of the boathouse. Olivia shivered at the wild savagery of the sound. "C-Can you hear what they're saying?"

"They're yelling, 'His head is off, his head is off!' " Portia said knowledgeably. "They've just executed the earl of Strafford."

"But why?" Phoebe asked.

"Lord, don't you know anything?" Portia was genuinely shocked at this ignorance. "Strafford was the king's closest advisor and Parliament defied the king and impeached the earl and now they've just beheaded him."

Olivia felt her scalp contract as the bloody, brutal

screech of mob triumph tore into the soft May air and the smoke of bonfires lit in jubilation for a man's violent death rose thick and choking from the city and its surroundings.

"Jack says there's going to be civil war," Portia continued, referring to her father with her customary informality. "He's usually right about such things . . . not about much else, though," she added.

"There couldn't be civil war!" Olivia was horrified.

"We'll see." Portia shrugged.

"Well, I wish it would come now and save me having to go back to the wedding," Phoebe said glumly. "Are you going to come, Portia?"

Portia shook her head, gesturing brusquely to the door. "Go back to the party. There's no place for me there."

Phoebe hesitated, then followed Olivia, the ring clutched tightly in her palm.

Portia remained in the dimness with the cobwebs for company. She leaned over and picked up the piece of gingerbread that Phoebe had forgotten about in the events of the last half hour. Slowly and with great pleasure, she began to nibble at it, making it last as long as possible, while the shadows lengthened and the shouts from the city and the merrymaking from the house gradually faded with the sunset.

Prologue

*Brian Morse moved swiftly through the dark alley lead-*ing away from the port. The man followed him; his cloak was drawn tightly around him, the hood pulled low over his forehead. He blended into the shadows as he hugged the damp stone walls of the houses pressing close on either side of the lane. The opposing roofs almost joined over his head, but the steady rain still drenched him as he picked his way silently over the slimy cobblestones.

The Englishman was aware of his pursuer. But he gave no indication, not by so much as a stiffening of his shoulder blades, that every nerve was stretched taut and alert. He came abreast of a narrow doorway and hesitated. Then he raised his hand as if to knock and stepped swiftly into the dark nar-row space, out of sight of the lane, pressing himself against the closed door.

His pursuer stopped, frowning. The Englishman was not supposed to make a stop on this street. He was supposed to be going to the Black Tulip to meet with the agent of the Dutch king, Frederick Henry of Orange. The man swore under his breath. How could his informers have made such an error? Dolts, the lot of them.

He moved forward again, hunching into his cloak. As he approached the doorway, Brian Morse stepped out in front of him. The man was aware first of a pair of small brown eyes, cold and flat as a viper's. Then he saw the flash of steel. He reached for his own poignard but was somehow paralyzed by the icy recognition of the hopelessness of his position.

The tip of the swordstick entered his breast, sliding through cloak and shirt and flesh with the ease of a knife through butter. The pain was acute, a piercing cold intensity in his vitals. He slid down the wall, his hands scrabbling for purchase on the wet stones, and crumpled in on himself, inert, blood spreading beneath him, mingling with the dark rain puddles on the cobbles.

Brian Morse turned him over with the tip of his boot. The eyes, glazing now, stared up at him. A thin smile touched Brian's mouth. Leisurely, he drew back his arm and drove the point of the sword deep into the man's belly. He drove it down and up and a gray and crimson mass of viscera spilled to the cobbles.

Brian looked down at the bleeding lump of meat for a second, then with a contemptuous grunt and a curl of the lip, he turned away and continued his journey up the alley.

At the top, he turned to the right. This street was broader than the lane and light spilled from the upper windows of a cross-timbered inn. The sign of the Black Tulip creaked and swung in the wind.

Brian pushed open the door and entered the crowded noisome space. The reek of stale beer, unwashed humanity, and boiling pigs' feet hung heavy in the smoke-filled air. The lime-washed walls sweated great gobbets of moisture and tallow candles burned in the sconces that hung from the massive rafters.

Brian pushed his way through the raucous throng, making for a low door behind the bar counter where a red-faced man was drawing ale with steady, unbroken movements, setting the filled tankards in a line on the counter. A harassed tavern wench retrieved them, carrying them on a tray held high above her head as she dipped and dodged the grasping fingers and the slapping hands of the tavern's customers.

The man at the counter looked up as Brian edged past. He gave him a curt nod and gestured with his head to the low door behind.

Brian raised the latch and entered a small, low-ceilinged room. A man sat at a small table beside the fire, nursing a pitch tankard. The room had a damp chill to it despite the sullen smolder of the fire and the man still wore his cloak and hat. He glanced up as Brian entered the room and gave him one sweeping appraisal.

"You were followed," he stated, his voice curiously flat and nasal. His eyes rested on the swordstick that Brian still held unsheathed. Blood dripped from the point and clotted in the sawdust strewn across the wooden floor.

"Aye," Brian agreed. He raised the swordstick and scrutinized the rusty stains with the air of one examining and approving his handiwork. Then he thrust the blade back into its sheath with a decisive thud and pulled out the chair opposite the man at the table.

"One of Strickland's agents?" the man asked, picking up his tankard.

"I assume so. I didn't take the time to inquire," Brian returned. "It was not a social occasion." He reached for the jug of ale on the table and in the absence of a tankard tipped the jug to his lips and drank deeply.

"Killing's thirsty work," he offered. His tongue flicked over his lips as he set the jug back on the table.

The other made only a noncommittal grunt and reached inside his cloak. He withdrew a paper from a pocket in his woolen jerkin and tapped it thoughtfully on the stained planking of the table.

Brian's small brown eyes watched the man's hands, but he said nothing, containing his impatience.

"So," his companion said after a few long seconds. "His majesty has been most generous."

"His majesty's son and heir is married to King Charles's daughter," Brian Morse reminded him with a caustic edge.

His companion's eyes narrowed at the tone. "Be that as it may, Holland is neutral in your civil war," he stated. "The king is making a great concession in this offer of aid."

"It will be acknowledged." Brian picked up the jug again and carried it to his lips.

The other man nodded as if satisfied. He unfolded the paper and silently slid it across the table.

Brian set down the tankard and picked up the paper. He ran his eye down the neat columns. The king of Orange was indeed being generous. The munitions he was offering to supply the embattled and impoverished king of England would go a long way toward redressing the difference in strength between Cromwell's New Model Army and the Cavaliers.

"His majesty will not stint his gratitude," Brian said slowly. He reached into his pocket for a letter of his own. It bore the seal of Charles of England.

His companion took it and examined the seal closely. He'd been told what to look for and there was no mistaking the royal insignia. He thrust the document inside his jerkin and drained the contents of his tankard.

His chair scraped on the planks as he stood up, pulling his gauntlets from his belt. "You will be contacted with exact details about delivery after the king has read the letter and consulted with his advisors. The ship will leave from Rotterdam. You should hold yourself in readiness."

He strode to the door and it banged closed on his departure.

Brian Morse finished the ale in the jug. Once this mission was successfully accomplished he would go home, bearing with him in triumph the fruits of his negotiations. And at last he would come to the attention of the truly powerful around the king. He would be noticed. He would be recognized as a man of ability. And there would be some reward. A reward, if he played his cards right, that would enable him finally to pursue personal interests under the guise of working for the king's cause.

1

*Lady Phoebe Carlton lay very still listening to her bed-*mate's even breathing. Olivia was a very light sleeper and woke at the slightest sound. And tonight, Olivia mustn't know what Phoebe was about. They never had secrets from each other and were as close if not closer than sisters. But Phoebe couldn't afford for her dearest friend to know about her present enterprise.

Phoebe pushed aside the coverlet and slipped to the floor. Olivia stirred and turned over. Phoebe froze. The fire in the grate was almost out, and it was so cold in the chamber that her breath formed a pale fog in the dim light from the guttering candle on the mantel. Olivia was afraid of the dark and they always kept a candle burning until she was asleep.

Olivia's even breathing resumed and Phoebe tiptoed across the chamber to the armoire. She had left it partly open so it wouldn't squeak. She took out the bundle of clothes and the small cloakbag and crept on her freezing bare feet to the door. She lifted the latch and opened it just wide enough for her to slide sideways through and into the dark passage beyond.

Shivering, she scrambled into her clothes, pulling them on over her nightshift. There were no candles in the sconces in the passage and it was pitch dark, but Phoebe found the darkness comforting. If she could see no one, then no one could see her.

The house was silent but for the usual nighttime creaks of old wood settling. She dragged on her woolen stockings and, carrying her boots and the cloakbag, crept down the corridor towards the wide staircase leading down to the great hall.

The hall was in shadow, lit only by the still-glowing embers in the vast fireplace at the far end. The great roof beams were a dark and heavy presence above her head as she tiptoed in her stockinged feet down the stairs. It was a mad, crazy thing she was doing, but Phoebe could see no alternative. She would not be sold into marriage, sold like a prize pig at the fair, to a man who had no real interest in her, except as a breeding cow.

Phoebe grimaced at her mixed metaphors, but they both nevertheless struck her as accurate descriptions of her situation. She wasn't living in the Middle Ages. It should not be possible to compel someone into a distasteful marriage, and yet, if she didn't take drastic action, that was exactly what was going to happen. Her father refused to listen to reason; he saw only his own advantage and had every intention of disposing of his only remaining daughter to suit himself.

Phoebe muttered under her breath as she crossed the hall, the cold from the flagstones striking up through her stockings. Reminding herself of her father's intractable selfishness buoyed her up. She was terrified of what she was about to do. It was absolute madness to attempt such a flight, but she would not marry a man who barely noticed her existence.

The great oak door was bolted and barred. She set down her boots and cloakbag and lifted the iron bar. It was heavy but she managed to set it back into the brackets at the side of the door. She reached up and drew the first bolt, then bent to draw the second at the base of the door. She was breathing quickly and, despite the cold, beads of sweat gathered between her breasts. She was aware of nothing but the door, its massive solidity in front of her filling her vision, both interior and exterior.

Slowly she pulled the door open. A blast of frigid air struck her like a blow. She took a deep breath . . .

And then the door was suddenly banged closed again. An arm had reached over her shoulder; a flat hand rested against the doorjamb. Phoebe stared at the hand . . . at the arm . . . in total stupefaction. Where had it come from? She felt the warmth of the body at her back, a large presence that was blocking her retreat just as the now closed door prevented her advance.

She turned her head, raised her eyes, and met the puzzled and distinctly irritated gaze of her intended bridegroom.

Cato, Marquis of Granville, regarded her in silence for a minute. When he spoke, it was an almost shocking sound after the dark silence. "What in God's name are you doing, Phoebe?"

His voice, rich and tawny, as always these days sent a little shiver down her spine. For a moment she was at a loss for words and stood staring, slack-jawed and dumb as any village idiot.

"I was going for a walk, sir," she said faintly, absurd though it was.

Cato looked at her incredulously. "At three o'clock in the morning? Don't be ridiculous." His gaze sharpened, the brown eyes, so dark as to be almost black in the shadowy dimness of the hall, narrowed. He glanced down at the cloakbag and her boots, standing neatly side by side.

"A walk, eh?" he queried with undisguised sarcasm. "In your stockinged feet, no less." He put his hands on her shoulders and moved her aside, then shot the bolts on the door again and dropped the bar back in place. It fell with a heavy clang that sounded to Phoebe in her present melodramatic mood like a veritable death knell.

He bent to pick up the cloakbag and, with a curt "Come," moved away towards the door at the rear of the hall that opened onto his study.

Phoebe glanced at her boots, then shrugged with dull resignation and left them where they were. She followed the marquis's broad back, noticing despite herself how the rich velvet of his nightrobe caressed his wide, powerful shoulders and fell to his booted ankles in elegant black folds. Had he been about to go up to bed? How could she possibly have been so stupid as not to have noticed the yellow line of candlelight beneath his door? But it hadn't occurred to her that anyone would still be up and about at this ungodly hour.

Cato stalked into his study and dropped the cloakbag on the table with a gesture that struck Phoebe as contemptuous. Then he turned back to her, the fur-trimmed robe swinging around his ankles. "Close the door. There's no reason why anyone else should be forced into this vigil."

Phoebe closed the door and stood with her back against it. Cato's study was warm, the fire well built and blazing, but there was little warmth in the marquis's gaze as he regarded her in frowning silence. Then he turned back to the bag on the table.

"So," he began in a conversational tone, "you were going for a walk, were you?" He unclasped the bag and drew out Phoebe's best cloak. He laid it over a chair and continued to remove the contents of the bag one by one. His eyes beneath sardonically raised brows never left her face as he shook out her clean linen, her shifts and stockings and chemises, laying them with exaggerated care over the chair. Lastly he placed her hairbrushes on the table, together with the little packet of hairpins and ribbons.

"Strange baggage to accompany a walk," he observed. "But then, anyone choosing to go for a walk at three in the morning in the middle of January is probably capable of any oddity, wouldn't you think?"

Phoebe wanted to throw something at him. Instead she went over to the table and began stolidly to replace the pathetic assortment of her worldly goods in the bag. "I'll go back to bed now," she said colorlessly.

"Not quite yet." Cato put a hand on her arm. "I'm afraid you owe me an explanation. For the last two years you've been living, I assume contentedly, under my roof. And now it appears you're intending to flit away by moonlight without a word to anyone. . . . Or is Olivia a part of this?" His voice had sharpened.

"Olivia doesn't know anything, my lord," Phoebe stated. "This is not her fault."

Olivia's father merely nodded. "So, an explanation, if you please."

How could he not know? How could she possibly be so drawn to this man . . . find him so impossibly attractive . . . when as far as he was concerned she was of no more importance than an ant . . . merely a convenient means to an end. He hadn't looked at her properly once in the two years she'd been living under his roof. She was certain the idea for this marriage had come from her father, and Cato had simply seen the advantages.

His wife, Diana, Phoebe's sister, had died eight months earlier. It was common practice for a widower to marry his sister-in-law. It kept dowries in the family and maintained the original alliance between the two families. Of course it was to Cato's advantage. Of course he'd agreed.

No one had consulted Phoebe. They hadn't thought it necessary. There had not been even the semblance of courtship. . . .

Cato continued to frown at her. Absently he noticed that the buttons of her jacket were done up wrongly, as if she'd dressed in haste and in the dark. Her thick, light brown hair, incompetently dragged into a knot on top of her head, was flying loose in every direction. The clasp of her cloak was hanging by a thread. She was very untidy, he caught himself thinking. He realized that he'd noticed it often before. He remembered now that Diana had complained about it constantly.

"Phoebe . . ." he prompted with an edge of impatience.

Phoebe took a deep breath and said in a rush, "I do not wish to be married, sir. I've never wished to be married. I won't be married."

It seemed that she had silenced the marquis. His frown deepened. He ran a hand through his close-cropped thatch of dark brown hair, back from the pronounced widow's peak to his nape. It was a gesture with which Phoebe was achingly familiar. It was something he did whenever he was deep in thought, distracted by some detail or contemplating some plan of action. And these days it never failed to turn her knees to water.

Cato turned and went over to a massive mahogany sideboard. He poured wine from a silver decanter into a pewter cup, took a thoughtful sip, and then turned back to Phoebe.

"Let me understand this. Do you not wish to marry *me* in particular . . . or do you have a generalized dislike of the marital state?" His voice had lost its edge and sounded merely curious.

If I thought there was the slightest chance you might pay me as much attention as you pay your horses, or find me as interesting as politics and this godforsaken war, I would probably marry you like a shot, Phoebe thought bitterly. All her often touted opinions on the myriad disadvantages of marriage for an intelligent woman of independent thought would have gone for nothing if the marquis had shown so much as a spasm of interest in her as a person instead of as a convenient means to an end. As it was . . .

She stated flatly, "I'm not interested in marrying anyone, Lord Granville. I don't see the advantages in it . . . or at least not for me."

It was such an extraordinary, ridiculous statement that Cato laughed. "My dear girl, you cannot live without a husband. Who's to put a roof over your head? Food in your belly? Clothes on your back?"

The laughter faded from his eyes as he saw her wide, generous mouth take a stubborn turn. He said brusquely, "I doubt your father will continue to support an undutiful and ungrateful daughter."

"Would you refuse to support Olivia in such a situation?" Phoebe demanded.

Cato responded curtly, "That is not to the point."

It was to the point, since Olivia had even less intention than Phoebe of submitting to the dictates of a husband, but Phoebe held her tongue. It was not for her to say.

"So rather than find yourself the marchioness of Granville, living in comfort and security, you choose to fly off into the night, into a war-torn countryside infested with roaming soldiers who would rape and murder you as soon as look at you?" The sardonic note was back in his voice. He took another sip of wine and regarded her over the lip of his cup.

Phoebe, never one to beat about the bush, asked bluntly, "Lord Granville, would you please tell my father that you don't wish to marry me after all?"

"*No!*" Cato declared with a degree of force. "I will tell him no such thing. If you held me in distaste, then I would do so, but since your reasons for disliking this marriage are utterly without merit . . . the mere whims of a foolish girl . . . I will do no such thing."

"I am not foolish," Phoebe said in a low voice. "I am surely entitled to my opinions, sir."

"Sensible opinions, yes," he snapped. Then his expression softened somewhat. Although she was the same age as her sister Diana had been at her marriage, Phoebe was somehow less protected, he thought. She had fewer defenses. Diana had never exhibited the slightest vulnerability. She had glided through life, as beautiful and perhaps as brittle as the finest porcelain. Graceful and regal as any swan. Cato didn't think she had ever questioned herself, or her entitlement. She knew who she was and what she was.

Diana's rounded, tangled little sister was a bird of a rather different feather, he thought. A rather ragged robin. The comparison surprised him into a fleeting smile.

Phoebe caught the flicker of the smile. It was surprising

coming after that uncompromising statement. But then it disappeared and she thought she'd been mistaken.

"Go back to bed," Cato said. He handed her the cloakbag. "I'll not mention this to your father."

That was a concession. But she couldn't quite bring herself to thank the marquis. The fact that he had the power to make her life miserable and chose not to exercise it didn't strike her as a matter for congratulation. She sketched a curtsy and left his study, making her way back to bed.

She undressed in the passage again, so as not to awaken Olivia. If Olivia awoke, Phoebe would have to tell her everything. And she had no idea how to explain this bolt from the blue that had felled her just before Christmas.

She'd been sitting in the apple loft, overlooking the stable yard, wrestling with a recalcitrant stanza of a poem she was writing, when Cato had ridden in with a troop of Roundhead cavalry. For two years Phoebe had seen the marquis of Granville go about his daily business and he'd barely impinged on her consciousness. And she'd known she hadn't impinged on his. But that crisp December day something very strange had happened.

Once more in her shift, Phoebe crept into bed beside Olivia. Her side of the bed was cold now, and she inched closer to Olivia. She was wide-awake and lay looking up at the dark shape of the tapestry tester, idly picturing the bucolic scene of a May Day celebration that was depicted above her.

But her mind wouldn't let go of the memory of that moment before Christmas when she'd fallen in love . . . or lust . . . or whatever this hideous inconvenience was . . . with Cato, Marquis of Granville.

She'd watched him ride into the yard on his bay charger—something she'd seen many times. He'd been at the head of the troop, but when he'd drawn rein, Giles Crampton, his lieutenant, had come up beside him. Cato had leaned sideways to talk to him.

He was bareheaded and Phoebe had noticed how in the sunlight his dark brown hair had a flicker of gold running through it. He'd moved a gauntleted hand in a gesture to Giles, and Phoebe's heart had seemed to turn over. This kind of thing happened in poetry all the time. But, poet though she was, Phoebe was rarely plagued by an excess of sentiment, and she had never imagined that verse was a veritable expression of reality.

And yet she'd sat in the apple loft, her quill dripping ink on her precious vellum, her apple halfway to her mouth, while the entire surface of her skin had grown hotter and hotter.

He'd dismounted and she'd gazed, transfixed, at the power behind his agile movements. She'd gazed at his profile, noticing for the first time the slight bump at the bridge of his long nose, the square jut of his chin, the fine, straight line of his mouth.

Phoebe grimaced fiercely in the darkness. It should have gone away . . . should have been a moment of angelic lunacy. But it hadn't gone away. She heard his voice, his foot on the stair, and a deep throb started in her belly. When he walked into a room, she had to leave or sit down before her knees betrayed her.

It was absurd. Yet she could do nothing about it. For a rational being, it was the ultimate injustice. And then two days ago her father had informed her that she was to replace her dead sister as Lord Granville's wife. For a moment the world had spun on its axis. The glorious prospect of achieving her heart's desire lay before her. Love and lust with the man whose simple presence was enough to set her heart beating like a drum.

The marquis had been standing beside her father.

He had nodded to her.

Lord Granville had said nothing to her. Not one single word. He had simply nodded to her when her father had completed his announcement. After the announcement had come a brief catalogue of details relating to her dowry and the marriage settlements. And Cato had listened impassively. It was clear he'd heard it all before. Indeed, Phoebe had had the impression that he was either bored or pressed for time. But then he was always pressed for time. If he wasn't conducting some siege of a royalist stronghold somewhere in the Thames valley, he was meeting with Cromwell and the other generals of the New Model Army, planning strategy in their headquarters outside Oxford.

Phoebe and Olivia rarely saw him. They lived their own lives in the comfortable manor house that Cato had acquired in Woodstock, eight miles from Oxford, when the theatre of war had moved from the north of England to the south and west. He had not wanted to leave his family unprotected in Yorkshire and had brought them with him. Diana's death had made little or no difference to his life, it seemed to Phoebe.

It had, however, made a significant difference to Phoebe's and Olivia's. Freed of Diana's tyranny, they'd been able to pursue their own interests without hindrance, and until two days ago . . . or rather until just before Christmas, Phoebe amended . . . nothing had occurred to disturb their peace.

Now she was condemned to marry a man who would as soon marry a healthy sow if she came with the right dowry and the right breeding potential. Not even Dante's inferno had created such a fiendish torment. She was to be compelled to spend the rest of her life with a man whom she loved and lusted after to the point of obsession, and who barely acknowledged her existence.

And the unkindest cut of all—there was no one in whom she could confide. It was impossible to explain any of it to Olivia. There were no words . . . or at least none that Phoebe could think of.

Portia would understand, but Portia was in Yorkshire. Ecstatically happy with Rufus Decatur. And if Cato Granville hadn't been up and about at three in the morning, Phoebe would be on her way to Yorkshire.

With something resembling a groan, Phoebe flung herself onto her side and closed her eyes.

*D*ownstairs, *Cato snuffed the candles in his study, all* but a carrying candle, and bent to poke a slipping log to the rear of the grate. He straightened and stood absently staring down at the fire. The full impact of Phoebe's crazy intention was only just hitting him. What kind of woman would hurl herself out into the freezing night, without the slightest regard for the obvious dangers? Where had she been going, for God's sake?

And for what a reason! A young woman of Phoebe's wealth and lineage not wishing to marry . . . actually prepared to reject the suit of a marquis! The girl had windmills in her head.

He could perhaps understand it if her father was compelling her into marriage with some monster. If he was proposing to wed her to some repulsive ancient . . .

Surely Phoebe couldn't see *him* in such a light?

The thought brought his head up. Of course that was an absurdity. He was in his prime, a man of five and thirty. True, he'd had ill luck with his wives—or they had had ill luck with their husband, he amended wryly. While it was hardly unusual for a man to have lost three wives before his thirty-fourth summer, it could perhaps strike an ominous note for an impressionable young woman preparing to become the fourth.

But Phoebe had claimed to have no personal objections to him, only to the state of matrimony. And that, of course, was ridiculous.

So was she perhaps unstable? Maybe he should think again. An hysterical wife given to irrational impulses was hardly a comfortable prospect. What kind of mother would she make?

And that, after all, was the crux of the matter. He needed an heir of his own blood. Daughters were all very well, but they could not inherit the title or the estates.

If he did not produce a male heir, then the Granville estates would pass to his stepson, his first wife's child, whom he'd adopted as an infant because it had seemed the generous thing to do. It had never occurred to Cato in his own exuberant youth that he would fail to produce a son of his own loins to inherit his family name. By adopting the child, he had thought he was merely ensuring the boy's future.

A foolhardy gesture it had turned out to be.

Cato's mouth thinned as he thought of his first wife's child. He would not trust Brian Morse further than he could throw him. He was plausible, charming, but his small eyes were shifty, his tongue too smooth for truth. There was something about him that set Cato's teeth on edge, and had done since the boy was little more than a child. And for the crowning touch, Brian Morse was on the wrong side in the civil war raging through the land. He supported the king.

Cato had long decided that the king must bow to the dictates of his subjects. He could no longer be permitted to lay waste the country's resources for his own ends. He could no longer be permitted to ignore the will of the people. King Charles must be compelled to enact the reforms that Parliament had laid before him. Sooner than do that, the king had gone to war with his people. And even those who, like Cato, were reluctant to take up arms against their sovereign had met his challenge.

The king's cause was all but lost, in Cato's informed opinion. The Parliamentarians had reformed their armies under Oliver Cromwell, and the New Model Army, disciplined and well paid unlike its royalist opponents, was sweeping victoriously through the country.

Which brought Cato back to Brian Morse.

In these dangerous times it would take very little—a skirmish, a stray musket ball, a sweeping sword cut, a fall from his horse—to leave Brian Morse as head of the Granville clan. So, Cato would marry Phoebe. She was at hand and he was in a hurry. For all practical purposes the alliance could not be bettered.

At eighteen the girl was still young enough to be influenced by her husband. He would be able to control any skittish tendencies.

He pursed his lips, considering Phoebe with cool dispassion. She had a robust air, a sturdy figure with generous hips. A good childbearing figure. Much stronger, much less fragile seeming than her sister. She looked like a woman who would bear sons.

No, she would make him a good wife. He would make sure of it. Cato went to the door, his carrying candle throwing a soft light ahead of him.

*P*hoebe was awakened at first light by Olivia's hand on her shoulder. "Phoebe, why are your clothes all over the floor?"

"Wh . . . what?" Phoebe struggled onto an elbow. She blinked blearily at Olivia. She felt horrible, as if she hadn't slept a wink. "What's the time? It's the middle of the night!" she protested. It certainly felt like the middle of the night.

"No, it's not. It's nearly six o'clock," Olivia stated. Her black eyes were sharply appraising in the pale oval of her face. She took a deep breath, concentrating on controlling the stammer that had plagued her from childhood.

"Your clothes. They're in the middle of the floor. They weren't when we went to b-bed."

"I couldn't sleep, so I went for a walk," Phoebe said.

"Out of the house!" Olivia stared in patent disbelief.

Phoebe shook her head. "No . . . I was going to but then it seemed too cold and dark, so I came back to bed again." Which was not exactly a lie, she thought.

Olivia was not convinced. "You're fibbing," she declared.

Phoebe flopped back on the pillows again. Her eyes felt gritty, filled with sand, and she rubbed them with the heels of her palms.

Olivia sat up, hugging her knees to her narrow chest. She frowned fiercely, her thick dark brows meeting over the bridge of the long Granville nose. "I suppose you really don't wish to marry my father," she said matter-of-factly.

If only it were that simple! But Phoebe couldn't see how to explain the complexities of her present dilemma to Cato's daughter. "I don't wish to get married at all. You know that," she replied. "We agreed we wouldn't ever marry . . . that day in the boathouse, with Portia."

"I know, b-but that was a long time ago," Olivia said. "Things change. Look at Portia. Would you ever have believed Portia, of all of us, would have married?"

"Portia's a law unto herself," Phoebe said. "She married because she chose to. I'm being made to."

Olivia contemplated this melancholy truth. "I know," she said simply. "B-but at least it means we'll always be able to live together."

"Until you get married," Phoebe pointed out.

"I'm not going to," Olivia stated flatly.

"That's what we all said," Phoebe reminded her again. "If it can happen to Portia and me, what makes you think you'll be able to hold out?"

Olivia's fine mouth took an obstinate turn. Her pale cheeks became a little flushed. "No one will be able to force me to marry!" she said with low-voiced intensity.

"Don't you believe it," Phoebe said glumly, dragging herself up against the pillows. "What say do women have in these matters? No one asked me for my opinion; quite the opposite. My father and yours just told me it was going to happen. I could have screamed and torn out my hair, but it would have made no difference. It's the way things are, and it'll be just as bad after I'm married. Probably worse."

She wrinkled her snub nose. "To add insult to injury, your

father can't possibly really wish to marry *me*. How could he?" She grabbed at her waist with a grimace. "Look at all this flesh! Diana was so slender and elegant and I'm as round as a sugar bun!"

"You're curvy and womanly," Olivia said, as always stubbornly defending her friend, even against herself. "That's what Portia said."

"Your father just wants a son, and I'm a convenient vehicle," Phoebe said bluntly.

Olivia regarded her in silence. She could think of no way to refute this very obvious truth. "You might like having a child," she suggested after a minute.

"It's not going to happen in a hurry."

She sounded remarkably definite to Olivia. "How d'you know?" she inquired, her eyes curious.

Phoebe stared into the middle distance. "There are ways to stop it happening."

"How?" Olivia gazed at her in wide-eyed fascination.

"You know my friend Meg?"

Olivia nodded eagerly. Meg was a herbalist and had a certain reputation for benign witchcraft in the village.

"Well, she's told me how to do it," Phoebe said. "There are certain herbs that can prevent conception. She says it's not foolproof, but usually it works."

"But why don't you wish to give my father a child?"

Phoebe looked into the distance again. "I just told you that he's marrying me because I'm convenient. An accidental convenience. Until he stops seeing me in that light . . . *really* stops seeing me in that light . . . then I'll not conceive."

She looked straight at Olivia now and there was a grimly determined set to her mouth. "Once I give him what he wants, he'll never need to try to understand me, or see me for *who* I am. D'you see that, Olivia?"

"Yes, of c-course I do."

"I would be a partner in his life," Phoebe continued. "Not a dependent with limited uses."

"Married women are always dependent," Olivia stated. "They can't help but be . . . well, except for Portia," she added.

"What Portia can do, I can do," Phoebe said.

"But once you give my father an heir, I don't expect he'll trouble you much. He's always so busy . . ." Olivia's voice trailed off. She was not offering much in the way of comfort to her friend, who was facing the one situation they had always agreed to avoid. A situation that Olivia herself couldn't bear to contemplate.

"Not so busy that he won't expect me to honor and obey implicitly in exchange for a roof over my head and clothes on my back," Phoebe said, swinging her legs over the side of the bed. "He said as much. Wives aren't people, they're chattels."

Olivia shrugged helplessly. "I don't know what to say."

"There isn't anything," Phoebe declared. "I'm stuck with it. Unless I can do something about it. So I'm going to try."

2

"*Oh, do stand still, Lady Phoebe. How can I set these* pins when y'are wrigglin' around like an anthill . . . and just watch where you put your 'ands, now! Filthy, they are. They'll leave great dirty marks all over, they will."

Phoebe sighed and curled her grime-encrusted hands into fists, holding them away from her skirts. She'd been in the village helping one of the young widows muck out her stable, and the time had run away from her, so she'd been late for the fitting and hadn't had a chance to wash.

"Do you think Portia will get here in time for the wedding, Olivia?"

Olivia, from the window seat where she was alternately reading and watching the progress of the fitting, shook her head. "My father said it would b-be impossible for her to make the journey in less than four weeks, and we only sent to her three weeks ago."

Phoebe nodded glumly. She was in sore need of some robust counsel of the kind that only Portia could provide.

The wedding night. She could think of little else these days. She had only a hazy knowledge of the whats and wheres of the business, but when she imagined being in the great four-poster bed with Cato, her body caught fire. Whatever it was exactly that they would do, she reasoned that they had to be close to do it. Skin to skin . . . mouth to mouth. She could run her fingers through his hair, press her lips to the deep hollow of his throat. Inhale that rich masculine scent that he had. An indefinable mélange of aromas that she had come to associate just with Cato. It was his hair, his skin, the tang of leather and musk, the lavender of his linen, and the fresh, clean scents of the open air.

"Oh, Lady Phoebe, keep still, do," the seamstress exclaimed as Phoebe took an involuntary step forward with one foot off the stool she was standing on.

"Let me look at the gown," Phoebe said, brushing the woman aside and stepping down completely. She picked up the trailing hem and walked over to the console glass.

Phoebe examined her reflection critically. "Hand-me-down gowns for a hand-me-down bride," she remarked with a somewhat bitter smile. "Why on earth should people assume that what looked wonderful on Diana on her wedding day would look as wonderful on *me*?"

The gown was of pearl-encrusted ivory damask and was caught under her breasts with a girdle of silver tissue. Five years before, Diana had married the marquis of Granville in this very gown. And she had looked exquisite, ethereal. Not so Phoebe, who looked dumpy and insipid.

"And no one asked me if I wished to wear it!" she complained. "My father just said how economical it would be, and Lord Granville merely shrugged as if it didn't matter a tinker's damn what I wore to the altar."

"I don't suppose he thinks it does," Olivia said from an accurate knowledge of her parent. "He's much more likely to think that a new gown would cost as much as outfitting three troopers of his militia. I wish the war would be over," she added with a melancholy sigh. "It's all my father ever thinks about."

"It's a little difficult to ignore," Phoebe pointed out. "But even if it was over, my father would still be trying to save money. He just wouldn't have the same excuse."

She frowned at her reflection, muttering, "You know, I think I'd rather wear one of my old gowns." She turned sideways and pressed the material to her body. "I'm so fat," she wailed.

"Oh, now don't you be silly, Lady Phoebe." The seamstress bustled over. "A lovely little figure you've got. Round in all the right places. Men like a bit of body to get ahold of."

"Do they?" Phoebe asked hopefully. Would Cato like a bit of body to get hold of? The man who'd once been married to Diana? Highly unlikely.

She cupped her full breasts just above the girdle. The neckline was lower than most of her gowns, but it had a wide lace collar falling over her shoulders and concealing the upper swell of her bosom. She thought her shoulders looked fat and her breasts pushing against the ivory damask were as shapeless as pouter pigeons.

"Don't you go an' complain at what the good Lord gave you," the seamstress said severely. "Now, let me fix this hem, then you can take it off."

"Don't you think I'd be better off in one of my old gowns, Olivia?" Phoebe pressed.

Olivia frowned as she looked up from her book. "They're all so shabby, and they don't fit you," she pointed out with devastating candor. "At least that's a pretty c-color."

"But it doesn't suit me. It suited Diana. It doesn't suit me."

Olivia considered and was forced to agree. "It's not as if you're in the least like Diana. Not in *any* way! Thank heavens." She examined Phoebe with a speculative air. "Actually, I think you should wear darker c-colors. Something that would accentuate your eyes and make the most of your hair."

Phoebe looked a little surprised. Olivia in general evinced very little interest in clothes herself. "Well, much chance of that," she said with a sigh. "Hurry up and take it off, Ellen."

Tutting, the seamstress edged the gown over Phoebe's hair and hurried away with it, leaving Phoebe still in her shift.

"Perhaps if you told my father that you hated the gown, he would ask your father to b-buy you another one," Olivia suggested.

"If I had money," Phoebe stated, "I could buy my own gowns." She sat down on a three-legged stool and stretched her legs in their woolen stockings to the fender. Absently she wriggled her big toe that was sticking out of a rather large hole. "The devil of it is, I do have money. From my mother's jointure. But you think anyone's going to give it to me?" She shook her head vigorously.

"I suppose it's part of your dowry," Olivia said sympathetically.

"To be managed by my husband, because what could a woman . . . a mere wife . . . know of such complicated matters?" Phoebe gave a snort of disgust.

"Maybe you should show my father some of your poetry," Olivia suggested. "That would show him how c-clever you are."

"Men aren't interested in poetry," Phoebe said glumly.

"But most poets *are* men," Olivia pointed out.

"Well, soldiers aren't interested in poetry."

"But you won't stop writing, just b-because you're married!"

"No, of course not. It's my life," Phoebe stated. "I don't intend to stop doing any of the things I do now. I shall go on helping out in the village, and learning to be a herbalist with Meg, and I shall go on writing my poetry."

"Then you'll hardly feel married at all," Olivia said. "It'll almost be as if you're not."

Phoebe gave her a quick glance. How could she tell Olivia that that outcome was the last one she wanted? It was impossible to explain this stupid dilemma. On the one hand she wanted more than anything to feel married to Cato, to *be* married to Cato, and all that her lusting imagination told her that could mean. But because she couldn't see how it could ever become what she wished for with such desperate passion, she could hardly bear the prospect of going through the motions.

"Well," Olivia said, with uncanny intuition, "perhaps not exactly as if you're not."

"No," Phoebe agreed. "Not exactly."

• • •

$\mathcal{P}$hoebe awoke on her wedding morning as exhausted as if she hadn't slept a wink. Her head had been full of dreams . . . dreams bordering on nightmares. Twisted strands of excitement, of hope, of a dread certainty of disappointment. And she opened her eyes onto a torrential rain, slashing against the windowpanes, sending gusts of drops down the chimney to sizzle on the embers of the fire.

"What a horrible day!" Olivia declared in disgust. "Horrible weather for a horrible day. They'll have to hold the wedding feast for the tenants in the b-barn."

"It'll be warmer than in the courtyard, anyway," Phoebe said. The weather, as Olivia said, seemed entirely appropriate. She could have predicted it herself. "I shall get very wet going to the church," she added with a certain grim relish. "It'll ruin my gown . . . or rather, Diana's gown."

It was to be a small wedding, a far cry from the grand affair that had been Cato's marriage to Diana on the day when Parliament had executed the king's favorite, the earl of Strafford, on Tower Hill, and civil war had become inevitable. On that occasion divisive political opinions had still been in their infancy, and there had been nothing to disturb the harmony of celebration. But now many of those who had celebrated with the marquis of Granville would sooner meet him on the battlefield than break bread with him. And many another had fallen in the great pitched battles that had been fought before the strife became as it was now, mostly one of sieges and attrition.

The wedding was to be a small affair, an economical affair. Phoebe's father, Lord Carlton, was not one to waste his money. Phoebe was not her sister—a diamond of the first water. She was making a convenient alliance for her father, but there was no need to go overboard in the middle of a war.

In these unusual times it had seemed practical to both

Lord Granville and his father-in-law for Phoebe to be married from the house where she'd been living for the last two years. But the marquis had graciously stepped aside in his own house and allowed the bride's father to make all the arrangements.

"My father won't let you get wet," Olivia stated.

"He can't stop the rain with a wave of his hand," Phoebe pointed out with much the same gloomy satisfaction.

Olivia's confidence was not misplaced. At dawn Cato took one look at the leaden sky and the sopping ground and decided that no one was going to walk to the church as had originally been intended. Within an hour bevies of soldiers from his militia were laying straw thickly the length of the drive between the front door of the house and the little village church just outside the gates, so that the iron wheels of a carriage wouldn't sink into the mud.

The guests would be transported to the church in groups by carriage, and the bride and her father, with Olivia in attendance, would follow last. As a final touch, a makeshift awning of tent canvas was constructed over the path from the lych-gate to the church door.

Cato inspected the arrangements himself, ignoring the rain that drenched his cloak and dripped from his soaked hair down the back of his neck. He returned to the house for breakfast, shaking water off himself like a dog who'd been swimming.

Phoebe and Olivia were breakfasting in a square room at the rear of the house, generally known as the young ladies' parlor. Or rather, Olivia was eating in her usual absentminded manner, her eyes glued to the book she was reading. Phoebe for once had no appetite. She crumbled bread on her plate, sipped from the cup of small beer, and wandered back and forth between the window and the table, as if hoping that the rain would have stopped between one circuit and another.

Cato rapped once on the door and entered on the knock.

Olivia jumped up from the table. Phoebe, already on her feet, stared at him in startlement and mortification.

She was wearing an old nightrobe that was too small for her, straining across her bosom in the most unflattering fashion and reaching only to mid-calf. She knew the short length made her exposed calves and ankles look thick and lumpy. To make matters worse, it had lost half its buttons, the fur trimming was now mangy, and there were some intractable stains down the front.

Cato had seen her looking scruffy before, but somehow on her wedding morning it seemed worse than usual.

"My lord, it's unlucky for a man to see his bride before the wedding," she said, the words tumbling forth. "Please go away."

"That's an old wives' tale, Phoebe," Cato said impatiently. "I came only to put your mind at rest about the weather."

"But it's still raining," she pointed out.

"Yes, it's still raining," he agreed, striving for patience. "But since you will travel to the church by carriage, you won't get wet."

"Oh . . . Thank you, my lord. But would you *please* go away now."

Cato hesitated, frowning, then with a brief headshake he left the parlor.

"I look such a mess," Phoebe groaned. "Why did he have to come in and see me like this? Today of all days."

Olivia regarded Phoebe in surprise. "You always look like that in the morning. Why should it matter?" Then, when that didn't appear to have the intended reassurance, she added comfortingly, "I expect he'll be up and out of the house long before you most mornings . . . if it really c-concerns you."

"I'm a bundle of nerves," Phoebe said in faint explanation. "Of course it doesn't really matter what I look like."

"Well, you'd better go and get ready now anyway," Olivia

stated. "It's close to nine o'clock and you have to b-bathe and wash your hair."

In reinforcement, another knock on the door brought the housekeeper, Mistress Bisset. "Lord, Lady Phoebe, are you still in your nightrobe? Come along now. The bath is all ready for you." Tutting in reproof, she swept Phoebe down the passage to the bedchamber where her maid was adding dried lavender and rose petals to the steaming tub before the fire.

Phoebe gave herself up to the ministrations of maid and housekeeper and seamstress. She followed instructions without conscious thought, barely hearing their stream of chatter bubbling around her. Her entire body was tingling, her skin sensitized as if someone had scraped over every inch with an oyster shell.

As she watched the maid curl her thick brown hair and roll it over soft pads on top of her head, hope warred with despair. Maybe her dread of disappointment was unfounded. Maybe everything would be all right. Maybe this night she would discover what she knew was there to be discovered. Maybe this night Cato would discover what was there to be discovered in his bride.

And then again, probably not.

"There now, Lady Phoebe, take a look at yourself." The housekeeper stepped back after fastening at Phoebe's throat the string of pearls that had belonged to Phoebe's mother, then to Diana, and now to Phoebe. She gestured to the mirror.

Phoebe cast only a cursory glance at her reflection. Close study would only add to her already raging anxiety. She moved to the door. "I'm ready. Is it time to go downstairs? Olivia, where are you?" A note of panic edged into her voice.

"I'm here," Olivia said calmly, stepping away from the bedcurtains. "Where I've been all along."

"Oh, I wish you could stay with me the whole time." Phoebe grabbed Olivia's hand in a convulsive gesture. "If only I didn't have to have the aunts to attend me at the end. If you were there, I wouldn't feel so much like a *sacrifice!*"

Olivia squeezed Phoebe's hand. "It's a horrible ritual," she said feelingly. "But it'll be over quickly . . . once you g-get out of the hall."

"I suppose so." Phoebe gripped Olivia's hand so tightly the other girl winced, but did not complain.

Lord Carlton was waiting for his daughter in the hall, pacing impatiently. The bridegroom had left before the first group of guests had been ferried to the church, and the earl was tired of his own company.

"Ah, there you are." He came to the foot of the stairs as Phoebe came down. "Such a long time as you've been . . . but then, I suppose the bride's entitled to take her time," he added with an attempt at a bluff smile. "Very well you look, m'dear," he said, but he sounded slightly doubtful. "Strange, when Diana wore . . . But come, we must be going."

Phoebe curtsied, but could find no words. She laid her hand on her father's arm, aware that her face seemed suddenly numb, as if frozen.

"I think it's stopped raining," Olivia announced from the front door that was held open by a servant. "That's a good omen, Phoebe." She looked anxiously at her friend. Phoebe didn't even look like herself, and it wasn't just the elaborate hairstyle and the stiff formality of her unsuitable gown.

"Yes," Phoebe said with a fixed smile. She climbed into the waiting carriage, managing only with Olivia's swift intervention to keep the full folds of ivory damask from dragging in the straw. Throughout the short journey she stared straight ahead, feeling like someone else. Someone she didn't know at all.

Cato was talking casually with a knot of guests at the front of the church when the bustle at the back told them that the bride had arrived. He moved without haste to the altar rail and turned to look at his bride as she came down the aisle. It was his fourth such ceremony and held neither terrors nor surprises for him, but he noticed that Phoebe was moving as awkwardly as a marionette with an unskilled manipulator.

He had a flash of compassion for her. Her best features were her eyes, her rich, luxuriant hair, and the delicate peach of her complexion, but somehow they were not shown to advantage. Diana had looked so wonderful in that gown, but it did nothing for her sister.

The poor girl didn't have her sister's taste any more than she had her style and beauty, he reflected. But she would do.

Phoebe took in a swirl of emerald green. He had shed his usual black in favor of this brilliant velvet doublet over white silk. And he was *magnificent*. And he was about to become her husband.

When he took her hand, her eyes were riveted on the square emerald signet ring, and then on the strong, lean fingers and the clean, pared, filbert nails. He'd never held her hand before.

She raised her eyes to his face. His expression as he spoke his responses was cool, courteous, and totally without sentiment.

3

*P*hoebe couldn't eat at the wedding feast. Not even the gilded marchpane cakes or the sugarplums and almonds could tempt her. She regarded the silver platters as they passed before her down the long table with complete indifference, mildly astonished that her usual sweet tooth had deserted her so completely.

Minstrels played in the long gallery above the great hall, and as the afternoon turned to evening, myriad wax candles cast a softening golden glow over the crimson-hued faces of the revelers.

Cato sat beside Phoebe in the center of the high table. He showed no inclination to drink deep, his chalice was only rarely refilled, and he struck Phoebe as distanced from the joviality, although he was attentive to his guests, keeping a close eye on the servants as they circled the long tables with flagons of wine and great platters of smoking meat. When his two youngest daughters, Diana's children, showed drooping heads and eyelids, he caught it immediately and signaled for a nursemaid to take them back to the nursery.

Despite this, Phoebe had the dismal impression that he would rather be anywhere than at this table, hosting a wedding party. He barely seemed aware of her sitting beside him, and her own father, Lord Carlton, was sinking ever deeper into the plentiful burgundy. The bride seemed an irrelevancy for all the notice anyone but Olivia took of her.

Olivia was sitting opposite Phoebe, too far away for any intimate conversation, but her dark gaze rarely left her friend's strained countenance. Olivia thought of the night to come.

The wedding night. Was that why Phoebe was looking so taut? Was she thinking of the coming hours? Of that moment when she'd cease to belong to herself? Olivia's fine mouth set hard. That would not happen to her. She was determined.

Phoebe with desultory hand waved away a basket of comfits, and Cato glanced sideways at his bride as he realized that she'd been ignoring all the succulent offerings that had passed before her.

"Not hungry?" he asked in some surprise. Phoebe's healthy appetite was a household fact.

"I don't seem to be," Phoebe responded, dragging her eyes away from their studious contemplation of the emerald on his signet finger and looking up at him for the first time since they'd left the church.

She was aware of his closeness over every inch of her skin. They sat side by side in state upon a high velvet-padded double chair, and she could feel Cato's thigh against hers; his arm brushed hers whenever he moved it. The sheer physical sense of him made her head spin. His dark eyes filled her vision as she gazed up at him. She could see her reflection in the irises, and it seemed as if she were drowning there. Her tongue was unaccountably stuck to the roof of her mouth, and she couldn't begin to form a sensible sentence.

And she was behaving like a mooncalf . . . a village simpleton touched by the full moon, she thought crossly, reaching for her goblet of wine. Her arm jerked and the goblet flew from her fingers, splashing crimson over the snow-white linen.

"Oh, I'm so clumsy!" she exclaimed in mortification, dabbing at the spill with her napkin.

Her frantic dabbing served to spread the mess perilously close to Cato's white silk-clad arm, resting on the table. Just in time he seized her mopping hand. "Phoebe, don't do that! Can't you see you're making it worse? Leave it to the servants."

With a swift movement he twitched the sodden napkin from her hand just as she was about to return it to her lap. "*No!* If you put this on your dress now, you'll stain your skirt!"

His tone was sharply impatient and produced an enlivening flash of annoyance in Phoebe's previously dull eyes. He had been as responsible as her father for the disastrously economical choice of wedding gown. "I fail to see what difference it could make, sir," she responded acidly. "It's a hideous gown and it doesn't suit me."

"What on earth do you mean? It's an extremely elegant and expensive gown," Cato said, frowning. "Your sister—"

"Yes, precisely!" Phoebe interrupted. "On Diana it was exquisite! On me it's hideous. The color doesn't suit me."

"Oh, don't be silly, Phoebe. It's a very fine color."

"For some people."

Cato had given her only a cursory glance as she'd come up the aisle. Now he looked at her closely. She was looking so flustered and rumpled, with her hair escaping from its elaborate coiffure; even the matchless pearls had somehow become twisted around her neck. Maybe the gown didn't suit her as well as it had Diana, but there was no excuse for such untidiness. She just seemed to become unraveled before his eyes.

Phoebe continued savagely, "But of course new gowns are a frivolous waste of money."

Cato felt unaccountably defensive. "There is a war on, Phoebe. Your father felt—"

"He felt, my lord, that the money should be spent on pikes and muskets and buff jerkins," Phoebe interrupted again. "And if I have to wear this ghastly ivory concoction, then so be it."

"You're making mountains out of molehills," Cato declared. "You look very well in that gown. There's nothing wrong with the color at all."

Phoebe merely looked at him in indignant disbelief, and the appearance of a servant with a cloth and a clean strip of linen to lay over the stain ended the exchange, much to Cato's relief.

Phoebe had to lean in toward Cato to give the man room to work. Her cheek brushed his emerald velvet shoulder, and all her indignation vanished like straws in the wind. Her heart began its drumbeat again. His scent of wine and lavender and the pomade that made his hair glow burnished in the candlelight set her senses reeling. The servant deftly removed Phoebe's napkin and replaced it with a clean one.

"My thanks," she murmured faintly. She was suddenly aware of how her legs on this high seat didn't quite reach the floor so that her feet were swinging at about the level of Cato's calves. She felt silly and clumsy and overwhelmingly inexperienced.

When she saw Cato and her father exchange a nod, she felt her cheeks grow hot. Lord Carlton gestured significantly to Phoebe's aunt, one of the two female relatives who'd risked the journey from London across the war-torn Thames valley to attend their niece's wedding, and to assist in the essential ritual of putting the bride to bed.

Phoebe swallowed. "Is it time?" she whispered.

"Aye, it's time," Cato replied softly. "Go with your aunts. They will look after you."

Phoebe regarded the aunts bearing down upon her shoulder to shoulder. They were a grim-faced pair, sisters of the mother Phoebe could not remember. They had adored Diana. And without exception, those who adored Diana had little time for Phoebe.

Phoebe cast Olivia a desperate look. If only Olivia could be beside her at this sacrificial rite. But it was a ceremony to be conducted only by women who'd gone through it themselves.

Cato rose to his feet, took his bride's hand, and courteously assisted her to stand. All eyes were upon her. He raised

Phoebe's hand to his lips, then stepped aside, passing her over to her aunts. The guests were smiling; knowing little smiles, and in some cases broad anticipatory grins with a touch of lasciviousness that brought them close to a leer.

Phoebe's face flamed anew. She hated to be the focus of attention. Usually it was because of some awkward or embarrassing faux pas, but this was worse than anything. She wanted what was about to happen, wanted it with a bewildering urgency, but she couldn't bear to imagine the thoughts going on behind those drunken prurient grins.

Olivia took something from her pocket and laid it carefully and prominently on the white cloth above her plate. Phoebe gazed at it. It was Olivia's friendship ring, one of the three that Portia had made all those years ago by twining their three locks of hair into a circle. Phoebe's hand went to the tiny pocket in the skirt of her gown and closed over her own ring. The moment of panic receded. She gave Olivia a half smile and allowed herself to be swept away on the tide of her aunts.

She stood still in the middle of Cato's bedchamber. She'd never entered this room before. Everything in it seemed dark and massive. The armchair drawn up before the blazing fire, the carved chest at the foot of the bed, the mahogany sideboard against the wall, the huge armoire with its great brass key. The curtains at the windows were of dark red velvet, hanging from massive oak rods. The floor was of almost black oak, highly polished, scattered with embroidered Elizabethan rugs.

Her gaze moved almost reluctantly to the bulk of the carved bed with its tapestry hangings. It seemed very high and she saw the little footstool that had presumably been put there for her benefit. Cato would hardly need it. The head and feet of the bed were carved in a tangle of what looked like serpents and dragons. The coverlet was of rich dark blue silk. Phoebe felt pale and dwarfed.

"Come now, child, there's no time for gawping," Lady Morecombe scolded, beginning to unhook Phoebe's gown. "Your husband won't expect to be kept waiting."

Phoebe shivered and moved closer to the fire, while her aunt followed her flapping her hands as she tried to finish unhooking the gown.

"Keep still, do!"

Phoebe came to a halt in front of the fire and then stood, still and mute as a doll, while the two women bustled around her, handing her clothes to the maid who stood ready to receive them. When she was naked, they brought a wet washcloth from the nightstand and sponged her body from head to toe, even though she'd bathed that morning. She was dried briskly.

"Now, rinse out your mouth with this essence of cloves," one of the aunts instructed, passing Phoebe a small cup filled with dark brown liquid. "Fresh breath is most important in the bedchamber. Make sure you remember that."

"But don't expect your husband to remember it himself," Lady Morecombe declared with asperity. Her own lord was a renowned drunkard who smoked a pipe and had a passion for pickled onions.

Their words washed over Phoebe. Obediently she rinsed out her mouth and spat into the basin. Then they dropped the soft white nightrail over her head and buttoned it at the back.

"That's very pretty," Lady Barett said. It was the first word of approval Phoebe could remember hearing all day. "Now, let's take down your hair."

Phoebe sat on the chest at the foot of the bed while they unpinned her hair, and then both stood aside as the maid brushed the long light brown hair with strong rhythmic strokes until it rippled down her back in gleaming strands.

"Now, get into bed." The aunts both turned down the coverlet, smoothing their hands over the crisp sheet beneath and the white cover on the bolster. Sprigs of lavender had been strewn over the pillows.

Phoebe climbed in with the aid of the stool. They told her to sit up against the pillows, and they smoothed the coverlet over her and arranged her hair over her shoulders.

"There, you'll do," they announced almost in chorus.

Lady Morecombe turned to the maid. "Clear away the mess, quickly now, girl. We shall go down and tell Lord Granville that his bride is ready for him."

With one last inspection of the sacrifice they had prepared, they left Phoebe alone to wait.

Lord Carlton was regaling his immediate neighbors with a particularly ribald joke as the aunts returned to the great hall. Cato's expression bore a look of faint distaste of which he was unaware as the gales of drunken laughter gusted over the gentler sounds of the minstrels in the gallery.

"Your bride awaits you, Lord Granville," gravely announced one of the aunts.

"Ah, to business!" bellowed Lord Carlton, pushing back his chair with such vigor that it crashed to the floor. "Come, gentlemen, let us accompany the groom to his feast."

Raucous laughter greeted this sally. Cato's smile was a mere flicker of his lips and came nowhere near his eyes.

They encircled Cato, sweeping him before them towards the stairs, flourishing their wine goblets, and singing and laughing as they escorted him up the curving flight to the landing above.

Phoebe heard the gusts of merrymaking, the loud laughter, the chanting voices. She sat bolt upright in bed, sick with apprehension and a strange excitement. The tangle of lusting dreams that had plagued her nights for so many weeks was about to become unraveled.

The bedchamber door burst open. A crowd filled the doorway. She stared at the blur of red glistening faces in shock and horror. Sitting up high in the big bed, she felt as exposed as if she were naked, bound to the stocks on the village green.

Then Cato turned to the crowd at his back and with a great shove with both arms, slammed the door closed on the face of the throng. He threw the bolt across as a hammering protest began on the far side of the oak. He waited, his arms spread wide across the door, hands firmly planted on the frame at either side. Finally the hammering ceased and the sounds of ribaldry drifted away as the wedding guests returned to the bottles below.

Cato turned back to the room. "For some reason, weddings make animals of men," he observed, coming over to the bed.

He regarded Phoebe keenly. If she was frightened and tense, it was going to be a messy and painful business.

His first wife, Brian Morse's mother, had been a widow, and the wedding night had been notable mostly because of his own inexperience. At seventeen he'd had relatively few sexual encounters, and all of those had been mere fleeting grapples leading to a short burst of satisfaction. He had had no idea of how to please a woman.

Olivia's mother and then Diana had both been virgin on their wedding night. And both nights had brought little satisfaction to any of them. On both occasions he'd tried without success to please them. Olivia's mother, Nan, had tried to disguise her dislike of the conjugal bed. Their marriage had been a deeply affectionate one, but Nan had never enjoyed the hungry grapplings of sex. Diana had never even tried. She had simply performed her duty.

It seemed that women of breeding, the women who became wives, disliked bedsport, and Cato had learned not to expect the uninhibited responses he enjoyed on occasion with women for whom lusty sex was both profession and pleasure. He had learned not to linger.

He turned away and eased off his boots against the bootjack.

Phoebe felt the first wash of disappointment. He hadn't said anything to her. He'd just looked at her in that speculative, almost cold manner, as if sizing her up. Then he'd turned from her as if finding her wanting.

She watched as he removed the emerald green doublet and threw it carelessly onto a chair. He wore no sword, only a small dagger sheathed at his belt. He unfastened the belt and tossed it onto the chair. His long, full britches of the same velvet as the doublet were fastened below the knee with wide black ribbons. She watched as he unbuttoned them at the waist, bent to unfasten the ribbons, and pushed them off his hips, stepping out of them in one fluid movement.

And now Phoebe was holding her breath. He glanced over at her as he stood in his knee-length drawers, stockings, and white silk shirt with its full lace-edged sleeves. Phoebe's gaze was riveted on his throat, on the pulse beating at its base. She was aware of the expanse of his chest beneath the thin silk. Her eyes slid timorously down to his hips, to the bulge clearly visible beneath the drawers. She bit her lip.

Cato moved swiftly and blew out the candles, plunging the chamber into darkness lit only by the fire. Then he threw off the rest of his clothes. His body was in deep shadow as he approached the bed. Reaching out, he drew the bed curtains tight, so that no chink of light entered the enclosed space.

The thick feather mattress yielded to his weight. Phoebe could make out nothing in the darkness. She wished she could see him. She'd wanted to know what he looked like without his clothes. But it seemed these couplings took place in the dark.

She could feel him above her now, though. Could feel the warmth emanating from his body. She could distinguish the dark shape looming in the darker shadows as he knelt over her. She wanted to touch him. Tentatively she raised her hand, laid it on his chest.

Cato didn't even notice the fluttering caress. "It will be over soon," he murmured. "I don't want to hurt you, but it's inevitable the first time. Lie still and try to relax."

He didn't want her to touch him. He didn't want to touch

her except where it was strictly necessary. Surely that wasn't right. It just couldn't be! Confusion and protest welled deep within Phoebe even as he moved her thighs apart.

The sharp pain of penetration made her cry out. He whispered to her, promising that it would be over in a minute. He moved once or twice within her, then withdrew with a clear and obvious sigh of relief. He rolled away from her and there was silence.

That was it! Phoebe lay still in shocked dismay. That was all there was to it . . . to this happening she'd imagined, fantasized about, dreaded, longed for. Just that in and out and then *nothing!* It wasn't supposed to be like that. She knew with every fiber of her being that it wasn't. Was it that he found her so unappealing, so unattractive, this man who'd had Diana in his bed, that he obviously couldn't endure to spend more than the necessary seconds with her? And once she conceived, he wouldn't even want to do that.

She lay rigid under the wash of outraged frustration. She wasn't Diana, but she had so much to give . . . so much more than her sister had ever offered anyone! But Cato was blind to what lay beneath what he saw.

Cato lay beside her rigid frame feeling like a brute. He heard the outrage in her silence. The act had obviously shocked her. Had no one prepared her? He felt as if he'd violated her . . . raped her . . . and yet such a concept was ridiculous in the marriage bed.

His mouth set in a thin line as he lay in the darkness. It was done now. And this union, distasteful though it was to both of them, would bring him a son. As soon as that was achieved, he would leave his wife alone.

He thought she was asleep now. The rigidity seemed to have left her, and her breathing had deepened. It had been close to two years since he'd shared his bed with a woman. Diana had been ill for many months before her death. Paradoxically in the circumstances, he found it rather pleasant to have a warm body so close to him.

He drifted to sleep while the sounds of revelry from down-stairs continued until well into the night.

When Phoebe awoke in the morning, she was alone in the big bed. And when she went downstairs, there was no sign of her husband and no indication in the quiet, orderly house that she had been married the previous day.

Even her father had left without so much as a word of farewell. Gone back about the business of the war, happy to leave his daughter in the charge of her husband—in more ways than one, Phoebe thought with a bitter little smile. His daughter was no longer *his* expense.

4

"That's the last one, Granny!" Phoebe threw the last cabbage from the trench into the basket and straightened her aching back. She leaned on the spade and pushed her hair out of her eyes with a gloved hand. The day was sunny, and despite the cold Phoebe had worked up quite a sweat digging up Granny Spruel's winter cabbages from the straw-lined trench where they'd been stored in the autumn. Mud from the glove mingled with the dew on her brow and streaked down her cheek, but she didn't notice.

"Eh, lass, you've got a right good heart on ye," the elderly woman said. "With the lads at the war, there's no one to 'elp a body these days."

"Any news of your grandsons?" Phoebe hoisted the basket and set off up the garden path towards the kitchen door.

"Nothin' since afore Christmas." Granny Spruel followed Phoebe into the kitchen. "Set 'em down in the pantry, dearie. . . . A fellow what was comin' through said he'd met up with Jeremiah down in Cornwall somewhere. Fightin' was somethin' awful, he said. But Jeremiah was still upstandin' when 'e left him."

"They're saying there's no support left for the Royalists in Cornwall," Phoebe said, returning from the pantry. "They've practically given up. I'm sure you'll be seeing your grandsons back again soon."

"Aye, we can but 'ope and pray, dearie. Ye'll have a slice of my fruitcake, now, won't you? And a cup of cider?" Granny Spruel bustled to the dresser and lifted the lid on an earthen crock. She took out a cloth-wrapped cake and cut a hefty wedge. "Help yourself to cider, dearie."

Phoebe did so and took a healthy bite of cake. She knew that while her physical assistance was welcomed by Granny and the other women of the village left without a male back to aid them, her company was as important for the elderly women who craved a chat in their long, lonely days. Younger women had no time to chat, left as they were with broods of small children and all the work of house, garden, and small-holding to take care of. So in these months of civil war the elderly suffered an isolation most unusual in the close-knit community of the countryside.

The chimes of the church clock brought Phoebe to her feet with a mortified cry. "Surely it isn't eleven-thirty already!"

"Oh, aye, that it is. That old clock never misses a minute," Granny said as if this was somehow comforting. "We all expected you'd 'ave no time for helpin' out the old folks after your marriage." Granny chattered as she accompanied Phoebe to the garden gate. "Quite the grand lady we thought you'd be." She chuckled as if at an absurdity.

"Some chance of that," Phoebe said with a responding grin. She raised a hand in farewell as she opened the gate. "Nothing's going to change, Granny. I'm just the same as ever."

For some reason this statement sent Granny Spruel into a fit of laughter, her lined, weather-beaten face crinkling like a wrinkled apple. "Aye, we'll see about that, m'dear," she said, and still chuckling turned back indoors.

Phoebe flew down the village street, holding up her skirts to protect them from the mud, although it was already too late, she reflected ruefully. The hem of her brown stuff gown and the once-white petticoat beneath were thickly coated with the mud from the cabbage trench in Granny Spruel's garden. Cato had said he wished to dine at noon, and unpunctuality always produced one of his sardonic comments. Now she wouldn't have time to change out of her muddy clothes. But when was that a novelty?

As she approached the village green she saw a small knot of people gathered around the stocks. The unmistakable figure of Cato Granville on his bay charger towered over the group.

Phoebe's heart did its customary erratic dance. He was bareheaded and the wind ruffled the close-cropped dark hair. As usual he wore black, except for the pristine white stock at his throat. And how it suited him! It suited the straight-backed, commanding posture of the soldier. It rendered his dark brown eyes almost black and gave his tanned complexion an almost olive tinge.

Her step slowed involuntarily as she drew closer. For all the marquis's plain dress, everything about him bespoke wealth. He held whip and reins in hands gloved in lace-edged leather. Those hands rested on the pommel of his tooled-leather saddle. His feet were encased in boots of the finest doeskin. The black velvet folds of his cloak were pushed carelessly back from his shoulders, revealing the white shirt with its ruffled sleeves, the lace-edged stock, the great silver buttons on his black coat, and the chased-silver scabbard of the curved cavalry sword at his hip.

How could any man be so beautiful? Phoebe asked herself. Was it his power that drew her? Was it his aura of absolute command that made her knees weak? And if it was, why was it? Why should she be so swept with lust because the man held the world at his feet?

It was absurd! Incomprehensible. And yet it was a fact. A fact not in any way diminished by the vast disappointment that her marriage had brought her.

She realized that she'd been drawing ever closer to the outskirts of the group, without any clear intention of doing so. But at the same moment, she also realized that she didn't want Cato to see her. If she hurried, she would be ahead of him at the dining table. She turned away, but a moment too late.

Cato, who in his position as Justice of the Peace was overseeing the imprisonment of a vagrant in the stocks, happened to glance up just as Phoebe edged away from the throng. What on earth could have brought her there? It wasn't meet for a young woman of Phoebe's position to be wandering on foot and alone through the countryside. And she certainly had no place witnessing the punishment of rogues and ruffians.

He turned his horse aside, leaving the beadle to see that justice was done, and rode after his wife.

Phoebe heard the soft clop of hooves on the damp grass. Her spine prickled and her scalp contracted. She didn't know whether it was with anticipation or apprehension. She never knew these days whether she wanted to be in Cato's company or not. She stopped and turned.

"Good morning, my lord." She greeted him with solemn formality.

"What are you doing out here, Phoebe?" Cato drew rein as he spoke. He frowned down at her. There were streaks of dirt on her face, and her hair was a veritable bird's nest. "What's happened to you? You look as if you've been dragged through a hedge backwards."

"I've been digging cabbages," Phoebe explained.

"Cabbages? Did you say cabbages?"

Phoebe nodded. "They were stored in a trench to keep them from the frost, and now Granny Spruel wants to pickle them, so I dug them up for her."

Cato stared at her. Nothing she said seemed to make any sense. He leaned down from his horse and commanded brusquely, "Give me your hand and put your foot on my boot."

Phoebe looked up at him with large blue eyes the color of speedwells. Cato was struck by the intensity of their color as he waited impatiently for her to obey him.

"I beg your pardon, my lord," Phoebe said after a hesitant moment, "but I don't like horses. They frighten me. They have such big yellow teeth and when I'm riding them they seem to know I can't control them and they run off with me."

"This horse isn't going to run away with you," Cato declared. "Now, do as I say. Lady Granville cannot refuse to ride, it's absurd." He snapped his gloved fingers impatiently.

Phoebe swallowed. She took the hand and hoisted up her leg, trying to get her foot on his boot. It seemed very high up and the length of her legs was not exactly one of her stronger features. Unlike Diana, whose legs had reached her armpits, Phoebe recollected resentfully as she hopped and finally managed to get purchase on the toe of Cato's boot.

Cato pulled her up, catching her around the waist and settling her on the saddle in front of him. "There, see. You're quite safe."

Phoebe bit her lip and offered only a jerky little nod in response. Her heart was apatter again, and she couldn't control the little quiver along her spine at the sensation of his body so close and warm at her back. Fortunately, the charger moved forward, gathering speed, and her quivering flesh had another excuse.

"Now perhaps we can discuss cabbages," Cato said after a minute. His arm tightened around her waist as the bay jumped the narrow ditch that separated the lane from the home farm.

"Well, there are no men in the village. They're all either killed or at the war," Phoebe replied when she could catch her breath. "Someone has to help the old women do the things that the men would have done for them. Like digging up cabbages," she finished with an all-encompassing gesture.

"It's right and proper that you should involve yourself in the welfare of the tenants," Cato responded when he'd absorbed this explanation. "Providing medicines and food for the sick and indigent, for instance. But the marchioness of Granville is not a farmhand. She does not dig up cabbages, or do any other kind of manual labor."

"Then who's to do it?" Phoebe asked simply.

Cato did not reply. They trotted into the stable yard and he dismounted, reaching up to lift Phoebe down. He took her face between his hands and examined her in frowning silence.

"It is not meet that my wife should go around looking like a scarecrow who's been standing in the field too long," he stated flatly. He wiped a smear of mud from her cheek with the pad of his thumb.

"Do you consider it meet that there are tenants in need on your farms, sir?" Phoebe's blue eyes held a militant sparkle. "If you can find someone else to help them, then I'll try to learn to sit at home sewing fine seams."

"That tone ill becomes you," Cato declared, an angry flash in his own eyes.

Phoebe took a deep breath. "Then I beg your pardon, my lord. But I would say it ill becomes a landowner to ignore the plight of his tenants." She dropped him a curtsy and hurried from the yard.

Of all the damned impertinence! Cato stared after her retreating figure. The hem of her gown had come down and was trailing over the muddy cobbles, picking up stray straws and other unsavory refuse common to stable yards.

"Beggin' yer pardon, m'lord." Giles Crampton's broad Yorkshire vowels brought Cato swinging round. "Summat the matter, m'lord?" The marquis's lieutenant looked askance.

"What's the situation in the village . . . with the tenants in general?" Cato demanded abruptly.

Giles gave the question some thought, but he wasn't quite certain to what situation exactly it referred. "Much as usual, I reckon," he offered eventually.

"Yes, but what's usual?" Cato sounded impatient. "Is there any particular hardship that you know of?"

"Oh, as to that, it's same as usual, sir." Giles shrugged. "The womenfolk are 'avin' t' manage as best they can. There's little enou' 'elp they'll be gettin' from the menfolk these days."

"How bad is it?" Cato gazed into the middle distance over the other man's head. Giles was a good half a head shorter than his lord.

"Worse fer the old folks and the youngun's with babbies, I reckon."

Cato clasped the back of his neck, deep lines corrugating his brow. "Why wasn't I told of this?"

Giles looked puzzled. "Was you interested in knowin', then, sir?"

He hadn't been, of course. "I am now," Cato said shortly. "Send some men into the village to find out how they can be of help with farm labor and suchlike."

"Right y'are, sir." Giles raised a hand to his hat in salute. He half turned and said casually over his shoulder, "We'll be 'eadin' out fer the siege at Basing House soon, then, shall us, m'lord?"

Cato understood what was implicit in the question. Giles Crampton did not consider farm labor appropriate for his highly disciplined and drilled troops. He'd been kicking his heels for the four weeks since the wedding but now clearly considered that the honeymoon should be over.

"We'll leave in the morning. Just tell the men to do what they can for today," Cato said and was rewarded with a broad beam.

"Aye, m'lord. I'll get right onto it."

Cato nodded and went in for dinner.

"*D*ivide *and conquer.*"

All eyes turned to Sir Jacob Astley, who stood beside an arched window overlooking the quadrangle of the college of Christ Church. He drummed his fingers on the thick stone sill. The ruby on one finger clicked against the stone.

"Not sure what you mean, Astley." King Charles raised heavy-lidded eyes and turned his head towards the man at the window. The king's fine-featured face was weary in the lamplight, his thick curling hair lank on his shoulders. He'd ridden into the city of Oxford the previous afternoon, hotly pursued by a cavalry brigade of Cromwell's New Model Army. It had been a narrow escape and His Sovereign Majesty had still not recovered his equilibrium. To be pursued by his own subjects, to escape capture by inches, had brought home to him as almost nothing else had done, that he now reigned England in name alone.

"I mean, Sire, that if we could cause trouble among Parliament's leaders . . . if we could somehow arrange for them to fall out among themselves, then we would find them easier to deal with." Sir Jacob turned from the window, his eyes in his pale face ablaze with conviction.

"Aye, Sire. And I heard talk already of some dissension among their high command." Brian Morse stepped out of the shadows, where he'd been standing silent up to now, listening and awaiting the moment when he could draw himself to the king's attention.

King Charles regarded the young man with a slight frown, trying to place him. The slender frame clad immaculately in dove gray silk was vaguely familiar, the little brown eyes, hard as pebbles, more so.

"Brian Morse, Your Majesty." Brian bowed low. "Forgive me for speaking out."

The king waved a hand in vague disclaimer. "If you have something useful to say, sir, don't stand on ceremony."

"Mr. Morse was responsible for bringing the offer of munitions from the king of Orange, Sire. You may remember congratulating him on his return from Rotterdam." The duke of Hamilton spoke up from the window embrasure at the far end of the paneled room, opposite the window looking onto the quadrangle. He was chewing at his thumb, carefully peeling back loose skin with his teeth and spitting it onto the floor at his feet.

The king seemed to consider this for a minute, then he smiled. It was a smile of surpassing sweetness. "Indeed I do remember. You have served us well, Mr. Morse. Your counsel is most welcome."

Brian felt a surge of triumph. He was there, at last. Into the holy of holies. He stepped a little further into the chamber. "My stepfather is the marquis of Granville, Sire."

A pained frown crossed the king's countenance. There had been a time when the marquis had been both friend and most loyal subject.

"A man is not responsible for his treacherous relatives," declared Prince Rupert, the king's nephew, in what could have been an attempt at heavy comfort. His florid, handsome face was flushed from the contents of the chalice he held between his beringed hands.

"And even less for a stepfather," agreed Sir Jacob. "Does Granville still receive you?"

"He has done up to now, sir." Brian's mouth thinned to the point of invisibility, and his hard eyes seemed to grow even smaller. He would not soon forget the humiliation visited upon him the last time he'd stayed under his stepfather's roof. The marquis's bastard niece, Portia Worth, now the countess of Rothbury, had played him for a fool, and the brat Olivia had had her part in it too.

He still squirmed at the memory of his stepsister's laughing, taunting eyes as she'd enjoyed his mortification. A true case of turned tables. In the past he had held the upper hand, subjecting the child to a reign of terror and uncertainty purely for the amusement it afforded him, and he had every intention of regaining that control. Once he stood as head of the Granville family, he would have ample opportunity to seek revenge upon the girl.

"I had thought that perhaps I might work some mischief

to good purpose under my stepfather's roof," he continued smoothly. "He will receive me again, and with open arms if I imply that perhaps my allegiance grows uncertain?"

He glanced around the room, watching for reaction. The king looked merely weary, Rupert interested, Sir Jacob and the duke clearly reserving judgment.

"A spy in the enemy camp?" queried Rupert.

"In a manner of speaking, sir." Brian shrugged easily. "Someone to plant misinformation, perhaps. To look and listen. To find something useful, perhaps. Something that might make trouble between Granville and the others."

There was a short silence, then the king said, "D'ye have a clear plan, Mr. Morse? Or are you catching at straws?"

"No straws, Sire. I don't have a clear plan as yet, but, if I might say so, I have a certain . . . a certain facility for seizing the main chance. Things occur to me that might not occur to someone else."

"To a less devious mind," said Prince Rupert with a chuckle. "Aye, I heard tell of your dealings with Strickland in The Hague. Fooled him completely for a while, I understand."

"For long enough to gather the information we needed," Brian agreed without undue modesty. This was neither the time nor the place for such.

"Granville's married again, I hear," Sir Jacob said suddenly.

Brian's face became as smooth as polished marble. "To his late wife's sister," he replied. "The alliance of Granville and Carlton thus continues as strong as before."

King Charles rubbed his temples. "Which brings us back to Sir Jacob's plan of divide and rule."

"Cromwell and Fairfax are as close as two peas in a pod," the duke pointed out. "And as Morse says, the alliance between Granville and Carlton is well cemented."

"But if they were obliged to take sides over one of their number," suggested Brian. His mind was racing. He hadn't expected to be given such an opportunity so quickly. But he

could see his way clear now to making a dramatic contribution to the king's cause. A contribution that would further his
own ends.

He stepped up to the table and stood with his hands lightly
balled into fists resting on the gleaming satinwood.

"My stepfather's trusted by both Cromwell and Fairfax,
but supposing his loyalty came into question. If Cromwell
supported him and Fairfax didn't . . ." He glanced around the
paneled chamber, an eyebrow raised interrogatively.

Sir Jacob kicked a slipping log back into the grate. "Granville's an honorable man." The quiet statement lay untouched for a moment in the dusty, crowded chamber.

"You would call a man who has risen against his sovereign
honorable, sir?" demanded Prince Rupert, his eyes flaring
under the lamplight as he pushed back his chair and jumped
to his feet. He glared angrily around the chamber, his flush
deepening. He was an impetuous man, as jealous of his
reputation as a brilliant commander in the field as he was
passionate in defense of King Charles's divine right to rule
England.

"Granville's a traitor and he'll lose his head when this is
over," the prince continued. "As they all will." He refilled his
silver chalice from the wine flagon on the table, his movements jerky so that ruby drops scattered over the long table.

Sir Jacob shrugged. He had little interest in defending
the marquis of Granville against the passions of the king's
nephew.

Rupert drained the contents of his chalice, throwing his
head back, his powerful throat working, the rich curling flow
of his hair cascading over his wide lace collar. He set the cup
down with a snap.

The king coughed gently, reminding his lords of who really
made the decisions in this company. "Gentlemen, let us return to the matter in hand. I find myself imprisoned in this
city, chased into it by a troop of Cromwell's cavalry. Our armies
are in disarray, our loyal supporters are being besieged in

their own houses. To enlist further support from the Scots, I will have to agree to the covenant. . . ."

He leaned his elbows on the table and steepled his fingers. The covenant would compel him to agree to establish the Presbyterian Church in England. A sin he was convinced would bring down upon him divine justice. It was not a course of action he could contemplate except in extremis.

"I am open to any suggestion. Astley's has merit, it seems to me. And in Mr. Morse, here, we seem to have the perfect instrument to hand." He bestowed another of his smiles upon Brian, who only barely managed to restrain a crow of triumph.

"Aye, then we'll start with Granville." Sir Jacob's voice was now brisk. "But you'll need more than ordinary trickery, Mr. Morse. I repeat that Granville is as honest as he's clever." He regarded the prince for a minute, one sardonically raised eyebrow inviting dissension, but when Rupert maintained silence, he continued.

"If we bring down the marquis, I believe the entire house of cards will topple. They'll turn against each other. Granville has many supporters, but there are those who wouldn't mind seeing him fall." His mouth took a cynical quirk. Human nature and its foibles could always be relied upon.

"If you will entrust this matter to me, Your Majesty, I give you my word I will not fail you." Brian spoke earnestly, a throb of sincerity in his voice.

"We put our trust in you, sir." The king rose to his feet. "Gentlemen . . ." He gestured in brief farewell and walked to the door. An equerry jumped to open it for him, and the king departed his bowing subjects, Prince Rupert on his heels.

"Lay your plans carefully, Morse," Sir Jacob advised, moving to the door himself. "Granville's no fool."

"No, but he's a newly married man," one of the others said with a cynical chuckle. "He'll have a few other things on his mind I daresay . . . for a month or two at least."

Brian made no response to this sally. He walked to the window opposite the quadrangle. This one looked out over the broad sweep of Christ Church meadow and the line of winter-bare trees along the riverbank. It was a peaceful scene, one that made it hard to imagine the war raging beyond the city walls. Tom Tower struck five, its hollow, sonorous chime booming out over the city.

Cato had a new bride. New brides meant children. Brian's luck couldn't hold forever. One day Granville was going to get a son, unless something intervened. So far and against many odds Granville had survived the war, and with his luck he might well continue to do so. But Brian's first priority must be the new bride. The wedding had been a month ago and she could well have conceived by now, be even now carrying the child that would disinherit him.

He stared out into the lowering dusk, his mouth pinched and hard. He had managed to dispose of the other one before she could produce more than squalling girl children; her sister should be no more difficult. He'd never met the girl, but if she was anything like Diana, she'd be easy to cozen, without a thought in her head but pleasure and fashion. Once under Granville's roof he would find the way to remove her. But first, maybe he could use her. He had nearly succeeded in using Diana to work against Cato. Why not this one? And then once she'd served her purpose, he'd get rid of her . . . her and whatever embryo she was carrying.

And then, if the war hadn't taken care of Cato, he'd have to turn his attention that way. Accidents were easy to arrange for a fertile and imaginative mind.

Brian nodded to himself as the last chimes of Tom Tower died in the dusk.

*C*ato and Giles Crampton rode into the stable yard at midday. It was a bright, clear day with even an intimation of warmth in the early March sunshine.

" 'Ow long d'ye reckon we'll be at 'ome this time, m'lord?"

Giles inquired with apparent casualness. He whistled tune-lessly between his teeth as he looped the reins over his mount's neck and dismounted.

Cato was well aware that Giles was seething with the need to get back to the business in hand—the long and dreary siege of Basing House. They'd only managed to spend three days there before Cato had received a message from Cromwell to attend a briefing in the general's camp outside Oxford. Giles, his most trusted lieutenant, had perforce to accompany him. Giles as usual was torn between his need to oversee the health, welfare, and discipline of the Granville militia and his need to be at his commander's side.

On the way to Cromwell's headquarters, Cato had made the detour to his own house in Woodstock. It was hard to tear his mind away from its constant preoccupation with the war, but he could not ride right by his house without checking up on the health and welfare of his wife and daughters

"A couple of hours today, then we'll ride into Cromwell's camp this evening. After the meeting I'll probably spend a day or two here. You may return to the siege." Cato dismounted as he spoke, handing the reins of his bay charger to a groom. As he did so, his two small daughters, riding Shetland ponies whose leading reins were held by a stolid groom, came into the yard.

They smiled shyly at their father as he came over to them, and solemnly informed him that they had been learning to trot. At four and five that was impressive, Cato reflected as he congratulated them with appropriate gravity. But their mother had been an intrepid horsewoman. So very unlike her little sister.

He left the children and made his way back to the house, thinking how he must teach Phoebe to overcome her fear of horses. It was absurd that she would only ride pillion behind a groom. There wouldn't be time this visit, but as soon as he had a few days clear, he would begin.

The soft weathered brick of the manor house was mellow in the sunshine, the mullioned windows gleaming. He caught himself thinking as he approached the house how welcoming it looked. He caught himself remembering how much he'd enjoyed coming back to Nan after an absence. Her dislike of the bedchamber hadn't ever dulled the warmth and affection of their companionship. He knew he'd been fortunate in the comradely pleasures of that marriage, and her death had grieved him terribly. Much more so than the death of Brian's mother. Their marriage had been too brief for any real emotional attachment. The marriages of his friends and his own to Diana had taught him how rare were the conjugal ease and affection he'd enjoyed with Nan. It had taken him a few bitter and disillusioning months to realize he wouldn't get it from Diana; he wouldn't set himself up for disappointment with her little sister.

The housekeeper glided across the hall to greet him as he entered, blinking to adjust his eyes after the brightness outside.

"Good morrow, Your Lordship. We wasn't expecting you for another week."

"No, but I have business outside Oxford and stopped on the way," he said, tossing his whip onto the long bench beside the door and drawing off his gloves. "Is Lady Granville within?"

"She's abovestairs, I believe, m'lord. I believe she's not yet risen this morning."

Cato frowned. Phoebe was never a slugabed and it was now past midday.

"Good morrow, sir." Olivia came down the stairs, the inevitable book in her hand. "We weren't expecting you t-today."

"No, I have a summons to headquarters," Cato replied, regarding his daughter with a smile that sprang directly from his earlier thoughts. Olivia was so very like her mother, except for the long Granville nose. She had the same habit of drawing her brows together and pursing her lips when she was considering something.

"I c-came down for some reading candles," Olivia informed him. "It's hard to see to read in the parlor even though the sun's shining."

"What are you reading?"

"Caesar's *Commentarii*." Olivia showed him the spine of the book. "It's m-most interesting. About the Gallic wars."

Cato nodded. "I remember it."

"D-didn't you find it interesting?" Her black eyes shone.

"Not particularly," Cato said with a reminiscent smile. "I think any recognition of its finer points had to be flogged into me."

Olivia regarded him in patent disbelief. "How c-could you *not* find it completely absorbing?"

Nan had never evinced her daughter's passion for scholarship, she'd been far too down-to-earth, but she'd had a needle-sharp wit that Olivia had certainly inherited. Cato reached out and lightly patted his daughter's cheek. "The military history interested me," he offered.

Olivia gave him a shrewd look. Despite his smile, she could detect a constraint in his eyes, a slight tension between his brows. "Are you sad about something?"

Cato shook his head. "No, but the siege is grim . . . grimmer even than most."

Olivia nodded and reached up to touch his hand. The bond they shared was usually unspoken, but there were times when a fleeting gesture expressed the inexpressible.

Cato's fingers briefly closed over Olivia's. "Where's Phoebe?"

Olivia frowned. "I haven't seen her this morning. Perhaps she's writing her p-play."

"Play?"

"Yes, she's writing a play." Olivia stated this as coolly as if it were the most natural thing in the world. "She's a very good poet."

Cato had had no idea his wife had literary pretensions. It didn't sound like Phoebe at all.

He shook his head as if to dismiss this puzzle and made for the stairs, taking them easily two at a time without even appearing to hurry. He strode down the corridor leading to the east wing and opened the door to his bedchamber.

The room was in darkness, the curtains still pulled across the windows, and still shrouding the bed. The fire was almost out in the grate.

Cato went to the bed and drew aside the curtain. "Phoebe, are you ill?"

She was a curled mound at the furthest edge of the bed, and as he spoke she turned with a little groan onto her back. Her face was pale in the gloom, her eyes heavy. She certainly didn't look well.

Sick . . . pregnant perhaps?

"What is it?" he asked, keeping the eagerness from his voice as he drew the curtain further back so that he could see her more clearly.

Phoebe turned again on her side, but this time facing him, drawing her knees up with another little groan. "It's my terms," she muttered, sending his hopes plummeting. "It's always bad the first day, but this is worse than usual."

So a month of duty-filled nights had produced no fruit. He looked down at her, frowning.

"Oh, I'm so indiscreet," Phoebe wailed at his frown, closing her eyes with another groan.

Cato could not immediately think of anything to say. His previous wives had always been very discreet about their monthly inconvenience. One evening he would discover that they had taken themselves to the bed in the dressing room, and there they would sleep until they made an equally explanationless return to the marital bed.

Phoebe opened her eyes again into the continuing silence. "Your pardon, my lord, if I shocked you," she said apologetically, struggling up against the pillows and pushing the tumbled hair from her face. "I can't seem to help what I say, particularly during my terms, when everything about me's all topsy-turvy, and I feel so cross and irritable, and then in the next instant so gloomy, I want to weep . . . oh, what am I saying? You don't wish to hear all that, do you?"

For a moment it looked as if Cato might laugh. Then he glanced around the darkened chamber. "It's no wonder you feel miserable. It's dark and cold as charity in this room, while the sun's shining almost like spring."

He drew the curtains right back from the bed as he spoke, then went to the window and flung the heavy velvet aside, letting in a stream of sunlight. He turned to the fireplace, raked over the embers, and took a handful of kindling from the log basket, throwing it onto the dim glow.

Phoebe watched his domestic maneuvers wanly, one hand unconsciously massaging the cramping in the base of her stomach. "Could you ask Mistress Bisset to make me a posset, my lord? If it wouldn't be too much trouble," she added.

"A posset? In the middle of the day . . . I hardly think that's wise . . . but, well . . . I suppose if it helps your . . . your . . ." His words trailed off as he busied himself with rather more energy than the task warranted, poking at the kindling until it spurted and crackled. He threw a log on the flame before he straightened and strode hurriedly to the door.

"Have you come home for long?" Phoebe's bright blue gaze followed him hungrily as he went to the door. He was wearing black again, relieved only by the crisp white of his shirt collar and the emerald on his finger.

"No, I have a meeting with Cromwell this evening. But I was passing and thought to see how you were doing."

"And then you'll return to the siege?"

Cato turned to look at her. Was she so eager to see him go? Her heavy-eyed gaze was intent despite her wan pallor and the shadows beneath her eyes.

He had been intending to spend a few more days with her, but there seemed little point in her present condition. "Yes," he said. "I'll return there for a week." He opened the door. "I'll send Mistress Bisset to you."

Phoebe surveyed the now closed door with lackluster eyes. So it was to be another week before she would see him. She pulled the covers up to her chin under a renewed wave of misery as her belly cramped fiercely.

The pain really was much worse than usual. She wondered if it could be because of the herb-drenched sponges Meg had given her to prevent pregnancy. Phoebe had been religiously using them when she went to bed in the evening, before Cato came up, and then sliding out of bed when she was sure he was asleep to cleanse herself again of all residue of their union. It had worked this month, anyway, she thought with another groan.

Had Cato been disappointed? It had been impossible to tell from his expression. But then, so often his countenance gave away nothing of his thoughts. The dark brown eyes would be unreadable, his features smooth and impassive. She had rarely seen him angry, although he could on occasion be unpleasantly sardonic.

The door opened again and Olivia came in carrying a tray with a covered bowl.

"My father's just left again, but he said you're unwell," she said in concern. "I wondered where you were when you didn't c-come for breakfast, but I thought perhaps you'd gone into the village to help out one of the women."

She set the tray on the bedside table. "He didn't say what was the matter. Is it your terms?" Until the last month, they'd shared a bedchamber and were both as familiar with each other's cycles as they were with their own.

Phoebe nodded. "I was just feeling sorry for myself," she said. "I wouldn't have been good company even if you had come in."

Olivia looked doubtful. Phoebe was so wan, lying in the big bed, somehow swallowed up by Lord Granville's invisible presence in a chamber that bore little evidence of Phoebe's occupation. No little feminine touches anywhere; not even her hairbrushes were visible; no discarded clothing; no flowers; no ribbons; no little pots of creams and oils and perfumes.

"It's funny," she observed, "but when Diana was alive, this chamber seemed more hers than my father's. But it doesn't seem as if it b-belongs to you at all." She lifted the cloth from the porringer and handed the bowl to Phoebe.

"I don't feel as if it does," Phoebe responded bluntly, inhaling the rich, comforting steam of the posset. "I don't really feel like a wife at all."

"Does my father not make you feel like one?" Olivia asked tentatively. "He is preoccupied a lot of the time, I know. But isn't it b-better that way? You can get on with your own life without interference? Just as you always said you would."

"Yes, of course it's what I want," Phoebe said hastily. "It's just the usual depression, you know how it is. It's like a black dog on my shoulder." She took a deep gulp of the hot milk curdled with wine and smiled reassuringly. "That's much better."

Olivia was not completely convinced, but she wanted to be, so she sat down on the end of the bed and began to regale Phoebe with a piece of kitchen gossip as the hot drink did its relaxing work, easing the cramped muscles.

The sound of horses and the insistent barking of a dog from the gravel sweep below the window brought Olivia to her feet. "I wonder who that could be."

She went to the window then gave a cry of pleasure. "It's Portia!"

"Truly?" Phoebe flung aside the bedcovers and scrambled to her feet, her pain miraculously easing.

"Well, that's Juno down there," Olivia said excitedly. She

grabbed Phoebe's cloak from the hook on the wall and thrust it towards her. "Just put this on; you can dress later."

Phoebe needed no urging. She pulled the cloak over her shoulders as she thrust her feet into a pair of slippers, hopping her way to the door as she did so.

5

A week later Cato walked into the great hall in the middle of a rainy morning and for a bemused moment thought he'd come to the wrong house. Whoever it was, it resembled a madhouse.

Explanation appeared in the shape of a large mustard-colored dog. Once encountered, Juno was not easily forgotten. And Cato had encountered her on several memorable occasions. She flung herself upon the master of the house with an excited bark, utterly confident of her welcome.

"Down!" Cato commanded in a voice that was as soft as it was meant to be obeyed.

Juno sat at his feet with a breathy sigh and gazed up at him, tongue lolling.

Having handled that situation, Cato turned his attention to the remaining causes of this bedlam. Two smallish boys were sliding down his banisters with an excess of exuberance, tumbling to the floor at the bottom and instantly scrambling up again and racing back to the top of the stairs. A very tiny little girl was stolidly clambering up the stairs in their wake, with a single-minded purpose that Cato could only admire. The boys ignored her until she reached the top step, at which point one of them heaved her up and tried to lift her onto the banister.

It seemed a suitable moment for intervention. Cato reached the head of the stairs in the nick of time and swept the little girl off the banisters the instant before she was about to be set in motion with a helpful brotherly hand on her back.

Cato surveyed Rufus Decatur's natural sons with a raised eyebrow. They stared back at him with their father's bright blue eyes under tangled thatches of strawberry curls.

"That was not a good idea," Cato declared.

"But Evie likes it," one of the pair informed him solemnly. "She cries if we won't let her do what we do."

"Clearly her mother's daughter," Cato muttered. Still carrying the child, who seemed perfectly content to be sitting in a stranger's arms, he turned back down the stairs. At the bottom he became aware of his own two small daughters standing to one side of the hall, eyes as round as saucers. They were clearly too timid to participate in the circus—Diana's daughters, although a year or two older, lacked the intrepid nature of Portia's—but there was no mistaking their fascinated envy.

They came forward when Cato beckoned them, offered him shy little curtsies, and then scampered back up the stairs to their own domain. Eve wriggled to be set down, obviously intending to follow them.

Cato hung on to her. "Portia!" he called in ringing accents.

A door burst open to the right of the hall and a thin young woman with a shock of orange hair, a mass of freckles, and bright green eyes seemed to leap into the hall. She was wearing leather riding britches, boots, a white linen shirt, and doublet. Cato found nothing surprising in this attire. Portia Worth had been married in britches on a battlefield with a sword at her hip.

"Oh, Lord Granville, I do beg your pardon. If I'd known you were coming, I wouldn't have let them loose like this. You must have wondered if you'd come to the right house." She came towards him, holding out her hand.

Cato took it and leaned over to kiss his niece. "It had crossed my mind."

"It's been raining, you see, and they haven't been able to go out." Portia offered the explanation with a cheerful smile.

"They were about to launch this little one hurtling to perdition down the banisters." He regarded her quizzically, reflecting that marriage to the earl of Rothbury had wrought no obvious changes in his half brother's illegitimate daughter. She looked no different now from the scrawny, undernourished creature who'd turned his house upside down that memorable first winter of the war.

"Oh, they're very careful of her," she said blithely, taking Eve from him. "But she really doesn't like to be left out."

"Mmm. Her mother's daughter," Cato repeated, half to himself.

Portia's responding grin was complacent. "She's Rufus Decatur's daughter too, sir."

"Is your husband here with you?" A note of gravity entered his quiet voice.

"No," Portia answered in much the same tone. "He left us at the gates. He had business in London. A meeting with Lord Manchester about pressing men for the army. Rufus is not in favor," she added.

"Neither am I, but I see little choice," Cato responded. War talk with Portia was so natural he didn't even realize how unusual it was for him to share such thoughts with a woman.

"He said he'll come back for us at the end of the week."

Cato nodded. He and Rufus Decatur had buried the blood feud that had torn their lives and their families asunder for two generations. They had buried it on the battlefield when Portia Worth, Cato's brother's child, had married Rufus Decatur at a drumhead wedding. Now they would be courteous to each other in company, had worked together in amity in the interests of negotiating a peace between the king and his parliament and would do so again, but they would not seek each other out in private, and Rufus would no more accept Granville hospitality than Cato would accept his. But Rufus did not prevent his wife and his children from accepting that hospitality, and that was enough. The old vendetta would not touch the new generation.

"My lord, you're back. I wasn't expecting you." It had taken Phoebe a minute to compose herself at the unexpected sound of Cato's rich, tawny voice. Now she hurried into the hall aware that her cheeks were warm and that the pulse in the base of her belly was beating a drumbeat of anticipation and delight.

"I didn't expect to be . . . *careful!*" Cato saw the danger in the nick of time and stepped forward just as Phoebe's foot caught in the fringe of a tapestry rug. She tripped, arms flailing, and he grabbed for her before she tumbled in an ignominious heap.

Instinctively Phoebe hung on to him, her arms tightly encircling his waist, and for a minute neither of them moved. She inhaled his scent, heard the beat of his heart beneath his jerkin, reveled in the firm hands planted squarely at her back. He had never held her before. Maybe clumsiness had its advantages, she thought wryly. At present it seemed the only way to achieve her heart's desire.

Then Cato righted her, his hands fell from her, and she was obliged to step back on her own two feet.

"Your pardon, sir," Phoebe said breathlessly. She managed a curtsy and tried to think of some appropriate greeting for a returning husband. "Did your business fare well, my lord?"

Cato did not immediately answer. He surveyed her with a little frown. Something was wrong with her face. He peered at her a little more closely. Her mouth was blue with ink.

"Is something wrong?" Phoebe asked a mite anxiously.

"Have you been drinking ink?"

"Oh!" Her hand flew to her mouth. "I was writing my pageant." She scrubbed at the stain, succeeding only in spreading blue across her chin. "I must have been sucking the wrong end of my quill." She gave a little shrug as she examined her now blue palm. "It often happens when I'm concentrating."

Cato supposed it sufficient explanation. Phoebe certainly

seemed to think so. He noticed absently how his wife was dwarfed by Portia's height and, he thought, overshadowed by her vibrancy. Phoebe's pale coloring and light hair were lost against Portia's orange halo and bright green eyes. Not that one would ever consider Portia to be beautiful, and she certainly wasn't pretty. But there was something striking about her.

However, it occurred to Cato, rather to his surprise, that Phoebe didn't lose on the comparison. Her style was altogether gentler, but it had its own appeal. Odd that he should have noticed it now for the first time despite the ink and her unprepossessing stuff gown that looked, like so many of her clothes, as if it had been made for her when she was an altogether different shape. Another example of Lord Carlton's economy presumably.

"As I was saying, I didn't expect to be back so soon. But we stormed Basing House three days ago." A shadow crossed Cato's countenance. It had been a grim business. The house had held out and Cromwell had showed them no mercy once he'd forced their surrender. They'd put most of the garrison to the sword, taken the household prisoner, marching them away in chains. It would set an example for the other royalist houses holding out against their besiegers throughout the country. The war was now mostly one of sieges—a tiresome and long, drawn-out business that wasted manpower and resources. Cato understood the strategic importance of the lesson of Basing House, but he deplored it nevertheless.

There was a thud behind him. The two boys had tired of adult conversation and had resumed their banister sliding. A gleeful shriek from the head of the stairs was joined suddenly by the insistent wail of a baby from somewhere above.

"Oh, it's Alex. He's woken up." Portia set Eve on the floor and hurried to the bottom of the stairs. "Luke, Toby, that's enough now," she instructed, to Cato's relief. "You can go outside. It's almost stopped raining."

With whoops of joy the boys raced for the front door, Juno plunging ahead of them. A manservant moved with alacrity to let them out.

A nursemaid was coming down the stairs, a baby in her arms. Portia took the infant, who had stopped wailing and was regarding the occupants of the hall with grave blue eyes. His hair was as red as his father's.

"This is Viscount Decatur, sir." Portia introduced her infant with maternal pride.

So Rufus Decatur had a legitimate heir. Cato felt the sharp stab of envy. He glanced at Phoebe, whose speedwell blue eyes returned his look without so much as a flash of self-consciousness.

"A handsome child," he said with as much warmth as he could muster. "I'm glad you've had company in my absence, Phoebe. Is there anything else I should know about?"

"Ah, well, yes . . ." Phoebe began with enthusiasm. "Gypsies. You should know about the gypsies, sir."

"And what should I know about them?"

"I found two of their orphaned children in a ditch."

"A ditch?"

"Yes, it's a little complicated." Phoebe pushed a stray lock of hair out of her eyes. "But I know you'll agree that I did the only thing I could do."

Cato remembered the cabbages. "Were you perhaps digging in this ditch when you found these orphans?"

"No, of course not," Phoebe said with some heat. "It was a ditch on the home farm and it was full of mud and water."

"Ditches do tend to be," Cato murmured.

"You are not being serious, sir," Phoebe accused with that militant gleam in her eye again. "It's a *very* serious matter."

Cato ran his hand through his hair, ruffling the crisp dark thatch from the widow's peak to his nape with the familiar gesture that as always made Phoebe's belly lurch with desire.

"I stand corrected," he said dryly. "Perhaps we should continue this in my study."

He moved away from her across the hall to the door to his sanctum. Phoebe followed with impetuous step, her words preceding her.

"You see, as I understand it, there had been a fight for leadership in the tribe, and the children's father, who had been the chief, was overthrown in a knife battle and he died of his wounds. So his children were left in the ditch, because the new chief took his enemy's wife for his own and he didn't want the other children to be a threat . . . in case one of the other families in the tribe decided to challenge his leadership. Like Romulus and Remus exposed outside Rome."

Cato closed the door. "Why is my wife concerning herself with internecine strife among the Romanies?"

"I could hardly leave the poor little things to die in the ditch," Phoebe pointed out. "They were on your land, my lord, apart from any humanitarian considerations. You wouldn't wish it said that—"

"Now, just a minute, Phoebe. These are gypsies. They are not my tenants and they have no claims on my charity."

"Well, what's that got to do with it?" Phoebe demanded. "They're little children. Of course I had to help them."

"And just how did you help them?" Cato went to the sideboard to pour himself wine.

"I fostered them in the village, but I had to promise that we would pay for their keep. No one has enough to spare for two more mouths. But *you* do." She regarded him with the air of one who has delivered the coup de grace.

"I don't care for your tone, Phoebe, I've told you that before," Cato said coldly.

"Then I ask pardon, my lord. But when you seem not to understand the importance, how else can I make you see what has to be done?" Phoebe met his frigid gaze steadily.

"And you are to be a judge of my actions, of course," Cato said. "I think you have said all you can possibly have to say." He bestowed a curt nod upon her and very deliberately picked up some papers on his desk.

Phoebe hesitated, then she accepted her dismissal and left the study, closing the door with exaggerated care behind her.

Cato let the papers fall to the desk. He felt as if he'd been run over by a juggernaut. *Pathetic, starving, homeless orphans in a ditch! For God's sake!*

He reached for the bellpull and paced the study until the summons was answered.

"Send for the bailiff at once," he ordered curtly. Presumably Phoebe would have informed the bailiff of her actions. The man would know where the children were housed and what outlay was necessary to keep them clothed and fed.

Phoebe stood in the hall for a minute, wondering if she'd made any impact on Cato. But he'd dismissed her so firmly there wasn't much else she could do at present. Where were Olivia and Portia?

Portia was probably feeding the hungry Alex in the parlor. She ran up the stairs to the bedchamber, where she scrubbed the ink from her mouth with ferocious vigor. Then she made her way to the square parlor at the back of the house.

Portia was ensconced on the deep window seat, Alex contentedly nuzzling her breast. Eve was sucking her thumb dreamily, leaning against her mother's drawn-up knees.

"This would be the very picture of a maternal idyll if you didn't look so unlikely," Phoebe observed. "Do you never wear dresses anymore?"

"Only if Rufus expresses a preference," Portia said with a wicked little grin. She moved Alex to her other breast.

"Where's Olivia?"

"In her chamber reading Pliny, I believe." Portia cast Phoebe a shrewd look as the other woman paced restlessly from the fireplace to the door and back again.

"So, what do you think of the state of matrimony, then, duckie?" Portia inquired. "As I recall, you were as much agin it as I was."

"I still am," Phoebe stated. "It's damnable not to be your own person anymore, Portia. To *belong* to a husband."

Portia nodded her understanding. "Laws made by men are going to favor men," she observed with a cynical smile. "But we aren't helpless, you know. Even husbands can be cut to fit."

"Maybe . . . if they notice you exist," Phoebe said tightly, coming to a halt by a worktable. She flipped open the lacquered lid of the workbox and began to trawl through embroidery silks with her fingers, not looking at Portia.

"What do you mean?" Portia lifted the satiated baby and held him against her shoulder, patting his back.

Phoebe's color was high, but there was no one but Portia in whom she could confide.

"Do people always make love in the dark, with the curtains closed, and they don't say anything, and it's all over so quickly, you barely realize it's happened, and . . . ?"

"Wait! Wait a minute!" Portia interrupted the flow. "Is that what happens?"

"Every night," Phoebe said dismally. "And it'll happen every night just like that until I conceive. He doesn't find me appealing, don't you see. How could he after Diana?"

"Diana was a bitch . . . hard as nails," Portia stated. "I expect she preferred the dark. She probably would have preferred it if it could have happened in her sleep when she didn't know anything about it." Her lip curled with scorn.

This struck Phoebe as remarkably shrewd. "I hadn't thought of that," she said. "Maybe Cato thinks I'm the same."

"But you're not?" It was clearly a question.

"*No!*" Phoebe cried. "No, I'm not. I ache, Portia. I'm so hungry for him to touch me. I want to see him naked, I want to touch him, every inch of him. I could *eat* him," she added with another wail. "It's such torment."

Portia's jaw dropped slightly. It wasn't that she didn't understand the need, it just surprised her coming from Phoebe. "Are you saying you love Cato?"

"Love, lust, I don't know!" Phoebe dropped the lid of the workbox with a clatter. "All I know is that when I hear his footstep, my stomach drops. When he pushes his hair back with his hand in the way he does, my thighs go all quivery, and when he touches me, even accidentally, I start to thrum like a plucked lute. I turn into a jelly. I want him . . . all of him."

"Lord, that's a powerful lust." Portia cradled the now sleeping baby to her bosom, and reached with her free hand to stroke Evie's pink curls. She was frowning, thinking of what torment it must be to feel what Phoebe had so graphically described and be unable to satisfy the hunger.

"But what am I to do?" Phoebe demanded. "There must be some way I can get his attention . . . some way I can show him how I feel without disgusting him."

"Oh, I don't think he'd be disgusted," Phoebe said. "Flattered more like."

"But women of my . . . our . . . breeding aren't supposed to feel desire like that."

"Your breeding, not mine," Portia reminded her dryly. "I'm the bastard, remember. And anyway, breeding doesn't have anything to do with it."

"Doesn't it?"

"No," Portia stated definitely. She regarded Phoebe thoughtfully for a minute. Then she said, "I think you have to do something dramatic."

"Yes, but like what?" Phoebe perched on the end of the table. She had the feeling Portia was about to unlock the key to Pandora's box. Would it let loose a plague or a swarm of heavenly secrets?

"Games," Portia said. "Play."

This was not making sense. Phoebe stared at her.

"Well, what I was saying earlier about Rufus's preferences. Sometimes he likes me to dress in certain ways . . . or pretend to be some other kind of person . . . we play games. Sometimes I'll surprise him by devising a play, a scene . . . oh, it's hard to describe. But that's what I think you have to do if you really want to get Cato's attention. You have to surprise him. Show him another side of yourself."

Phoebe's eyes were very wide. She began to have an inkling of the possibilities. But supposing it didn't work. Supposing Cato was horrified, disgusted. Supposing he found her so unappealing in any guise that . . .

"It might be a bit risky," Portia said, reading her mind. "I don't know how straitlaced Cato is. Anyone who'd marry Diana has to be pretty rigid, I would have thought."

"He married Diana for the alliance with my father," Phoebe pointed out. "Just as he married me. For that and an heir," she added.

"Mmmm." Portia nibbled her bottom lip, thinking. "I have an idea," she said, swinging her legs off the window seat. "We'll try something first, just to see how he reacts."

"What?"

"Clothes," Portia declared, heading for the door, carrying Alex. "Bring Evie, will you? It's time for her nap. And then I'll show you what I mean."

Phoebe scooped up Eve and followed Portia, agog to discover exactly what Portia had in mind. But Portia said nothing until both children had been handed over to the nursemaid and Phoebe and Portia were in Portia's chamber with the door firmly closed.

"Now, do you have money?"

"Money?" Phoebe frowned. "What do I need money for?"

"To buy things with, of course. Rufus left me with some, but I don't think it's enough for what I have in mind." Portia opened a small leather pouch and shook the contents onto the bedcover as she spoke. A shower of gold coins scattered over the green taffeta quilt.

"Five guineas. It might do."

"I can't use your money." Phoebe was bewildered and growing impatient. "Even if I knew what it was for."

Portia hitched herself onto the end of the bed. "New

clothes," she said distinctly. "What you're wearing now must have been made for you when you had no bosom or something."

"It was," Phoebe agreed, unperturbed by this brutal truth. "My father didn't believe in wasting money on *my* wardrobe. Diana's was a different matter," she added acidly. "But I've never really cared about such things. There's too much else to think about."

"Well, it won't do," Portia said firmly. She surveyed Phoebe with her head on one side. "You need gowns that make something of your figure."

"No, I don't," Phoebe said with asperity. "I need to hide it. There's too much of it."

Portia shook her head. "That's where you're wrong, duckie. You have all the right curves in all the right places. You need to make the most of them, not cover them up. And you shouldn't walk with your shoulders hunched as if you're trying to hide your breasts. They're beautiful and round and firm. I wish I had a bit more on offer . . . although," she added, patting her own bosom with a speculative air, "they do seem bigger than usual these days because of feeding Alex."

"Does Rufus like big breasts?" Phoebe asked, growing fascinated by this discussion.

"I expect so . . . most men do. But he has to put up with what he's got," Portia said cheerfully. "Anyway, we're not talking about Rufus, we're talking about Cato. If you want him to notice you, then you're going to have to force yourself into his line of vision. Which brings us back to money."

Phoebe shook her head. "I don't have any. I've never needed any. When the peddler comes, Olivia and I buy what we need and Cato pays him. There aren't any fairs because of the war. There's nothing to spend money on."

She frowned. "I suppose I could get the seamstress here to make me up a new gown. I don't think Cato's quite as parsimonious as my father." She remembered his indifferent acceptance of the economical wedding dress and added a shade doubtfully, "Although I'm not certain."

"That won't do at all," Portia declared. "You don't want a homegrown gown. We want something exotic. And for that we need money. What about pawning something? Jewels or something?"

Phoebe thought. "There are some rings that belonged to my mother." She knew she ought to find the idea of pawning her mother's rings horrifying—wicked almost—but somehow she couldn't summon up a shred of conscience.

"Good." Portia jumped off the bed. "Now, where's the nearest sizable town? I don't know this area."

"Bicester or Witney. But how do we get there?"

"Ride, of course. How else?"

Phoebe could think of several objections to this plan. She didn't like to ride. They'd have to take a military escort; no one traveled the roads unarmed these days, and so Cato would have to be told of the excursion without being told its purpose. And he'd be bound to find that peculiar, and then things would get very complicated and she'd be bound to let something slip. But her imagination was fired, and the prospect of taking some kind of action was too heady to be given up for the sake of minor details.

"I'll ride pillion with you, and we can take Decatur men as escort, so I don't have to tell Cato. I'll just tell the housekeeper that we're going for a ride. The housekeeper's used to me going out all the time anyway. No one will think anything of it, as long as we're back by dark."

Portia nodded her approval. "You fetch the rings and I'll see if Olivia wants to come too."

Olivia was as intrigued at the prospect of the excursion as Phoebe. Town visits had been very few and far between in her sixteen years. "I think you should get a velvet gown," she announced. "B-black velvet. Or something really dark."

"Since when have you been interested in such things?" Portia asked in surprise.

Olivia considered. "I don't really know," she said, sounding as surprised as Portia. "It just seemed to happen. But I'm sure I'm right."

"Yes," Portia agreed, surveying Phoebe with a speculative eye. "I think you are."

6

$\mathscr{P}$hoebe *gritted her teeth as a groom helped her onto the* pillion pad behind Portia. It was all in a good cause, she told herself. And kept telling herself throughout the ride into Witney, some five miles' distance. Portia made no concessions to her passenger's fears and gave the mare her head across the flat fields.

They rode into the small market town just after noon and left the horses and their Decatur escort in the stable yard of the Hand and Shears. Portia for once was wearing a riding skirt over her britches, but it did nothing to constrain her long, rangy stride as they set off in search of the golden balls that would denote a pawnbroker.

Phoebe was astonished to find herself behaving as if she did this kind of thing all the time. She seemed to be driven by a compulsion that had come from nowhere and was as exciting as it was irresistible. She marched into the gloom of the pawnbroker's, unwrapped the silk scarf that contained the rings, and laid the small hoard on the cracked pine counter. "I want twenty guineas for them," she heard herself say, bold as brass.

"Oh, do you now?" The pawnbroker peered at her through a monocle. He was wondering what straits could have brought three such young women of obvious breeding to his door. Most unlike his usual customers. They seemed very self-possessed, and not in the least supplicant. The dark girl was strolling around his shop examining his wares with an air of purposeful curiosity. The tall redhead merely stood against the door, arms folded, as coolly as if she owned the place.

He turned his attention to the rings. The settings were old-fashioned, but the rings were worth a deal more than twenty guineas. He wondered why the young woman hadn't asked for more. She was tapping her fingers on the counter in obvious impatience as he made his examination, and he came to the odd conclusion that she'd fixed on the sum she wanted and wasn't in the least interested in anything more. She couldn't be in some kind of trouble, he thought. People in trouble behaved very differently. It was most intriguing.

However, after his inspection he merely nodded and unlocked a silver-bound chest. He extracted twenty guineas and gave them to her without a further word.

"My thanks." Phoebe scooped the coins into her pocket. She turned to the door. "Come on, Olivia. We don't have much time."

"I was looking for a pair of c-compasses," Olivia said. But she abandoned her search and followed Phoebe and Portia out of the shop.

They found a dressmaker's shop halfway down the High Street. Phoebe peered in the window. "I've never bought a gown ready-made before," she said, assailed by her first moment of doubt since the expedition had started, but Portia was already striding into the shop.

The dressmaker looked as if she'd found a treasure trove as she hurried out of a back room at the tinkle of the bell. "What can I do for you, my ladies?" It was very clear from dress and posture that they were ladies. Although it was strange that they should be unaccompanied.

"Lady Granville wishes to buy a gown," Portia announced, indicating Phoebe with a wave of her hand. "She wishes to be able to take it home this afternoon, so perhaps you could show us what you have."

The dressmaker looked closely at Phoebe. She saw a voluptuous young woman in a shabby, ill-fitting gown and unhappily revised her expectations. Expensive high fashion didn't seem to be in order here. She disappeared into the sewing room, reappearing in a very few minutes with several pallid gowns, all with delicate lacy shawl collars that covered the bosom almost to the throat. She laid them on a chair.

Phoebe felt a surge of disappointment. Portia said, "No, they won't do at all. We want a gown that will make the most of her advantages."

Phoebe was so unaccustomed to thinking of herself as having advantages that she felt embarrassed, imagining that the woman would be wondering what on earth Portia was talking about. Once again this didn't seem like such a good idea.

But the woman, looking immediately more cheerful, was now nodding as she walked all around Phoebe. "Yes, a lovely little figure, if I may say so, my lady. A touch of Rubens about you. It will be a pleasure to dress you."

"Oh, I like this one." Olivia had wandered off with her usual blithe curiosity into the back room and now came out with a gown of orange silk edged in black. "Isn't this lovely?" She held it up.

"The color would suit you, m'lady, with your black hair," the dressmaker said, "but it's too harsh for Lady Granville."

"Is it?" Phoebe asked with disappointment. "It's very . . . very bold. I wish the gown to be bold," she asserted as her ideas crystallized.

"Bravo." Portia applauded softly.

The dressmaker stroked her chin where a little cluster of whiskers sprouted, much to Olivia's fascination. "Blue," she pronounced. "Dark blue for the eyes. I have just the gown. It was made for a customer's trousseau, but alas, poor lady, her betrothed was killed at Naseby and she hadn't the heart to take any of the trousseau." She turned and dived into the back regions again.

"I wish I c-could buy this." Olivia held the orange gown against her and examined her reflection in the mirror.

"It certainly suits you, but I don't think we want to give Cato too many surprises all at once," Portia said.

"Is that what you're doing? Trying to surprise my father?" Olivia turned slowly from the mirror. "Is that why Phoebe won't have a g-gown made up at home?"

"Exactly," Portia said. "Men need to be surprised now and again. It's good for 'em."

Olivia couldn't imagine her father surprised. He was always so much in control of things. If any surprises were to be dished out, he'd be doing the dishing. Or so she had always thought.

"Now, try this, Lady Granville." The dressmaker bustled back. She held a gown of midnight blue velvet. The color was so dark, the material so rich, it shimmered in the light of the oil lamp hanging from the low ceiling.

"Oh!" Phoebe said with a tiny gasp. She touched the gown, brushing the velvet with her fingers. "It's like a river."

Portia was already unhooking Phoebe's dimity print. It fell to her feet and she stepped out of it, kicking it away impatiently.

The dressmaker dropped the velvet over her head and expertly hooked it at the back. She adjusted the skirts that looped over an underdress of figured blue silk.

"Now, that," Portia declared, "is what I call dramatic."

"I knew I was right," said Olivia with satisfaction.

Phoebe stepped to the mirror and gasped. Her bosom rose creamy white from a décolletage so low her nipples were almost visible. A stiff embroidered collar rose at the back of the gown, framing her head and somehow accentuating the plunging décolletage. The gown was bound beneath the bosom with a girdle of braided silk and fell in luxuriant folds to caress the swell of her hips.

"I don't look like me," she said. "But it's shocking. My breasts are going to tumble out."

"No, they won't, m'lady," the dressmaker assured her. "But

it does need a few minor adjustments. The sleeves are a little long, and the skirts. If you'll leave it with me for an hour, I'll have it ready for you." She had a pincushion fastened to her wrist and was pinning and tucking as she spoke.

"How much is it?" Phoebe asked. Uncertainty mingled with exhilaration. She looked like a wanton. Cato would be horrified. And yet she was fascinated by this new image of herself. Wanton perhaps, but also undeniably fashionable. And she'd never noticed how white her bosom was, or how truly deep the cleft between her breasts. Her waist was not defined by the gown, and somehow that made it seem smaller than she knew it was. But that was the contrast surely between the swell of her breasts and the curve of her hips.

"Ten guineas, m'lady." The dressmaker was on her knees pinning up the hem of the underskirt.

"That means you can have two," Portia said practically.

"No!" Phoebe exclaimed, then said almost without volition, "Unless . . . well, unless the poor lady . . ."

"I have just the very gown, m'lady." The dressmaker disappeared into the back room again, reappearing with a dress of dark red silk. "The very thing," she repeated, holding the garment up for inspection. "And I can let you have it for ten guineas."

"Oh, yes," Phoebe murmured. "What a wonderful color."

"It'll certainly look well on you," Portia stated.

Phoebe glanced at Olivia, who was examining her with wide eyes.

"What do you think of this one, Olivia?"

"I think if you mean to surprise my father, you'll certainly succeed," Olivia replied. "In b-both gowns." She hesitated, then asked somewhat tentatively, "But why do you wish to?" She had the feeling there were mysteries here to which she was not party.

Portia and Phoebe exchanged a glance, then Portia said, "Wait until you're married, duckie. Then you'll understand."

"But I'm never getting married," Olivia pointed out.

"What d'you think are the chances of that, Phoebe?" Portia said with a grin.

"Minimal," Phoebe replied promptly. "Look what happened to us."

"It doesn't have to happen to me," Olivia declared. "My father won't compel me, not like yours, Phoebe. And I'm never going to fall in love like Portia, so of course I'm not going to get married." She gave them a look as if defying them to disagree with her.

Portia chuckled. "No, of course you're not."

Phoebe turned back to the looking glass. She surveyed her image in the blue velvet gown with an almost fearful awe. "Do I dare?" she breathed.

"Dare all to win all," Portia responded. "It really does look lovely . . . but . . ." She grinned. "It's a very different you. Now you have to think of the games to follow."

"Games . . . what games?" Olivia asked.

"If you're never going to get married, you'll never need to know," Portia said with another grin.

Phoebe turned so the dressmaker could unhook the gown at the back. "I don't really know what you mean, either." Her voice was muffled in velvet as the gown came over her head. She stood still for the red silk and then examined herself in the glass with her head on one side. She gave an involuntary gasp of delight, forgetting all about games for the moment.

"Oh, it *is* gorgeous. I don't know which one I like best. But are you sure I don't look like a whore in them?"

"They're very fashionable," Portia said definitely and diplomatically. "Let's go to the inn and find something to eat; I'm ravenous. We'll come back for the gowns after."

Phoebe scrambled into her old gown with something like relief at the return to normality. Portia and Olivia linked arms with Phoebe and bore her out into the street again before she could have second thoughts.

• • •

*R*ufus Decatur's sons careened into Cato as he crossed the hall. "Where's Portia? Do you know where she went?" they clamored in chorus.

"I have no idea. When did you see her last?" He regarded them with a faint smile, thinking that for all their unruly grubbiness they were a very attractive pair of tykes.

"Oh, ages ago," Luke informed him. "She went out with Phoebe and Olivia on horses and said she'd be back soon. But she isn't."

"Riding? They went riding?" Phoebe voluntarily on horse-back? Cato's eyebrows lifted. "Did they say where they were going?"

Toby shook his head. "An' we forgot to ask."

"Well, they can't be too long." Cato glanced out of the window beside the front door. The afternoon was drawing in. "I'll go to the stables and see if they told anyone where they were going."

He moved to the door, the two boys trotting at his heels, Juno exuberantly bounding ahead. "We'll all come too," Toby informed him unnecessarily.

They reached the stables just as the small cavalcade trotted in. He saw with approval that the three Decatur men accompanying them were well armed, but he wondered why they hadn't taken an escort of his own men.

"Where have you been? The boys were growing anxious."

Phoebe was clinging to Portia's waist, and when Portia dismounted, she gave a little squeal of dismay and grabbed for the pommel. "Don't leave me up here, Portia! This beast'll run away with me!"

"Don't be absurd, Phoebe," Cato chided, reaching up to loosen her death grip. "Let go now."

Phoebe did so and instantly tumbled into his arms, so suddenly he staggered back before he regained his balance.

"Oh, thank you for catching me," she said.

"I didn't have much choice," he observed, aware of her rounded arms encircling his neck and her swift breath rustling against his cheek.

He set her on her feet, but kept a hand on her shoulder for a moment. He looked down at her with a quizzical gleam in his eye.

He was close enough for Phoebe to see the little creases around his eyes, white against the weathered tan, and she could smell leather and wood smoke on his skin.

Portia said cheerfully above the excited barks of Juno and the insistent clamor of the boys, "I wanted to see some of the surrounding villages, sir. I don't know this part of the world and once it stopped raining it seemed a good opportunity."

The Decatur men were not about to contradict her.

Cato's hand dropped from Phoebe's shoulder and he moved away.

"How long will you be staying, my lord?" Phoebe found her voice again.

He paused and glanced back at her. "A while," he said. "Now that Basing House has yielded, I'll be working with Cromwell in headquarters for some time. There'll be no need for me to spend too much time from home in the next weeks."

Phoebe's heart leaped. There was nothing stopping her now from implementing Portia's advice. Her eyes darted to the package still fastened to Portia's saddle.

Then she caught Portia's eye. Portia winked as if she could read her thoughts, and Phoebe lifted her chin in answer. Dare all to win all.

"*You* need to do something with your hair," Portia said later, prowling around Phoebe like a tiger on the scent of prey. "It looks too demure and innocent in that ribbon. It doesn't go with the gown."

Phoebe caught the thick mass at the nape of her head and lifted it on top, twisting it into a knot. "Like this?"

"Yes, precisely." Portia rummaged through the little box on the dresser. "There's only pins in here. What you really need are some combs to hold it in place. Silver ones, if you've got them."

"Oh, I have some," Olivia said. "They were my mother's. I've never worn them. I wonder if I can find them."

"Well, go and look, duckie."

Olivia hurried off and when the door shut behind her, Phoebe said, "Portia, I'm scared. Diana never wore a dress like this. She was always so elegant. This isn't very elegant, is it?"

Portia considered this, her head on one side. "Diana couldn't have worn it," she pronounced finally. "It's a different kind of elegance, and only someone with your shape could wear it."

Phoebe wasn't sure that this did much for her confidence, but Olivia's return with two silver combs studded with tiny sapphires distracted her.

"I forgot they had sapphires," Olivia said. "They'll pick up the c-color of the gown. Isn't that good?"

"Perfect," Portia agreed, taking them from her. "D'you want me to do it, Phoebe?"

"Oh, yes, if you would. I'm no good with my hair. I can never get it to stay in place whatever I do with it."

"I'm not exactly expert myself. But I'll try." Frowning in concentration, Portia positioned the combs in the thick knot, then she stood back. "That should do. How does it feel?"

Phoebe moved her head gingerly. "As if it's going to come tumbling down at any minute."

"Well, don't move your head too much," Olivia suggested.

"I can't sit like a stuffed dummy all through supper. I have to move my head to eat . . . not that I think I'm going to be able to eat a thing," she added. Her stomach felt as if a field of butterflies had taken up residence there.

Portia added a few pins to her handiwork, then said, "That'll have to do. I'm sure it'll hold."

"We'd b-better go down." Olivia went to the door. "It's close to six o'clock."

The clock was striking six when Cato emerged from his study. As he crossed the great hall he glanced up at the stairs and stopped dead. Portia, for once in female attire, his daughter, and someone else were descending the stairs. His first thought was that this was some unknown guest about to be sprung upon him, and then he stared.

"Phoebe?" He stepped to the foot of the stairs.

Phoebe's heart pattered, her knees trembled, but she kept on down the stairs. "We haven't kept you waiting for supper, I trust, my lord."

"Phoebe?" repeated Cato, stunned.

His wife was wearing the most unsuitable gown. He had never seen one like it . . . no, that was not true. He had seen women of the court dressed with such blatant sensuality. But never a wife of his.

He shot an outraged look at his niece. It had to be Portia's fault. Phoebe could never have chosen such a gown for herself.

Before he could gather his thoughts, even begin to express himself, a servant crossed the hall to the dining parlor with a laden tray and the butler, husband to the formidable Mistress Bisset, emerged from the kitchen regions.

"My lord, supper is served."

Cato could say nothing in front of the servants. "Thank you, Bisset." He strode toward the dining parlor and opened the door, holding it for Phoebe, Portia, and Olivia to pass through.

Phoebe's midnight blue skirts brushed against him in a fluid ripple of velvet. His eye fell on the deep cleft of her breasts. He could see the faint shadow of her nipples just below the neckline.

Portia took her seat with a demure air so out of character

Olivia almost choked into her napkin. She glanced covertly at her father, wondering what he was thinking. It was hard to tell. His features were as well schooled as always, but there was something remarkably like shock in his dark eyes as he pulled out Phoebe's chair at the foot of the table before taking his own place at the head.

Phoebe's gown had certainly surprised him, Olivia reckoned. Not that it could have failed to. It was difficult to tell whether he liked it or not. She glanced at Portia, who gave her a lazy wink before solicitously offering Lord Granville the wine decanter. It was obvious to Portia that despite the even facade, the marquis was in sore need of fortification.

It was also obvious that the servants were fascinated by Lady Granville's new incarnation.

"You may leave us," Cato said curtly to the butler. "We'll serve ourselves."

The butler bowed and hustled his minions from the room. Cato regarded Phoebe over the lip of his goblet. He couldn't help noticing how the candlelight threw a rosy glow over the creamy white flesh of her bosom. The high collar at the back accentuated the smooth column of her throat. The sleeves of the gown were puffed, and banded in paler blue velvet. They ended just below the elbow in three layers of white ruffles.

He noticed her shoulders in the gown. They were prettily rounded, and her forearms emerging from the ruffles had a very graceful line. She seemed to be holding herself differently. Instead of hunching over as if to shield as much of herself as possible from observation, she sat with her shoulders back, her head up, her back very straight.

Phoebe was aware of Cato's eyes on her throughout the meal. Even when he was addressing some innocuous remark to Portia or to Olivia, his gaze would dart to Phoebe, a speculative gleam in the dark depths. She'd wanted his attention, and she certainly had it.

Phoebe was concentrating so hard on not spilling anything on her gown that she didn't notice at first when her hair started to come down. It trickled in little wisps at first, then she felt one of the heavy loops in the knot beginning to slip out of the comb. She put a tentative hand up and tried to push the comb back in, but her hair as always had a springy life and strength of its own. The more she touched it, the looser it became.

She blushed, picked up her goblet, took an overhasty sip of wine and choked. Coughing and spluttering into her napkin, she cursed her clumsiness. It always let her down in the end.

Cato threw down his napkin, pushed back his chair, and came around the table. He patted her back until the coughing fit subsided and then held her goblet to her lips.

"Take a slow sip this time."

Phoebe was so furious with herself she almost snatched the goblet from him. Her hair under the violence of her coughing was now tumbling unrestrained down the back of her neck, and she felt like screaming with annoyance.

"Keep still a minute," Cato instructed softly, and with swift and deft fingers he twisted the knot securely again and inserted the silver, sapphire-studded combs. They seemed familiar and he paused in his work with a slight frown. Then he remembered. They were Nan's. Olivia must have lent them to Phoebe. Nan, of course, had always been neat as a new pin, never a hair out of place.

As his hands moved intimately through her hair, Phoebe seemed to catch fire and her breath stopped in her lungs. Only when he took his hands away and returned to his seat could she breathe again.

Never had he touched her with such intimacy before. One could not call the swift and distant act of their marriage bed intimate. She glanced at Portia, who raised an eyebrow even as she blithely continued deboning a river trout.

Cato rang the bell for the second course. He was impatient to have Phoebe to himself. Before he told her exactly what he thought about the unsuitability of her attire, he wanted a few explanations. Not least how she'd paid for the gown. He'd assessed the quality of the velvet and the lace and could make a fair guess at what it had cost her. It was also, for all its daring cut, a very fashionable garment, and fashion did not come cheap.

He sat back in his carved chair, tapping his fingernails on the glowing cherrywood of the table while the servants cleared platters and placed a raised venison pie, an apple tart, a compote of plums, and a basket of mushroom tarts on the table.

His impatience throughout the second course grew more obvious, and it was a relief to all when he decided it was time to bring this interminable meal to a close. He pushed back his chair with a scrape on the parquet and stood up. It was the signal for the rest to lay down their spoons and forks, whether they'd finished or no.

"Forgive me, but I have work to do," he said. "If you wish to continue with supper, please do so."

He turned to his wife. "A word with you, Phoebe, if you please."

"Yes . . . yes, of course, my lord." Phoebe stood up in a rush.

Cato bowed in acknowledgment and moved to the door. He held it for her, saying quietly as she passed through, "Let us go abovestairs for this."

Phoebe felt a little tremor of alarm. He looked remarkably like a judge about to don the black cap.

7

Cato ushered Phoebe up the stairs. She could sense the tightly coiled impatience in his body as he walked just behind her. Her skin tingled as he laid a hand on her arm, turning her into the corridor at the head of the stairs that led to the east wing and the bedchamber that Phoebe still thought of as belonging only to Cato . . . a place where she was only a guest.

He leaned over her shoulder to open the door, and she felt his breath on her cheek as he raised the latch and pushed open the door. The fine hairs along her spine lifted. The room was candlelit, the fire a bright glow, the curtains at the windows drawn against the night. The handle of a warming pan stuck out from the foot of the bed. The maids would come in and remove it soon.

Phoebe thought this as she took in the familiar details of the chamber as if from some distant plane. Her body seemed to be oddly separate from her mind.

Cato closed the door quietly. He stood with his back to it, regarding Phoebe in frowning silence for what seemed to her an eternity. Without realizing how provocative was the posture, she put her shoulders back and rested her hands lightly on her hips, facing him across the length of the room.

It drew Cato's attention to the curve of her hip beneath the sensuous folds of the gown. Absently he massaged the back of his neck. *It was a damnable garment!*

"You don't care for my gown, my lord?" Phoebe broke the silence when she could no longer bear it.

Cato said brusquely, "At the moment, I'm more interested in where you acquired it, and how you paid for it. Assuming you did pay for it." He raised an eyebrow.

It was the tone and gesture Phoebe hated. Purely sardonic. She'd rather have anger any day.

She felt herself flushing, which she also hated, and said with an almost unconscious hauteur, "I paid for it myself, sir."

"How?" he demanded. "You have never asked me for money. All your wants and needs are taken care of within the household. Apart from ribbons and pins . . . peddler's wares." He gestured dismissively.

"If you have need of money, you have only to ask. But since you didn't, you must forgive my curiosity." The sardonic note was more pronounced.

"I couldn't ask you for money or you'd have wanted to know what it was for," Phoebe pointed out. "I wished to surprise you."

"Hell and the devil!" Distractedly Cato ran his hands through his hair. "Why am I to be subjected to surprises? I don't *like* surprises!"

"Oh," said Phoebe, somewhat nonplussed. "Most people like them . . . at least pleasant ones."

"Just answer the question please!"

"Oh . . . well . . . well, I had money of my own," she offered. "From my father." Such a possibility was laughable, but it was still an oblique shot at the truth.

Cato frowned at her. It didn't sound likely. Lord Carlton, traditional father that he was, would have informed the husband if he'd given his daughter a financial wedding present before he'd left her under her husband's roof. Another explanation came to mind.

"Did Portia give you the money?" He would not have *his* wife taking Decatur charity. His dark eyes were suddenly ablaze, a tiny pulse beating in his temple.

Phoebe shook her head hastily. "No . . . no, indeed not, my lord."

"Do not fob me off with tales of your father's generosity," he said curtly. "The truth if you please."

It seemed there was nothing for it. "I pawned some rings of my mother's."

Cato stared at her. "You had dealings with a pawnbroker?"

"It was very easy and discreet," she said in what she hoped was reassurance. "No one saw us in Witney. It only took a minute."

"In God's name, Phoebe! If you needed a new gown, why didn't you have one made here?"

"But I couldn't have had one like *this* made here." Phoebe had the air of one stating the obvious. "Ellen doesn't know anything about high fashion. And why would I want another countrified gown?"

"Why wouldn't you?" Cato demanded. "What could have possessed you to purchase a gown best suited to a courtesan at the king's court? You don't seem to have the slightest notion of propriety."

"So you *really* don't care for it, my lord?" Instinctively Phoebe turned slowly, her hands still on her hips, allowing the skirts to flow fluidly around her, the luxuriant darkness shimmering in the candlelight.

Cato passed a hand over his mouth. Completely without volition he muttered, "It's growing on me." Instantly he regretted the admission.

Phoebe spun round to face him, her face aglow. "I *knew* it! It *was* a good surprise, admit it, my lord."

Cato realized that this infuriating, unpredictable muddle of a girl had swept the ground from beneath his feet. If she hadn't looked so triumphant, so smugly jubilant, he could almost have been beguiled, but he wasn't about to give her the satisfaction of seeing him crack a smile. It struck him as a fairly demented response anyway. The girl had visited a *pawnbroker*, for God's sake.

So he said in what he hoped were cutting accents, "It is not . . . repeat *not* . . . a suitable gown for you. And it's quite inappropriate for the quiet country life we lead here. You have no need to dress as if you're going to court."

He turned on his heel and went to the door. "I have work to do . . . dispatches to send to headquarters. I'll come to bed later."

Phoebe stood still in the middle of the room after the door had closed. At last he had truly noticed her. For once he had seen her clearly as a woman. It had angered him, but that was a small price to pay.

"*I* feel just like the proverbial square peg being hammered into the round hole," Phoebe complained to her friend Meg, the herbalist, the next day as she stripped branches of fresh thyme for drying. "Why would Cato be so determined to keep me in some mold he's designed for me when it's obvious to a blind man that I don't fit it?"

Mistress Meg pursed her lips. "Men," she stated, as if the entire sex lay behind all the problems of the universe.

She was about ten years older than Phoebe, a tall, dark woman, brown as a berry from days in the woods gathering the herbs and simples of her trade. Laugh lines crinkled the skin around her clear gray eyes. Meg was surprised by nothing and regarded the world's vagaries with wry humor. She dispensed advice and medicine in equal parts to all who came knocking at her door, and she was Phoebe's confidante and most trusted advisor.

Phoebe waited for expansion and, when none came, inquired, "Yes, but what about them?"

Meg stirred the fragrant pot of herbs on its trivet over the fire. "The male of the species in general is an unfortunate creature," she pronounced. "Generally the poor benighted soul can't see further than his nose, but at least that saves him from knowing what he's missing."

"That's so harsh," Phoebe protested, chuckling. "And you've never even had a man in your life."

"Precisely," Meg said serenely. "I practice what I preach. No man is going to start telling me what I may or may not do, as if for some reason he has a God-given right to do so. Narrow-minded bigots, most of them. Hidebound, habit-ridden, conventional . . ."

"Oh, stop!" Phoebe cried, flinging up her hands in protest. "Cato's not like that."

"Oh, no?" Meg regarded her in disbelief. "He has an image of what a wife should be like and he won't look outside it. You've just said as much."

A one-eared black cat jumped onto Phoebe's lap with a demanding cry, and she obeyed the command, digging her fingers into the deep groove at the back of the animal's neck, then down his spine. The cat purred ecstatically and arched his back against Phoebe's scratching fingers.

"Well, that's true," Phoebe conceded. "But he's not stupid, Meg."

"Oh, you think he can learn?" Meg scoffed. "Then he's a rare case indeed. Take my word for it. Men are far too arrogant and self-satisfied to change their minds about anything. Why should they? They've arranged everything just the way they want it."

"Oh, you're impossibly prejudiced," Phoebe said. Meg was never less than forthcoming with her robustly unflattering opinion of the male sex. Phoebe regarded her with curiosity. "Did some man offend you once . . . or something?"

Meg shook her head. "Never gave 'em the chance." She stood up and reached up to the rack of herbs drying above the fire. She selected several strands and dropped them into the pot before resuming her slow, rhythmic stirring.

Phoebe absently pulled at the cat's single ear. She'd met Meg when she'd first arrived in Woodstock, after Cato had acquired the manor house. She was known to everyone simply as Mistress Meg, and she was very reticent about her background and parentage, but her diagnostic skills and great talent as a herbalist had quickly earned her a place in village life, despite the occasional mutterings about the oddity of a single woman flying in the face of convention, living totally independent of any man. There were those who called her a witch, but Meg just laughed at such superstitions and continued about her business, dispensing earthy advice with her potions.

Phoebe was fascinated by simples and the arts of the herbalist. She'd proved an apt apprentice, absorbing Meg's blunt opinions and down-to-earth wisdom, including Meg's advice on avoiding conception.

Now Phoebe watched Meg curiously, contemplating the puzzle of her friend's antipathy towards the male sex.

"You never felt passion?" she inquired.

"For a *man*! My stars, no!" Meg shook her head with an expression of horror. Then as she stirred, she added calmly, "There *was* a woman once."

Confounded, Phoebe could only gaze at Meg until she found her tongue. "A woman?"

Meg smiled to herself. "Not everyone's the same, Phoebe. As we were just saying."

"No . . . but . . ."

"No, but what?" There was a hint of mockery in Meg's smile now.

"Well, what happened? Who was she? Where is she?"

"Oh, she succumbed to convention . . . yielded to the power of man," Meg said with a twisted grin. "She went off to become a farmer's wife with a brood of squalling brats."

"I'm sorry." Phoebe could think of nothing else to say.

Meg shrugged. "It wasn't really Libby's fault. It's hard to be strong enough to withstand the whip of convention when it's wielded by those who have the power of compulsion."

"But you haven't yielded."

"No. I haven't."

A loud knock at the door broke the moment of silence.

Phoebe, relieved at the interruption, jumped to her feet. The black cat leaped from her lap in the same instant, needing catlike to prove that the decision to leave his perch was only his. His back claws scored her thighs as he took off.

Phoebe opened the door and a shaft of morning sunlight lit the dim, smoky interior of the little cottage.

An elderly man in rough homespuns stood on the threshold. He looked worried as he asked, "Is Mistress Meg within?"

"Yes, indeed." Phoebe stepped aside to allow the man entrance.

"Good day, Grandpa." Meg looked up from her stirring. "How's the little one?"

"That's what I come about." He twisted the cap between his hands. "He's wheezin' summat chronic. Think you'd better come an' take a look. His mother's at 'er wit's end."

"I'll come at once." Meg rose and reached for her basket of simples that she kept ready packed beside the door. "I'll see you later, Phoebe." She hurried past Phoebe and strode off down the path, the elderly man half trotting to keep up with her.

Phoebe closed up the cottage, leaving a window ajar for the cat, then she left the small clearing in the woods.

Ordinarily she would have noticed the young man standing in the doorway of the Bear Inn as she hurried past along the main village street. Strangers were few and far between, particularly those dressed with such obvious finery, but she was too preoccupied with the afternoon's intriguing revelations.

Brian Morse watched her turn the corner into the lane running alongside the churchyard. "That's Lady Granville?" he asked over his shoulder.

"Aye, sir." The man behind the counter in the tap-room didn't look up from the keg he was tapping. "Like I said 'afore."

Brian scratched his chin in thought. The barman had pointed her out to him on her way through the village an hour earlier, and he'd been watching for her return. How could that shabby, dumpy little creature be the stately Diana's sister? How could Cato have taken such an unprepossessing girl to wife?

But of course she was still a Carlton, and came with all that family's advantages of wealth and lineage. That's all that would interest Cato. That and getting an heir.

Brian's little brown eyes grew speculative. This visit to Woodstock was intended as a reconnaissance. He wanted to gauge the lie of the land and decide on the best approach to Cato and his wife. Perhaps the girl's lack of obvious attraction could work to his advantage. She might well be susceptible to flattery, since it was hard to imagine much came her way.

Once ensconced beneath Cato's roof, he would try an appeal to her sympathy. Involve her in a clandestine little enterprise that would excite her, make her feel special. Women were so easy to manage.

Except for Jack Worth's bastard, Portia. The familiar worm of mortification squirmed in his gut, and he turned back to the taproom, demanding curtly, "Ale!"

He took the leather pitch-coated pot and drained it in one long swallow before tossing a coin on the bar counter and calling for his horse. He would return to Oxford and make his preparations to enter his stepfather's household.

*P*hoebe *was about to climb the stile leading to the home* farm and the back entrance to the house when the deep thunder of hooves, the chink of bridles, reached her on the crisp air. It sounded like a large cavalcade cantering down the ice-ridged ruts of the Oxford road. Curious, she sat atop the stile and waited for whoever it was to come around the corner. A party of Parliament's militia, she guessed. Such troop movements were constant in the Thames valley.

The standard snapping in the wind caught her attention first. It flew above the hedge as the horsemen drew close to the corner. It was the eagle of Rothbury. Rufus Decatur had come back to collect his wife and children.

Phoebe forgot all about the events of the morning. She half fell off the stile in her eagerness to conceal herself before Rufus caught sight of her. She knew exactly how she intended to greet the earl of Rothbury, and it was not in her present guise.

She scrambled across the field, tugging her cloak loose when the hem caught on a thornbush. There was a harsh rending sound but Phoebe ignored it. She raced through the orchard and darted into the house through the kitchen.

Mistress Bisset gave her a startled look as she ran past the linen room, then shrugged and returned to her inventory of sheets. Lady Granville was still Lady Phoebe as far as the household was concerned.

In the bedchamber, Phoebe tore off her old gown, tossing it into a corner. There was water in the ewer and she splashed her face and hands. How long did she have before they arrived? She'd come cross-country, but they were a good mile away along the road, and then another half up the drive. And then there would be all the flurry of dismounting. She had twenty minutes.

She opened the linen press and took out the dark red silk. Cato had not seen this one. She had been going to spring it upon him at dinner, but how much better to show it off as she greeted her first real guests as lady of the manor. Not that Rufus Decatur would notice particularly. A man who preferred his wife in britches was not likely to appreciate the glories of the dark red silk. But then, Phoebe was not seeking to impress the earl of Rothbury.

She dropped the gown over her head and struggled desperately with the hooks at the back. Her arms ached as she twisted and turned, trying to see over her shoulder in the mirror as she fiddled with the tiny fastenings, but at last she had them done.

She smoothed the rich folds of silk. They felt wonderful, soft and caressing. Her hair was already in a thick plait hanging down her back. She twisted it against the nape of her neck and stuck some pins in it, hoping that the coil would hold rather more effectively than it had done the previous evening.

Her image in the mirror was most satisfactory. She patted the lace collar, making sure it lay flat, then hurried to the door. She could hear the sounds of commotion from the hall below, and at the head of the curving sweep of stair she paused to look down on the scene, gauging the moment for her entrance.

Rufus Decatur stood on the threshold. Cato Granville came forward to greet him. The two men were of much the same height and build, but Rufus's red hair and beard, his plain jerkin and britches, the serviceable but dull leather of his boots and gloves were in startling contrast to the other man's darkly aquiline looks, the elegant cut of his black velvet doublet, the fall of lace at his throat. But the same controlled power emanated from both men, and they both held themselves and moved with the sinuous assurance of those who were accustomed to command.

"I bid you welcome, Rothbury." Cato extended his hand.

Rufus pulled off his glove and took the hand in a brief clasp. "I've come to relieve you of my brood, Granville. Not a moment too soon, I'll be bound."

Cato's polite disclaimer was lost in a wild shriek as Luke and Toby tumbled through the front door. "We heard you . . . we knew you was here." They grabbed for their father's knees.

He ruffled their bright heads, but his eyes had found Portia, who came out of the parlor, Alex in her arms, Eve's hand in hers.

Eve followed her brothers' example, tugging her hand free of her mother's and flinging herself upon Rufus, who caught her up and swung her through the air as she shrieked joyously.

"I give you good day, gosling," Rufus said to his wife, as he settled his daughter on his hip and caught Portia's chin on the tip of a finger, tilting her face for his kiss. He moved his mouth from her lips to the baby's cheek in one smooth movement.

Cato watched the scene with a strange tug that he identified reluctantly as envy. His own small daughters, Diana's babies, never greeted him with such unbridled joy as Decatur's children greeted their father. And the emotion that flowed between Portia and Rufus was a palpable current.

"I hope you'll break your journey with us overnight, Rothbury." Cato issued the invitation even though he was sure it would be declined.

"My thanks, Granville, but we'll be on our way," Rufus responded. "As soon as this gypsy caravan of mine can be assembled."

He raised an eyebrow at Portia, who said swiftly, "Not more than an hour. I've been expecting you these last two days."

Rufus nodded.

"Lord Rothbury." Phoebe came slowly down the stairs. "I bid you welcome."

"Ah, Phoebe." The surprised flash in his eye was unmistakable, as was the instant of swift and approving appraisal. "Lady Granville," he said, and bowed with grave deliberation.

Phoebe's head lifted. She glanced at Portia, who was grinning wickedly. Olivia gave her an infinitesimal nod of encouragement even as her dark eyes shone with curiosity as she waited for her father's reaction to Phoebe's stunning entrance.

Cato turned slowly. Briefly he closed his eyes and his fingers fleetingly brushed his mouth, before he said, "I trust we can persuade Lord Rothbury to break bread with us before he resumes his journey, Phoebe."

"Yes, indeed." Phoebe, with regal grace, swept past Cato to curtsy to her guest.

Cato gazed at his wife's back with astonishment. The hooks at the back of Phoebe's latest revelation were missing several connections, and those they had made were not all correctly paired.

Cato slipped a casual arm around her. "If you'd excuse us for a minute, Rothbury . . ." He moved Phoebe away, his hand sliding to the small of her back as he steered her towards the library, concealing the middle of her back view from the occupants of the hall.

Phoebe shivered at the easy intimacy of his touch. She had no idea what he was about, but she was not complaining.

In the library, out of direct sight of the hall, Cato put his hands on her shoulders, keeping her back to him. "Why didn't you get your maid to help you with these hooks?"

"Why? What's the matter?" Phoebe peered over her shoulder.

"It's more a question of what's right," he said, beginning to unhook the gown from the top.

Phoebe felt the air stir the thin cotton of her shift. "Oh dear, are they done up wrong?"

She stood on tiptoe as she continued to peer over her shoulder as if the extra height would enable her to see better. "I was afraid they might be," she added dolefully. "It's very difficult if you don't have arms like an octopus."

"Which is why you have a maid," Cato pointed out.

"I was trying to hurry. I knew Lord Rothbury was coming; I saw him on the road when I was coming back from the village, and I wanted to be able to greet him dressed properly."

"As against dressed for digging up cabbages," Cato said sharply. "For God's sake, girl, why can't you find a happy medium? This gown is as inappropriate as the blue vel—that other one."

"But it's very elegant," Phoebe pointed out.

"It depends who's wearing it," Cato said with a hint of

savagery. He finished fastening the hooks and placed his hands on her hips as he checked that he hadn't missed one.

Phoebe felt the imprint of his hands on her skin beneath the silk. Each finger seemed to burn against her flesh. She stood very still.

Cato's hands dropped from her hips. "So," he inquired, "how many more of these sartorial surprises am I to expect?" The sardonic edge was again in his voice.

"I don't have any more money," Phoebe said simply.

"On which subject." Cato reached into the pocket of his britches and drew out the three rings. "If you ever visit a pawnbroker again, madam wife, you will rue the day."

"You redeemed them?"

"Of course I did. You think I would permit some thief of a pawnbroker to hold *my* property?"

"I thought they were mine," Phoebe said softly. "They belonged to my mother."

"And neither will I permit a pawnbroker to hold *your* property," Cato said acidly, tossing the three gem-studded silver circlets onto a sidetable. "If you let them out of your possession again, you will forfeit that possession. Understand that."

He left the library and after a minute Phoebe scooped up the rings and dropped them into her bosom. It seemed she had her currency returned.

*T*he Rothbury clan was ready to leave within the hour as Portia had promised. The countess of Rothbury was accustomed to military maneuvers and could marshal a brood of children and nursemaids as efficiently as she could a troop of soldiers.

Phoebe held her in a tight embrace and whispered urgently in her ear. It was her last chance for concrete advice.

Portia murmured, "If you can't tell him what you want, duckie, you're going to have to show him."

"How?" Phoebe whispered with the same urgency as before.

"Use your poetic imagination," Portia responded, her green eyes alight with mischief.

"Easier said than done." Phoebe gave her one more convulsive hug, before stepping back to give Olivia room for her own farewells.

8

"*A*re you working on your play, Phoebe?" Olivia looked up from her books at the table in the square parlor. She realized that Phoebe hadn't spoken a word in a very long time, which was unusual.

The house seemed very flat in the wake of the Rothbury party's departure. Ordinarily Phoebe, who had little patience with moping, would have made an effort to lighten things, but she was so absorbed in her work that she'd barely raised her eyes from the page for several hours.

"How far have you g-got?" Olivia persisted.

"It's not a play anymore, it's a pageant," Phoebe said, nibbling the end of her quill. "It's to be a midsummer pageant, I've decided."

"What about?" Olivia closed Catullus over her finger.

"Gloriana. Scenes from her life."

"Queen Elizabeth, you mean?"

"Mmm." Phoebe's voice grew more animated. "In verse, of course. I'd like to stage it on Midsummer Eve, if I can have it written by then," she added, looking down at the scrawl of lines in front of her. "There are so many parts. But the three important ones are Elizabeth, Mary, Queen of Scots, and Elizabeth's lover, Robert Dudley, Earl of Leicester."

"Who's to take them?" Olivia got up and came over to the window seat where Phoebe was sitting cross-legged, heedless of the creases in the red silk.

"Oh, all of us, of course, and for the minor parts members of the household and the village. I have it in mind to include as many people as possible. The village children and of course your little sisters. I hope it'll cheer people up, give them something other than gloom and doom and war to think about. Oh, and you're to be Mary, Queen of Scots, and . . ."

"Am I to lose my head?" Olivia clapped her hands to her head in mock horror. "Shall I g-go around with it under my arm?"

"You could, I suppose," Phoebe said doubtfully. "But I hadn't thought to stage the execution. It might be a bit too difficult to do convincingly."

"Well, who's to play Elizabeth? It had better be you, don't you think?" Olivia sat on the window seat and picked up a sheet of vellum already covered in Phoebe's black writing. "Although Portia has the right c-color hair. . . . Oh, I like this speech of Mary's! You're so talented, Phoebe."

She was about to declaim when Phoebe snatched the paper from her.

"It's not finished," Phoebe said. "I'm not satisfied with it yet. You can't read it until I am."

Olivia yielded immediately. She knew what a perfectionist Phoebe was over her work. "Well, are you going to play Gloriana?" she repeated.

Phoebe shook her head. "Hardly. I'd be a laughingstock. I'm too short and plump and I don't scintillate. The virgin queen was dignified and elegant and she definitely scintillated."

"When you're not untidy, you c-can be elegant," Olivia said seriously.

"Well, thank you for those few kind words," Phoebe said. It seemed like a backhanded compliment to her.

"It's true, though," Olivia insisted. "People aren't the same, Phoebe. You know what they say: one man's meat is another man's poison."

"I suppose so," Phoebe said, suddenly remembering her conversation with Meg. "Have you ever heard of women who like women more than men?"

"Oh, you mean like Sappho on Lesbos," Olivia said matter-of-factly. "Although the Greeks were mostly known for men who liked men, or boys. It was part of the c-culture."

She grabbed up a book from the table. "And then of course there were the Romans. This passage in Suetonius about the minnows . . . little boys that were trained to act like minnows in the Emperor Tiberius's swimming pool. Look, here it is." She began to translate the scandalous passage.

"And some of Sappho's verse is really passionate." Olivia jumped up and went to the bookshelf. She took up a book and flicked through pages, then came back to the window seat. "See, here it is."

Phoebe looked at the hieroglyphics on the page and was at a loss. "I can't read that."

"No, but I c-can. She's saying how sweat pours down her and there's a fire beneath her skin when she's with this woman. . . ."

"Well if that's not lust, I don't know what is." Phoebe turned sideways and glanced down at the rear courtyard below. Cato in riding dress was crossing towards the stables. Her gaze drank him in.

A fire beneath her skin. Oh, yes, it was a very precise description of passion.

What if she wrote Robert Dudley's part for Cato? She would write the love scenes, put the passion into Cato's mouth . . . And she would play Gloriana opposite him. . . .

Phoebe nibbled her pen as the impossible idea took hold.

"*Dammit, what's that?*" *Later that day, Cato raised his* head and sniffed the wind. It was bitterly cold; the earlier sunshine had given way to snow-laden clouds. Cato's instincts for approaching trouble were well honed, and Giles Crampton stiffened in readiness.

They could hear nothing, yet Cato was convinced danger lay close by.

"Run for it?" suggested Giles. It went against the soldier's grain, but there were only two of them, and the first flakes of snow now fell onto his mount's glossy coat.

"Aye," Cato said shortly. He put spur to his horse but it was a moment too late. A party of yeomanry in the king's colors broke out of the trees. In grim silence they spread out across the narrow path, blocking the horsemen.

Cato's horse reared as he was about to break into a gallop. Cato steadied the charger with one hand as he drew his sword. Giles had his musket in his hand in the same instant. For a long moment there was an impasse, the line of men with swords and pikes holding steady across the road, the two horsemen watching them, every nerve stretched.

Then one of the yeoman raised his pike, and in the same moment, Cato spurred his horse straight at the line of men. Giles, with a skirling yell of pure gleeful exhilaration, charged alongside. His musket cracked and a man went down to the path beneath the hooves of Giles's mount.

Cato's cavalry sword flashed down from side to side. Blood spattered onto his boots and britches. A man went for the charger's neck with his pike. Cato wrenched the beast to one side and the animal screamed as the point tore a superficial cut in his hide. He reared, using his hooves as weapons, and it was men who were screaming now.

Giles unloosed his pike and drove it into the upturned throat of one of his assailants the same instant the man raised his musket. The gun wavered and the ball exploded into the air.

Then they were through and the path ahead was clear under the now thickly falling snow.

"Well done," Cato said, his teeth flashing in a smile that was as exhilarated as his lieutenant's. "Quite a scrap."

"Aye, m'lord. That it was." Giles nodded complacently. "Reckon their insignia was the King's Own Foot. They've been a right menace these last weeks, patrolling the road between our headquarters and the city."

"Well, maybe we gave them something to think about," Cato said cheerfully, leaning over to examine the scratch on his charger's neck. "Doesn't look too bad."

"Ted'll patch 'im up at home," Giles said. "A rare wonder 'e is with injuries." He pulled the brim of his hat down against the driving snow, and they galloped the rest of the way in silence, anxious now only to get out of the worsening blizzard.

It was close to six o'clock and Phoebe was standing at the window in the hall looking out at the white flakes swirling ever more thickly from the sky. Even on a clement evening the roads were too dangerous for nighttime travel unless in the company of an armed cavalcade, and Cato had gone out only with Giles as escort.

"Did Lord Granville say how long he'd be away, Bisset?"

"No, Lady Phoebe. But I doubt his lordship will return for supper now. Will you take it in the dining parlor or in the little parlor abovestairs?"

Phoebe glanced again at the long-case clock in the hall. The pendulum swung inexorably as the hands approached six o'clock. If Cato hadn't returned at six, he wouldn't return tonight. And if he didn't return tonight, she didn't know whether she'd ever have the courage again.

Then as she hesitated, she heard the sound of hooves on the gravel sweep before the front door. Giles Crampton's robust tones carried through the oak. Where Giles was, Cato would be also. Her heart beat fast and she wiped her suddenly clammy palms on her skirt.

"In the dining parlor, Bisset," she said in her most stately tone.

Cato came in, his face reddened with cold. Snow dusted his black cloak. "Damned March weather!" he announced, taking off his hat and shaking snow from its crown. "Brilliant sunshine this morning and now it's readying for a blizzard. Put supper back for half an hour, Bisset, and bring me a tankard of burned sack into the library. I'm cold as a corpse's arse."

His eye fell on Phoebe still in her red silk. "Are you and Olivia starving, Phoebe, or can you wait supper for half an hour? I need to thaw out."

"There's blood on your boots and your britches," Phoebe said, barely hearing the question. "Are you hurt, sir?" She touched his arm, raising anxious eyes to his face in searching inquiry.

"It's not my blood," Cato informed her.

"Oh, then who else is hurt? Where is he . . . they?" She took a step towards the door as if expecting to minister to a party of wounded.

"I didn't exchange introductions," Cato said dryly, having little difficulty guessing her thoughts. "They may well be lying in a ditch for all I know."

"Oh, but—"

"No, I did not bring them home wrapped in blankets to be housed and tended like your tribe of gypsies. As it happened, there were eight of them against the two of us, and *they* started it. Believe it or not, my dear girl, war has no room for philanthropy." He dusted his hands off in a gesture of finality.

"It wasn't a tribe of gypsies," Phoebe protested. "It was just two . . . two very little ones. And they didn't have anything to do with the war."

"Maybe so," Cato was obliged to concede. "But little ones grow."

Phoebe considered this, then said with a sunny smile, "Well, when they're grown up a little, they can earn their keep and they won't be quite such a charge upon you, will they?"

Before Cato could find an adequate response to this insouciant impertinence, Phoebe was saying, "I'll fetch the sack for you, my lord, if you'd like. I'll bring it to the library."

It was the first time she'd assumed the domestic duties of

a wife in his household, and he was so surprised he could manage no more than a faint "Thank you."

"Bisset, will you tell Lady Olivia that we'll be taking supper a little later?" Phoebe asked the butler as she went past him towards the kitchen regions. "She's in the parlor abovestairs."

Bisset looked as surprised as his master at this assertive tone, but he went with measured tread to the stairs.

Cato threw his damp cloak onto the bench beside the door and went into the library. He bent to rub his hands at the fire, then turned to warm his backside.

Phoebe came hurrying in carrying a silver tankard. "I hope it's to your liking, sir." She handed it to him with a small curtsy.

"Did you prepare it yourself?" He took the tankard and sipped appreciatively.

"Well, not exactly," Phoebe confessed. "I don't have quite the right touch with the poker. But I watched Mistress Bisset."

"I see." Cato sipped again. "I expect you'll be adept at it the next time."

"I'm not sure about that," Phoebe said frankly. "You have to be so careful that the poker doesn't touch the side of the tankard, and you have to stir the liquid just so, to get the heat all the way through the sack. I expect I'll have to practice."

Cato agreed solemnly, his eyes flickering over her. There was something touching about her candor, something altogether appealing about her at the moment. She had an air almost of suppressed excitement. Her eyes were even brighter than usual, and her cheeks had a soft glow.

Phoebe moved around the room, adjusting things that didn't appear to need adjusting. Straightening perfectly straight papers, rearranging a jug of dried leaves, trimming the wick of a steadily burning candle.

"Was it an ambush, then, my lord?"

"Aye. We were on our way back from headquarters and a party of yeoman jumped us."

"Why didn't you take an escort?" she demanded.

"It wasn't necessary," he responded crisply.

"Oh, but it was! If you'd had an escort, you wouldn't have been in danger . . . or at least not so much."

"There's danger abroad every minute of every day in wartime," he told her.

"When will it be over, do you think?" Phoebe asked wistfully. It seemed to her that her entire adult life had been spent in the disjointed troubled times of civil war. She had never known the ordinary carefree pleasures of a prewar girlhood, any more than had Olivia.

Cato shook his head in a gesture of regret. "I wish I could say for sure. But even when it's over, it'll be many a moon before the country is truly at peace."

"But the king won't win?" She looked at him, her gaze intent.

Again Cato shook his head. "No," he said. "But the question is, will Parliament?" He drank deeply.

Phoebe frowned. "I don't understand."

"It will be a Pyrrhic victory at best," he said with a sigh.

Phoebe hesitated. The conversation seemed to make him gloomy and that was not the mood she wanted for this evening.

"Well, I'm glad you managed to get home," she said, swiftly changing the subject. "When I saw the snow, I wasn't sure whether you'd be able to." She swooped suddenly on the fire and, seizing the poker, began to stab at the logs with businesslike ardor.

"Be careful. You don't want sparks flying onto that tenguinea gown," Cato observed.

"Do you like it . . . the gown, I mean?" Phoebe dropped the poker with a clatter in the hearth and straightened, facing him.

Cato considered her with a quizzical eye. "Why is it so creased? It wasn't this morning."

"Oh." Chagrined, Phoebe looked down at her dark red skirts and saw how the silk was crumpled. "I expect it's because I was sitting cross-legged all afternoon." The explanation was so helplessly resigned that Cato smiled. What a ragged robin she was. And what an amazingly intense blue were her eyes. Quite magnificent with their thick fair lashes.

"Should I ask why?"

"I was writing my pageant. I can't seem to write at a table like ordinary people. I don't get inspiration that way."

Cato regarded her over the lip of his tankard. "So, what's the subject of this pageant?"

Phoebe's cheeks took on a deeper pink. Could he be mocking her? He'd never expressed any interest before.

"It's about Gloriana," she said cautiously. "Queen Elizabeth, you know."

"Yes, I do know. That's a big subject."

"Oh, it's huge," Phoebe agreed, unable to hide her enthusiasm now, her eyes star-bright.

"You must be very ambitious," Cato observed.

"Well, I think I am," Phoebe confided. She glanced up at him from beneath lowered lids. "I was hoping you would take a part, my lord."

Cato laughed. "As if I have time for such playacting, my dear girl."

"No," Phoebe said, "I don't suppose you do. I'll go and tell Olivia to come for supper."

The clock on the mantel struck nine. Phoebe stopped her restless pacing around the bedchamber. When would he come? It seemed an eternity since they'd left the supper table. The maid had removed the warming pan and turned down the coverlet. The fire was banked; only the candles on the mantel remained lit. The chamber was prepared for the night. It wanted only the master.

Phoebe repositioned the fireside chair for the fifth time, moving it so that its back was more fully turned to the window. She was going to conceal herself behind the heavy velvet curtains. Cato would not go near them when he came to bed. The night was dark as pitch, snow still falling heavily; he'd have nothing to see if he looked out of the window.

She went to the bed again and checked that the bedcurtains were completely drawn, not a chink showing. He never touched them until he came to bed, after he'd snuffed the candles. But supposing tonight he did. Supposing tonight he looked behind them for some reason when he first entered the chamber. The fact that he'd never done it before didn't mean he would never change his routine.

In a panic, Phoebe flew behind the bedcurtains. She shoved the bolster into the bed, pulling the cover up over it. It didn't look in the least like a person, but it would be dark and the mound would surely satisfy him. He would be expecting to see a shape and that's what he would see.

But when would he come? Most nights it was soon after nine o'clock. Phoebe grimaced. She guessed that he came up early out of consideration for her. Their coupling was a perfunctory enough business without waking her up for it. So he got it over with before she went to sleep. Quite often, afterwards, he would get up again and go to work in his study. And most mornings he was awake and out of the house before she stirred. Indeed, one could hardly tell that they shared a bed at all.

But that was about to change.

She went to the door and opened it a crack. The corridor was dimly lit by the candles sconced at either end. She could hear nothing. The household rose at first light and went to bed as soon as the supper dishes were cleared away.

Phoebe tiptoed into the corridor and crept soundlessly to

the stairs. The hall was lit only by the fire. Then she heard a door open. The study door. She caught the flicker of a carrying candle.

Phoebe turned and raced back to the bedchamber. She dragged off her nightrobe and, naked, dived behind the window curtains. It was freezing! Icy drafts needled through every tiny gap in the window frame. Her teeth chattered. How could she possibly hope to be seductive when her skin was all pimpled like a plucked goose? she thought in despair. Why did things never work out the way they were supposed to?

But there was no time to remedy the situation even if she knew how. The door opened and Cato came in.

Phoebe glanced down at her feet. She couldn't see her toes. Oh God! They were sticking out from under the velvet curtain. She scrunched them tightly, inching them backward. Her heart was hammering so hard she couldn't understand how Cato could fail to hear it.

Cato set his carrying candle on the small table and glanced around the chamber. The bedcurtains were tightly drawn as usual. A small sigh escaped him.

He pulled off his boots against the jack and began to undress methodically, hanging his clothes in the armoire as he removed them. Shirtless but still in his britches, he sat down in the chair to take off his stockings.

And something fell across his eyes, blinding him. His hands flew to his eyes as the thin silk was suddenly pulled tight across them. *"What the hell . . ."*

He made to jump up and then something landed in his lap, forcing him back into the chair. His hands encountered soft but chilled skin. The unmistakable contours of a naked female body.

For one astounded instant Cato thought he was in the midst of a delusion—either that or he'd fallen asleep without knowing it and was having some extraordinary dream bred of frustration.

Then the body in his lap twisted slightly and he was vibrantly aware of soft breasts pressed against his bare chest. This was no dream. He reached to tear off the strip of silk covering his eyes.

"No, please don't. Not for a minute." Phoebe spoke softly but urgently against his ear, her hands closing over his wrists, trying to prevent him from uncovering his eyes. A ludicrous shyness prompted the request. Sitting naked in his lap was one thing, but she didn't want him to see her, not yet.

Cato let his hands fall. He didn't know what was happening, but his body was responding to the warm weight in his lap, and the desire to discover what she would do next drove reason from his mind.

He closed his eyes beneath the silk and his hands began to roam of their own accord.

"Why are you so cold?" he asked, cupping the curve of a breast in his palm.

"I was standing in a draft, behind the window curtain," Phoebe replied, her voice muffled against his throat. For so many weeks she had longed to press her lips against the fast-beating pulse, and now tentatively, shyly, she did so.

"Of course. Such a simple explanation," Cato murmured. "Why didn't I think of it myself?" He circled the nipple with his finger and it rose hard beneath his touch.

Phoebe felt the first tug in her loins, a deep and wonderful sense of fullness. She moved in his lap, an unconscious little wriggle of pleasure.

Cato scooped her other breast into his free hand, teasing the nipple with his thumb. His blindness seemed to heighten his sense of touch. He had never explored her body, not with his eyes nor with his hands, and it was now as if she were quite new to him. Untouched and unknown territory waiting to be discovered. And indeed this softly sensuous, deeply responsive girl in his lap bore no resemblance to the stiff, taut woman who had endured his sexual invasions, rigid with revulsion, night after night.

He moved his hands down to her belly, smoothing over its soft roundness. It was tender and sweet like a juicy plum. He dipped a finger into her navel, a surprisingly deep indentation, soft as the silk covering his eyes.

Phoebe stirred again in his lap, her thighs parting in involuntary invitation. Little spasms of pleasure were darting through her loins now, and she was aware of a strange little ache of need between her thighs. It was hard to tell where it was centered, impossible to describe exactly how it felt, but it seemed to intensify as Cato's hands slid over her belly.

"Untie the scarf," Cato commanded softly. "I don't know what's going on here, but it's no longer a game of blindman's buff."

Phoebe obeyed, her fingers fumbling with the knot at the back of his head. The scarf fell away but her hands stayed where they were, her fingers straying through his hair, getting to know the shape of his skull, tracing the curve of his ear. She wanted to know every part of him. Not a hair or an inch of skin could be ignored. She wanted to know his eyebrows, the little frown lines crisscrossing his forehead, the grooves beside his long nose, the little cleft in his chin.

Cato's own exploration ceased for a minute. He rested his head against the back of the chair, regarding her with a puzzled half smile. She bent and kissed his eyelids, the tip of her tongue moistening the thin skin.

"Just what is going on here?" he inquired. "And no . . ." He raised a forestalling finger. "Don't tell me you wanted to surprise me."

"I wanted to show something to you," she said. "I couldn't think of any other way to do it. Does it matter? Is this not good?"

"Oh, yes, it's good," Cato said. "And it's an ungrateful man who'd look such a gift horse in the mouth, even if he doesn't have the first damn inkling of how or why it's been given to him." With a lazy smile he put his hands at her waist and repositioned her on his lap, so that she was leaning back against him. Then he slid his hands inside her thighs and parted her legs.

"I think it's time I surprised *you*."

Phoebe's eyes widened. She felt suddenly exposed, as if her secret places were laid open, and with a jerky little movement tried to resist the pressure of his hands.

Cato moved one hand to her belly again, stroking and kneading the silken flesh. His other found her breast and tugged gently on her nipple, rolling it between finger and thumb.

The ache sprang fresh and new again and the little pulse in Phoebe's loins began to throb. Her thighs fell open of their own accord and she offered no resistance this time as the hand on her belly slid between them.

He touched her, gently opening the flower of her sex. Phoebe moved against his fingers, aware now only of the hot, wet center of her being. He found the erect little bud of pleasure and teased it with the tip of a finger, flicking delicately until she moaned, hovering on the brink of a maelstrom of sensation, her belly and thighs tightening, her loins quivering. His fingers slid within her as his thumb continued to play on the swollen little nub.

Phoebe gave a little cry almost of surprise as the first sweet ripple of ecstasy radiated from his fingers, moving up into her belly and along her thighs. She twisted on his lap, pushing herself against his hand under the spiraling urgency of pleasure. Then something astounding burst deep within her, making her cry out, her breathing swift and shallow, as streamers of delight shot through her body.

Cato held her as she quivered in his arms, the entire surface of her skin flushed and damp against his chest.

Phoebe's loins were filled with a delicious languor and yet deep inside her the faint stirrings of desire renewed themselves. She brushed his mouth with hers. Her lips touched the tip of his chin then trailed down the strong brown column of his throat. Her tongue darted against the pulse at its base and then painted downward. She found his nipples and her lips closed over them, her tongue flicking, her teeth lightly grazing.

The scent of him filled her with heady need. It was musk and leather and lavender. She wanted him . . . all of him. She could feel his hardness pressing against her bottom and she moved seductively against it as she played with his nipples.

Cato gave a little sigh as he yielded to the irrational power of desire. It was a tiny sound that filled Phoebe with an almost triumphant satisfaction. Following blind instinct, she squiggled her hand between their bodies, her fingers pulling at the fastening of his britches. Her hand slid within the loosened waistband to close over his erection.

His penis jumped against her palm. It was hot and hard and her finger brushed the jewel of moisture at its tip. Cato slipped a hand beneath her bottom and lifted her off him just enough to enable him to release his swollen flesh. It sprang forth, and Phoebe with a little moan of delight moved her thighs to take him between them.

Cato's head fell back against the chair with a soft murmur of satisfaction. He scooped her breasts into his palms, playing with her nipples as she squeezed him between her thighs, pressing her sex against him, bringing the ripples of delight in her belly to dancing life again.

Phoebe swiveled on his lap until she was facing him. Again she seemed to know instinctively what to do. She brought one leg over so that she was sitting astride him and then raised herself and lowered her body onto the hard, thrusting shaft of flesh. She took him deep within her moist and opened body, feeling him touch her womb as she pressed down on his thighs.

Cato grasped her hips and stretched his legs beneath her. The movement changed the sensation inside her and she gasped. He smiled and drew his legs up again. He moved his hard muscled thighs, bouncing her on his lap.

Phoebe gazed at him, her eyes locking with his in astounded wonder. She leaned forward, wrapping her arms around his shoulders, so that every part of her sensitized body was touching him. His tongue snaked over the mounds of her breasts, licked down through the deep cleft between them. Phoebe threw back her head as sensation ripped through her, seeming to tear her apart, hurling her through space into star-shot oblivion.

Cato cried out with the strength of his own climax; his penis throbbed deep within her velvety sheath as her inner muscles closed around him with a life all of their own.

Phoebe fell forward, her head on his shoulder, her sweat-slick skin pressed to his. He laid a hand on her curved back as if to soothe her, and for a moment her eyes closed and she seemed to sleep. But it was only a moment. Then she felt his hands beneath her bottom, lifting her slightly as he slid from her body.

She raised her head from his shoulder and looked down into the dark eyes. A smile still lingered there but there was a question behind the smile.

"I think . . . yes, I really think you have to explain," he said. "Just what is all this, Phoebe?"

Phoebe climbed from his lap. She stood looking down at him, the sweat cooling on her skin, her expression now uncertain. "I thought . . . Portia thought . . ."

"*Portia!*" Cato exclaimed. "I might have known. She has a hand in everything."

"Well, I had to ask someone!" Phoebe said, stung. "I knew it wasn't right, the way every night we did this . . ." She threw her hands in the air. "I don't know what it was that we were doing, but it wasn't making love. And I wanted to *make love*. I didn't know how to tell you that, so I had to show you."

Cato regarded her in frowning silence. He felt as if his entire world had turned upside down. The frigid girl he had believed he had taken to wife was no such thing. She was as lusty as any of the women of the night he had enjoyed, as uninhibited and, it seemed incredibly, as knowing. Yet he knew she'd been virgin on their wedding night. He didn't know what to make of it. He didn't even know whether he liked it. Which was pure contrary ingratitude, he recognized, but it was such a shock to find a gently bred young woman possessed of such an earthy sensuality.

He saw her shiver and said swiftly, "You're cold. Climb into bed now." He drew back the bedcurtains and then stared at the hump of the bolster in the middle. "Phoebe, what on earth . . ."

"Well, I was afraid you might look in the bed before you undressed and if I wasn't there . . ." She shrugged.

Cato shook his head, at a loss for words. He pulled out the bolster and turned down the covers. "In."

Phoebe clambered into bed and nestled against the pillows. The deep feather mattress cradled her languid body and the crisp sheets were wonderfully cool and fresh against her still-overheated skin.

She watched as Cato turned away and kicked off his unfastened britches. The moment of unease disappeared as her eyes drank in every glorious inch of his back view. The long sweep of his back from the broad shoulders, the sinuous ripple of his shoulder blades beneath the muscled flesh. His backside was glorious. So different from a female bottom, Phoebe thought with a little hug of delight. It was smooth and taut rather than rounded, and startlingly white against the darker line at his waist. Obviously he had spent time shirtless in the sun. His thighs were long and hard; even the backs of his knees and the muscled swell of his calves delighted her.

And then he turned to come to the bed, and she gazed at the wide expanse of his chest, the points of his nipples nestled in the light dusting of dark hair, the narrow waist and the slim hips. Her eyes followed the trail of black hair that began at his navel. His quiescent sex now looked small and almost vulnerable, she thought, like a dormouse asleep in its nest of crisp curling black hair. A little tremor went through her as she remembered the feel of its thrusting hardness deep within her.

"Why didn't you wish to make proper love with me?" The question spoke itself.

Cato paused, one hand resting on the bedpost. "I didn't expect you to enjoy it," he said after a minute.

"But . . . but why not?"

He ran a hand over the back of his neck. "In my experience, wives are not particularly . . ." He paused, searching for words. "Particularly lustful," he said finally. "In truth I hadn't expected you to be any different."

"Is it inappropriate for a wife to feel lust?"

Cato considered the question. "You're an exception to every rule in the book, Phoebe."

Phoebe wasn't quite sure how to take that. "What about love?" she asked, tentatively now.

Cato turned away and snuffed the candles on the mantel. "Love has nothing to do with such alliances."

The mattress shifted beneath his weight as he climbed in beside her. After a minute he stretched out an arm and drew Phoebe against him, twining his fingers in her hair as he turned her face into his shoulder.

Cato Granville was going to learn to love her, Phoebe thought as sleep claimed her.

9

Brian Morse rode up to the front door of Cato's manor under a lowering sky. The snow lay thick on the ground except where a party of soldiers had cleared a narrow path along the driveway.

He looked up at the house, with its mullioned windows and gabled snow-covered roof. It was a substantial pile of stone, and he wondered how much Cato had paid for it. Not that it would have been more than a bagatelle for the marquis of Granville, whose wealth was almost legendary.

A wealth that was within Brian Morse's grasp.

He dismounted, tethered his horse to the hitching post beside the door, and banged the great brass knocker. A well-dressed retainer opened the door. He was not one of the servants from Castle Granville whom Brian would have recognized, and he regarded the stranger with an air of polite if aloof curiosity.

"Is Lord Granville within?" inquired Brian, stamping the snow off his boots against the edge of the step.

"May I say who's asking for him, sir?"

"Who's at the door, Bisset?" Cato's voice came from behind the butler. He stepped out of the dimness of the hall. His dark eyes narrowed over a flash of disquiet when he saw his visitor. But he spoke pleasantly.

"Well, Brian, this is a surprise. Come in out of the cold."

Bisset stepped aside and Brian entered Cato's house, drawing off his gloves. "You must indeed be surprised," he said in somewhat ruefully apologetic tones. "I trust it won't be an unpleasant surprise though, when I've explained myself."

He extended his hand to his stepfather, who took it in a firm, cool grasp.

"Bisset, have Mr. Morse's horse taken to the stables. Have you breakfasted, Brian?"

"Not as yet, sir. I left Oxford before dawn. I had no wish to meet any patrols and thought to travel under cover of dark and snow."

Cato raised an eyebrow. Only something of vital importance would have sent a man out alone, even armed, on horseback and in such foul weather. "Come." He gestured towards his study at the rear of the hall. "Bring bread and meat and ale, Bisset."

Olivia stood at the bend of the stair looking down into the hall, hardly breathing.

"Who's that?" Phoebe murmured behind her. She didn't know why she was whispering, but there was something about Olivia's posture that seemed to encourage secrecy.

"The pig," Olivia stated.

"Who?"

"The swine . . . the g-guttercrawler." Olivia's mouth was compressed, her dark eyes flaring. "Brian Morse," she expanded. "My father's stepson. He's a loathsome, belly-c-crawling *snake*."

Phoebe had heard the famous story of how Portia and Olivia had squashed this particular snake back in Castle Granville two years earlier. Cato's stepson had had the malicious habit of making fun of Olivia's stammer.

"I wonder what he wants. Isn't he supposed to be for the king? I'm sure Cato said so."

Olivia shrugged. "I don't c-care what he wants, just so long as he doesn't stay." She turned and ran back upstairs.

Phoebe remained where she was for a minute, then she went down to the hall. She paused outside Cato's office, trying to think of an excuse to go in. She was most curious to make the acquaintance of her husband's stepson. Cato had told her that he had adopted Brian Morse as a small child and the man was at present his heir. He had sounded as if he found the prospect distasteful. It would be very interesting to discover why.

Resolutely she raised her hand and knocked.

"Come in." Cato's tawny voice as always brought the fine hairs on her nape to life. She hadn't seen him this morning. Would he look any different . . . be any different . . . after the glories of last night?

She opened the door and put her head around. "Forgive me for intruding, but Bisset said we have a guest. I wondered if I should have a bedchamber prepared for him." She addressed Cato but she was looking only at the visitor with unabashed curiosity.

"Why don't you bring the rest of yourself in here," Cato suggested in his cool way. "And allow me to present Mr. Brian Morse, my stepson."

Phoebe didn't need a second invitation. She stepped into the room and offered a curtsy as Cato presented her with punctilious formality. She didn't think she'd ever seen anyone dressed in such extravagant style. Mr. Morse's coat and doublet were of crimson cloth edged with silver lace, and his lace collar was an elaborate fall of pleated ruffles. His hat, which he'd cast onto a chair, sported a flamboyant plume of crimson dyed ostrich feathers.

"Lady Granville." Brian bowed, his small brown eyes assessing her. She looked a little different from the last time he'd seen her, a dumpy unfashionably clad creature, hurrying through the village. In a fashionable gown of blue velvet, she was more voluptuous than plump, he amended. But there was still something awry about her appearance; he just couldn't put his finger on it.

Cato, however, saw the problem immediately. The three-tiered lace ruffles on her right sleeve were all rucked up inside the bottom of the sleeve instead of falling smoothly over her forearms. She must have dressed in haste, thrusting her arms into the gown anyhow. He took her right arm and patiently released the lace, smoothing it down. "It's all creased," he said. "You had better take off the gown and . . ."

The vivid image of Phoebe's naked body rose with stirring effect to his mind.

"Yes, my lord?" Phoebe prompted softly.

Cato blinked in an effort to dispel the image. "Tell your maid to use the flatiron on those ruffles," he finished firmly.

"Yes, my lord." Phoebe curtsied, her gaze turned up to him. "But maybe there won't be time before church."

Time to . . . His own gaze drifted to the seductive swell of her bosom and then back to her smiling countenance.

Dear God, her eyes were the most amazing color.

"Go," he said. "The bells will be ringing soon."

"Oh . . . yes . . . very well." The radiance of her smile remained undimmed, her gaze unfaltering. For a minute she didn't move. She was thinking that Cato, in his somber black velvet and pristine white shirt with its plain lace collar, was so much more elegant than Brian Morse for all his rich garments.

Cato went to the door and pointedly opened it for her.

"Uh . . . yes, right away," Phoebe said and hurried past him.

Cato closed the door firmly and with a certain sense of relief. He turned back to Brian.

"These documents you've brought are very interesting." He picked up a sheaf of waxed papers from his desk. "This list of munitions from the king of Orange, for instance. But . . ." He shuffled through the papers. "To be frank, I'm not sure how much new information is in here. We've known about the munitions for several weeks now."

"I thought you probably had," Brian said with a tentative little smile. "But I don't suppose you knew the exact figures that I supplied?"

"No," Cato agreed, his eyes on the documents.

"I'm sure you must understand that I didn't dare risk

too much. If you refused to trust me . . . have faith in my conversion, as it were . . ." Here Brian laughed a little self-consciously. "Then I couldn't risk giving up truly vital information. This is just an earnest of my intent."

Cato raised his eyes and examined his stepson thoughtfully. "Careful as ever, Brian?" he murmured. "Don't risk too much until you're sure it's safe."

Brian flushed darkly. "Do you blame me, my lord?"

Cato stroked his chin, still thoughtful. "It argues a less than wholehearted conversion," he observed. "However, I can see your point, if it's any comfort. But by the same token, I assume you'll not accompany us to church? It's probably not in your best interests to advertise your presence here just yet."

Brian had no choice but to agree. His stepfather had always seen through him . . . had always had the ability to cut the ground from beneath his feet.

Cato nodded briefly. "This afternoon we'll ride to headquarters, where you may present your case to the high command. This is not a decision I can make alone, and I'm sure they'll have a great many questions for you." He gestured that Brian should precede him from the study and then locked the door, dropping the key into his coat pocket.

"I'll introduce you to Mistress Bisset. She'll take care of you until I return."

The bells from the village church had already begun to peal when Cato, Olivia, and Phoebe left the house.

From a window in the front bedchamber allotted to him, Brian watched them go. Cato walked a little behind the girls, his cloak blowing back in the wind revealing the somber richness of his doublet and britches. His high-crowned black felt hat had no adornment, and the fur-edged collar of his cloak was turned up at the back, covering his ears. Brian knew that the serviceable elegance, the casual richness of his stepfather's dress were merely an extension of the man himself. The marquis of Granville was assured, commanding, powerful, and he looked every inch of it. Every inch as formidable as Brian remembered. He would not be an easy victim.

As Brian watched, Phoebe slipped on an icy patch. Cato seemed to have predicted it and moved almost before it had happened, an arm around her waist, steadying her. She looked up at him with a rueful smile, catching her bottom lip with her teeth. Cato shook his head, straightened her bonnet that seemed to have gone askew beneath the capacious hood of her cloak, and tucked her hand into his arm.

Interesting, Brian thought, remembering the almost automatic way Cato had adjusted his wife's rucked sleeve earlier. It seemed to bode an easy familiarity that was unlike Cato.

Brian frowned, pulling at his chin. It had been easy enough to dispose of Diana. She'd been all too willing to accept the gifts he sent her in secret, and he guessed she had enjoyed the thought of her clandestine correspondence with an admirer.

Poison was such a versatile weapon, Brian reflected. It could be administered at a distance and in any number of ways. The gloves had been the most elegant trick, he thought. They had been of the softest doeskin, lace-edged and studded with tiny seed pearls. Very beautiful, and quite deadly. Every time she wore them, the poison would seep into her skin.

There had been silk stockings too—the kind of intimate loverly gift that would excite a woman as susceptible to flattery and courtly gestures as Diana. And the little boxes of comfits. Little jeweled boxes of lethal sweetmeats.

He had been in no hurry and it had taken about eight months before she died. The poison had mimicked a wasting disease and the bloody flux, symptoms too common to arouse the suspicion of foul play, particularly when there was no obvious reason for it.

Brian smiled to himself. The refinements of Diana's death had pleased him almost as much as the fact itself. And then, of course, Cato had to marry her sister and undo all his good work.

Well, he might have to be a bit cruder in his methods this time, but that should pose no problems . . . now that he was firmly established under Cato's roof.

All but the sick were straggling down the village street, wrapped against the cold, shuffling booted feet through the drifts. No God-fearing soul would neglect Sunday service, even for the snow, and the lord of the manor, if he was in residence, would never neglect the observance for fear of setting a bad example.

The congregation in Woodstock, as in so many other villages across the land, was mostly women, old men, and small children. The able-bodied men for the most part had been pressed into the army regardless of their views on the civil strife. The women bobbed little curtsies, the old men touched forelocks as the manor party walked up the path to the church door. Phoebe greeted them by name and would have stopped to chat if Cato hadn't been holding her arm so securely, propelling her inexorably to the church door, where he moved his gloved hand to her shoulder, easing her in front of him.

Cato was thinking about Brian Morse. What was the real reason for this visit? A change of allegiance seemed unlikely. He didn't want the man under his roof, but without good cause he couldn't refuse to shelter his adopted son and heir. Well, he would play a waiting game. Brian would reveal his hand soon enough.

The vicar's sonorous boom broke abruptly into Cato's reverie.

"The arm of the devil has a long reach. His servants are to be found everywhere. And, my people, they are to be found among us now. Here in the very bosom of our village lurks evil, a follower of the devil. Her vile hand has fallen upon the innocent and the weak and we must cast her out."

Here the vicar paused and raised his eyes to heaven, his arms flailing as if in ecstasies of prayer. "You have taken your children to this woman, in times of trouble; in times of weakness you have sought her help. And she has preyed upon your sorrows with the devil's art."

Phoebe felt the first icy shaft of premonition. It was something she had always feared, something that Meg risked with every act of healing. And it had to be Meg. She had been called a witch before, but before it had been almost an affectionate description, never accusation. There was no other member of this community who would fit the vicar's diatribe. She glanced around. There were nods and whispers and grim faces. She glanced up at Cato, sitting beside her in the Granville pew, and saw that the vicar now had his full attention.

Something must have happened since Phoebe's visit to Meg's cottage the previous morning. Ordinarily she would have heard of anything untoward, but the blizzard had kept her and the household, her usual source of rumor and gossip, within doors.

Meg should be in church, Phoebe thought. Meg knew full well how the village was suspicious of and swift to censure anyone who didn't obey the unwritten rules, but she persisted in flying in the face of convention. And her absence from the altar of God gave credence to these wild accusations.

Cato grew increasingly angry as the vicar's invective continued. The fire-and-brimstone kind of sermon was becoming

ever more popular as the strong Puritan element in Cromwell's New Model Army took hold over the looser morality of
the royalist Cavaliers, encouraging a rabble-rousing fanati-
cism that did little good and had much potential for harm.

When the service was over, he said rather curtly to Phoebe,
"Stay here with Olivia. It's too cold to wait outside and I wish
to talk with the vicar."

Phoebe buried her gloved hands in the deep pockets
of her cloak and slumped down in the pew, huddling for
warmth. She needed to go and find Meg, but it would have
to wait until after dinner.

"It's as c-cold inside as outside," Olivia stated glumly.
"What a dreadful sermon." She was right about the cold.
The two small braziers in the nave did nothing to relieve the
icy dampness.

"He was talking about Meg," Phoebe stated.

"Oh, but he c-couldn't be!" Olivia exclaimed. "She's never
done any harm to anyone."

"It had to be her, there's no one else in the village it
could be. I'm going to see her this afternoon. Will you come
with me?"

"Yes, of c-course." Olivia often accompanied Phoebe on
her visits to the herbalist, although despite her fascination
she regarded Meg with a faint degree of alarm.

"Come," Cato called from the door. There was an edge to
his voice that brought them hurrying to join him. His expression was dark, his mouth thin, his jaw set.

"What did you say to the vicar?" Phoebe asked.

"Watch your step," Cato said shortly instead of answering
her question. "You don't want to slip again."

"Why did you wish to talk to him?" Phoebe persisted, lifting her feet with exaggerated care on the path.

"I don't like all that fire and brimstone. If the man gets a
sense of power out of stirring the crowd . . . For God's sake,
Phoebe!" He grabbed at her arm as she stepped knee-deep
into a snowdrift.

"Oh!" Chagrined, she dragged herself out of the snow. It had gone into her boots and soaked the hem of her cloak and gown. "I didn't see it."

"Why didn't you look where you were going?" he snapped.

"I don't think it's just," Phoebe stated, "to be cross with me simply because you're cross with the vicar." She looked down at her sodden feet with a grimace. "It's bad enough as it is."

"What a ragged robin you are! I'd better carry you home."

"No, thank you," Phoebe said. "And anyway I'm too heavy." She stalked ahead, trying to ignore the horrid cold squelching of the snow in her boots.

Cato forgot his annoyance with the vicar. In two paces he came up with Phoebe, swung her around, lowered his shoulder, and hoisted her up and over. "Not in the least heavy," he said cheerfully, patting her upturned bottom in reassurance. "Keep still, and we'll be back in the warm and the dry in no time."

"You can't carry me through the village like this!" Phoebe squawked.

"Oh, no one will think anything of it," he assured her, striding out. "Besides, everyone's gone home to fires and Sunday dinners."

Behind them, Olivia gazed at the sight of Phoebe disappearing around the corner over her husband's broad shoulder. She'd never seen her father do anything quite like that before. Of course, it would ensure Phoebe didn't fall into another snowdrift. Olivia hurried in her father's footsteps.

At the front door Cato eased Phoebe off his shoulder. Games were all very well in their place, but Lady Granville couldn't appear before the servants in her present position.

"Ugh!" Phoebe said, shaking out a foot. "I'm sure I'm frostbitten." She moved through the door that Bisset now held open and said mischievously over her shoulder, "My thanks for the ride, sir."

Cato shook his head at her retreating back, then, drawing

off his gloves, turned to the butler. "Bring a decanter of madeira to my study, Bisset. Ah, Brian . . . I trust you've been made comfortable." He greeted Brian, who was coming down the stairs. "You'll forgive me if I leave you to your own devices until dinner. I have to gather some papers and change my dress for the ride to headquarters this afternoon."

"Of course, my lord." Brian offered the rigid Olivia a half bow. "Olivia, my little sister. You do seem to have grown up since I saw you last." He regarded her with a faint smile.

"I do hope you won't find the c-climate in Woodstock as unhealthy as you found it in Yorkshire," Olivia said sweetly. "You had such an uncomfortable t-time. Was it fleas . . . or lice, Brian? I don't recall."

A mottled flush spread across Brian's thin, pointed countenance. Cato was already halfway across the hall and didn't hear Olivia's mockery.

"And as I recall, you also ate something that disagreed with you," Olivia continued. "I do t-trust you won't have a similar problem on this visit."

Brian's thin mouth flickered. The fine line of his eyebrows lifted in a supercilious question mark. "You talk in riddles, little sister. I'm sorry to see that you haven't managed to overcome that unfortunate stammer. It makes you sound like a simpleton. I wonder you have the courage to open your mouth at all. But at the very least, you should *try* to make sense. It might lessen the unfavorable impression."

Olivia felt the old surge of frustration and the nasty cold tremor in her belly that Brian had managed to engender as far back as she could remember.

With curled lip and mockery in his eye Brian watched her struggle. "Poor little girl," he murmured. "But so amusing."

Olivia's hand closed over the friendship ring in her pocket. Portia had exorcized this demon once and for all. Now Olivia met Brian's smile with her own and concentrated fiercely.

"Excuse me. I have to take off my cloak." There, she'd managed the stumbling block. It was the hardest sound of them all for her. With a little nod of satisfaction she turned to the stairs.

She was feeling so pleased with herself that she almost skipped down the passage towards Phoebe's bedchamber.

Phoebe was sitting on the chest at the foot of the bed, wriggling her white numbed toes at the fire in an attempt to get the feeling back, when Olivia came in. "I'm sure I'm frostbitten," she declared.

"They do look rather dead," Olivia said, peering at Phoebe's feet with some fascination. She hitched herself onto the edge of the bed, observing cheerfully, "It was funny to see my father c-carrying you like that."

"My feet *were* wet," Phoebe offered, a slight flush blooming on her cheeks.

"I've never seen him do anything like that before," Olivia said. "He doesn't tend to be spontaneous. Maybe all these surprises you k-keep giving him are having an effect."

"What kind of effect?" Phoebe hopped off the chest to fetch clean stockings from the linen press.

Olivia considered. "Well, he laughs more," she said finally. "He never used to laugh when Diana was around, but now he's often amused. I like it," she added. "I used to think he was sad a lot of the time. But he doesn't seem so now."

"Really?" Phoebe paused, her clean stockings in her hand. "Do you really think so?"

"Mmm." Olivia nodded. "Haven't you noticed how his eyes seem to gleam sometimes?"

"Yes, they do, don't they?" Phoebe smiled to herself.

"Well, I'd better take off my c-cloak before dinner." Olivia jumped up. "We'll go and see Meg this afternoon." She went to the door just as it opened to admit Cato, intent on changing into riding dress.

"Excuse me, sir," she said with a curtsy. "I was just talking to Phoebe while she changed her stockings."

Cato nodded a mite absently. He had rather a lot on his mind at present. He closed the door behind Olivia.

"How are your feet?"

"Warmer now." Phoebe eased her stockings over her toes, then slowly pulled them up, stretching her leg in front of her as she did so, flexing her foot.

Cato watched her. There was something undeniably sensuous about the whole maneuver. She fastened her garters just above the knee and then looked up as if aware of his scrutiny for the first time. Her teeth closed over her bottom lip, and a smile touched her eyes, a smile where diffidence blended with invitation.

"I've ordered dinner for noon," Cato said slowly. He began to unbutton his doublet. "I have to ride to headquarters this afternoon."

"Will you ride home today when you've completed your business, sir?" Phoebe remained perched on the bed, her skirt still hitched up above her knees.

They were very prettily rounded knees. Cato's fingers were now on the waistband of his velvet britches. "I had not thought to be absent this night," he said.

Had the previous night really happened? Had it just been a trick, an artful pretense? He had a sudden mad impulse to test the waters.

"Come here," he said, crooking a finger at her.

Phoebe slid off the bed, her rich velvet skirts sweeping once more to her ankles. She came slowly towards him, her eyes as brilliant as a sun-filled midsummer sky.

10

*C*ato stood very still, *making no attempt to touch her. He* wanted to see what she would do.

Phoebe looked a little puzzled at the lack of a lead. She hesitated, then as if of their own accord, her hands went to his waist, to the fastening of his britches. She pressed her hand against the hard bulge at the apex of his thighs, feeling it stir beneath the rich dark velvet. Her face was upturned to his and Cato watched her, his eyes glittering with an almost predatory light that flooded her with excitement, set her loins pulsing, her stomach tightening.

Slowly she lowered her eyes and unfastened his britches, button by button. She slipped her hands into the opened waist to hold the slim hips, before sliding behind to the taut muscular slopes of his buttocks. She was breathing fast, her hands operating as if without instruction from her brain. Slowly she peeled his britches and drawers away from his hips, slipping to her knees in almost the same movement.

The turgid shaft of flesh jutted from its bush of black curling hair. Phoebe placed her palms flat against his hips and her face against his belly. The earthy fragrance of his arousal filled her nostrils, sending her senses spinning. She licked the column of dark hair running down from his navel, enjoying the rasp on her tongue as taste mingled with scent. Her hand slipped between his thighs to grasp the tender globes. She felt their weight, the softness of the taut skin.

She ran her hand up the shaft of flesh, enclosing it in her palm, feeling the blood pulse strong against her hand. Her tongue darted, to lick the dew clustering at the dark swollen tip. The salty taste of him entranced her. Taking him fully within her mouth now, she drew her lips up the length of the stem as her hands continued to stroke and knead between his thighs.

Cato was lost. He had been pleasured thus by women for whom sex was both a toy and a commodity, but this young woman with her flawlessly knowing touch was unlike any other he had experienced. There was a paradoxical innocence to the instinctive deftness of her touch, to the clear delight she was taking in pleasuring him. When she looked up at him, her blue eyes were sparkling with her own excitement, her cheeks delicately flushed, her parted lips offering a near irresistible invitation.

He grew closer to the brink and then with a sudden movement caught her head, moving her mouth away from him. "You will share this with me," he rasped, his voice sounding oddly harsh with the effort of restraint. He bent and caught her up beneath his arms and toppled her backward onto the bed.

Phoebe writhed, her entire body suffused with need. His hands were rough on her thighs as he pushed up her skirts. He seized her ankles and lifted her legs onto his shoulders, kneeling between her thighs, his eyes fierce as he drove deep within her.

He leaned over her and pushed her gown off her shoulders, catching her full breasts in his hands. She moaned and bucked beneath him as he played with her nipples. The corded muscles in his neck stood out as he held himself on the brink for as long as he could. Then, when he could wait no longer, he ran his hands down the backs of her thighs, grasped her buttocks with hard fingers, pulling her closer against him. Phoebe's eyes flew open, pure wonderment in their depths. Then her back arced off the bed and her body convulsed around him.

Cato fell forward with a groan, gathering her against him

in a tangle of skirts and petticoats, his mouth buried against the softness of her throat. Phoebe quivered beneath him.

And into this dark and sweat-tangled world of their own came a knock on the door.

Cato pulled himself up. "What is it?"

"Me, m'lord." Giles Crampton's robust tones called through the oak. "You ordered me 'ere fer dinner at noon, sir. We're to set off after, you said."

Cato uttered a barnyard expletive and got off the bed. "I'll be down in five minutes, Giles."

"Right y'are, m'lord. I'll tell Bisset to put the meat back in the warmin' oven, shall I?"

Cato glanced at the cloak on the mantel. It was a quarter past noon. "Damn his impertinence!" Cato muttered, stripping off his disordered clothing. Giles always found a way to make his point.

"I don't think I can get up," Phoebe murmured, stretching languidly. "I seem to be dissolved."

Cato looked down at her as she lay in an abandoned sprawl on the bed, her skirts pushed up, exposing the sweet white plumpness of her thighs and the small curve of her belly. The dark bush at the base of her belly glistened with the juices of their loving. Clearly her responses the previous night had been no artful pretense.

"Where did it come from?" he muttered.

"Where did what come from?" Unconsciously Phoebe passed her hands in a long caress over her body.

"Your wantonness," he said, tapping his mouth reflectively with his fingertips. "I've never come across it before in a woman of your breeding."

There was a note in his voice that made Phoebe sit up, pushing down her skirts. "Is it wrong, then?"

Cato hesitated for a minute too long before he shook his head. "No . . . no, of course not." He gave a half laugh that didn't sound particularly mirthful and went to the armoire for his leather riding britches and woolen jerkin.

Phoebe dragged herself off the bed. Why had he hesitated?

Cato dressed swiftly, saying as he strode from the room, "Hurry, Phoebe, I don't relish any more of Giles's veiled impertinence."

Phoebe dipped the washcloth into the basin and wrung it out. He'd been as eager for that passionate lust as she had. So why did she feel this unease? Thoughtfully she tidied herself and hurried down to the dining parlor.

Everyone was already at table when she came in. Giles Crampton cast her a knowing sidelong glance which infuriatingly made her blush. She took her seat with a somewhat incoherent apology for having kept them waiting and hastily reached for her wine goblet.

"Have you decided to play Gloriana, Phoebe?" Olivia inquired, helping herself to roast mutton and onion sauce. She studiously ignored Brian Morse, who sat opposite her.

"I'm thinking about it." Relieved at this ordinary turn of conversation, Phoebe looked over at Cato, "Do you think, sir, that some of your soldiers would be willing to take part? I'm writing the scene where Elizabeth addresses the troops and says those things about having the heart of a man in the weak body of a woman, and it would make a better spectacle if there were some real troops for her to address."

Giles snorted. "Over my dead body, m'lady! They're soldiers, not play actors."

Phoebe was too used to Giles to take offense, but she could mount her own spirited defense. "I thought a midsummer pageant might cheer people up," she said. "Life's so gloomy and hard for everyone with the war, and it's been going on for so long. Raising morale is an honorable enough task for a soldier, I would have thought."

"You're writing a play, Lady Granville?" Brian sounded amused.

"A pageant," she corrected.

"Oh, I do trust you'll find a part for me," he said in the same tone.

"Surely you won't still b-be here at midsummer?" Olivia said in undisguised horror, looking at him for the first time since the meal began. "That's *months* away!"

Phoebe broke in as she saw Cato's expression. "I'm sure I can find a part for you, Mr. Morse, if you're still here. But what about the soldiers, my lord? Real ones would be much more effective than villagers dressed up, don't you think?"

"Undoubtedly," he agreed, quelling Olivia with a glare. "But I have to agree with Giles that the men have better things to do than play at amateur dramatics, however worthy the motive."

"So, you're an amateur playwright?" Brian pressed, before Phoebe could respond to Cato's careless dismissal of her enterprise. "It was always quite a popular activity at court before the war. But not too many ladies indulged in the pursuit, as I recall." He offered a humoring smile and sipped his wine.

"Phoebe is a very accomplished poet," Olivia declared. "I dare swear no c-court poet would be ashamed to acknowledge her writing."

"Indeed." Brian's eyebrows rose. "I hadn't realized you had frequented court circles."

"Phoebe has and she told me about the empty-headed courtiers," Olivia said.

Brian ignored this. "Maybe you would show me some of your work, Lady Granville. I have, after all, some experience of what's considered good poetry at court. And, of course, you must please the court if you are to succeed."

"I write to please myself, sir," Phoebe said with unconscious hauteur. "I have no particular desire to shine at court, if indeed the court is ever reinstated. Indeed, as Olivia said, my few visits there at the beginning of the war gave me a great dislike for its posturing and pretensions."

Brian recognized a snub when he heard one. Strangely, instead of infuriating him, it piqued his interest. Little sister had nothing at all in common with big sister, it seemed. He regarded her over the lip of his glass. Her hair was tumbling from its pins; the upstanding collar of the blue gown was rather limp. In fact, it almost looked as if she'd slept in it. It hadn't looked quite so bad earlier that morning before the trip to church. He wondered what on earth she could have been doing in it.

"Perhaps you didn't meet James Shirley," he suggested. "A man of little or no pretension."

"Oh, yes, I most particularly admire Mr. Shirley's dramas," Phoebe interrupted, forgetting her moment of irritation. "He has no pretension at all."

"You'll need music for your pageant, Phoebe," Olivia said, refusing to be shut out of the conversation by Brian. "Have you thought about it?"

"Not really. I wish I could find a composer like Henry Lawes." Phoebe passed Olivia a dish of buttered salsify.

"Ah, the incomparable Mr. Lawes," Brian murmured. "I saw him at a performance of *Comus* once with John Milton."

"Oh . . . you've met John Milton?" Phoebe's fork hung neglected halfway to her mouth.

"The gentleman has a great conceit of himself," Cato observed.

"Well, he's a very fine poet," Phoebe's fork continued its journey. "That must be some excuse."

"But I hardly think you're aspiring to such exalted literary circles," Cato commented with a slight smile.

"I might be," Phoebe muttered.

Cato raised his eyebrows incredulously. "I confess my interest in this pageant grows apace. Perhaps I could persuade Henry Lawes to cast a glance over it with an eye to composing the music."

"Do you know him, sir?" Phoebe regarded him across the table with a distinctly martial gleam in her eye. She heard the sardonic note.

"Actually, quite well," Cato said. "Before the war, I met

him many times at court. I also have some acquaintance with Mr. Milton these days. He is now staunchly for Parliament."

"Well, you may rest assured, my lord, that I have no in-flated sense of my own poetic abilities," Phoebe stated, taking up her glass and drinking deeply.

Cato contented himself with a nod. He tossed his napkin to the table and pushed back his chair. Giles with clear relief followed suit. Talk of poets and composers was way outside his sphere of interest.

"We should be on our way, Brian. It's an hour's ride," Cato said.

"Yes, of course." Brian bowed his head in agreement. Things were moving swiftly but he was under no illusion that Cato trusted his change of heart. He would be interrogated this afternoon, but he had every confidence that he would convince his interrogators.

It was close to two o'clock that afternoon when Phoebe and Olivia left the house. The sky was heavy, a black-edged gray that looked as if it held more snow. Phoebe, mindful of the morning's accident, had changed into one of her old woolen gowns and armed herself with a stout stick with which to test out snowdrifts. They took the road into the village. It was longer than across the fields, but the fields were impassable.

The snow was thick in the woods and Phoebe plowed ahead, plunging her stick into the snow before each step. Olivia followed, carefully stepping into Phoebe's footprints, until they emerged in the small clearing.

"Meg's at home." Phoebe pointed to the smoke curling from the cottage chimney.

"She hasn't been out at all." Olivia gestured to the virgin expanse of snow leading from the gate to the front door. Cat prints zigzagged among the bushes, but there was no other indication that anyone had been around. "Although of c-course a broomstick wouldn't leave tracks," she added mischievously.

It was not a successful joke. Phoebe glared at her and stalked off up the path.

Olivia stumbled after her. "Oh, c-come on, Phoebe. It was in jest."

"I didn't think it was funny." Phoebe raised her stick to bang on the door.

"I'm sorry," Olivia said. "Forgive me?"

Phoebe glanced at her and then smiled. "Of course. Come on, let's go in before we turn into icicles." She banged on the door with her stick.

It was a minute or two before they heard the bar being lifted and the door creaked open. Meg, wrapped in a thick blanket, her head swathed in flannel, tried to smile and grimaced instead. She stood back, gesturing that they should come in.

"What is it? Are you ill?" Phoebe asked in concern.

"Toothache," Meg mumbled. "You have to help me draw it." She laid a hand to her flannel-wrapped cheek. "I've tried everything. Oil of cloves, witch hazel. It has to come out."

"My father pulled one of my teeth when I was little," Olivia remarked. "He tied string around the door latch and slammed the door. It hurt," she added rather doubtfully.

"It won't hurt as much as it does now," Meg declared. "Come now, Phoebe, put me out of my misery." She sat on a small stool beside the fire, and the one-eared cat jumped onto her lap.

Meg's teeth were a constant source of trouble for her. Phoebe had performed this service for her friend before and knew how to be both swift and gentle. She found the string, located the rotten tooth, and the task was over in a second. Meg rushed to the basin in the corner of the cottage, while Phoebe stared at the tooth dangling from the string. The cat jumped onto the windowsill and began to wash himself.

"What a lot of blood," Olivia observed with habitual curiosity. "You wouldn't think such a small thing could c-cause so much."

"You wouldn't think it could cause so much pain," Meg said thickly, raising her head from the basin and reaching up for a vial on the shelf above. She rinsed out her mouth with the contents and then sighed with relief. "Such agony . . . you can't believe."

"Do you want the tooth?" Phoebe handed it to her.

Meg took it and tied a knot in the string, slipping it over her head. "Maybe it'll act as a talisman against future toothache." She grimaced and touched her still-swollen face. "Thank heavens you came."

"There's something I came to tell you." Phoebe's face was suddenly very grave. "There's talk of a witch in the village. The vicar was raving this morning."

Meg nodded slowly. "That's no surprise. You remember when you were here last I was called to a sick child?"

"Yes." Phoebe perched on the edge of the table.

"Well, the child died soon after I physicked him."

Olivia ceased her examination of Meg's alabaster jars and glass vials of potions. "What of?"

Meg shrugged and drew her blanket closer around her. "I can't say. He was fine when I left, but according to his mother fell into convulsions an hour later. He was dead when I reached him."

"Sometimes there's nothing you can do," Phoebe said hesitantly.

"You and I know that," Meg said dourly. "The child's mother cursed me. The father spat at me. There was a crowd there, murmuring and whispering."

Phoebe crossed her arms over her breast with an involuntary shudder. There was a jolt of fear deep in her belly. "What were they saying?"

"That I had laid a curse on the child."

"So it *was* you the vicar was bellowing about," Olivia said, coming over to Phoebe. She laid a hand on her shoulder.

"Like as not," Meg said. "Superstition is an unpredictable evil." She reached up to the drying rack for a handful of thyme and another of verbena. "Set the kettle on the trivet, Olivia. I need some tea for the swelling."

"It seems to have come out of nowhere," Phoebe said. "It was but last week that you cured the Bailey girl's fever. . . . And look at the Harvey children. Last month they could barely walk with the rickets, and now they're running all over the village."

"That was then. This is now."

"Maybe on the way home I'll pay a visit to the Bear in the village, hear what people are saying. If they are talking such foolishness, I'll have a few things to say of my own." Phoebe's eyes snapped.

Meg shook her head. "Have a care, Phoebe. Tar sticks." She dropped herbs into an earthenware teapot as the kettle began to steam.

"Tar doesn't stick to Lady Granville," Phoebe said stoutly.

"This tar is no respecter of rank," Meg replied. "You remember Lady Constance . . . she was not spared the witch finder."

Phoebe frowned. "But she was accused by her husband's mistress. And when that was known, she was released."

Meg inclined her head in faint acknowledgment, but Phoebe could tell that she was unconvinced. "She was still not spared the witch finder," Meg repeated. "In open court."

"That would be terrible," Olivia said, turning pale. To be exposed naked in open court for the minute examination of the witch finder with his long pins was a horror not to be contemplated.

"An understatement," Meg said dryly. "But we must hope it won't come to that." She poured water on the herbs in the teapot, and the fragrant steam filled the small space.

"Well, I shall see what I can discover." Phoebe bent to kiss Meg. "Are you sure there's nothing else you need this afternoon?"

"No, my dear." Meg patted her cheek. "Sleep is my greatest need and that I can get alone."

"Well, send word to the house if you're uneasy. Unless . . ." Phoebe paused. "Unless you'd consider coming back with us now. No one will harass you under Lord Granville's roof. And when it blows over, you can return."

Meg shook her head decisively. "No, indeed not. I thank you, but I'm not about to leave my home because of some ignorant mischief makers."

Phoebe had expected nothing else and didn't press the matter.

"I wonder what my father would say if we brought Meg home with us," Olivia said thoughtfully as they made their way back down the path.

"What could he possibly say?" Phoebe asked in genuine puzzlement.

Olivia cast her a quick look. "He might not see things the way you do."

Phoebe frowned. She had noticed that Cato did not see the issues of the village and his tenants the way she did.

"My father is a very just magistrate and very generous to his tenants," Olivia said. "But he doesn't like to g-get personally involved. He's the lord of the manor; it's not his business."

"Well, it's my business," Phoebe said after a minute's thought. "I do like to get personally involved."

"Perhaps you c-can change his view," Olivia offered but without much conviction.

"Perhaps," Phoebe said. They had reached the lane leading back to the manor. "You go on home. I'm going to make a detour in the village, ask some questions about Meg, and I'll follow you."

"Should you go alone?" Olivia sounded doubtful.

"They might not talk so freely if you're there," Phoebe said. "And no one's going to molest me. These are my friends."

"Yes, you see, that's the difference between you and my father," Olivia pointed out. "He would never c-consider that his tenants were his friends."

Phoebe contemplated this insight as she hurried through the village. She had no doubt that Olivia was right, but how to reconcile that attitude of Cato's with her own? Therein lay the puzzle. She was firmly convinced her own view was the only correct one, so if someone had to change, it would have to be Cato.

Still frowning, she turned into the Bear Inn, where all gossip put down its roots.

"Afternoon, Lady Phoebe." The landlord greeted her as she entered the dark hallway. "What can I do for you?"

Phoebe had decided on the direct approach to her errand. "I was wondering if you'd seen anything of Meg, Ben," she said.

The man's face darkened and he turned and spat into a corner. "I'd not be wantin' to," he muttered. "Saving your presence, Lady Phoebe, that one's got the evil eye."

Phoebe clenched her gloved hands. "You know that's nonsense, Ben. Don't you remember how she cured your mother's rheumatism? Singing her praises from the rooftops, you were then."

The landlord looked a little self-conscious and he avoided her eye. "Aye, but bad things're 'appenin'. First there was the child, and now there's been a murrain out Shipley way."

"What's that to do with Meg?" Phoebe demanded.

Ben shrugged. "There's those that saw 'er in the dark o' the moon, walkin' the field. The cows fell sick days after."

"Oh, you know better than to spout such fairy stories!"

"Aye, well, 'appen the witch finder'll discover the truth," Ben said.

Phoebe felt the blood drain from her face. "He's been sent for?"

Ben shrugged. "Don't know about that. But they say he's over Banbury way."

Phoebe had heard enough. Banbury was but fifteen miles away. "We'll see what Lord Granville has to say about this foolishness."

"Beggin' yer pardon, Lady Phoebe, but the vicar don't answer to his lordship in matters of the church." Ben's tone was one of surly defiance, one that Phoebe had never heard before. It made her more uneasy than ever.

"We'll see about that," she said and turned on her heel, making her way to Granny Spruel's cottage, where she hoped to get a second opinion.

When she left, it was already growing dark even though it was only just four o'clock, and the snow-charged sky was so low it was as if it were pressing upon the earth. She hurried down the lane towards the manor, jumping at every crack of a twig or rustle of a small animal in the hedgerows. The world seemed suddenly a very inhospitable place.

It was almost full dark when she turned into the gates of home. Her visit to Granny Spruel had taken much longer than she'd realized and had brought no reassurance. She broke into a run as she made her way beneath the bare overarching branches of the oak trees that lined the long, curving drive.

It was a sinister corridor at this dark and lonely hour, and the lights of the house were still hidden from her by the bend at the head of the carriageway.

She was a dark figure huddled in her cloak, blending so perfectly into the shadows that Cato, Brian, and Giles nearly ran her down as they cantered up the drive. They came up so fast that Phoebe wasn't aware of them until the drumming of hooves made her jump sideways with a cry of alarm.

"Holy Mother!" Cato reined in his horse. "Who the hell is that?" He stared down from atop the bay charger. "Who has business at Granville House at such an hour, on such a filthy night?"

"It's me," Phoebe said, stepping out of the shadows. "You nearly ran me over."

"What in the devil's name are you doing out here?" Cato demanded. "You're nearly invisible in the shadows."

"I didn't realize it was so late," Phoebe explained. "The night seemed to come on much faster than usual."

"Aye, it's black as pitch and barely five of the clock," Giles agreed. He looked up into the darkness and sniffed the wind. "More snow, I reckon."

Cato leaned down, extending his hand to Phoebe. "Come," he commanded.

Phoebe didn't argue. Her husband seemed less than pleased to see her at the moment. She took the hand and struggled to get her foot on his boot in the stirrup. He hauled her up onto the saddle in front of him and encircled her lightly with his arm as he nudged the horse into motion.

Phoebe leaned back against him, unable to resist the opportunity to feel the beat of his heart beneath his cloak and doublet, to inhale his mingled scents of horseflesh and leather, the almost lemony tang of his skin and hair. She turned her head and gave him a sunny smile, reaching up a hand to caress his cheek in a gesture of delightfully unconscious intimacy.

There was something irresistibly sensual about that smile, about the touch. Sensual and *still* surprising. Cato cast a sideways glance at Brian Morse, riding beside him. There was only one surprise he wanted from his wife, he thought a little grimly. One that would take his stepson out of the picture.

Welcoming light poured from the front door as they drew rein. The ever attentive Bisset stood in the doorway to greet them. Cato dismounted, handing his reins to Giles, before lifting Phoebe from the saddle.

"To go out without an escort at this time of day, Phoebe, is foolish beyond permission," he chided as he urged her into the house with a hand on the small of her back.

"It was the middle of the afternoon when we left," she protested. "But in truth, I didn't intend to be out so late. There's something I need to discuss with you."

Cato frowned at her for a minute. Then he said shortly, "Come, then," and turned aside towards his study.

He closed the door behind them and said, "Well?" He took up a decanter and filled a goblet with wine.

"I went to see a friend," Phoebe told him, adding somewhat irrelevantly, "I had to help her draw a tooth."

"Draw a tooth?" Cato paused, the goblet halfway to his lips. "Talk sense, Phoebe."

"She had a toothache. I had to draw the tooth for her," Phoebe said, articulating each word with exaggerated care. "Is it so hard to understand, my lord?"

"Yes," Cato said forcefully. "I find it impossible to understand why Lady Granville should be going about the countryside performing the tasks of a barber! Who is this friend?"

"I believe," Phoebe began slowly, "that Meg, my friend, was the subject of the vicar's sermon. She wasn't in church this morning, so I went to see if she was all right, and to warn her. There's much talk in the village and now Ben at the Bear said there's talk of sending for the witch finder from Banbury." She looked up into her dumbfounded husband's face and said simply, "We have to help Meg, sir."

"You are associating with a *witch*?" Cato demanded when he could find his tongue.

Phoebe shook her head. "No . . . no, Meg isn't a witch. Of course she isn't. It's just that the rumors have started and they're taking hold. We have to help her. I tried to persuade her to take shelter here, but she's too stubborn and proud."

"You offered my roof to a woman accused of witchcraft?" Cato could barely believe his ears. "Phoebe, this is beyond anything."

Olivia had been right. "Why would you not offer her

shelter?" Phoebe demanded. "You're a Justice of the Peace. You're the law here."

"It is precisely for that reason that I could not possibly offer an accused individual my personal support. I have to be an impartial judge. Surely you understand that?"

"Meg is unjustly accused, sir."

"If the woman is accused, then she should face her accusers," Cato said shortly. "If the accusations are unjust, they will be proved to be so."

"How can you *say* that?" Phoebe cried. "You know justice doesn't always prevail. You said yourself this morning how the vicar was trying to rouse a rabble."

He had, of course. The reminder didn't please him but it caused him to moderate his tone.

"I commend your generosity, Phoebe, but it won't do. I will ensure that there is no miscarriage of justice. From here on, you must let matters take their course."

"You are asking me to abandon my friend?" Phoebe shook her head. "Indeed, I cannot, sir."

Cato's lips thinned. "Even you . . . even *you* must see how inappropriate it is for my wife to consort with someone of such unsavory reputation."

Phoebe's jaw dropped. "Unsavory!" she said. "Meg is a healer. She has done so much good in the countryside. It is not her fault that the child died, or the cows at Shipley have the murrain."

"Child . . . cows?" Cato was for a minute mystified. He drank down the contents of his goblet and enlightenment came. "The evil eye! So that's what this is all about."

"Yes, but Meg wasn't walking in the field in the dark of the moon. And she certainly didn't put a curse on the child."

"Such nonsense!" Cato exclaimed. "I have no time for such ignorant stupidity. You will keep away from all such talk, if you please."

"You will excuse me, sir," Phoebe said through compressed

lips. "I must get ready for supper." She offered him a stiff curtsy and marched from the room.

She closed the door at her back and stood fiercely frowning in the passage. Her thick fair eyebrows almost met across the bridge of her snub nose as she chewed her bottom lip. Obviously nothing would be gained by further protest. Her husband, for all his many wonderful qualities, was clearly very stubborn even when he was wrong. She had no choice but to ignore him on such occasions.

"Stubborn, pompous man!" she said aloud.

"Yes, he is, isn't he?" A soft voice spoke from the shadow of the stairs. Brian Morse stepped into the golden glow of the candles sconced on either side of Cato's study door. "Trouble, Lady Granville?" He raised an eyebrow with an air of complicity.

"Oh, call me Phoebe," she said with a touch of impatience. "Everyone does and I usually forget to answer to anything more formal."

"Then, Phoebe . . ." Brian bowed. "Forgive the impertinence, but I know well what it is to run up against Lord Granville. However just and reasonable one's arguments, if he doesn't agree, nothing will move him."

Phoebe's chin lifted. "In general he's right in his views," she stated.

"In general, yes," Brian said with a slight smile. "But in the particular . . . ?" He left the question mark in the air.

"Not always," Phoebe admitted. She twisted a lock of hair around her finger, still frowning. Then she shrugged. "I have to get ready for supper. Excuse me."

Brian followed her into the brighter light of the hall. She was wearing the gown he'd first seen on her. Too small, straining across her deep bosom, the sleeves too short, the hem dipping, and an ugly color to boot. And yet when he looked at her closely, to his surprise he could see the potential. It gave him an idea.

"Have you thought of coiling your hair over your ears?" he asked suddenly. "I believe such a style would frame your face very prettily."

Phoebe spun round to look at him in some astonishment. "I always wear it like this." She put her hands to the loose knot on top of her head. Of course, it's always coming down," she added.

"If you'll permit . . ." Brian put his hands on her head, deftly unpinning the knot. He divided it into two and then took two swatches and twisted them around her ears. "Yes, I'm right," he said nodding. "You should try it."

"Do you know much about fashion and such?" Phoebe asked with a surge of interest. It seemed likely, judging by his clothes.

"I used to advise your sister," he responded. "I have frequented the court for close on five years, and I believe I'm considered something of an arbiter. Many women ask my opinion on such matters." He offered a deprecating smile that concealed the flash of calculation in his hard eyes.

"I'm something of a lost cause," Phoebe said dubiously. "I try but it often doesn't work out right."

"Oh, but you have so much potential," he said warmly. "If you'd permit me to advise you on your wardrobe . . . that gown, for instance . . ."

"It's a very old one," Phoebe said, a mite defensively. "I didn't wish to wear one of my best gowns out in the snow."

"Quite so," he agreed with a smooth smile. "But must you wear something so *very* old? Could you not have the seamstress make up some gowns for everyday? More hard-wearing materials than silks and velvets, but with a more fashionable cut?"

Phoebe looked rueful. "I suppose I could. This one is really too small, isn't it?"

"It is." He smiled again. "I hope you don't consider me impertinent."

"No," Phoebe said after a second's hesitation. "I need all the help I can get."

"I will draw some sketches for you to give the seamstress, if you'll permit. Styles that will look well in wool and linen."

"Yes . . . yes, thank you." Phoebe shook down her loosened hair again, feeling somewhat stunned. She hurried away, leaving Brian looking after her.

11

"*A*h, *there you are, Phoebe. I've been looking all over for* you. I assumed you'd be in the parlor, but Olivia said you'd be in here for some reason."

Startled, Phoebe looked up from her perch on the linen shelf in the stillroom. She'd been so absorbed in her writing that the sound of a voice, even Cato's voice, was for a moment almost an unpleasant surprise.

"Sometimes I like to write in the stillroom, my lord," she explained, nibbling the tip of her quill pen. "It's very quiet and the scent of the herbs seems to aid the muse. At the moment the meter keeps escaping from me. It's not exactly classical to change meter in the middle, but iambic pentameter feels awkward . . ." She stopped. "But why should that interest you?"

"I certainly know little of poetry," Cato agreed. It was fragrant and very warm in the stillroom, and tendrils of hair clung damply to Phoebe's forehead. Cato was suddenly vividly aware of how desirable she was looking. She'd done something different with her hair, and her breasts were soft creamy mounds, bared almost to the nipples in that outrageously sensual blue gown. Pure seductive sophistication and her youthful innocence offered an irresistible paradox.

"It doesn't go with soldiering, I suppose," Phoebe said. Her gaze drifted back to the vellum. "I wonder if maybe hexameter or perhaps sapphic would work here," she mused, scratching out a line and scribbling rapidly.

It seemed she had little time for her husband while in the throes of composition. The light in her round blue eyes, the light of pure desire and promise that he was growing accustomed to seeing whenever she looked at him, was conspicuous by its absence. Cato missed it.

"I would think it must be a more than daunting subject," he suggested, leaning casually against the closed door. "A pageant of such scope."

"Oh, you don't know the half of it," Phoebe said with a sigh. She looked up. "I'm just beginning to think about costumes. Can you imagine what a headache they're going to be?"

She shook her head mournfully. "I don't know why I didn't come up with something simpler. Something with the Greeks and the Romans . . . togas and laurel wreaths would be so much easier to contrive than ruffs and farthingales, don't you think?"

"Without a doubt," he agreed.

"Maybe Caesar and Pompey . . . or Tiberius, perhaps . . . but then he was such an unpleasant man; and of course if you do Rome you'd have to find lions from somewhere because you couldn't ignore the Games, could you?"

"I suppose not." Cato regarded her with fascination as she pursued her train of thought, a little frown drawing her eyebrows together over her smidgeon of a nose.

"And then, of course, you'd have the problem with the minnows, wouldn't you?"

"Minnows?" He stared at her.

"Yes, Olivia and I were reading about it just the other day. Tiberius had these little boys trained to swim in the pool and pretend to be minnows. They had to nibble—" Phoebe stopped short in confusion as she saw his astounded expression. "Well, you know what I mean."

"Dear God!" Cato exclaimed. "You and Olivia have been reading about the depravities of the Roman empire!"

"Well, they're hard to miss if you're reading the classics," Phoebe offered. "But there's a lot more of it in Greek. They didn't seem to think it was depraved, just part of normal life.

But, I was wondering . . . what exactly did they do, sir? I can't quite imagine how they . . ." She paused and shrugged, searching his expression for enlightenment.

"You can't imagine *what*?" he demanded.

"What they did," Phoebe said simply and when he merely stared at her, expanded, "how?"

Suddenly it was too much. Cato threw back his head and laughed.

"Get off that linen shelf and come here," he commanded.

Phoebe did so somewhat hesitantly. He took her shoulders in a firm grasp. "I will answer your question. Don't interrupt, and when I'm finished I want no further questions. Just hear it, accept it, and then it would very much please me if you would forget it. Understand?"

Phoebe nodded, her eyes wide. They grew wider as she listened to the explanation delivered in measured tones.

"Oh," she said when he fell silent. "How uncomfortable it sounds."

Cato's lips twitched. "Each to his own," he said.

Phoebe looked up at him and now the familiar little shiver of pleasure ran down her spine. He was dressed in leather britches and doublet, with a plain linen shirt and stock, sword and dagger at his belt. It was a gusty day and his hair was ruffled by the wind, and she noticed how even his strong dark eyebrows were askew, as if the wind had caught them too. She had the urge to lick her finger and smooth them down. He'd been to a horse fair in Bicester and had risen well before dawn, so she hadn't seen him since the previous night. It was too long. All his absences were too long.

"Did you want me for something, my lord?" she asked as her thoughts took her along a pleasant road.

"Oh, yes, I did." Cato remembered what he'd come for. "I'd like you to accompany me to the stables."

"The stables!" Phoebe exclaimed. "Why would I wish to go there?"

"Because I have bought you a horse. A very quiet, docile

little mare." Cato was pleased with his purchase and it showed. Phoebe, however, was horrified.

"I don't wish for a horse."

"I am going to teach you to ride, Phoebe."

Phoebe shook her head and said firmly, "No thank you. Indeed, I'm sure it's very kind of you, but no thank you, I really don't wish to do any such thing."

Cato sighed. "I promise you that the mare is as well mannered and as gentle as a horse could be. You will enjoy riding her."

"No," Phoebe said. "No, I will not. I know I will not."

"Oh, don't be silly." Cato grew impatient. "It's absurd to be afeared. How can you get about without being able to ride?"

"I walk," Phoebe said simply. "I like to walk."

Cato surveyed her in some frustration. "You've never been taught properly . . . if at all," he said. "I assure you that when you know how, you'll find it as easy as writing your poetry."

Phoebe's eyes flashed. "Writing poetry is not easy, my lord," she stated. "I am no mere rhymester."

"Your pardon," Cato apologized with a careless gesture. "But you have nothing to fear, Phoebe. I'll not let you come to harm. And it's a beautiful day," he added.

"I have no clothes for riding," Phoebe pointed out with an air of finality, as if that would put an end to the matter.

"The dressmaker in Witney could perhaps be persuaded to make up a riding habit . . . a fashionable riding habit," he added deliberately. "I believe such a garment might suit you well."

"Oh!" Phoebe cried. "I take leave to tell you that that is the most devious, shameless trick, sir. Just because you know that I've discovered high fashion, it's most dishonorable to use it to try to manipulate me."

Cato couldn't help chuckling. "Come, a riding habit for a riding lesson. How's that for a bargain?"

"A truly fashionable riding habit?"

"The most fashionable that can be found in the whole Thames valley," he declared extravagantly.

"Well, I suppose I could try," she muttered but still doubtfully.

Cato turned to open the door. "Come. I will show you that you have nothing to fear."

Phoebe reluctantly gathered up her quill and paper. "If I don't like it, you will not insist I go on?"

"I will undertake to ensure that you do like it," he said with conviction, ushering her into the corridor. "Go and change that gown to something a little less suited to a palace drawing room . . . oh, and don't forget britches. You cannot ride astride without them. Borrow Olivia's if you have none of your own."

"Olivia's a different shape," Phoebe pointed out. "Her legs are longer and she has no hips."

Cato dismissed this irrelevance with a wave, and Phoebe went off in search of Olivia with something less than enthusiasm.

Cato was waiting for her in the hall, tapping his riding whip against his boots, when she trailed downstairs again twenty minutes later, her expression martyred. Olivia's britches were a disaster; she'd had to roll them up at the waist and leave all the buttons undone. The muddle wasn't visible beneath her old gown, but she felt like a particularly ill wrapped parcel nevertheless.

"What took you so long?" Cato turned to the front door impatiently.

Phoebe ignored the question. She tugged uncomfortably at her bunched-up waist. "Why must I do this? I've managed perfectly well until now." She hesitated on the bottom step. "I ride pillion if I must ride."

"Trust me." Cato turned back and took her hand. He led her firmly to the stable.

Phoebe was relieved to see that the mare was quite small and had a reassuringly broad back. The horse stood docilely at the mounting block, her bridle held by a groom. She turned her head in an incurious stare as Phoebe, still firmly led by her husband, approached across the straw-strewn cobbles.

"Touch her nose," Cato instructed.

Obediently Phoebe darted a finger, brushed the velvety tip of the mare's nose, and then retracted her hand with the air of one who has done a job well.

"Stroke her neck . . . here." In demonstration, Cato drew his hand down the hollow of the mare's neck. The animal raised her head and whickered.

Phoebe jumped back.

"Don't be silly, Phoebe!" Cato took her hand and placed it on the hollow. "Now, she's called Sorrel. Just speak to her. Call her by name so she gets to know your voice."

"I don't see any point talking to horses. It isn't as if they can talk back," Phoebe said, trying to pull her hand free. Cato's fingers closed more tightly over her wrist and kept her hand where it was. Phoebe eyed the little ripples running along the mare's withers. The smell of horseflesh filled her nostrils and Phoebe's nose wrinkled. She was very conscious of the heat of the mare's skin beneath her hand. She tried again to pull it free and this time Cato released his hold.

But the reprieve was only momentary.

"Mount up now," Cato instructed. "Use the block."

There seemed nothing for it. Phoebe lifted her leg onto the block and stepped onto the hem of her full skirt. There was a rending sound as the hem tore.

"Now look what's happened!" She glared at Cato. "It's ruined. I can't do this in an ordinary gown. Why don't I wait until I have a proper habit?"

The hopeful suggestion fell on stony ground. "You go around looking like a scarecrow most of the time as it is," he said without a flicker of sympathy. "Just get on with it, we don't have all day." He put both hands beneath her rear and shoved her unceremoniously upward onto the mounting block.

"Put your foot in the stirrup, hold the pommel, and pull yourself up and over . . . surely you've mounted a horse before."

"Why won't she run away with me?" Phoebe demanded. "Every other horse I've ever mounted has done so. Why's this one going to be any different?"

"Because I'm going to be holding her," Cato said, taking the bridle from the groom. "She's not going anywhere. Just hitch up your skirts; the britches will ensure decency."

"That's what you think," Phoebe muttered. She hitched up her skirts, thrust her foot into the stirrup, grabbed the pommel, and heaved herself up, swinging her leg over the saddle and thumping down. The horse shifted on the cobbles as it felt her weight. Phoebe gave a cry of alarm and clung to the pommel.

"Relax," Cato said, which struck Phoebe as a senseless command. Cato attached a long leading rein to the mare's bridle and led her across the stable yard towards the home paddock, Phoebe muttering to herself and hanging on for dear life.

In the paddock, Cato stepped away from the mare, paying out the leading rein. Phoebe gazed at him in alarm. "Where are you going?"

"I'm still holding her. Let go the pommel and take up the reins."

"This is such a bad idea," Phoebe complained, doing as she was told. "I can't tell you what a bad idea this is."

"On the contrary, it's an excellent idea."

Cato instructed the mare to walk on, and she started forward placidly around the paddock at the end of the long rein while Cato remained standing in the center of the field.

There seemed nothing for it but to grit her teeth and endure. Phoebe clung grimly to the reins, closed her eyes, and prayed for it soon to be over.

"You're sitting like a sack of potatoes," Cato chided. "Sit

up straight . . . put your shoulders back. There's no need to grip the reins so tightly. . . . For God's sake, Phoebe, *open your eyes!*"

Phoebe opened them. There didn't seem anything of the least interest to see. She closed them again and jounced in the saddle, her jaw aching with the effort to keep her teeth from clattering under the unstable motion of the horse.

"Oh, this is ridiculous." Cato signaled to the horse to stop. He came across the paddock, reeling in the leading rein. "I have never seen anything so pathetic, Phoebe! I am losing patience."

"Well, what do you expect me to do?" Phoebe exclaimed.

"I expect you to keep your eyes open, your hands off the pommel." Cato spoke with exaggerated patience. "I expect you to sit up straight, grip the saddle with your knees, and for God's sake, girl, *relax!*"

"Well, where do I put my hands if I don't hold the pommel?"

"You hold the reins loosely, fingers like this." He reached up and grabbed her hands, roughly adjusting her fingers. "The reins have to lie just so. D'you see?"

Sorrel, taking advantage of the break in the proceedings, bent her head to crop the grass, and Phoebe grabbed the pommel again with another cry of alarm as the mare's neck offered a glossy slide to the ground.

"Pull her head up," Cato said tautly.

"It won't come," Phoebe said as she gave a little tug on the reins. "She's not going to take any notice of me."

"No, of course she's not if you sit there like a blancmange. You have no more backbone than a vanilla custard." Cato put his hand against her spine. "Sit up straight!"

Grimly Phoebe straightened her spine against his hand.

"Now take a firm hold of the reins and pull her head up. She needs to know who's master."

"Oh, I think she knows that already," Phoebe muttered

again, giving a tentative tug on the reins. To her relief, Sorrel had decided she'd had enough of the icy grass and lifted her head apparently to order.

"That's better. Now we'll try a trot." Cato stepped back again, paying out the leading rein. "You have to rise up in the stirrups . . . no, for heaven's sake. What's the matter with you? Feel the rhythm of the horse. Can't you *feel* it?"

Phoebe could feel it in her teeth. She couldn't imagine a more uncomfortable, unnatural motion for a human to be involved in.

"This is just ridiculous," Cato declared, drawing Sorrel to a halt again. He came back towards her. "I have never seen anyone so completely at odds with a horse. I have been trying to explain—"

"No, you haven't. You've been shouting at me!" Phoebe cried, now pushed beyond bearing. "I'm doing the best I can, but I take leave to tell you, my lord, that you're a horrid teacher! You have no patience at all! No one could learn anything from you."

Cato was taken aback. He had always been the soul of patience, an impeccably understanding teacher. "That's nonsense," he said. "You're just not concentrating."

"Oh, I *am*! And it's not nonsense." Phoebe's eyes were filled with angry tears. "If I must do this, I want someone else to teach me." Impulsively she kicked her feet free of the stirrups and tumbled from the mare's back.

Cato caught her as she half fell, half scrambled from the saddle. "For God's sake, girl! What the devil d'you think you're doing? That's no way to dismount. If you slip, the horse might accidentally kick you or trample you."

"*Oh!*" It was too much. Phoebe planted her hands on his chest and pushed him away with all her strength. "You haven't heard a word I've said!" she exclaimed. "Why must you scold and command all the time? You're just a damned tyrant!" She glared at him, her eyes still sheened with furious tears.

Cato was reduced to astonished silence. He could still feel the pressure of her hands on his chest as she'd thrust him from her.

As he stood trying to make sense of her outburst, Phoebe turned and marched towards the paddock gate.

"Phoebe!" He dropped the leading rein and went after her. "Just where do you think you're going?" He caught her, spinning her round to face him. He cupped her chin on his palm and tilted her face up so she had to look at him. "You don't swear at me and shove me away, and then stomp off without a word of explanation."

Phoebe's temper was rarely aroused and always short-lived. "You made me so angry," she said, swiping the back of her gloved hand over her damp nose. "I was doing the best I could, and you know how scared I am. And all you could do was criticize and command. You didn't give me one word of encouragement. I don't know how you can expect anyone to learn anything like that."

"That's beside the point! How dare you swear at me?"

"You were doing everything but swearing at *me*," Phoebe pointed out, the fire still in her eyes.

Cato hesitated, looking down into her upturned countenance. He hated leaving things half done, but Phoebe's expression was thoroughly unyielding. Reluctantly he said, "Very well, we'll stop for today. You've obviously had enough for the first lesson. We'll try again tomorrow."

"Must we?" Phoebe groaned. "Can't you see it's pointless?"

"No, I can't," he said shortly, releasing her chin. "You will learn to ride, if it takes me a year."

"Then you owe me a riding habit," Phoebe declared. "A riding habit for a riding lesson is what you said. And if I've got to go on with this torture, then you have to keep your promise."

Cato would never renege on a debt. "Very well. We will ride into Witney and you may have your habit." He turned from her and went over to fetch the mare, once more placidly cropping the grass where it poked through the thin crust of snow, all that remained of the earlier storm.

Phoebe watched him take up the reins, and had a sudden awful thought. "I'm not ready to ride all that way on my own."

"Oh, believe me," Cato said with a short laugh, "I know that. You may ride pillion with me."

An hour later Cato lifted her down from his charger in the stable yard of the Hand and Shears. "You know your way to the dressmaker's, I assume?" He reached into his pocket and drew out a leather pouch.

"Yes, it's on High Street," Phoebe replied.

Cato handed her his purse. "There's close to thirty guineas in there. It should be sufficient."

"Thirty guineas!" Phoebe's jaw dropped as she felt the weight of the purse. It would buy half a dozen muskets and goodness knows how many buff leather jerkins. "May I spend all that?"

"Judiciously," he said with a slight smile. "I doubt you'll bankrupt me."

Phoebe considered. There was no reason why only she should benefit from this largesse. "The dressmaker has a gown that Olivia loved," she said. "Orange and black. It would look splendid on her."

"Olivia wishes to wear an orange and black gown?" Cato tried to imagine his solemn and intense daughter in such a frivolous garment.

"Yes, the color suits her beautifully. I was wondering . . . well, perhaps you could buy it for her. Ellen could make adjustments to the fit. It could be her birthday present." Phoebe was warming to her theme. "It's her birthday next month, you know."

"Uh . . . yes, I did know that," Cato responded. "I'm not in the habit of forgetting important dates."

"Oh, I wasn't saying you were," Phoebe assured him hastily. "I just thought to give you an idea in case you didn't have one."

"How kind," Cato murmured.

"May I purchase it for her?"

"You may. Just make sure that what you choose for yourself has some practical application. I'll bespeak a private parlor in the inn here. Try not to keep me waiting too long."

"These things can take time," Phoebe said, but she was speaking to his back as he went in search of ale.

An hour later Phoebe returned to the Hand and Shears. "Where's Lord Granville?" she demanded of the landlord.

"Allow me to escort you, my lady." The man bowed low with a deference that made Phoebe grin. For once she felt like the marchioness of Granville. She tossed her head in its fine plumed new hat and followed the landlord with regal dignity.

He threw open a door on the first landing. "Lady Granville, my lord."

Cato, deep in thought, was in a chair before the fire, his feet propped on the andirons, his hands curled around a tankard of ale. He turned his head, then rose slowly to his feet.

"Well, my lady, you've certainly not wasted your time."

Phoebe glowed. "Isn't it handsome?" She stepped into the chamber, patting the folds of the dark green broadcloth skirt. She gave a little tug to the fitted jacket as it sat on her hips. "The silver lace was very expensive, but the dressmaker said it was the height of fashion."

"Fashion does tend to be expensive," Cato agreed. This incarnation of his wife he could not fault. She cut an impeccably elegant figure.

"And the britches are a perfect fit. Wasn't that lucky?" Phoebe pivoted and was about to haul up the back panel of the skirt when she realized the landlord still stood in the door, rather wide-eyed. "Thank you, mine host," she said loftily and waited until he'd bowed himself out.

Then she scooped up the rear panel. "Do they look all right, my lord?"

Cato considered that his wife's voluptuous curves delineated by the britches constituted a sight to be kept for his eyes only. He said repressively. "It's more a question of how do they feel? No one's going to see them, I trust."

"I suppose not." Phoebe peered over her shoulder. "Do you think my backside's too big?"

Cato briefly closed his eyes. "There's a time and a place for all subjects, but this is neither the time nor the place for that one."

"Oh. I just wondered," she said, allowing the skirt to fall back. "I'm not the same shape as Diana."

"No," he agreed dryly. "Come and eat." He went to the table set with cold meat, bread, and cheese. "Shall I carve you some ham?"

"Thank you," Phoebe said. Not a subject to be pursued, clearly, but he might have given her some kind of disclaimer. "I purchased the gown for Olivia," she said. "But the dressmaker wished to add some more lace to the collar, so she'll send it to the manor when it's finished."

"Good," Cato said.

They were almost at the end of their meal when the landlord knocked at the door. "Beggin' yer pardon, m'lord, but there's soldiers in the taproom who've jest outrun a raidin' party of deserters from the king's army. The deserters were in search of plunder . . . well armed, they say." He adjusted his cravat with an air of importance. "Thought you might like to know, sir."

"You thought right," Cato said. "My thanks." He rose from the table. "Finish your meal, Phoebe. I need to talk to these men." He left her as he spoke, and Phoebe looked down at her plate of ham with a moue of distaste.

She seemed to have no appetite anymore. And it wasn't the prospect of skirmishers on the road. That held no terrible fears, at least not in Cato's company. But why did he always relegate her to some fuzzy nest where the hard realities of life weren't to intrude? Had he learned nothing about her?

In the taproom, Cato listened to the troopers account. Ordinarily a party of disaffected royalist soldiers, one of the many who'd taken to the country roads around the city in search of plunder, would have caused him little concern. His bay charger could outrun almost any horse in the country. But with a pillion passenger, one who was terrified of horses, things could be a little more difficult.

He gestured to the landlord. "Have my horse saddled and ask Lady Granville to meet me in the stable yard." He counted out coins and tossed them onto the counter. "Gentlemen, I'm in your debt."

"Watch for them on the Eynsham road, sir."

"Aye. And have a drink on me." Cato raised a hand in farewell and left the taproom amid a chorus of goodwill.

Phoebe, obeying the summons, emerged into the stable yard. Cato looked her over. "In that habit, you'll be able to ride astride the pillion pad now. We'll be able to make more speed."

"Because of the renegades?"

"Perhaps," he said, helping her onto the horse. He mounted in front of her.

Phoebe slipped her hands beneath his cloak and gripped his belt. She felt much more secure riding astride, and there was something very solidly comforting about Cato's back. She leaned forward and rested her forehead for an instant between his shoulder blades.

12

The shot crossed the bay's withers just as they were approaching the village of Eynsham. It was so close it almost ruffled the animal's mane, but the charger was accustomed to the fire of a battlefield and didn't so much as start in alarm.

Phoebe didn't immediately realize what had happened. She heard the crack and the whine but for a minute couldn't place the sound. Then there came a bloodcurdling shriek of triumph, and a party of men broke from the trees on the path just behind them.

"What is it? Is it the deserters?" Phoebe gasped, swiveling to look over her shoulder.

"I imagine so," Cato said, sounding utterly calm. "I've been expecting them these last two miles. Hold on tight now, because we're going to outrun them."

Phoebe circled his narrow waist and clung on as the bay broke into a gallop. Another musket shot whistled close to Phoebe's ear, and she couldn't hold back a little scream.

"There's nothing to be alarmed about," Cato said, as coolly as before, over the thundering of the bay's hooves on the lane.

"There isn't?" Phoebe found that hard to believe, but Cato's calm was infectious. She glanced over her shoulder again. "Some of them have gone off into the field at the side."

"I was afraid of that. They're going to try to cut us off at the corner." Cato abruptly swung the bay to the left.

Phoebe stared at the massive hedge looming up before them. There was no way through it. And then she understood. They were going over it.

"Oh God!" she whispered, closing her eyes tightly, burying her face against Cato's back, her hands gripping his belt at the front so that she felt as if her body was an extension of his.

The bay rose into the air. Phoebe's stomach dropped, her gut turned to water. She bit her lip and tasted blood. The hedge scraped the bay's belly as he soared over. His back hooves caught the top and then he thundered down into a stream the other side of the hedge. Icy water flew upward, soaking the hem of Phoebe's skirt as the animal stumbled to his knees.

Cato hauled him up and the bay struggled onto the bank. Cato swore when he realized the horse was limping. There were shouts from the far side of the hedge, but their pursuers were clearly not going to follow them over the jump.

Cato glanced around. There was a copse at the back of the field. Their attackers might well give up, assuming their quarry would be well away by now, but then again they might seek a way around the hedge. From the copse he'd be able to hold them off. The bay could walk, but nothing faster.

Cato dismounted, took the bridle, and led the animal towards the copse.

"Should I get down too?" Phoebe asked, automatically grabbing for the pommel as she found herself unsupported atop the great horse.

"No," he said. "I don't want you running off."

"But where d'you think I'd go?" Phoebe looked anxiously over her shoulder in search of pursuit.

"Knowing you . . . anywhere," he said.

"That's unjust," Phoebe accused.

"Is it?" Cato gave a short laugh. "Just sit still. If you wriggle, it'll aggravate his limp. When we get into the copse, I'll have a look and see what the damage is."

"But what if they follow us?"

"We'll cross that bridge when we get to it." Cato sounded to Phoebe as if it were a matter of sublime indifference whether a pack of murdering deserters pursued them or not.

The bay limped into the gloom and concealment of the copse. Cato led him into the center and stopped. He glanced around, assessing the situation, then he looked up into the spreading branches of an old conifer. "All right, now. Phoebe, I want you to climb up there."

Phoebe looked upward. "Why? Because you'll know where I am?"

"That too," Cato responded with a dry smile. "But also because you'll be safe out of the way if those bastards do follow us. And while you're up there, if you go high enough you'll be able to tell me if they come into the field." He reached up to lift her to the ground.

"I knew you'd find I could be useful if you thought about it," Phoebe remarked. She looked up at the tree. "I just wish I was wearing one of my old dresses, though." She brushed at her new riding habit. "My skirts are all wet from the stream, and now they're going to get dirty up the tree." She gave a philosophical shrug.

She took off her hat and cloak and laid them on the ground, then surveyed the tree again a mite dubiously. The bottom branch was a long way off the ground. "You'll have to boost me up. If I can reach that bottom branch, I think I can climb up the rest of the way."

"Get on my shoulders." Cato knelt and held up his hands so that she could hold them as she clambered onto his shoulders.

"Aren't I hurting you?"

"No." He stood up slowly, transferring his hands to her waist to balance her. When he was standing, Phoebe could reach the bottom branch easily. She scrambled into the tree and went on up, heedless of the fir tree's prickly greenery.

"What can you see?" Cato called softly.

"Nothing . . . oh, yes, I can. There's two of them in the field."

"Well, tell me if they come in this direction." Cato turned

to the bay and began to run his hands down the animal's forelegs. He could feel nothing there and turned to the rear limbs. The right fetlock was hot to the touch, and he swore under his breath. The bay wouldn't make it home to Woodstock with such a strain.

He straightened and looked around the darkening copse. They could hardly spend the night here. He could see but one option and it wasn't one that appealed. "What's happening, Phoebe?"

"There's about six of them in the field now, but they're just milling around. It's getting quite dark."

"Mmm." Cato took a brace of pistols from the straps buckled to his saddle. "Stay right where you are. I'm going to get rid of them."

"But there's six of them and only one of you," Phoebe pointed out.

"I assure you that I'm more than a match for that rabble," Cato told her with some considerable scorn. He walked away towards the outskirts of the copse.

For some reason Phoebe had little doubt that despite the odds her husband would make short work of the opposition. She watched from her perch, interested rather than frightened. Then came the sharp crack of a pistol. One of the men in the field dropped to his knees with a cry, a hand pressed to his shoulder. The others gazed around in confusion. There was a second shot, and another fell.

The remaining four took to their heels and ran as if all the devils in hell were in pursuit.

Phoebe applauded and scrambled back down the tree, reaching the ground just as Cato reappeared, the still-smoking pistols hanging casually from his hands.

"What cowards they were! But you're a wonderful shot," Phoebe said in awe.

Cato looked surprised rather than gratified by the compliment. "Did you doubt it?"

"Well, no, not really. But I've never seen you in battle before." She gathered up her hat and cloak.

"That was hardly a battle," Cato corrected. He stood for a minute in thought, whistling idly through his teeth. There really wasn't an alternative.

"I think the bay will be able to carry you. It's only about a mile."

"What is?"

"Cromwell's headquarters. We'll spend the night there. It's a damnable nuisance, but I don't see any option tonight. The bay will need to rest that fetlock for at least a week, so I'll pick up another horse in the camp to get us home tomorrow." He slid his pistols back into the saddle straps.

Phoebe absorbed this information. "Are there any women in the camp?"

"None that you'll be consorting with," Cato said shortly. "Mount up, now." He cupped his palm for her foot.

"Whores, are they?" Phoebe hauled herself inelegantly into the bay's saddle. With only one rider, there was no need to use the pillion pad.

"Camp followers," Cato agreed, taking hold of the bridle at the bit. "And," he continued with some force, "you will steer clear of them and speak only to those people to whom I present you. Indeed, it would please me if you didn't speak at all unless you're in my company. Do you think you could manage that?"

"But why?" Phoebe was bewildered at this abrupt and rather harsh turn to the conversation.

"Because, my dear girl, you have the most exasperating habit of getting involved in unsavory situations," he informed her. "I am beginning to understand that you don't seem to be able to help it, but I dread to think what you could get up to in an army camp. I'm not even sure what I'm going to do with you . . . where I'm going to put you."

Phoebe didn't bother to defend herself. It seemed he was

thinking of Meg, and she had no desire to reopen that subject. When someone was so patently wrong, you didn't argue with them. "But won't I stay with you?" she asked mildly.

"You'll have to, I suppose. But we live a communal existence in the house. It's not arranged for privacy." He led the bay out of the copse, in the opposite direction from the field and the wounded men.

Phoebe said no more. She found the idea of spending the night in an army camp intensely interesting, but if Cato realized that, he'd probably be even more disagreeable.

It was almost full dark when they turned through the gates of the Cotswold stone farmhouse that served as Cromwell's headquarters. The tented camp spread out across the surrounding farmland, and lamps and fires sparked through the trees. The strains of a fife and the martial beat of a drum drifted on the frosty air.

Phoebe looked around curiously from her high perch. She was no longer gritting her teeth in fear and was sitting quite relaxed as the bay limped slowly up the driveway. He seemed to know where he was, and raised his head and whickered hopefully.

Cato patted his neck. "Not long now, old boy."

The animal turned and nuzzled into Cato's shoulder before picking up his pace a little.

The farmhouse was a squat, square, two-story building of yellow Cotswold stone. A courtyard in front was formed by outbuildings on two sides and the house itself at the rear.

Men were moving purposefully around the courtyard, carrying sacks, loading and unloading carts, under the flickering lights of pitch torches. Cato hailed a soldier, who immediately dropped what he was doing and came hurrying over, offering a brisk salute.

"Yes, m'lord." His eyes darted once to Phoebe, then returned to the marquis.

"My horse is lame. Take him to the stables, have them

poultice the fetlock and give him a bran mash. The poultice is to be changed every hour throughout the night. Understand?"

The soldier listened to the crisp instructions and saluted again before taking the bay's bridle from Cato, who reached up to help Phoebe to the ground. The soldier glanced at her more openly now and with unfeigned admiration.

Phoebe responded with one of her customary friendly smiles. The soldier grinned back. Cato took her elbow and said briskly, "Come."

He hurried her across the court to the house. "It's inevitable that you'll draw attention, Phoebe, but there's no need to invite it," he said curtly.

"I didn't realize I was," she responded. "I didn't speak to him. I only smiled at him after he'd started looking at me." She paused to look around, fascinated by the scene.

"There are a lot of things you don't realize," Cato said. She had no idea of the effect her lushly sensual appearance was going to have in this world of an army camp.

He put a hand on the small of her back and propelled her in front of him to the front door of the house.

The man guarding it jumped to attention and flung open the door. Phoebe found herself in a beamed, stone-flagged hall that took up the entire ground floor of the house. It was filled with men, most of whom were sitting on benches along a long plank table in the center of the room. Great smoking platters of meat and leather flagons of wine were on the table.

"Cato!" someone bellowed from one end of the table. "Welcome, man! We weren't expecting you." A tall man pushed back the bench and stood up, coming over to them, his ale mug still in his hand.

"Aye, my horse went lame after an encounter with some deserters, and I was afraid we'd be benighted." Cato shook the man's hand. "We'll seek shelter here till morning, Oliver." He turned to Phoebe, who was unclasping her cloak. "This is General Cromwell, Phoebe. Oliver, may I present my wife."

Phoebe curtsied. So this was Oliver Cromwell. He was ill dressed, she thought, in a very plain suit of poor cut and material. His linen was grimy and there was a speck of blood on his collar band.

"Lady Granville, I bid you welcome," he said with a short bow. He had a grating voice and his countenance was rather red and seemed swollen to Phoebe. She wondered if it was drink. He certainly cut a poor figure beside Cato. She took off her hat and stood a mite awkwardly, unsure what to do next.

"We're ill equipped to entertain a lady," the general continued, "but come to the table. You'll be glad to sup, I'll be bound."

"Aye, we're famished." Cato took Phoebe's cloak and hat and tossed them both over a settle close to the fire, before urging her towards the table. "Gentlemen, may I present my wife." He moved her in front of him as they reached the table. The man gathered there all half rose from their benches, nodding to Phoebe, who curtsied shyly.

"Sit down, Lady Granville." An aesthetic-looking gentleman, rather older than the others, and dressed with impeccable style, brought a stool and set it at a corner of the table. "You'll have to forgive our rough manners, but we're an army camp and ill used to gentle company." He smiled as he gestured to the stool.

"This is General, Lord Fairfax," Cato said. "Sit down, Phoebe. And when you've supped, I'll find somewhere for you to sleep."

To Phoebe's alarm, he moved away from her as soon as he'd provided her with a platter of roast suckling pig, a mound of buttery boiled potatoes, a hunk of wheaten bread, and a pewter cup of wine. He took a place on one of the long benches some distance from her and was soon deep in conversation. No one took any notice of her after that.

Phoebe ate and listened to the buzz of voices, the occasional burst of laughter. She felt both neglected and seriously out of place. She understood now why Cato had been reluctant to bring her here, but she wished he had not abandoned her.

Cato cast her a quick glance now and again, relieved to see that for once she was behaving with perfect propriety, eating in silence and making no attempt to draw attention to herself. The men around the table were considerately ignoring her, knowing how uncomfortable she must be feeling. The main problem was where she was to sleep. He frowned, ladling vegetable soup into his bowl.

Phoebe had finished her platter of suckling pig, but she was still hungry and the rich aroma of the soup was tantalizing. The great tureen, however, seemed to have come to a stop beside Cato. She tried casting a speaking look in his direction, but he was deep in conversation about horse breeding, a subject that clearly interested him more than the welfare of his wife.

She hesitated for a second, then lifted her chin and got up from her stool. There were a few surprised glances as she came around the table to Cato and the tureen.

"What is it?" Cato asked, with a quick displeased frown.

"May I have some soup?" She met his frown with another little tilt of her chin.

It was hardly an unreasonable request, although it had done what he'd been trying to avoid and every eye was now upon her. "Sit down, then," Cato instructed with a crisp edge to his voice. He inched up on the bench and put an arm at her waist as she clambered over.

"There's a shortage of bowls and spoons, so you'll have to use mine." He refilled his bowl and passed it to her with the spoon. "Take what you want and I'll finish it. Then I'll find you somewhere to sleep."

He wanted her to hurry and Phoebe obliged. She didn't think she could endure many more minutes in this uncomfortable situation. Even Cato's proximity was for once no help, and the impatience he was radiating destroyed her pleasure in the soup.

She put the spoon down and said, "I've finished, thank you, my lord."

"Good. Let's go abovestairs." He swung off the bench with alacrity and helped her to her feet.

"Good night, Lady Granville. I trust you won't be too disturbed," Cromwell said. "We're not all the quietest of sleepers." Someone guffawed at this and there were a few more muted chuckles.

Now, just what did that mean?

"I bid you good night, gentlemen," Phoebe said with a little curtsy to the company.

She followed Cato across the room to a narrow staircase at the far end. She understood the significance of Cromwell's comment when they got to the top of the stairs. There was one long room under the eaves. It was lined with cots and leather-bound trunks.

"Does everyone sleep up here?" Her eyes widened at the implications. "All those men?"

"I did tell you there wasn't any privacy," Cato reminded her, holding up the lamp he'd carried up from the hall below. "It's the very devil of a situation!"

"I didn't make it happen," she pointed out, stung. "If you like, I'll go and sleep with the horses."

Cato shot her a swift appraising glance. "This is hardly the time for jesting," he observed aridly. He returned to his examination of the long room. "We'll just have to make the best of it. Over here will do as well as anywhere." He moved to the rear of the loft.

Phoebe followed, threading her way through the lines of cots. "But don't the beds belong to people?"

Cato shook his head. "No. There'll be folk moving in and out of them all night as the watch changes. No one lays claim to any one space."

"Oh." Phoebe looked around a mite helplessly.

"Here, this one'll do. It's against the wall, so you'll only have one neighbor." He gestured to a cot in the corner. "There's a blanket and a pillow of sorts. Don't strip down beyond your shift."

"I wasn't about to," Phoebe said. "Where will you sleep?"

"I'll decide when I come up.later." He set the oil lamp on one of the chests at the foot of the cot. "Turn down the wick when you're in bed."

"Yes, but . . . but I need the privy," Phoebe said in sudden panic. "I can't go to bed without using it."

Cato swore.

"I can't help it," Phoebe protested. "Everyone has to go sometimes. Even soldiers!"

Despite himself, Cato's lips twitched. She had a point. "There's an outhouse at the rear of the kitchen garden. No one uses it. Take the lantern and go down that way." He gestured to a stairway that was little more than a ladder at the rear of the loft. "You shouldn't meet anyone, but if you do, don't talk, just be quick."

He hastened away, obviously in a great hurry to get back to his cronies, Phoebe reflected acidly. She took up the lantern and went to find the outhouse.

She returned to the long dormitory having met no one on her journey. She took off her outer garments, laying them tidily over the chest. Her shift felt very skimpy as she stood by the cot. She could hear laughter from below and lamplight showed through the spaces in the floorboards. If she listened hard, she could distinguish snatches of conversation and recognize some of the voices.

She extinguished the lamp and lay down on the narrow cot, pulling the thin blanket over her. The pillow and mattress were stuffed with straw and crackled when she turned over. She lay listening to the sounds from below. The laughter had ceased and there was a different tenor to their voices, as if, supper over, they had returned to business. Phoebe identified the rich, mellow cadences of Cato's voice interspersed with the sharp and unmelodious tones of Cromwell and the lighter tones of General Fairfax. It sounded as if they were in dispute.

"If a man hasn't the courage to take the ultimate step, then I can't help but question his commitment," Cromwell said, his voice nasal and strident.

"I trust it's not my commitment you're questioning." Cato's voice was even, almost amused, as if such an idea were laughable.

"You'd vote to depose the king?" Cromwell demanded.

Phoebe listened, straining to catch Cato's reply. "It's not a step to be taken lightly," he replied after a minute. "We force peace on our terms. I see no reason to do more."

"You think the king would abide by such an agreement?" The question came from General Fairfax and produced a buzz of response from the company.

"I think we must assume that he would." Cato's response was firm, rising over the buzz. "I didn't enter this war to establish a republic."

"Then this war has overtaken you," Cromwell declared. "It's no longer a gentlemanly exercise to persuade Our Sovereign Majesty to heed the wishes of his subjects." His voice was bitter and ironic. "It's a fight for the right to rule England. And I say the people's rule must hold sway."

"You go too far for me, Oliver," Cato said, as firmly and evenly as before. "But we can surely agree to differ on the final outcome without throwing accusations of disloyalty at one another."

"Aye, you have the right of it, Cato," Fairfax said warmly. "Oliver, 'tis foolish to fall out with your friends."

"I said nothing about disloyalty," Cromwell declared. "Only of a failure of commitment. But you're right, 'tis too early to talk of such things. Let us win first."

This was received with a rousing cheer and stamping feet and the sound of goblets being banged upon the table in resounding approval.

Phoebe drifted off to this lullaby.

She awoke in darkness, faintly aware through the clinging tendrils of sleep of the sounds of breathing, of snores, the creaking of straw palliasses as men shifted in sleep. For a moment she was disoriented, then she felt the hand on her back and she remembered.

"Cato?" she breathed.

For answer, he kissed the back of her neck. She was lying on her stomach, her shift tangled around her waist, and she could feel his length along her back, the hard throb of his erection against her bottom. She reached her arms over her head in a languid, luxuriant stretch as her body came alive, her skin began to tingle in anticipation.

He slid a hand between her thighs, feeling for her, caressing her until she opened to him, hot and moist with her own arousal. He moved his arm beneath her, lifting her buttocks towards him, and penetrated her with one deep thrust. He was lying along her back, his skin pressed to hers, as he moved within her, long, slow movements that filled her completely. His teeth grazed her nape, the points of her shoulder blades, and with his free hand he played with her breasts.

Phoebe buried her face in the pillow to stifle the moans of pleasure building in her throat. The sense of the men around them in the darkness seemed to increase her excitement. It was as if what they were doing on this narrow cot was forbidden, dangerous, no longer the legitimate if entrancing act of marriage. She could not move her own body, not by so much as a wriggle, for her own pleasure or for Cato's. She was held captive by the body above her, pressed into the mattress, able only to submit to the waves of pleasure that broke over her with increasing strength.

The ripples began deep, deep in her belly, at the very center of her being, it seemed, and spread in ever widening circles until they consumed her, every inch of her. Her body was rigid, taut, held for a moment in an exquisite vise of sensation, then everything seemed to burst and dissolve and she bit the pillow to muffle the unpreventable gasping cries of an inarticulate joy that seemed to go on for ever and ever.

Cato pulled her buttocks hard against him and moved his other hand from her breasts to clasp the back of her head, his fingers twined in the thick, luxuriant hair as his own climax throbbed deep within her. He buried his mouth against her neck, tasting the salt on her skin, inhaling her fragrance that always reminded him of vanilla. He felt as if he had never possessed a woman as completely as he now possessed Phoebe, in this dark loft amid oblivious sleepers.

Or were they oblivious? The thought that maybe someone was lying there listening to the muted sounds of their love-making had a strange and heady effect. It seemed to increase the power of his orgasm, and as he fell from the heights of pleasure back to reality, he wondered what on earth had happened to him. He who never lost control, would never consider making an exhibition of himself, had found something about the dark, illicit nature of that clandestine act utterly compelling and arousing.

He disengaged slowly, reluctantly, and rolled to lie beside her, gathering her against him. She pressed back, drawing up her knees so that they lay like spoons in the narrow space. His fingers were still twined in her hair, and his other hand was at her waist, holding her.

13

"*You've heard nothing further about Meg?*" *Phoebe asked* Olivia on their return the following morning.

"I haven't been out," Olivia said, "but no one's said anything in the house, and someone would have mentioned it if anything bad had happened. They know you're a friend of hers."

"Well, that's something," Phoebe said. "But I'll go and see her right away. Will you come?"

Olivia hesitated. "I'm in the middle of a very difficult translation. You go on ahead and I'll c-catch you up."

Phoebe laughed. "There's no need to tear yourself away from your books. I only wondered if you felt like the walk."

"Well, I do, but . . ." Olivia looked at the pile of books on the parlor table.

"But another time," Phoebe said, giving her a quick kiss.

"I'll c-come later," Olivia promised.

Phoebe stood on tiptoe to adjust the set of her new hat in the mirror above the mantel. She thought her eyes seemed heavy, languorous almost, still aglow with the memory of that loving on the narrow cot among sleeping men. Never in her wildest dreams would she have expected such a thing from Cato.

With a little smile, she left the parlor and went downstairs. She was intending to leave the house immediately, but somehow her feet took her to Cato's closed study door. She had no real errand but she found she wanted to see him. It seemed an irresistible urge. She raised her hand to knock and then realized that there were two voices coming from the other side of the door. Brian Morse was with Cato. The small passageway at the rear of the hall was windowless. The keyhole in the study door was very large. There was no key in it and Phoebe could see the stream of light falling onto the dark oak at her feet.

She had never listened at a door before. But now, without really knowing why, she found herself bending forward to press her ear against the keyhole. Their voices were very clear.

"We were discussing the situation in the West Country last even at headquarters," Cato was saying. "Your knowledge of the king's council's views would be invaluable . . . even your opinion if you have no definite knowledge . . ."

"The concern in Oxford is that the West Country is on the point of going over to Parliament," Brian replied after a moment. "The tyranny of the king's commander in the West has done more harm to the king's cause than a thousand enemies."

"Aye, we had heard tell of some such," Cato responded, his voice considering. "And what is the king proposing to do about it?"

"I believe he will recall Sir Richard."

"And replace him with . . . ?"

Again there was a pause, then Brian said slowly, "Hopton, I believe."

"Ah" was Cato's response.

"Have I satisfied the inquisition, sir?" Brian's voice sounded light and humorous.

There was another short silence. Phoebe's heart skipped a beat. She pressed her ear yet closer.

"You will understand our hesitation," Cato returned. "We have still to digest what you've given us."

"I'll leave you to reflect, then, and hope most fervently that after some thought you'll be convinced of my sincerity . . . and will be willing to convince your high command."

To her horror, Phoebe felt the door latch lift. She fell back into the shadows, her hand clapped to her mouth, as the door was suddenly flung open. Brian stepped out into the corridor. His eye fell on Phoebe, shrinking against the wall. He closed the door at his back.

"Well, well, what big ears we have," he murmured, his teeth glinting in a smile. "Hear anything interesting?"

Phoebe, terrified that Cato might suddenly open the door, darted past him into the hall, where she could reasonably have legitimate business. She stood casually with one foot on the bottom step of the stairs, her hand on the newel post, and said in carrying tones, "Have you completed your business with my husband, sir?"

Brian was still smiling as he approached the stair. "You're well suited to conspiracy, Phoebe," he said softly. "But you have no need to listen at doors. I will tell you whatever you wish to know."

"I wish only to know what interests my husband," Phoebe responded, casting a quick glance around. A servant appeared from the kitchen regions and went into the dining parlor.

"And of course he won't tell you," Brian said matter-of-factly. "Cato has always relied only on himself . . . oh, and on Giles Crampton," he continued. "He follows his own path. Something extraordinary would have to happen for him to confide in anyone apart from Giles. It's a point of principle with him."

"You know my husband very well, then," Phoebe said thoughtfully.

"Oh, aye. I've known him since I was in short coats." He laughed slightly. "I understand him very well, Phoebe."

"I wish I did," Phoebe said.

Another smile flickered over his thin mouth, and his eyes glittered like hard brown diamonds. "You may not like what you understand."

"Oh, now you're talking nonsense!" Phoebe declared, a

flare of anger in her eyes. "And I'll thank you not to say such things to me!"

"My, my . . . it's a lucky man who can inspire such loyalty," Brian murmured. "But forgive me, Phoebe. My own experiences with Lord Granville have not given me quite such a rosy view of him as yours."

Phoebe regarded him doubtfully. She could understand how one might find her husband distant and intimidating. She'd found him so herself until without volition she'd tumbled so violently into love and lust with him.

"I am his heir, Phoebe. And it pains me that we should be so constrained. It was inevitable when I took the other side in this damnable conflict, but now . . . now that I've seen the justice of Parliament's cause . . ." He shrugged eloquently. "I have provided him with vital information. And still I believe he hesitates to trust me."

"Yes, I can see that it must be hard to understand," Phoebe agreed. "But Cato is never unreasonable. He'll not hold past mistakes against you. I'm certain of it."

"Ah, one would hope so," Brian said. "One would hope so." Then he smiled and reached into his pocket. "But I was forgetting. I was in Banbury yesterday and I found this in a bookshop. I thought you might like it." He handed her a small leather-bound volume.

"Oh, the poems of Thomas Carew!" Phoebe exclaimed. "Why, how thoughtful of you. I am most particularly fond of his elegy on John Donne."

"I find 'The Rapture' most appealing," Brian said, watching her with a glint in his eye.

Phoebe regarded him suspiciously. "It is a very fine love poem," she said after a slight hesitation.

"But a trifle licentious; you're quite right," he said, his smile broadening. "Perhaps too much so for innocent sensibilities."

"I am no innocent!" Phoebe protested, feeling he was making fun of her. "I have read very widely, sir."

"Oh, forgive me. It was not meant as an aspersion," Brian said hastily. "Of course, as a poet yourself you would regard the more risqué literature with more sophistication than the average young woman."

"I do not know whether you're mocking me or not," Phoebe said frankly. "But you will not put me out of countenance, that much I can tell you." She dropped him a curtsy. "I thank you for the gift, sir."

Brian caught her hand, bringing it to his lips. "Forgive me. I meant no insult. Perhaps I was teasing you a little, but I find you quite enchanting."

Phoebe blushed. "Indeed, you should not say such things. I am a married woman." She pulled her hand free and turned to leave in some disarray.

Brian stood watching her. Absently he scratched his head. There was something about her . . . something elusive and yet curiously appealing. It was absurd that he should find such a tangled naïf attractive. And it was very dangerous.

His lips thinned. He was here to destroy her, not make love to her . . . much as it would amuse him to cuckold that cold fish Granville. His stepfather was not the kind of man to appreciate Phoebe's rich and vibrant brand of sexuality. Was she even aware of it herself?

Phoebe hurried from the house. Had he been trying to flirt with her? She gave a fastidious shudder. She could never imagine Cato flirting with her, or indeed with anyone. It was a pathetic game. So unstraightforward.

But it wouldn't do to alienate Mr. Morse, she decided. If she played her cards right, he could prove quite useful. His fashion sense couldn't be faulted, for a start. And if she could get him to tell her what Cato wouldn't, then maybe she could surprise her husband with her informed commentaries on all those matters that absorbed him.

That conversation she'd overheard last night, for instance. Cato and Cromwell had been at outs. The situation had been defused, but it had sounded serious. A difference of opinion on how to conclude the war. That had to be a most serious question. Perhaps Brian would have some insights if she approached him discreetly.

Phoebe strolled through the village, surprised at how quiet it was. Usually at this hour of the morning, particularly on such a fine day, there would be folk around, working in their gardens, tending their chickens, chopping firewood. She saw a few backs as people hurried into their cottages, and as she passed the Bear a murmur of voices drifted through the open door into the street.

They were male voices and Phoebe didn't pause. If the village men were gathered in the taproom, they wouldn't welcome a woman's presence. The men who remained in the village considered womenfolk irrelevant to their own manly pursuits, which were of course of supreme importance and quite beyond the ken of a mere female.

Phoebe gave a scornful little sniff at this reflection. She had seen too much of the way country women kept body and soul together, the sacrifices they made for their families, the selfless way they shouldered their own burdens and those of the menfolk, to have much time for the entrenched belief in the superiority of the male.

The woods were quiet, the snow covering long melted, and Phoebe thought she could smell the first faint intimations of spring. A snowdrop raised its fragile head above the moss-covered roots of an old beech tree, and a pheasant started from a bush heavy with berries at the side of the path.

Phoebe's heart lifted as it always did at this time of year. It always seemed as if there was so much to look forward to.

Meg's front door stood open, and the black cat sat on the threshold washing himself. He gave Phoebe an incurious stare from his greeny gold eyes.

"Meg!" She stuck her head in the door. There was no sign of Meg. "So where is she?" Phoebe demanded of the cat, who blinked and yawned, rose, stretched and arched its back, and stalked daintily away down the path, his tail aloft.

Phoebe shrugged and followed him. The cat always knew where his mistress was to be found. Hardly mistress, Phoebe corrected herself. Companion was probably the correct word. Cats acknowledged no superior. Good examples, perhaps, she thought with the same exuberant lift of her spirits that had accompanied her walk.

Meg was milking the goat in the little shed at the back of her kitchen garden. She looked up with a glad smile as Phoebe came into view, walking behind the cat.

"Well, and it's glad I am to see a friendly face." She squeezed the last of the milk from the teat into the pail and stood up, slapping the nanny on the rump with careless affection. "I haven't seen a soul since you were here last."

"No one's had need of you?" Phoebe kissed her.

"No one's come anywhere near me," Meg replied, picking up the pail. "Either everyone around is healthy as elves, or there's trouble still abrewing."

"I've heard nothing," Phoebe said. "Granny Spruel wasn't in her garden when I passed just now, so I wasn't able to get the latest gossip."

Meg shrugged philosophically. "Well, come and have some tea. That's a very elegant riding habit."

"Yes, isn't it?" Phoebe said complacently. "I'm astonished you recognized me."

"I wouldn't have, except the hem has a water stain, and your shirt is hanging down below your jacket, you're missing a button, and your hat brim is only half turned up," Meg pointed out.

"Oh, well, you know what they say about silk purses and sow's ears," Phoebe responded dolefully, tucking her shirt back into the waistband of her skirt. "Nothing stays done up on me for more than a minute. I doubt even Brian Morse can work the necessary miracle."

"And who's that gentleman?"

"Oh, let me tell you all about him."

They sat in Meg's kitchen, drinking blackcurrant tea

while Phoebe expounded her theory that Brian Morse could be put to good service. She would permit him to flirt with her, although why he would want to she couldn't imagine, but he could do so and she would pick his brains at the same time. He would surely be able to give her some insights into Cato's military preoccupations so that she could surprise her husband with her intelligent contributions. It could turn out rather well, she thought.

The cat had returned with them, but he was restless. He paced the kitchen, jumped onto the table, onto the shelf above the range, back to the floor. Then he stalked to the door and went off down the path.

"Going hunting," Meg said, refilling Phoebe's teacup.

The next instant, the cat came flying back into the kitchen, racing footsteps sounding on the path close behind him.

"Phoebe . . . Meg . . ." Olivia burst into the kitchen, her hair flying loose from its pins, her breath coming in gasps. "They're c-coming!"

"Who are?" Phoebe had jumped to her feet, sending her cup spinning to the floor in a dark splash of blackcurrant.

"The village . . . they have the witch finder," Olivia panted. "They're a few minutes behind me. Meg has to hide!"

Meg drew herself up to her not inconsiderable height. "I'm not hiding from a rabble," she said.

"But you *must*!" Olivia insisted, her eyes wild, darting around the small kitchen.

And then they heard the sounds. It was the sound of feet, the soft rumble of voices. Then the cat flew out of the cottage, fur on end, his tail a thick bush. He leaped onto the roof of the cottage with a loud meow of outrage.

The crowd appeared out of the trees. It was the whole village, Phoebe thought in stunned horror. The men were in front. They carried heavy staves; behind them swarmed the women, some carrying babies, some with children clinging to their skirts.

"Olivia! For God's sake, get out of here!" she cried before

the mob had reached the gate. "You can't be found here!" For some reason it didn't occur to her that what was not meet for Lord Granville's daughter might also be wrong for his wife.

"In the apple loft," Meg said calmly. "Go quickly. Phoebe's right. When they've gone, maybe you can go for help."

Olivia hesitated, then she turned and scrambled up the ladder into the loft.

Phoebe and Meg with one mind stepped out of the cottage, side by side, presenting a united front to the incoming tide.

In the middle of the front line strode a tall man in a frieze cloak and a flat-crowned, wide-brimmed black felt hat. He carried a thick walking stick and a large leather pouch at his waist.

"Is that the witch?" He stopped and pointed at Meg with his stick.

"No!" Phoebe exclaimed, pressing her foot on Meg's to gain her silence. "And just who might you be, sir?"

He stepped forward. "I, my good woman, am the witch finder. And I am here to find a witch." His voice boomed through the quiet, and the villagers at his back shifted and murmured in agreement.

"I am not your good woman!" Phoebe declared, incensed. Her only hope of prevailing was to intimidate this man and his rabble with her own status. "I am Lady Granville, and my husband is the representative of the law in this country."

"Aye, 'tis true," one of the leading men said.

"Indeed it is. And you should know better than to have truck with this nonsense, Bill Watson!" Phoebe jabbed a finger at him.

"Be silent!" boomed the witch finder. "I have the authority to seek out witches across the land. And I fear no one in the exercise of my holy work."

"Where's the vicar?" Phoebe demanded. "He's the one supposed to be concerned with holy work."

"The vicar has given his blessing. The devil is among us and must be cast out," the witch finder droned. "You will stand aside, woman, and let me do my work."

"I mostly certainly will not!" Phoebe planted herself in front of Meg, arms akimbo. Meg was silent, seeming to accept Phoebe's tactics. Phoebe had no idea whether the natural authority of her own position as Cato's wife would carry any weight in the face of this muttering crowd. But it was all she had if they refused to remember her as a friend.

The witch finder suddenly drew something from his leather pouch. It was a long, thin needle. "I smell not one witch but two," he said. "You did well to send for me, good folk."

"May the devil take you and damn you to hell!" Phoebe cried, not sure whether anger or terror was holding sway. She couldn't believe this was happening, and yet she knew it was a nightmare lived all too often across the land.

The witch finder spun around to face the crowd. "You heard her curse me. You heard her call upon the devil. Seize them both. We'll prick 'em and find the mark of the devil."

"You touch me and you will answer to Lord Granville." Phoebe raised her hands as if she could thus ward off the throng who had begun to move towards the two women.

There was an unmistakable hesitation and she had a moment of hope. But the witch finder knew how to command a crowd.

"If there be no mark, then they have nothing to fear. Only the guilty would resist the test. Will you go on with the devil in your midst and watch your children die, your crops fail, your cattle fall where they stand?"

"No . . . no . . . no devil!" a woman cried at the back. It was the woman whose child had died. She pushed forward, her face contorted with hatred, her eyes crazy with grief. "She killed my child." She pointed at Meg. "She put a curse upon him and my baby died." She spat directly into Meg's face.

It was the signal for the rest. They surged forward and

Phoebe and Meg were both surrounded. Hands grabbed at Phoebe, wrenched her arms behind her back, tied her wrists with rope. She cursed them, using every expression she had ever heard in barnyard and stables.

And yet rough as they were with Phoebe, they manhandled Meg with a savage brutality, scratching and punching her as they trussed her. A yowling shriek that truly sounded like the devil shivered through the air, and a black bundle, hissing, spitting, claws tearing, flew through the air to land on the back of one of Meg's captors.

He screamed as the cat's claws dug into his back, and the witch finder gave a bellow of satisfaction. "The familiar!" he cried. "I have no need of pins. We'll swim the witch."

"Aye, swim the witch . . . swim the witch." They took up the chant, and Meg's cat loosed his hold and leaped back up onto the roof again. For a second he was visible on the gable, and then he was gone in a black streak.

Phoebe struggled for breath. "You cannot swim for a witch without finding a mark," she said desperately. "It is not permitted. You cannot do that. You know you cannot."

She could think now only of buying time. If it meant they had to endure the ordeal of the pricking, then so be it. Once Meg was trussed, wrists to ankles, and thrown into the freezing river, she would drown. If she held her breath and came up again, seeming to float, then they would burn her for a witch. There was no salvation, short of a miracle. But while there was time, there was time for a miracle.

"Aye, she's right," Bill Watson said slowly. "We've to do this accordin' to law an' custom. 'Tain't right otherwise."

There was a murmur of agreement, and the witch finder, after a moment when he seemed to assess the mood of the crowd, said, " 'Tis all the same to me. I smell witches, but if you want proof, then you shall have it. Bring them."

He strode through the crowd, who parted before his staff like the Red Sea before Moses'. They surged around Meg and Phoebe and drove them after the tall figure of the witch finder.

Phoebe stumbled along, conscious not of her own ills but of Meg's. Meg's face was scratched and bruised. Her gown had been torn and her breast was exposed, but her expression was grimly determined. She would show this rabble not the faintest sign of fear.

In the apple loft, Olivia stared out of the small round window as the procession surged away. Then she half jumped, half fell down the ladder to the kitchen. Meg's carving knife lay on the breadboard on the table, and Olivia grabbed it up. She had no idea what she could use it for, but just possessing a weapon made her feel better.

She pulled the hood of her cloak close about her face as she set off after the mob, running through the woods parallel to the path until she came up with the stragglers. In their heated excitement they paid no attention to the tightly cloaked new arrival slipping into their midst.

14

They were borne in savage triumph to the village and onto the green where the stocks and the whipping post stood.

"Where's the beadle?" Phoebe demanded in a last-ditch attempt to avert this horror. "You cannot conduct this business without the beadle."

There was a moment's hesitation. "And you cannot conduct it without the Justice of the Peace," she continued on a rush of ascendancy. "Send for the Justice."

"The Justice has no say in the matter of witches," the witch finder declared in stentorian tones. "Strip her and seize her to the whipping post."

He advanced on Meg and was about to rend the collar of her already torn gown when he gave a shout of triumph.

"Aha! She carries a serpent's tooth at her neck." He grabbed the thin string that held the tooth Phoebe had drawn, and snapped it. He held it up for the crowd. "See, the serpent's tooth."

"Oh, don't be absurd!" Phoebe cried. "It's her own tooth. I pulled it for her myself."

"It takes a witch to defend a witch," the finder said in triumph. The crowd's murmur became full throated and Phoebe felt the terror she had so far held at bay begin to overwhelm her.

Two men rushed at Meg to seize her to the whipping post, and Phoebe closed her eyes under a wash of despair. Once the witch finder began his poking at Meg's naked flesh with his long pins, looking for the devil's mark, he would find it.

Not an inch of her skin would be left untouched; the most intimate crannies would be prodded. Every tiny blemish he would prick and they would bleed, but eventually he would find one that didn't bleed. This witch finder would ensure that he found his witch, but he would give the crowd a good show before he did so.

Phoebe knew as Meg did that there were witch finders who would use a pin with a retractable point. At some point, when the crowd was sufficiently worked up, they would apply that pin and it would draw no blood. Their fanatical love of their profession, if thus it could be called, permitted any subterfuge. And Phoebe knew that they had here such a witch finder.

And soon it would be her turn.

But for the moment she was standing ignored, her hands bound behind her, all her senses straining towards Meg, who was lost to view in the crowd.

Olivia glided away from the throng. Phoebe's heart jumped as she saw her. Olivia seemed to stroll away, casually, as if the scene no longer interested her. A couple of heads turned in her direction, but then the witch finder gave a cry and the mob surged forward jostling for a view.

Olivia stepped behind Phoebe. She knelt so that she was obscured by Phoebe's body and began to saw at the bonds with the awkward carving knife, terrified she would cut Phoebe's wrists. Phoebe held her breath and let her head droop as if in defeat, surreptitiously spreading her legs to give Olivia more of a shield.

The last strand broke. "Run!" Olivia hissed. "Before they finish with Meg."

"I can't leave her." Phoebe knew they were wasting precious time, but her feet seemed planted in the ground.

"You c-can't do her any good here!"

Phoebe saw her point. She turned and raced with her, across the green to the tangle of narrow lanes running off the main street. Every minute she expected to hear someone cry the alarm, but the interest in Meg and the witch finder was at fever pitch, and all eyes were riveted to the finder's long pins as they slid into Meg's flesh.

They reached the corner of Church Lane and stopped, panting for breath.

"What can we do?" Phoebe demanded on a gasp as she bent double trying to catch her breath. "We have to rescue Meg." She looked desperately towards the village green. "Dear God! What can we do?"

"If they swim her, she'll drown!" Olivia said, agonized. "Should we go for help? C-call my father?"

"There's no time," Phoebe said. She felt sick and exhausted and stupid.

A great shout went up from the rabble, and Phoebe and Olivia shivered at the surging triumph of the sound. And then the calls of "She has the mark . . . the devil's mark. Swim the witch . . . swim the witch . . ." went up.

The crowd parted as the witch finder came through, brandishing his long needle. And only then did they notice the absence of their other victim. "Where's the other witch?" he demanded in ringing tones.

A murmur grew from the crowd and it became clear to the pair in the lane that Lord Granville's tenants were having second thoughts about pursuing his wife.

The witch finder tried to arouse them once more, but now that Lady Phoebe was no longer in front of them, they had no stomach for a second round of pins. They had their witch, they didn't need two, and particularly one of Lady Phoebe's standing.

They turned back to Meg, who lay in a crumpled heap on the ground, and "Swim the witch" rang out anew.

"We have to get to the river first." It was all Phoebe could think of. Once at the riverbank maybe inspiration would come. "We'll move much more quickly than the mob." She turned and darted down Church Lane, leading the way through the lychgate and across the churchyard into the field beyond.

The field sloped down to the riverbank where Brian Morse was sitting his horse, his gun raised as he sighted on a flock of mallards that had broken cover under an onslaught from Cato's hounds.

Brian fired and a duck tumbled from the sky, its blue-green breast luminous as it fell through sunlight. The dogs shot into the rushes to retrieve the bird, and it was then that Brian saw the two figures racing across the field towards him.

"Well, well, what have we here?" he murmured, sliding his gun into the loop on his saddle. Something was awry.

"Oh, you have a horse!" Phoebe exclaimed as she reached him a few paces ahead of Olivia. "Thank God for that! We can do nothing without one."

"Yes, you have to help!" Olivia stated with a ferocious glare.

"They're bringing our friend to the river to swim her for a witch," Phoebe explained in a tumble of words. "You have to ride them down, pull her onto your horse, and ride with her to safety."

"I have to do *what*?" Brian stared at her in disbelief. "What in the name of the devil are you talking about, Phoebe?"

"Don't bring the devil into this!" Phoebe snapped. "We've had more than enough of him already. Oh, listen, they're coming." She grabbed his mount's bridle, completely forgetting her fear of horses. "You have to *do* it. Ride them down, particularly the witch finder, and get Meg. Do you understand?"

"Not really."

"Oh, don't be obtuse!" Olivia exclaimed, stamping her foot in exasperation.

The sound of the mob grew closer. Brian glanced down at Phoebe again and there was calculation in his eye now. Would it benefit him to help her in whatever this craziness was?

Probably, he decided. Banked favors had their uses. He turned his horse to face the crowd seething towards them along the bank.

Immediately he saw the woman they were dragging along behind the tall figure of the witch finder, who strode out in front. Brian recognized in his eyes the glitter of the fanatic. He'd met his like before. They too had their uses.

"Where should I take her when I have her?" He shifted in the saddle, gathering up the reins. The horse sidled beneath him, sensing the preparation for action.

"To the manor," Phoebe said. She and Olivia had moved behind Brian so that they were not immediately visible to the mob. "God knows what those bastards have done to her. She will need physicking. *Hurry!*"

"You'll need to take Phoebe too," Olivia stated. "They've lost her once. If they lose Meg, they may well lay hands on Phoebe again."

"They've taken you . . . taken Lady Granville . . . up for a witch!" Brian whistled through his teeth. He could almost find it in him to feel sorry for Cato.

"Don't worry about me!" Phoebe cried in an agony of apprehension. "Get Meg before they swim her."

Brian looked down at her for a second. Then he rode down the witch finder.

The man seemed to freeze as the piebald stallion pounded the bank towards him, clods of earth flying from beneath his great hooves. And then the animal was rearing over him and he could see the white underbelly, the thrashing hooves above his head. He flung himself sideways, but he was a hair too late and he went down with a shriek of pain beneath a flying hoof that caught him on the shoulder. The crowd was for a moment too stunned to move, then as the stallion reared again, they jumped to all sides and Meg was alone, naked and slumped in her bonds.

But she looked up as the horse came to a halt beside her.

Brian leaned down with his sword unsheathed and slashed the rope that bound her wrists. Meg needed no instruction; she jumped for his stirrup, grabbing the hand he held down to her. Brian hauled her up to the saddle in front of him and rode through the now milling bewildered mob.

"Up," he said to Phoebe, holding down his hand. She grabbed it and hauled herself up, scrambling for purchase on his boot.

"Meg . . . Meg . . . how hurt are you?" She tried to reach around Brian to touch Meg.

"Keep still, girl!" he commanded as his horse tossed his mane with a snort.

Phoebe retreated hastily, fighting her fear as the horse took off immediately.

"I'll follow you," Olivia called. She had her hands on the dogs' collars, holding them back as they strained towards the excitement of the mayhem on the riverbank.

Phoebe clung to Brian's belt as the beast hurtled up through the field, away from the river.

The wind whistled past her ears and she could find no breath to speak, and she was too scared to let go of Brian's belt long enough to try again to reach a comforting hand around him to Meg. It was cold, the wintery sun offering no warmth. Meg must be freezing; her own teeth were chattering, but that was aftermath rather than cold.

*C*ato had just mounted his horse at the front step of the house, preparing to ride to headquarters, when Brian's horse galloped onto the gravel sweep.

Cato couldn't believe his eyes. Brian held a naked woman on the saddle in front of him; behind him Phoebe clung for dear life, her face white as a sheet, her jaw clenched.

Brian reined in so suddenly, the horse skidded, digging in his rear hooves and nearly sending Phoebe sliding over his rump. She managed to save herself just in time and tumbled sideways instead, succeeding by the skin of her teeth in landing on her feet.

"Cato . . . my lord . . . the witch finder is come. They took us up and have hurt Meg so sorely." The words came through violently chattering teeth, and Cato could barely make head or tail of them.

He swung down from his horse and automatically put a steadying arm around her as she rushed up to him. He looked to where understanding might be found. "What's going on, Brian?"

Brian dismounted in almost leisurely fashion. "I was fortunate enough to effect a timely rescue, my lord. The witch finder and the mob were at the river. They had this woman—"

"Who would be grateful if someone would have the decency to give her something to cover herself with," Meg interrupted in sharp accents.

"Oh, Meg, how thoughtless of me. Take this." Phoebe moved out of Cato's encircling arm and tore off her cloak. She held it up to Meg. "How badly did they hurt you?" she asked distressfully. "I could do nothing—"

"Seems to me you did all that was needed," Meg broke in, wrapping herself in Phoebe's cloak. "I'm not drowned in a freezing river, am I?" She tried to smile but her mouth seemed numb and a violent convulsion of shivering ripped through her.

"Who is this woman?" Cato demanded.

"I can give you the answer myself, Lord Granville," Meg declared, her tone remarkably robust. "The bastard of a witch finder didn't take my tongue. I'm generally known hereabouts as Mistress Meg, the healer."

Cato grasped at a familiar straw. Phoebe had talked of such a friend in the village. A friendship he had forbidden.

The woman looked at death's door, wrapped in nothing but Phoebe's cloak.

"Come, you need to be in the warm." He reached up and lifted her to the ground, but when he set her down, her knees buckled and she would have slid to the ground if he hadn't supported her.

"You there! Trooper!" He called over one of the troopers who'd been observing the scene with unabashed curiosity. "Carry Mistress Meg into the house. Ask Mistress Bisset to have a care for her."

"Oh, you made it safely!" Olivia was shouting as she came round the side of the house, having taken a shortcut through the home farm. The dogs bounded ahead of her. "Is Meg badly hurt?" She arrived panting. Her face was very white, her lips so pale as to be almost blue.

"Olivia! What has happened? Are you ill?" Cato looked at his daughter in concern. "Tell me what's happened." He passed Meg over to the trooper and bent to take Olivia's cold hands in his.

"Oh, it was so frightening," Olivia said, catching her breath on a sob. "We were in Meg's c-cottage when the witch finder c-came for her. And they took Phoebe too, so I had to rescue her when they had her bound on the village green, but we c-couldn't save Meg from the pricking, and then . . . then . . ." Olivia hesitated fractionally. "Brian was at the river and he rode them down and rescued Meg."

Cato listened to this breathless explanation in astounded fury. "Bound on the village green?" he demanded in something akin to a bellow. His wife bound on the village green! He dropped Olivia's hands and swung around on Phoebe.

"Please . . . it wasn't for long," Phoebe said, wincing at his tone. She didn't think she could bear his anger . . . not now. She was shivering and her knees seemed to have turned to water now that the need for action was passed.

"Really it wasn't," she said, hearing the plea in her voice. "I must go and tend Meg." She turned to follow the trooper into the house.

Cato caught her arm in a steely grip. "You are going

nowhere until you've explained what's going on here. None of it makes any sense to me at all."

"It wasn't Phoebe's fault, sir," Olivia broke in passionately. "Indeed you c-can't blame her. She was so brave. They just took her up because she tried to defend Meg."

"They took you up *for a witch!*" At last Cato grasped the reality. His hands moved to Phoebe's shoulders and for a dreadful minute she thought he was going to shake her, there on the drive, in front of everyone.

"I *told* you it was going to happen. I *told* you if you didn't do something . . ." Her voice choked on a lump of tears and she massaged her throat, glaring up at him with unnaturally bright eyes.

"Come with me!" He released her and marched into the house. Phoebe hesitated, then followed her husband in. He stalked to his study and held the door for her, gesturing she should precede him.

Rage rode him like a jockey. The door shivered in its frame as he slammed it shut behind him.

"So, what have you to say?" he demanded, striding to the big desk.

"I told you it was going to happen. I told you about the rumors and that Meg was unjustly accused. If you'd stepped in earlier, it would not have gone so far. If you'd listened to me instead of talking about justice and unsavory reputations, none of this would have happened." Her voice shook, and there was a hard nut of nausea in her belly. "You *cannot* blame me!" she cried, her hand going to her throat again as if she could ease the tightness that was making it difficult to breathe.

Cato stared at her in disbelief. "You are blaming *me* for that shambles!" He was still carrying his riding whip, and he slashed it across the desk in livid emphasis.

"Yes, because you wouldn't listen to me! You're the Justice of the Peace; no one disobeys you. I told you they were going to bring that . . . that *devil incarnate* into the village, and you wouldn't listen. *You just wouldn't listen.*"

"I forbade you absolutely to have anything to do with the woman."

"And you really thought I would take notice?" Phoebe threw at him. "When you were so *wrong*! How could you possibly expect me to abandon my friend? You wouldn't do so yourself!"

Cato's voice was suddenly quiet and cold. "Do you think I will tolerate having my wife cast into the same mold as a village woman with an unsavory reputation? Look what you've done to yourself!" He gestured contemptuously at her torn and filthy raiment. "You expose yourself to the filthy hands and public mortification of the village green! You are *my wife*! Have you no pride? Look at you. I've never seen such an appalling sight! And not satisfied with disgracing yourself, you dragged Olivia into the mire with you."

Each staccato sentence was punctuated with a slash of his whip across the desk.

Phoebe didn't need to look at herself. She had a very good idea of what she looked like. "Olivia made her own decisions," she stated. "And I had no choice but to do what I did, and I don't understand why you can't see that. I *had* to defend Meg. They accused her of wearing the serpent's tooth, but it was the same tooth I'd drawn for her a few days ago. I *told* you about it. Meg was wearing it in jest. Like a talisman against another toothache. And the cat isn't a familiar, it's a perfectly ordinary black cat."

This was the first Cato had heard about cats, although he did remember something about a tooth. But none of it made any difference.

"I have no interest in your excuses. I do not know what to do with you. You refuse to honor my requests; you ignore my express orders; you rush headlong into whatever situation crops up. You never think before you act, before you speak.

You sweep everyone up in your impulses. I cannot imagine whatever could have led me to think you would make a suitable wife. How you could be so unlike your sister is a complete mystery. You shared the same parents. But you have none of Diana's poise, her grace, her innate sense of propriety. You have not the least vestige of a fine feeling, a sense of what's appropriate. Can you imagine your sister doing anything so disgraceful?"

And so it went on. Phoebe stood numbly and when it was over she turned and ran from his study.

Cato stalked after her, shouting for Giles Crampton, who appeared on the instant. He'd been expecting a summons once he'd pieced together the astonishing reason for that equally astonishing scene at the front door. Lord Granville wouldn't tolerate mob rule in his bailiwick.

"Arrest that charlatan and have him whipped five miles from the village boundary. And make damn sure the entire village sees it. Then bring me the vicar. This is his work too. And if there are any obvious ringleaders, arrest them and throw them in the stocks."

"Aye, sir. Right away, sir." Giles saluted crisply and strode off to do his master's bidding.

Phoebe had flown up the stairs, praying that Olivia wouldn't be waiting for her. She couldn't bear to see anyone. She couldn't even bring herself to go to Meg. She had no resources left to tend anyone's hurts but her own. She slammed the door of the bedchamber behind her and threw herself onto the bed.

She was sprawled facedown when someone knocked at the door. "Go away!" she called, her voice scratchy.

But the latch was lifted and the door swung open. "Forgive me, but I thought perhaps I might be able to help."

Brian stepped into the room, leaving the door wide open

behind him. If anyone did come along, he didn't want to risk the appearance of secrecy. "May I come in?"

"You seem to be in already," Phoebe said, sitting up. Her face was tear streaked, her eyes red and swollen, the once fashionable riding habit disheveled and dirty. "But please go away."

"You were very brave this morning," Brian said, ignoring this. "And I know that Lord Granville can be harsh. He wouldn't understand what you did for your friend. Believe me, I can sympathize. I've experienced the rough edge of his tongue on many occasions."

He placed a gentle hand on her shoulder. "Unfortunately, he has not a forgiving nature."

"He will understand when I can explain it to him . . . when he's not so angry," Phoebe said, shrugging his hand from her shoulder.

"Perhaps there's some way to win back his approval," Brian mused. "Some way to make him forget this morning . . . to forget such a terrible blow to his pride."

Phoebe winced but said nothing. She scrabbled for her handkerchief up her sleeve and, when she failed to find it, roughly swiped the back of her hand across her damp nose.

"May I?" Brian handed her his own pristine square of lace-edged linen.

"Thank you." Phoebe blew her nose with great vigor.

"No . . . no, keep it, I insist," Brian said hastily when she made to return his now soggy property.

"If you're sure." Phoebe scrunched it into a ball and shoved it up her sleeve.

She regarded him consideringly, her tears well and truly dried. He had done sterling service himself that morning. His rescue of Meg had been nothing short of heroic. "What do you suggest?"

Brian frowned, stroking his mouth with his fingertips. "I don't know, but there is something that I heard . . .

something that could cause trouble for Cato with his own high command if he doesn't avert it. I don't know if there's any way . . . But, no, how could you possibly do anything to help him there?"

"I can't tell if you don't tell me more," she said acerbicly. "What could you possibly know about Parliament's high command anyway?"

"You'd be surprised," he said dryly. "But if you don't want my help . . ." He turned to go.

"I didn't say that," Phoebe said. "I'm just not sure what kind of help you can give me."

He turned back to her. "Well, for a start, soak some pads in witch hazel and hold them over your eyes until the swelling goes down. Then put on one of your elegant gowns, dress your hair the way I showed you, and greet your husband as if nothing had happened. If you look guilty, he'll continue to treat you as such. You have to brazen it out."

Phoebe listened to this with her head on one side. It struck her as very sound advice. She wasn't ashamed of what she'd done.

"Perhaps," she said.

Brian bowed with an ironic glint in his eyes. "Any time I can be of further service . . ." The door closed softly behind him.

Phoebe sat down on the bed, frowning down into her lap, snuffling to clear her blocked nose. What Brian had said made sense. But how could things ever be right again? Cato's contemptuous words buzzed in her head like a swarm of angry hornets.

He didn't love her. He didn't even like her. He couldn't tolerate her. She disgusted him. He had said nothing so brutal and yet Phoebe knew that that truth lay beneath the tirade, beneath the scathing comparison with Diana.

Tears started anew and she bit her bottom lip hard. She would not cry again.

The sounds of a commotion on the gravel beneath the window was welcome distraction, and she slid off the bed to look. Giles Crampton and a trooper stood before the front door, where a cavalcade of Cato's militia were drawn up in a semicircle. Between Giles and the trooper stood the vicar, his black robes billowing in the breeze, his wide sleeves flapping with his violent gesticulations. He did not look a happy man, Phoebe thought with grim satisfaction.

As she watched, Cato emerged from the house in his soldier's buff leather jerkin, his sword at his hip, a short cloak swinging from his shoulders. Despite her wretchedness Phoebe felt the familiar throb as she gazed at him. Then she caught his expression as he turned to the vicar, and her spine prickled. She would not choose to be in the vicar's place at this moment.

She couldn't hear what Cato said, but she could see its effect. The vicar's self-righteous air became defensive, fearful, and then utterly crushed under the marquis's crackling eloquence.

At least Cato was defending her in public. And he would surely have dealt harshly with the witch finder. The village would never take the law into its own hands again. Phoebe looked for comfort in the reflection, but her own sense of betrayal was as sharp as the witch finder's pins. People she had helped, people she considered her friends, had turned on her with a blind vengeance. She could still feel their hands upon her as they'd bound her wrists. It would be a long time before she would forget . . . a long time before she would go among them with the same trust again.

Finally, with a curt order to the trooper who held the vicar, Cato mounted his horse. The vicar's shoulders drooped; his head was almost on his breast as the trooper led him away. Giles mounted his own horse. Cato raised a gauntleted hand in signal to move forward.

Phoebe watched the cavalcade canter up the drive, Lord Granville at its head. Her eyes stung and she turned from the window with a little gesture of defeat. So much for showing him a brave face in all her finery.

15

"*This war is no longer against the king's counsellors,*" Cromwell declared. "It began that way. Five years ago we all believed that once the king was no longer surrounded by self-serving men who gave him evil advice, then he would rule with truth and justice. But we all know that's no longer the issue." His words punched forth in a faint mist of spittle, and he paused to drink from his wine cup. No one interrupted him.

"The issue is the king himself," he continued, snapping his cup on the table. "This king will never be a just ruler. He will always surround himself with men whose advice he wishes to hear. He will never back down from his belief that he has a divine right to rule and any who challenge that right are hell-bound traitors."

He glared around the long table in the farmhouse at the somber faces gathered there. His gaze fell upon one countenance in particular.

"Granville, do you still maintain that our object in fighting this war is to return a reformed king to the throne he's dishonored? Are we to give him the right once more to rule the subjects he treats and has always treated with such disdain?" His tone was bitter and angry.

Cato raised his head and turned his frowning eyes upon the general. "Perhaps I still have hopes that the king can be brought to reason," he said slowly, absently almost. "Maybe it's a fool's hope, but I'll maintain it until I can no longer do so."

There was a murmur, some of agreement, some not. Cromwell's already heightened color deepened. "If you're not with us, you're against us," he stated.

Cato shook his head with a dismissive gesture. "You know better than that, Oliver, and you gain little by making enemies of your friends."

He pushed back his stool and stood up. "I have a militia to command. If we sit around debating such questions instead of fighting the war, this damnable strife will never be ended and the country will have good reason for believing that we have no interest in its ending. There are whispers already that some of us fight it simply for the power and influence it bestows upon us."

He snatched up his cloak and stalked from the large square room, leaving a buzz of voices in his wake.

Cato had spoken without his customary tact, and he was aware of it. Cromwell could well have taken his last comment personally, but Cato's mood was far from patient. He had ridden to headquarters after banishing the vicar from his parish, unable to rid himself of the image of Phoebe's face, her eyes so filled with hurt and something akin to betrayal as he'd vented his fear-fueled rage. She'd looked like a wounded fawn. He'd been savage, he knew. His anger had known no bounds, and he despised that lack of control. But who would blame him? What man could view with equanimity his wife's part in the morning's debacle on the village green . . . could even begin to contemplate what could have happened to her?

What man with a wife like Phoebe wouldn't be driven to distraction? he thought grimly, swinging onto his horse in the stable yard. If she would only conceive . . . a baby might slow her down somewhat, turn her thoughts and attentions to something other than this mad and impulsive need to rattle around the countryside offering help to all and sundry.

But that reflection was such a thorn in his side, he preferred not to dwell upon it. It was bad enough having Brian Morse under his roof, reminding him every minute of the day of what the future held if Phoebe remained barren.

"We goin' back to Woodstock, m'lord?" Giles Crampton sounded as if the prospect were less than enticing.

Cato glanced up at the sky; there were still a couple of hours of daylight left. He needed action of some kind. Something to clear his head, to restore his equilibrium. "Not immediately, Giles. We'll do a little scouting. See if we can't scare up a few of the king's men."

Giles beamed, and turned to bellow the news over his shoulder at the small troop of Granville militia who'd accompanied their lord to headquarters.

Cato raised a hand and gestured that they should move out, and the small cavalcade trotted away down the driveway to the road.

"We'll be takin' the Oxford road, then?" Giles drew abreast of Cato.

"Yes, but away from the city. We'll head towards Woodstock, but keep our eyes peeled for some excitement."

Giles muttered his assent although he would clearly have preferred to have headed towards Royalist headquarters rather than away from them. And as luck would have it, they met neither Roundhead nor Cavalier on the road until they reached the woodland outskirts of Woodstock. The evening star was showing in a clear sky, and Cato drew rein, looking around, listening intently to the beginning night sounds.

"The woman they took up fer a witch, 'er cottage's in the woods," Giles volunteered, gesturing with his whip. "Mebbe we should 'ave a look-see, make sure there's been no lootin' or suchlike." In the absence of real action, Giles would manufacture his own.

Cato nodded. He was curious to see where Phoebe had been spending so much of her time. Somehow, he had to find a way to understand her better. He still couldn't lose the image of her stricken little face, her great blue eyes filled with tears she had fought to hold back. After what she had endured at the hands of the mob, after what she'd seen them do to her friend, he might have kept a rein on his anger, however justified.

"*Cat . . . cat . . . where are you, cat?*" Phoebe held up her lantern, hoping to catch the animal's eyes in the light, as she circled Meg's cottage. She was sure he was here somewhere, and Meg was so anxious about her companion, Phoebe didn't think she could go back without at least being able to report a sighting. She had put out food and water for him so that he wouldn't feel abandoned, even though he was quite capable of foraging for himself among the small woodland rodents.

When he suddenly appeared, however, stealthily coming up behind her on the path and brushing against her legs, she gave a little squeal of shock and nearly dropped the lantern.

"Oh, you gave me such a fright, cat!" She bent to stroke him and he wound himself around her legs, purring as if nothing had happened to disturb the customary orderly turning of his world. He allowed her to pick him up, and she stroked his head, wondering if he would permit her to carry him back to Meg at the manor.

As if in answer to her unspoken question, he leaped suddenly from her arms and stalked in leisurely fashion to the cottage, jumping upon a windowsill and inserting himself through the narrow opening she'd left for him in case he returned after she'd left.

He was all right where he was, Phoebe decided, not relishing the prospect of carrying a squalling, scratching animal the mile or so home. She'd come back in the morning and replenish his food and keep him company for a while. Meg would be easier in her mind now.

Phoebe picked up the basket she'd left on the front step. It contained the fresh mint she would use to make dressings for the worst of Meg's wounds. The mint had a numbing, soothing effect. She also had mallow leaves for poultices and an assortment of herbs that Meg had listed to make the soothing drinks and jellies that would induce sleep and bring down the fever brought on by her exposure to the freezing elements.

Meg had no need of the leech, she was her own physician, and Phoebe was a competent physician's assistant. She slung the basket over her arm, turned the key in the door and pocketed it, then set off down the path, holding her lantern high. It was growing dusk, but it was a clear, soft, early spring dusk, not threatening even in the rustling world of the woods.

As she reached the gate, however, she heard the chink of bridles, the clopping of hooves, a murmur of voices approaching through the trees. Phoebe froze, her heart hammering against her ribs, all her terror of the morning returning in full flood. Who could be coming here at this hour?

She darted back down the path to the cottage, the key in her hand, but before she could reach the door, the first horsemen appeared at the gate and a voice bellowed through the gloom, "Hold fast! Who has business here?"

Phoebe recognized the voice instantly. Giles Crampton's tones were unmistakable. She felt first relief and then dismay. If Giles was here, it was odds on that Lord Granville wouldn't be far behind. They'd left together just before noon.

She would have to try to brazen it out, as Brian had suggested.

She turned back and said boldly, "It's me, Giles." Then she saw Cato. Her heart began to thump again despite her resolution.

"Phoebe, what in the name of the Almighty are you doing now?" Cato dismounted as he spoke. He came through the gate and down the path towards her, his step light and springing, the white collar of his shirt gleaming in the dusk against the dark leather of his buff tunic. He reached her and placed his hands on her shoulders.

For the first time, Phoebe found herself shrinking from him as he held her. A frown crossed his eyes, dark and glowing as they rested on her pale face.

"What are you afraid of?" he asked quietly.

"You." Phoebe forced herself to meet his eye. "Don't you think I have good cause, my lord?"

There was something both hurt and yet indomitable lurking in the depths of her eyes. "No," Cato said. "You have no cause to be afraid of me."

Phoebe dropped her gaze with an almost palpable air of disbelief.

Cato's expression grew taut, but he managed his normal calm tones as he asked, "What are you doing here at this time of night, Phoebe?"

"Meg needs her medicines and she was worried about her cat. I came to feed him and make sure he was all right. He ran off when the crowd came this morning." A slight shudder ran through her and she half turned from him as if to hide her expression.

Instinctively Cato moved a gloved hand up to clasp the back of her neck, his fingers closing warm and firm around the slender column. "Come."

The men of the cavalcade were grouped together on the narrow track, their horses shifting, shaking their bridles as they sniffed the evening breeze. The men carried pikes and muskets at their saddles, swords thrust into their belts.

Phoebe hesitated as they reached them. "You have no need to interrupt your business, sir," she said, her voice sounding stiff. "I can make my own way home."

"No," Cato said with finality. "You cannot." He took Phoebe's basket and lantern and set them on the ground. "Give me your foot." He bent and cupped his palm. "Grab the pommel as I send you up."

Phoebe scrambled into the saddle. She was wearing one

of her old gowns and a threadbare woolen cloak missing its clasp, so had no fear of tearing anything. She settled astride, hitching her skirts up to her knees without giving a thought for exposed stockinged legs.

"We'll head for home, Giles," Cato instructed as he extinguished the lantern and left it behind the gate. He handed Phoebe the basket and then mounted behind her. "Let's go, gentlemen." He moved forward and the cavalcade followed in single file along the track.

Phoebe wanted to lean back against him, into the encircling embrace of the arm that held her. But how could she?

"There's someone up ahead," she whispered suddenly. Her ears were particularly acute and she'd heard what she was certain was the chink of a bridle. "Listen."

Cato drew rein, signaling that his men should do the same. They all sat still, ears stretched into the darkness of the woods on either side of the track.

Then Cato heard it too, at the same moment that Giles raised a finger and pointed to the right. A twig cracked, then another. And then the faintest whicker of a horse. Then it was hushed and silent as the grave. Nothing stirred, not a squirrel, nor a rabbit, not a pheasant, not so much as a sparrow. And it was this silence, this total lack of ordinary sound, that told Cato they had company in the woods and it was company that didn't wish to be discovered.

He stared frowning into the trees. If it was a royalist party, he should engage them. In ordinary circumstances he wouldn't hesitate. He could feel Giles's eagerness as the man drew close beside him on the narrow path.

But Cato could not do battle with Phoebe on his saddle.

Phoebe took matters into her own hands. She would not be a burden to him when it came to military decisions, whatever else he thought of her. She leaned back and mouthed against his ear, "I'll wait up a tree. I've done it before."

Cato's teeth flashed white in the darkness. "So you have,"

he murmured. "Get down, then." He lifted her down to the path and Giles nodded with satisfaction.

Phoebe, still clutching her basket, slid into the trees to the left of the path. Whatever was going to happen would happen on the right, so she'd be out of their way. She felt a curious exhilaration mingling with her apprehension. Cato would be all right. She'd seen him in action. She had faith. No one could get the better of him.

She set the basket at the base of an oak tree with low branches and hauled herself onto the bottom branch. Her gown ripped under the arms as she reached upward to grab a higher branch. Phoebe gave a mental shrug. The dress was too small for her anyway.

She scrambled up until she could sit astride a branch that overhung the path. There were no leaves to obscure her view of the track below, and she leaned into the trunk so she wouldn't be easily visible to anyone passing underneath. Her gown was a dull gray and blended well with the bark.

She was barely settled before the evening quiet was riven with sound. Yells, then the clash of steel, the violent thudding of hooves. And now Phoebe was no longer exhilarated, she was terrified. Why should she believe Cato would survive a hand-to-hand battle? What made him immune?

A volley of musket fire, the smell of cordite on the soft evening air. A barrage of shouts, a whole confusion of sound. Phoebe tried to imagine what was happening from the noise, but it was hopeless.

Suddenly she couldn't bear to sit in her perch a moment longer. She had to see what was happening. She inched forward along the branch to give her room to swing her legs down to the branch below. Then she froze. Hooves thundered along the narrow track, coming away from the sounds of fighting.

Three horsemen hurtled along the path, spurring their mounts, whips slashing flanks as they urged the sweating beasts to greater effort. A gust of wind snatched at the plumed hat of the man in front. He reached to grab for it but it was lost, and his long, flowing hair cascaded free in the wind as they raced beneath Phoebe's tree. For an instant she saw his face clearly. And then they were gone.

Phoebe almost fell from her perch in her excitement. As she reached the track, Cato with Giles and four other Granville men came galloping towards her.

"It was the king!" Phoebe shouted as they reached her.

"*What!*" Cato hauled back on the reins and his horse came to a rearing, plunging halt, the others following suit. "What did you say?"

"The king! He just went past here." Phoebe pointed down the track.

"Are you sure?" Giles demanded, staring at her.

Phoebe's chin went up. She said with that faint hauteur that Cato had noticed before, "Do you doubt me, Lieutenant? I assure you I've seen the king many times."

Her tone had its effect. Giles looked for once a trifle discomfited. He coughed and then said, "We'd best be after 'im then, m'lord." He kicked his horse and it leaped forward.

"Follow me!" he yelled to his men, and they galloped in pursuit of His Sovereign Majesty King Charles.

"They won't catch them," Phoebe said to Cato, who had not followed Giles. "They were going like bats out of hell."

"I had an inkling," Cato murmured, more to himself than to Phoebe. "When those three didn't even stay to fight, I had a feeling one of them was of more importance than the rest. But fool that I am, it never occurred to me we had the king within our grasp."

"I saw him clear as day."

"Well, he's away now," Cato said with a vigorous oath. "And if I know anything, he's heading for the Scottish border."

This was a significant development. If Charles had fled Oxford and was heading for Scottish protection, it must mean he'd given up hope of prevailing against Parliament. He would surrender to the Scots, who would guarantee his safety and their support to regain his throne, in exchange for his commitment to establish the Presbyterian Church in England. A commitment Cato, from his knowledge of the king, was convinced Charles would not make.

He would prevaricate; he would negotiate; he might appear to agree; but in the end he would renege. The king's false dealings with both the Irish and the Scots were well known. He was a supreme wriggler, a past master at the art of making and breaking promises, of twisting his own words and those of his advisors to make a simple statement suddenly mean something quite other.

"We lost 'im." Giles's disconsolate shout preceded his reappearance. "Vanished into thin air. Should we search the countryside, sir?"

"We don't have enough men," Cato replied. "And we need to attend to the wounded. Get Jackson and Carter to organize a litter party, and have the others escort the prisoners to headquarters. You accompany me back to the manor. I'll write up a dispatch and you can take it straight off to headquarters."

"Aye, sir." Giles rode back to where the sounds of fighting had now ceased.

Cato reached down a hand for Phoebe, who hopped for his boot, clutching her basket, as he pulled her up.

"You're not hurt?" she asked, turning to look at him over her shoulder.

"Not a scratch," he said, absently removing a twig from her hair before licking his thumb and wiping a smudge of dirt from her cheek.

"It was the tree," Phoebe said.

"Yes," he agreed, looking back down the path, a frown in his eyes.

"What would have happened if you'd caught the king?"

"Good question," Cato said, his tone abstracted.

Phoebe didn't press for further information. The exhilaration of excitement was wearing off and her brave front with it.

"Right y'are, sir." Giles came up with them. "They're seein' to the litters. Job's got a nasty sword gash, but the rest is minor, I reckon. The prisoners is on their way."

Cato nodded and they started off back down the path towards the village.

"You think there'll be talk at 'eadquarters, m'lord, about us lettin' the king slip, like?" Giles ventured after a minute. His tone was unusually tentative.

"No!" Cato responded sharply. "Why should there be? We didn't even know he was there."

"Jest that I 'eard rumors, like," Giles said with a shrug. "Like what not everyone's fer gettin' rid o' the king."

"You mean, like I'm not," Cato said with a touch of acid.

"Well, summat like that."

Phoebe was listening intently now. This touched upon what she had overheard last night in headquarters, the altercation between Cato and Cromwell that she'd listened to as she lay upstairs on the cot. It had sounded serious to her then. Now it seemed there were ramifications.

Cato and Giles appeared to have forgotten her presence on Cato's saddle. "I'm not sure what I think, Giles," Cato said with a sigh. "But I'm not going to rush to judgment. There's too much at stake."

"There's those that would send 'im into exile," Giles observed.

"Aye. And it may come to that. But I'll reserve judgment for the time being."

"So you don't think anyone'll remark on our lettin' 'im slip, then?" Giles repeated.

"They might, I suppose." Cato shrugged. "It's of little matter to me. I answer to my own conscience."

Giles made no comment but began to whistle tunelessly through his teeth, and Phoebe had the sense that he questioned his lord's wisdom but was not about to say so.

"I'll write that dispatch, Giles. Give me half an hour and then come and fetch it," Cato said as they rode up the drive.

"Right y'are, sir." Giles turned his horse towards the stable block.

Cato dismounted at the front door and lifted Phoebe down. He didn't release her immediately, his hold moving instead to her upper arms. But Phoebe thought that he didn't seem to know she was there. He stared over her head into the dark line of trees along the driveway. She stood still under his hands, hardly breathing. He didn't seem to acknowledge her and yet she had the feeling he was about to say something. Then abruptly he looked down at her and his eyes were puzzled, as if she didn't look at all as he'd expected.

"My lord?" she prompted hesitantly.

"I wish . . . I wish . . ." Then he shook his head, released her, and strode into the house.

Phoebe followed slowly. *What did he wish?*

16

Cato finished his dispatch and then sat staring into the darkness beyond his window, his fingernails tapping a rhythm on the smooth polished surface of his desk.

What did he wish?

Peace? Quiet? The orderly existence of an ordinary marriage? A wife who would *not* follow her conscience regardless of danger and regardless of who she dragged in her wake?

He rubbed his eyes with the heels of his palms. *He just didn't know.*

Abruptly he rose from his desk and went in search of Phoebe.

The parlor was empty but his eye fell on the sheets of vellum scattered over the table. Idly he glanced down at the untidy, ink-splattered scrawl. It must be this pageant she was always talking about, he realized, picking up several of the pages.

The notes in the margin were elaborate and impressive, detailing costumes, positioning, gestures of the actors. His vague curiosity became genuine interest as he read, turning the pages, picking up others as he finished.

He was deep in a scene between the young Elizabeth and Robert Dudley, Earl of Leicester. It was a love scene. And somehow he found himself reading the rich flow of language aloud in the deserted parlor. So absorbed was he, he didn't hear the door open behind him.

"Oh, gentle lady, sweet queen, be kind. Stay awhile and let my hungry eyes feast upon thy beauty. To be absent from thy heart is torment. Take all my love, my heart, my soul, and make them thine."

"Indeed, fair friend, a queen will take such gifts and will not love the less. A sovereign no longer in your sight, but a woman bound in love, a love more powerful than the gilded thrones of princes."

Cato spun around as Phoebe's soft voice recited Gloriana's reply to her lover. He stared at her for a moment as if seeing her for the first time as she stood in the doorway, her hand still on the latch. Her eyes were aglow, her cheeks softly flushed, her expression almost dreamy. It was as if she'd been living the words she'd spoken, lost in the fantasy world of her play.

Then suddenly the dreamy look vanished, the glow faded. "I wrote Dudley's part for you, my lord," she said, not moving from the door. "I had hoped to persuade you to take the part, but I realize it was foolish of me. I know you have no time for my scribbling."

The words he'd spoken still sounded vividly in his brain. He remembered suppertime conversations about who was to play Gloriana. He remembered how Olivia had pressed Phoebe to play the role herself. How she'd appeared to shrug off the suggestion. He continued to look at her as if at an impossible revelation.

Phoebe came into the room and took the pages from his hand. "Did you wish to speak to me, sir?"

With an effort Cato returned to the hard clarity of reality. "We have some business best discussed in private, I believe." He went to the door and held it for her. "We will go abovestairs; we're less likely to be disturbed."

He led the way to the bedchamber and once again held the door for her.

What couldn't be avoided must be faced. Phoebe abandoned Brian's advice. She wasn't going to brazen this out but she would strike first.

She said in a low but firm voice, "I do not think I can live with someone who holds me in such dislike. I can never be like my sister, and so I can never be the kind of wife who will satisfy you. I think I should go away from here. Go back to my father, if he will have me. Or to Portia. She would let me stay with her and . . ." Her voice faded as she saw his expression.

Cato stared at her in disbelief. "What are you saying? You're telling me you would flee my roof, take shelter . . . Oh, don't be absurd, Phoebe!"

"I cannot stay with you," Phoebe repeated steadily. "You think I'm untidy and unappealing. Everything I do offends or exasperates you. You want me to be something that I'm not. I can't change for you. You don't like who I am, but I don't know how to be different."

"It's not that I want you to be different . . . not exactly . . ." Cato found himself feeling for words, but Phoebe swept his hesitant beginning aside.

"I don't even know if I *want* to be different," she declared. "I can't try to please you when it means doing things I don't think are right!" She turned from him with a tiny shrug that spoke volumes.

"Phoebe, you're my wife," Cato said. "You're not leaving."

"I don't think that's sufficient reason to stay where I'm not wanted," Phoebe flashed.

Cato inhaled slowly. "When did I say I didn't want you, Phoebe?"

"You didn't have to. You made it clear as day."

Cato ran both hands back through his hair, then linked them behind his neck. He stared up at the ceiling and the silence stretched between them. Then he lowered his eyes; his hands dropped to his sides. He moved towards her.

"I do want you," he said.

Phoebe felt his hands on her shoulders.

"Be very still," Cato said softly into her hair. "Just trust me now. I have to show you something."

His hands slid over her shoulders, his fingers moving up her neck, circling her ears, gently tugging on the lobes.

"Don't," Phoebe protested. "It only makes it worse. Can't you see that?"

"Trust me," he said, and there was a hint of sternness in his voice, an edge of determination that brought her to stillness again.

"I'm going to undress you," Cato said quietly. "And I don't wish you to do anything to stop me or to help me."

His fingers were on the hooks at the back of her disheveled gown. His hands brushed her shoulders as he drew the garment away from her. For an instant they lingered, cupping the sloping curve of her shoulder where it blended with her upper arm. She felt his lips warm on the back of her neck, his tongue painting upward into the untidy tangle of her hair.

A little quiver ran through her. Her brain felt thick and stupid, unable to grasp what was happening. It made no sense with what had gone before.

His hands reached over her shoulders again to unlace the bodice of her chemise. He scooped her breasts into his palms, stroking the soft underside, lightly brushing her nipples with a fingertip. And despite everything, Phoebe felt the rosy crowns harden.

She glanced down, saw how the deep blue veins stood out against the creamy opalescence of her breasts as he cradled them in his palms. She noticed how large and well formed were his hands, how the swordsman's callused palms were so much paler than the tanned backs. She had noticed all these things before, but never with such startling clarity.

He slipped the chemise from her body, and she was naked except for her stockings and shoes. Despite the fire-warmed air in the chamber, Phoebe felt her skin prickle and lift as if with cold. She obeyed the hands at her waist, urging her closer to the fire. Cato pushed her gently down onto the stool and knelt to untie her garters. He lifted her feet to take off her shoes, then rolled down her stockings, easing them over her feet.

The tapestry-covered seat of the stool was rough against her bottom and thighs, and the fire was hot on her back. What was happening still made no sense, but her mind now had gone awandering and she was aware only of physical sensations, so heightened it was almost painful.

Cato drew her to her feet. "Close your eyes," he murmured. And then he began to touch her as she stood naked in front of him.

She kept her eyes closed and felt as if she were swaying like a sapling in the wind as his hands moved all over her. The light brushing caresses seemed to come where least expected. Sometimes there was a pause and every sensitized inch of her waited in breathless expectation. Then she would feel the touch in the small of her back, the finger at the pulse of her throat, the light brush in the curve of her elbow, the soft tender flesh of her inner arm.

It seemed that not a part of her went untouched, and yet his caresses did not approach her sex. It was as if he were paying homage to her body just with his hands, and without the sexual urgency that had been so much a part of their lustful loving. Phoebe felt herself drifting in the crimson-shot blackness behind her eyes. She was in her body and yet she was outside it. Every touch magnified the feeling of unreality, of detachment from everything that was solid and grounded.

Then his mouth followed the path of his hands. Where before he had touched, now he kissed. And again the kisses came when and where least expected, and again the surging urgency of lust was absent, and only this loving homage held sway.

It seemed she had been standing with her eyes closed for an eternity when he kissed her eyelids and said softly, "Wake up, Sleeping Beauty."

She opened her eyes as if from a drugged trance and gazed into his face. He was smiling, but it was unlike any smile she'd seen in his eyes before. It was filled with tenderness. He caressed the curve of her cheek, ran the pad of his thumb over her mouth.

"Now, my sweet, tell me that I do not like you, that I do not want you, that I find you unattractive, that I take no pleasure in you."

Phoebe's body sang with the memory of his hands and mouth upon her, and she knew that he could not have done such things to her without desiring her, without wanting her for who and what she was.

Cato cupped her face in his hands. He spoke gravely, "You are lovely, Phoebe. Every inch of you is beautiful."

"Perhaps it's fortunate, then, that there are so many inches of me," Phoebe said with a tremulous smile.

"I would not have one ounce less of you," Cato said firmly.

He smiled and pressed the tip of her nose with his thumb. "But I do, however, agree that you're quite the untidiest individual I've ever come across. Nothing however elegant seems to stay done up on you for more than a moment." He raised a quizzical eyebrow. "But strangely I begin to find it appealing."

Cato drew her against him, his hands spanning her back. She turned her head against his chest and rested her cheek on his heart, hearing its steady rhythm beneath her ear. Cato spoke softly into her hair.

"I have a cold and savage tongue, Phoebe, I know it. I was unwontedly harsh this morning and I will try not to be again. But I need your word that in future you will come to me at the first sign of trouble."

"I did come to you about Meg," Phoebe reminded him, lifting her head from his chest to look up into his face.

"I won't fail you again," he promised quietly.

"But you're not always very accessible," Phoebe pointed out.

"Well, that probably won't change." His voice lost its earlier softness. "At least not while this damnable war continues.

And Cromwell and his ilk pick fights among—" He stopped abruptly. "But that need not concern you."

He scribbled down her spine with his thumbnail and then stroked her flanks in a quick light caress. "Let us put this behind us now, my sweet. Get dressed quickly. It's long past suppertime."

Phoebe had forgotten that she was naked. She glanced down at herself with an air of such surprise that Cato burst into laughter. "I really do believe that if I hadn't reminded you, you'd have wandered out of here without a stitch on," he declared. "Hurry now." He turned to the door. "Everyone will be waiting supper for us and then I must go back to headquarters."

"You won't be back tonight?" She couldn't hide her disappointment.

"No. This business with the king's escape will take hours to thrash out." He left the chamber.

Phoebe wrapped her arms around her body in a convulsive hug. Her skin seemed warmer, more alive than usual where Cato had touched her. And there was a wonderful warm spot deep inside her, as if a lamp had been lit.

In her head she could hear his voice reading Dudley's speech . . . her creation into which she'd poured so much of her heart's hunger . . . a world of her own where two lovers could express their love and their need without fear. She'd responded to his reading without thought, the words flowing so naturally from her lips. And for a moment, just a moment, she had thought that Cato had been living in that same dream world.

Much later, after Cato had left for headquarters, Phoebe went to Meg's bedside.

The room was lit by a single candle on the bedside table, but Meg was awake, her face white and shadowed against the pillows.

"How are you?" Phoebe sat on the edge of the bed and took her hand. It seemed thinner, almost clawlike, the fingers lacking their usual strength.

"I'll mend," Meg said.

Phoebe squeezed her hand. "Cato had the witch finder whipped for vagrancy and he's turned the vicar out of his living."

"Harsh," Meg observed.

"After what they did to you?" Phoebe exclaimed softly.

Meg shook her head. "Vengeance is mine, sayeth the lord." She gave a short laugh. "No, I have no sympathy with those two. But I'll be sorry if he took revenge on the villagers. They can't help their ignorance."

"No," Phoebe agreed, although she couldn't rid her mind of the image of those hate-filled faces seeming to press against her.

"Giles said at supper that he'd arrested Ben from the Bear and Gabriel Benson, and he was going to have them put in the stocks in the morning. His men had discovered that they'd incited the others, but Cato said he'd changed his mind, there'd been enough violence. He told Giles a night in the jail would give them enough of a fright. I think that's right, don't you?"

"Aye," Meg said. "Punishing superstition is no answer. We have to eradicate it."

"What will you do now?"

"Go back," Meg said. "Do what I always do."

"You could bear to help those people again?" Phoebe shook her head with a shudder of disgust. "I don't think I could bring myself to speak to any of them again. Except perhaps Granny Spruel."

"It's understandable."

"But you will go on helping them?"

"If I can gain their trust again, yes. There's more to physicking than herbs and simples, Phoebe. The mind is often as much in need of healing as the body. If I can show them the evil of superstition, then I'll not have wasted my time."

"You're such a *good* woman," Phoebe said fiercely. "They don't deserve you."

"As if that had anything to do with anything," Meg scoffed. She closed her eyes. "I'm tired, Phoebe."

"I'll leave you to sleep." Phoebe bent to kiss her. "I'll come back in the morning."

She went to her own deserted bedchamber and looked at the large empty bed. Then, grabbing up her nightrail, she picked up the candle and made her way to Olivia's bedchamber.

Olivia stirred and said sleepily, "Is something the matter?"

"Do you mind if I share your bed?"

"No, not at all." Olivia moved up accommodatingly and sat up, blinking sleep from her eyes. "I'd be glad of the c-company. Every time I c-close my eyes I see that dreadful man with his pins."

"I know." Phoebe threw off her clothes and scrambled into her nightgown. She slipped beneath the covers. "I wonder what'll happen now that the king's escaped."

"Maybe the war'll be over." But Olivia didn't sound too convinced. "I c-can't even remember properly a time when there was peace. Can you?"

"Just," Phoebe said. "But Cato once said that even when it's over it won't really be over. He said it would be a Pyrrhic victory at best."

"What did he mean by that?"

"I don't know. He wouldn't say. Just like he wouldn't talk about what's going on at headquarters. He started to say something and then stopped. Why won't he tell me these things?" She leaned over to blow out the candle and lay down beside Olivia.

"It's so maddening," she muttered.

17

"It's so frustrating, Meg!" Phoebe paced Meg's bedchamber impatiently, returning to her theme the next morning. "Why should men have this attitude? Women are just as capable as they are. Maybe we're not such good soldiers, although Portia's as good as any man, but there are other things we're better at. And we can have opinions, can't we?"

She came to a standstill beside the bed, where Meg sat up against piled pillows. Phoebe was glad to see that she was looking much more herself this morning, the light back in her shrewd eyes, the humor returned to her fine mouth. Her hair hung in long plaits over her shoulders, making her look younger than Phoebe had ever seen her. The long sleeves and high neck of Mistress Bisset's borrowed nightgown hid the bruises and puncture wounds of her ordeal, but the striped cambric swamped her, so that she looked much frailer than usual.

"We can have opinions and give advice and good counsel. Can't we?" Phoebe demanded.

"Without doubt," Meg said with a serene smile. "But I doubt that husband of yours will ever accept that."

"But he *must*!" Phoebe wailed. "I don't want to be left out of everything that matters to him . . . kept swaddled in some cocoon, told that I mustn't bother my pretty head with male concerns. Not that I have a pretty head," she amended.

"What you have is a deal more attractive than mere prettiness," Meg said, her smile broadening.

"Oh?" Phoebe's interest was piqued. "What's that, then?"

"Character," Meg replied.

"Oh." Phoebe was disappointed. Character seemed like a very dull endowment when compared with beauty and elegance.

"And brains," Meg continued.

"Well, much good they are if no one acknowledges them or lets me put them to good use," Phoebe said, aggrieved.

"Why would you want to be involved in your husband's self-important absorptions, anyway?" Meg said. "In my experience, men are always attaching too much importance to trivialities."

"But the war isn't trivial."

Meg shook her head. "It's about power, Phoebe. Wars are all about power and greed. Men's obsessions. Women deal in life and death; birth, sickness, health. Those are the warp and woof of existence, not the posturing and pronouncing and proselytizing that make men believe they're running the world as they kill each other for their own self-interest."

As always, Meg made sense. Phoebe frowned. "Maybe you're right, but I can't make miracles. I have to deal with what's at hand. Cato has to see that I have something to offer, that he can confide in me." She thumped down on the edge of the bed.

"Well, if you must pursue such an object, you'll have to prove your competence to your husband in some way . . . if you could rescue him from some dire peril, for instance . . ."

"Oh, now you're making fun," Phoebe accused. "Cato's never in dire peril, anyway, except perhaps on the battlefield. And I can't do much to help him there. . . . Now, who could that be?" She slid off the bed at the sound of a knock at the door. "Come in."

Brian Morse entered the chamber, a sheaf of papers in his hand. "Forgive the intrusion, but I've been looking all over for you, Phoebe. I wished to give you these." He behaved as if the woman in the bed didn't exist.

"Ah, my savior," declared Meg. "The scourge of witch finders the length and breadth of the country."

A flash of anger crossed Brian's little brown eyes at this cool irony, but he ignored Meg and continued to speak directly to Phoebe. "Mistress Bisset told me where to find you. I've brought you the patterns for those gowns I promised you." He held out the papers. "I need to show them to you and discuss the right fabrics to choose."

"My, my. Is there no end to your talents, young man?" murmured Meg. "The nemesis of witch finders is also a couturier."

Phoebe tried to hide her smile. She was well aware that Brian's arrogant attitude had annoyed Meg. And she could quite understand why. He was treating her as if she was utterly beneath his notice.

"Let us look at them here. Meg will be interested to see them too. And I should be glad of her opinion." Phoebe hitched herself onto the bed again and offered Brian a sunny smile that nonetheless held a grit of determination. She extended her hand for the drawings.

Brian looked comically astounded, as if the ground had been cut from beneath his feet when he wasn't looking. He remembered that she'd snubbed him once before. Her spirit had intrigued rather than annoyed him then, but to be finessed by her in front of an insolent, disreputable village woman . . . for her to imply that this *peasant's* opinion on *his* sketches would be of value to her . . . It was insupportable!

He held on to the drawings, saying coldly, "When you're not so busy, perhaps." He spun on his heel and left the bedchamber, closing the door gently, but not before a smothered chuckle reached him, making his ears burn.

"Oh dear," Phoebe said, her eyes alight with laughter. "He's so pompous, but he *did* rescue you. We must give him some credit."

"A man of an overweening conceit," Meg pronounced.

Then her expression sobered. "I wouldn't trust him an inch, Phoebe."

"Why not? What do you know of him?" She was immediately intrigued.

"I know nothing of him, but I assure you he's not trustworthy."

Phoebe had great respect for Meg's intuitions. "That seems to be everyone else's opinion also," she conceded. "But I had thought maybe to use him . . . to pick his brains, perhaps, to find out more about the politics and the tactics of the war . . . all the things Cato won't tell me. Then I could surprise Cato with what I know. What do you think?"

"I think," Meg said consideringly, "that if you play with fire, you'll burn your fingers."

"I'll be careful," Phoebe assured her, sliding off the bed. "I'd better go and placate him. I'm sure he knew we were laughing at him."

"Have a care," Meg said somberly. "He'll be a bad enemy."

"I'll bring you an infusion when I come back," Phoebe promised cheerfully as she left the room.

In the corridor she hesitated, wondering where Brian might have gone. She decided to try the library and hurried towards the stairs. But she didn't have to go very far. Brian Morse was coming up the stairs as she reached the head.

"Dare I hope you could spare me a few minutes?" he inquired, his face still dark, his eyes hooded. "I worked many hours on those drawings."

"I ask your pardon if I offended you," Phoebe said frankly. "But Meg is my friend and you insulted her by ignoring her."

"It is not my custom to engage in social intercourse with villagers," he stated. "But I have some things I wish to discuss with you, so we'll put it behind us."

Pompous was hardly an adequate description, Phoebe decided. But she merely offered a vague smile as she said, "Please do show me the drawings. I'm most eager to see them."

Brian handed them to her, saying as he did so, "There is another matter . . . one of great delicacy. I fear all is not well with your husband."

"What do you mean?" Phoebe demanded sharply, looking up from her perusal of Brian's sketches. All interest in playing games with the man had vanished. "What has happened? Has he returned from headquarters?"

"No, not as yet." Brian laid a hand on her arm. "But I've heard some disturbing information."

"What?" Phoebe looked at him in alarm.

Brian looked around, up and down the passage. "As I said, it's a matter of great delicacy. Where can we talk in strict privacy?"

"I was going to the stillroom to mix an infusion for Meg. No one will disturb us there." Phoebe hurried down the corridor, Brian on her heels.

In the aromatic quiet of the stillroom, where the late morning sun fell in a great golden swath from a round window high up in the wall over the orderly shelves of lavenderstrewn linens, Phoebe said without preamble, "So, what is it? What have you to tell me?"

Brian looked concerned. "I've heard that Lord Granville is facing difficulties among the high command . . . there are serious questions of his loyalty."

"Oh, what nonsense!" Phoebe exclaimed, her eyes flaring with indignation. "Who could have told you such a thing?"

"I have many sources of information," Brian told her gravely. "Believe me, I know much that goes on in both headquarters."

"You mean spying?" Phoebe's nose wrinkled unconsciously. "How could you possibly have spies in Parliament's camp? You're a Royalist."

"Was," Brian reminded her gently. "But believe me, Phoebe, my work has always been one of digging for information. Distasteful, you may think it, but it's a vital part of warfare. But then, a woman couldn't possibly be expected to understand," he added with a smile that was meant to be kind but that appeared as flagrantly patronizing.

"Oh, pah!" Phoebe said. "You sound just like Cato. I fail to see the male mystery involved in killing and being killed."

"Well, perhaps we men like to think of it as our preserve," Brian said pacifically. "Historically it always has been."

Phoebe's expression seemed to indicate that she was unimpressed with historical precedent.

He continued. "But in truth, Phoebe, Cato is in difficulties and I would like to help him, to prove my loyalty to him."

"Why don't you talk to him about it, then?"

"Because he won't listen to me! God knows, I've tried, but he's as stubborn as a mule. And he still doesn't trust me, I'm certain of it, despite all the information I've given him."

"What is it exactly that you've heard?" Phoebe turned from him and began to select jars from the shelf behind her. She was trying to hide the keenness of her interest. Perhaps this was her opportunity to prove herself to Cato.

"I know that Cato has come under suspicion by his party's high command. Cromwell has questioned his commitment. It's a very dangerous situation and the king's escape yesterday has only made it worse. It looks as if he might have allowed him to slip away."

"How do you know this?" Phoebe realized she was holding her breath.

"There was a skirmish several weeks ago and the king's men took several prisoners. They became quite voluble . . ." Brian shrugged and left Phoebe to come to her own conclusions as to the means by which they became so.

"It's also been reliably said that Lord Granville has questioned Cromwell's motives in waging this war. That's not an accusation to make lightly."

That was a master stroke, Brian reckoned. He'd heard two troopers discussing the rumor the previous evening, when tongues were running loose over jugs of ale around the brazier in the stable yard. It might or might not be true, but it was still powerful fuel to the fire he was building here.

Phoebe measured herbs into the mortar and took up the pestle. She said nothing as she worked, and the rich aroma of crushed juniper, thyme, and lovage filled the stillroom. Brian's words had the ring of truth, but she was mindful of Meg's warning and determined to tread lightly.

"Do you think your husband would listen to you?" Brian asked into the fragrant silence.

"No. He considers his affairs to be solely his preserve."

Brian nodded in silent satisfaction as he heard the disgruntled note. He was on the right track. "Perhaps there's a way around that," he mused, watching her profile from beneath lowered lids.

"What way?"

"Well, if Lord Granville refuses to see any need to convince his own party of his loyalty, perhaps his true friends should convince them for him."

Phoebe turned slowly, the pestle still in her hand. "What do you mean?"

Brian appeared to ponder the question for a minute, then he said consideringly, "I'm thinking that if someone sent a document to Parliament under the Granville seal . . . something that proves Cato's loyalty conclusively. That would be one way. But one would need access to his seal, of course . . ."

Phoebe frowned. "What kind of a document?"

"A piece of information from the king's camp," Brian said promptly.

"And where would we get that?"

"I would supply it." Brian pursed his lips. "The king is going to seek help from the Scots. But to get it, he must make certain promises. I have conclusive proof that he'll not keep those promises. If the Scots knew that, then they'd hand the king over to Parliament. If Cato provides Parliament with that information, his loyalty and commitment would go unquestioned."

Phoebe shook her head. This was too much to take in. She felt utterly out of her depth. She knew that Brian had been supplying Parliament with information from the king's camp, but how could he know so much about Parliament's affairs? But then, he was right. What did she know of the devious workings of a spy?

One issue, however, seemed simple enough. "But why don't you give this information to Cato yourself? Then he can put to rest any suspicions himself."

"You really aren't much of a conspirator, are you?" Brian's smile was almost pitying. He laid a hand on her shoulder. "Let us be a little more devious here, Phoebe. I had thought to kill two birds with one stone. You feel excluded from his life, don't you?" His little eyes gazed intently into her own.

"I know how difficult that is, because I know how he holds himself apart from those who love him. He did it with my mother, and he's always done it with me. I would help you change that. If he once sees how capable you are, and how ready and willing to help him, to partner him, then he might change the habits that hurt so many people. Think about it."

Every word he spoke was true. It was what Meg had said too. She had to show Cato what she could do.

"You have this document? This proof of the king's intentions?" she asked slowly.

Brian nodded. "Of course, I could simply take it to Parliament myself and thus prove my own loyalty beyond question, but it hurts that Cato won't trust me. I'm his heir, after all."

He looked closely at her as he said this, and noticed the faint color blooming on her cheekbones, a slight quiver of her full mouth.

"Until, of course, you give him a son," he added with a

tiny smile. "Forgive the indelicacy, but it is a matter of some interest to me."

"Yes," Phoebe agreed. "I suppose it is."

Brian waited a heartbeat to see if she would say anything else, give him some clue as to whether she was carrying a child already, but she did not and he continued as if the previous exchange had never occurred. "So from my own point of view, this rather more devious approach might give him a reason to be grateful to me as well as to you."

It seemed to make sense. Phoebe had seen the constraint between Cato and his stepson, although Cato never referred directly to it. And the idea that Brian had his own motives for helping her was somehow reassuring. Total lack of self-interest, she thought, would have been suspicious.

"How do we do this, then?" Now she made no attempt to disguise her eagerness.

"We have to be able to use Cato's seal, as I said. The document must bear his seal, otherwise there'll be no proof that it comes from him."

"He seals things with his ring sometimes," Phoebe said slowly. "But he never takes it off."

"True, but he also has the big Granville seal. He keeps it locked in the drawer of the table in his study." Brian watched her through narrowed eyes. He had her now. The unwitting architect of her husband's downfall.

"If it's locked away, I can't see it's much use to us," Phoebe pointed out.

Dear God, the innocent! "We have to get it," he said patiently. "We have to get the key and borrow the seal. Affix it to the document, send the document to Cromwell."

Phoebe just looked at him in blank amazement. "That would be stealing," she said.

"Borrowing," Brian corrected as patiently as before. "Not stealing, but borrowing. And just for a very few minutes. He'll never know, or at least not until all the good has been done and you can explain it all to him."

"You don't think he'd be angry at my *borrowing* his seal?" Phoebe demanded incredulously.

"Perhaps a little," Brian conceded. "But the end justifies the means. He'll see that. He's a reasonable man, just rather stubborn about certain things." His expression became very grave again.

"I don't know how to convince you of how serious the situation is, Phoebe. If the high command decide Cato has betrayed them by letting the king slip, he'll be destroyed." He thumped a fist into the palm of his other hand. "It's so frustrating, because he refuses to acknowledge the seriousness of it. He can't see why anyone would question his loyalty."

"Well, neither can I," Phoebe said tartly.

"But they *are* questioning it."

Phoebe bit her lip. She knew it was true. However absurd it was. And Cato's careless dismissal was not helping matters. She'd heard the unspoken criticism in Giles Crampton's responses yesterday.

"Cato keeps his keys on his belt." Brian pressed his advantage as he saw her hesitation. "At night you could borrow them. Press them into a ball of wax, and I can have copies made very easily. Then we unlock the drawer and borrow the seal . . . just for a minute."

"Where's this document?" Phoebe asked. She was still unsure. It was all so smooth and convincing and sounded so easy. But it was also wrong! She couldn't imagine stealing Cato's keys while he slept. It was so . . . so impossibly *wrong*.

"Among my private papers."

"Well, I'd have to see it before I agreed to anything," Phoebe stated. "Maybe, as you say, the end justifies the means, but I want to see what that end is."

Every time he thought he'd got her, she wriggled away

again. Every time he thought he understood how to manipulate her, she suddenly threw an obstacle in the way. Naive one minute and infuriatingly down-to-earth the next. He had to learn never to take her responses for granted. She was unpredictable and definitely not the easy mark she appeared.

He wanted this business over and done with. He wanted to see Cato in the dust. He wanted to see him dead. He wanted to see himself the legal owner of title and possessions. And then he would find some way to deal with this odd, troublesome creature. She was an untidy, ramshackle apology for a woman, and yet she had this peculiar potential. Every time he looked at her, he saw it. He couldn't understand where it came from.

Now he'd have to produce a document that didn't exist, and produce it in a convincing form. It was a painstaking task that would take him hours even once he'd laid hands on the right materials.

"May I see it now?" she pressed.

"My private papers are not here. They're in safekeeping elsewhere," he said. "I'll fetch them and you'll see it in the morning."

"I would have thought they'd be safest under your eye," Phoebe said with her customary bluntness. "It seems strange to hide them elsewhere. You have no other shelter but your stepfather's roof, or so you've always said, now that you've been discredited with the king. Where would you put private papers? In a tree, or under a stone? Or are they with some friend? Although I didn't think you had any left after you switched sides."

Brian listened to this artless speech that had gone straight to the heart of the single flaw in his hastily concocted explanation.

"If I were to tell you, they would no longer be in safekeeping," he stated dismissively. "You know nothing about the work I do. It's beyond your ken, my dear girl."

Phoebe considered. If his work was all to do with stealing

and borrowing and spying and hiding, then she wasn't sure she wanted to know about it. But the fact remained that he knew what he was talking about, and he was offering to help her as a by-product of helping himself. Why shouldn't she take advantage of it?

"Show it to me in the morning, then," she said. "Now, can we look at your sketches?"

"Most certainly." Brian smoothed the papers out on the linen shelf. "This one should be made up in linen, a loose weave, to accentuate the flow of the skirts."

"What color?"

He looked at her consideringly. "A gold or bronze," he said. "Now, this one in cambric. A simple patterned cambric."

"They look very sophisticated," Phoebe said in some awe. "For everyday gowns, I mean."

"Compared with your present everyday gowns, they are," he said bluntly. "It shouldn't take the seamstress more than a week to make these up for you. Less if she has help. Then I suggest you throw away those dreadful garments you persist in wearing. And why don't you do your hair the way I recommended?"

"It takes so long," Phoebe said apologetically. "It doesn't seem worth it when I'm just doing ordinary things in the house or the village."

"Now that," Brian scolded, "is a great piece of nonsense. You should always look your best, whatever you're doing. Cato has always appreciated the finer points of women's dress. What do you think he must think when he sees you dressed like that?" He gestured to her old gown. "That you don't care to please him?"

"Oh, but I do!" Phoebe exclaimed. "Indeed I do."

"Well, I know that, but does he?" He smiled suddenly. "Come, now, Phoebe, you must make the most of yourself. You have much to make the most of."

He turned to the door before she could recover from the careless compliment, saying over his shoulder, "If your husband returns this night, maybe you'll have the chance to get the imprint of his keys. Do you have wax?"

"It's easy enough to acquire," Phoebe muttered, still taken aback by the turn in the conversation. In these matters she trusted Brian's judgment absolutely, and while, because she knew he was right, it was most unpleasant to be taken to task by him, by the same token, such a compliment had the ring of truth. And that was as disconcerting as the rebuke.

Brian nodded his agreement and left the stillroom, his mind swiftly turning to the next stage as soon as the door closed behind him. He needed materials in order to forge a document that would satisfy Phoebe. He'd have to ride into Oxford for what he wanted. There were those in head-quarters who could provide him with what he needed. A copy of the king's signature and the heavy parchment the king would use, paper that bore a convincingly important seal.

It could be done; it was just a nuisance. But it would be worth it in the end. Once he had the Granville seal in his possession, then he could wreak merry hell among Parliament's men.

Of course, no document incriminating the king would be forwarded to Cromwell, but Lord Granville would be responsible for any number of leaked documents contain-ing top secret information sent under his seal to the king. Once Brian had a key to the marquis's desk and thus to his private papers, there was no limit to what havoc he could wreak.

Brian had practiced over the years forging his step-father's signature, but the opportunity to use it had never before presented quite such heady possibilities. It wouldn't take long before the entire fabric of Parliament's com-mand structure was in tatters. And if Cato was executed for treason, then Brian's dirty work would have fallen to an-other hand.

It was all highly satisfactory, despite this minor inconve-nience. Brian set his horse to a gallop along the Oxford road.

• • •

"*The king's escape alters matters considerably.*" Lord Fairfax scratched his nose with the tip of his knife as he leaned over the map spread out on the long table.

"I see no way to intercept him on his way to the Border, although we'll send a party in pursuit. But there are any number of routes he could take," Cromwell said sourly.

"It prolongs matters some," Cato put in. "But eventually he'll renege on whatever promises he makes to the Scots . . . or they'll impose conditions that he can't even pretend to agree to . . . and they'll turn him over to us."

"You hope so, I assume?" Cromwell regarded him with a frown.

"I know so," Cato said firmly. "What we do with him when we have him will then be a matter for discussion. But I see little point in argument until he's in our hands."

"Granville speaks truth," Lord Manchester said. "Let's not squabble over the final outcome until we have the possibility of a final outcome to hand."

"We could have that now if the king had not been permitted to gallop away from a sizable troop of our militia," Cromwell stated.

There were only the four men in the large ground-floor room of the farmhouse. Cato said quietly, "Oliver, if it was a mistake, then I beg indulgence. It was growing dark. We came upon them suddenly. There was no indication that the king was among them."

"You wouldn't expect there to be," Cromwell growled.

"No, indeed not." Cato shrugged. "I doubt there's a man among us who hasn't seen an opportunity slip through his fingers."

"Aye, there's truth in that," Lord Manchester declared. "Let's move on to other matters, Oliver. Of pressing concern is this business with Walter Strickland. We've had no information from the Low Countries for two months now. The two agents we've sent to contact him have failed to return. It seems imperative to me that we discover if Strickland is still alive. If he is, then his dispatches are not getting through to us."

"And now, with this new development, it's of paramount importance we discover what position the king of Orange will take in supporting Charles in his bid for protection from the Scots," Lord Fairfax said.

"He'll support him if he agrees to establish the Presbyterian Church in England," Cato observed, moving away from the table, his hand absently stroking the hilt of his sword. "But will kinship ties prevail if Charles loses Scottish support?"

There was a moment of silence as the four men considered this. Then Cromwell said, "We need to send someone to find Strickland and bring him back if he's still alive. We need face-to-face discussions now; dispatches are too uncertain."

"I'll go," Cato said quietly. "This situation needs a more than ordinary ambassador. And there are no pressing military concerns while the king's pushing his way up to Scotland. Hopton in the West Country has thrown in the sponge. There are no more significant pockets of resistance."

Cromwell regarded him thoughtfully. "You have a point, Granville. But the mission carries some hazard, it seems to me."

Cato raised an eyebrow. His hand was now motionless on his sword hilt. "You think I might run from hazard, General?"

"No, of course there's no such implication, Granville!" Lord Fairfax exclaimed. "No man would ever question your courage."

"Not with impunity, certainly," Cato agreed coolly, but his eyes still rested on the general as gently he drew his sword an inch from its sheath.

Oliver Cromwell picked at a scab on his chin, then he

shook his head slowly. " 'Twas just an observation, Cato. We've sent two agents who've disappeared into thin air. Strickland has vanished, to all intents and purposes. It seems obvious there is hazard in the mission. But I believe you're well suited to take it if you're willing."

"I have already said so," Cato returned, pushing his sword back in place. The air seemed to lift and lighten.

"I'll take ship from Harwich to the Hook, then down to Rotterdam," Cato stated.

"The Black Tulip is the usual point of contact with Strickland," Fairfax said. "How many men will you take with you?"

"None." It was a crisp negative.

"Not even Giles Crampton?" Fairfax was incredulous.

"Not even Giles. I've no desire to draw attention to myself," Cato pointed out. "And clumping around Rotterdam asking questions in the company of a broad Yorkshireman will certainly make us conspicuous. Giles is a magnificent soldier, but espionage is not his forte."

He picked up his cloak and gloves from the settle beside the empty hearth. "I'll travel as an English merchant looking to find transport for lace and Delftware. It'll give me a good excuse to roam around the port. If there's information to be found, it'll be found where sailors and ruffians congregate."

"Aye," Cromwell agreed with a dour smile. "And by the same token, you'd best watch your back."

"I'm a past master at that, Oliver." There was a small pause as the possible significance of the remark sank in. "However, I don't expect to look for the knife in the hands of my friends," Cato continued deliberately.

"I've no wish for a falling out," Cromwell said gruffly after a minute. He held out his hand. "Godspeed, Cato."

Cato took it in a brief firm clasp, then shook hands with the others and left, calling for Giles Crampton as he emerged into the bright sunlight.

18

"*But how long will you be gone?*" *Phoebe asked in dismay,* pushing herself upright against Cato's bare chest.

"I can't say for sure." He reached up to pull her down again, but she resisted his encircling arm.

"But Italy is such a long way away. And this mission . . . it'll be dangerous, won't it?" She knelt on the bed, looking down at him.

"No more dangerous than anything else," Cato said. "Come now, Phoebe, if I told you I was going to be away at a siege, you wouldn't give it a second thought."

"Oh, yes I would," she declared. "I'd give it dozens of thoughts! You could be killed at a siege, and that's not a matter for indifference. How could it be?"

"Maybe it isn't," Cato conceded. "But this journey will be no more dangerous than anything else I've been doing in the last several years." He smiled up at her with a hint of placation, twining his fingers in the luxuriant fall of her hair obscuring her face. "And a damn sight less dangerous than a pitched battle. And I've been in a good many of those."

"But you could be gone *months*!" she wailed. "Across the sea. You could sink and be drowned."

Cato laughed. "No, that's not going to happen. Although I admit I'd sooner not have to go anywhere by ship. I'm a terrible sailor."

"How?"

"Sick," he said with a grimace. "Sick as a dog from the moment the vessel puts out of harbor."

"I wonder if *I* would be," Phoebe mused, her imagination caught by a whole range of possibilities.

"Well, you're not about to find out," Cato declared. "Now, come back down here and let's go back to where we were."

Thoughtfully Phoebe nibbled her lip for a second. Then she grinned mischievously and said, "I've a mind to try something different, my lord."

She swung herself astride him as he lay supine, and ran her hands up over his chest, her fingers playing in the dusting of dark curls clustered around his nipples.

Cato brought up his knees so that he was supporting her back and then watched her lazily through hooded eyes.

Phoebe moved her hands down over his flat belly and then up over his rib cage. She loved the feel of his body, the surprisingly soft skin stretched taut over the ridged muscles. She cupped his biceps in her palms, ran her hands down the corded sinews of his forearms where the hair grew thick and dark. She loved his wrists. They were slender, bony, amazingly strong; and his hands, broad yet elegant, hard yet so surprisingly tender, the fingers long, the nails pared and pink.

She caught her bottom lip between her teeth as she concentrated on an exploration that never failed to delight her, never failed to reveal new areas, new possibilities, however often she made it. Leaning against his legs, she reached behind her to run her hands down the long, firm length of his outer thighs, then behind to the backs of his legs, the deep hollow behind his knees, the corded muscles in his calves, the sinew that ran from his knees to his buttocks.

Playfully she kept her exploration away from his sex, even as she felt his penis harden and flicker against the base of her spine.

Cato reached up and took her breasts in his palms, caressing them languidly before he brought his mouth to her nipples, inhaling the delicate scent of her skin mingling with the sharper fragrance of arousal. The cleft of her body was hot and moist against his belly as at last she stroked his engorged and needy shaft of flesh. His teeth grazed the erect crowns of her breasts as he sucked upon them, flicking with his tongue, knowing how she loved such caresses, how they never failed to bring her to a peak of delight.

Phoebe moaned softly and when his hands slid down her body, beneath her bottom, lifting her, she guided herself onto him, taking him deep within her with a little crow of triumph that made Cato chuckle through his own pleasure.

Leaning back against his drawn-up knees, she moved herself upon him and around him, glorying in the control she had over her own sensation. Her eyes widened in delighted surprise as she understood how she could heighten her own pleasure by discovering where deep inside her the point of contact was the most sensitive.

Cato continued to play with her breasts, content to let her bring them both to fruition in her own time and at her own pace. Her movements became more rapid, her skin damp and glowing with the growing intensity of sensation. She pressed the heated cleft of her body hard into his belly and cried out with delight as the waves of pleasure radiated through her loins, streaming into every cell and pore.

At the same instant, Cato dropped his knees and drove his hips upward to meet her, and Phoebe fell forward, unable to contain a pleasure so exquisite it verged on pain. She felt his climax throbbing against her womb, and the hot flood of his seed laved the tight sheath that held him, and again, impossibly, the wave broke over her and she thought she couldn't endure such joy.

Cato stroked her damp back as she lay against him, her heart beating as fast as if it would burst from her chest.

"How was that possible?" she murmured after long minutes. "I don't know what happened."

He pushed her hair away from her forehead, catching it at the nape of her neck so that the cool air could get to her heated skin. "You have a gift for loving," he said with a soft laugh. "It's not given to everyone."

"I always knew I had to be a little lucky," Phoebe mumbled. "Diana couldn't have had *all* the advantages."

Cato slid his hands down between their slick bodies and gently lifted her off him. She fell on the bed beside him and lay breathing deeply, one round arm flung across his body.

Cato thought she was asleep. He continued to stroke her back with little circular caresses, thinking how he didn't wish to leave her. It was a revelation that had come slowly and one that he had tried to resist. But it was unavoidable. His offer to take the mission to Rotterdam would have been perfectly natural for the man he'd been before Phoebe had come into his life. He would not then have given a thought for his personal safety, and certainly not cared a farthing for leaving house and hearth, wife and children, for however long was necessary.

Even though he was keeping his destination a secret, offering a false trail for any malign ears, the hazards were undeniable. And for the first time in his military career he would have preferred to avoid them.

His hand stilled in the small of Phoebe's back. It was one of his favorite places. There was something so vulnerable and yet so sensual about the little dip, before it swelled into the rounded curve of her bottom.

To be absent from thy heart is torment . . .

A woman bound in love . . .

He couldn't forget those words she had written, could hear in his head his own voice reading them, could hear Phoebe's reciting the answering lines.

"I think it would be best if I came with you," Phoebe murmured.

"It most certainly would not be best," he said roundly.

Phoebe rolled over and sat up cross-legged on the bed beside him. She brushed her hair out of her eyes and fixed him with an appealing gaze. "I can't stay here for weeks and weeks without you. I shall go into a decline."

Cato laughed. "I'm immensely complimented, but the answer is still no."

Phoebe twisted a lock of hair around her finger as she continued to regard him thoughtfully, then she said, "So where will you take ship?"

"Harwich."

"That's several days' ride, isn't it?"

"Three days probably."

"Well, if I accompany you to Harwich, we'll have three more days together. I've never seen the sea."

"You couldn't possibly ride that far," he said.

"I will undertake to ride that far and ride back. You'll take an escort to Harwich; they can bring me home again." Her eyes were bright, her cheeks delicately flushed.

She leaned down and kissed his nose. "Why can't I?"

"Apart from the simple fact that you don't know one end of a horse from another?" he inquired dryly.

"How soon before you leave?"

"Two days. It'll take that long to put matters in order here and—"

"Then I have two days!" Phoebe declared. "I will spend the next two days on Sorrel and I'll prove to you that I can do it. If I can prove it to you, will you let me come?"

"No, Phoebe, it's out of the question. Your place is here, not racketing around the countryside with my troopers. Now let's go to sleep. I've been riding all day and I'm awearied."

Phoebe's mouth had taken a stubborn turn, but she lay down beside him as he reached out and snuffed the candle.

She lay listening as his breathing moved into the deep, regular rhythm of sleep. He was *impossible*! she thought. There was no logical reason why she shouldn't go with him if she was willing to ride.

Silver moonlight fell onto the chest at the foot of the bed and caught the bright gleam of his belt buckle. His keys were still hooked to his belt.

It would be the matter of a moment to take the soft wax that had fallen into the saucer that held the candle and take an imprint of the keys. She hadn't seen Brian's document yet, but with Cato about to leave, there was no telling when she'd have this opportunity again . . . at least before he returned from Italy.

She slid to the floor. She stood immobile, listening to his breathing. The rhythm didn't change. She crept on tiptoe around the bed to the candle and lifted it from the saucer. There was a goodly quantity of spilled wax, and it had not yet hardened.

Phoebe scooped the wax into her palm and kneaded it into a ball, then she tiptoed to the foot of the bed. She wouldn't even have to remove the keys from his belt. But which one was the key to his desk? One of the two smaller ones, it had to be.

She knelt, holding her breath, and gingerly separated one of the small keys from the rest of the bunch. There was a tiny chink as one slipped and knocked against its fellows. Phoebe held her breath. She had no idea how she would explain what she was doing on the floor in the dark, clutching a ball of wax, if Cato awoke.

Her blood was so loud in her ears it almost deafened her. Swiftly she pressed the key hard into the wax, then she turned the ball over and did the same with the second of the smaller keys.

It was done. The rest was simple. If she decided to go along with Brian's plan, he could have the keys copied. Cato would be away. It would be a simple matter to open the desk, borrow his seal, affix it to the document, and sent it to headquarters. She could tell the messenger who carried the paper that Cato had left it with her with instructions that she was to see it got to Cromwell as soon as possible. And they would sing Cato's praises to the skies, and no one would ever question his loyalty again. And he would have to look upon his wife, who had saved him from dire peril, as something other than a domestic encumbrance who should know her place.

It was simplicity itself.

Phoebe stood up, the ball of wax flat on her palm. Cato would have to acknowledge then that she was resourceful, able to help him even when he couldn't see difficulties himself. That she could be trusted to partner . . .

Phoebe sat down abruptly on the chest. Trusted? What in the devil's name was she thinking? How could she have been so stupidly naive?

How could he ever trust a wife who went to such devious and distasteful lengths to prove anything? It was a disgusting thing to do. The entire surface of her skin prickled with revulsion. How could she ever had allowed Brian Morse to persuade her that this was even possible?

But she knew the answer. She'd been so eager to find a way to impress upon Cato her worthiness to be taken into his confidence that she'd fallen for Brian's scheme like a ripe plum to the picker. She'd told herself she was using Brian, not the other way around, but of course it had been the other way around. Brian inhabited the nasty, dirty world of spies. Such schemes were second nature to him, and he'd manipulated her like a puppet handler. How had she so easily dismissed Meg's warning? Meg was always right about such things.

Phoebe glanced towards the bed, making out the shape of Cato's body beneath the coverlet. His head was a dark shadow against the white of the pillow, and one strong brown arm was thrust out of the sheet, his hand flung wide, palm up, the fingers curled loosely.

Her heart was swept by an invincible surge of love. And then the familiar wash of frustration. How could she love him so completely, so without condition, knowing that he didn't, perhaps couldn't ever, feel the same for her? Was it something she had to accept?

Her lips set firm. Not yet.

Perhaps there was another way, a more honest and straight-forward way. Perhaps she could catch him off guard. Surprise had always made him more susceptible before, more willing to listen to her. And then she would have something to tell him that would prove what a valuable ally she could be.

Phoebe couldn't imagine why she hadn't thought of this before. Brian had caught her off guard. He'd traded on her emotions to achieve his own ends. But what exactly were those ends? Phoebe now felt sure they had nothing to do with gaining Cato's trust.

Cato would be interested to know of his stepson's nasty little plan. And it would give her every excuse for surprising him.

Phoebe crushed the ball of wax in her hand, kneading it once more into an amorphous shape. She dropped it into the saucer and climbed back into bed.

*B*rian strode into the house the next morning and found it abuzz. "Lord Granville is going away, sir," Bisset informed him. "For quite some time, as I understand it."

"Where to?"

"I couldn't say, sir." Bisset moved off with an air of importance.

Brian stood frowning. How was this going to affect his own plans? And why hadn't Cato told him himself?

"Is Lady Granville in?"

"She went to the stables, I believe, sir."

Brian headed back to the stables. Phoebe, with an expression of grim determination, was stroking the nose of a rather pretty mare.

"Ah, there you are. I was looking for you," Brian said, dropping his voice as he came up to her. "Bisset says your husband's going away."

"Yes." Phoebe nodded.

"Where to?"

"You had better ask Cato," she replied, her tone cool as she forced herself to stroke the length of the mare's neck. Cato hadn't said his destination was a secret, but she had no intention of ever again confiding anything to Mr. Morse.

Brian frowned. Something was amiss. "I have the document to show you," he said, keeping his voice low. "When does Cato leave?"

"He said in two days." Experimentally Phoebe moved her hand up onto the horse's withers. Sorrel turned and nuzzled her neck.

Phoebe controlled the urge to jump back and stood very still. "I wish they didn't have such big yellow teeth," she muttered.

Brian was growing impatient, but he continued to keep his voice at a low pitch although with an edge of urgency. "You'll have to get the keys before he leaves. I imagine, if they're sending him off on some mission, they're trying to get rid of him. If they distrust him, they won't want him around during their debates over the king's future."

He paused for a minute, then added softly, "They might even intend that he not return from this mission. Of course, Cato's so stubborn he wouldn't consider such a possibility."

This had not occurred to Phoebe. Her hand stilled on the mare's neck. Could Parliament be deliberately putting Cato in danger?

"It's even more important now that you get the keys without delay." Brian's low insidious voice flowed over her. "We must convince Cromwell and his peers of Cato's loyalty before it's too late."

What he said made sense, but Phoebe was beyond Brian's seduction now. Somehow she would persuade Cato to listen to reason, persuade him to defend himself against these charges. Somehow she would manage to convince him that she knew what she was talking about.

"No, I'm not going to get the keys," she said, from the

other side of the mare where she was continuing her getting-to-know-you journey.

Brian was suddenly very still. He couldn't have lost her. Yesterday he would have sworn he had her in the palm of his hand. "What do you mean?"

Phoebe reappeared, ducking beneath Sorrel's neck, impressed with the confidence with which she accomplished the maneuver. "It's too dishonest," she stated with devastating candor. "It's a nasty, devious trick. I can't think why I ever thought I could do it. It may be something that *you* could do without conscience, but I can't. I'm not in the habit of it."

Brian could not believe his ears. He had lost her. Without her cooperation his carefully constructed plans were in ruins. How had it happened? What had he missed? What possible mistake could he have made?

"*Why, you stupid little ninny!*" he exploded in an undertone, unable to take in the depths of his disappointment. "You think you can prate ethics at *me*! What do you know of anything? You're a pathetic, infantile fool!"

Instinctively he found the words that would hurt the most. "Look at you . . . a walking disaster, a disgrace to your sex. I tried to help you, but it's hopeless. It would take a miracle to turn you into anything remotely approaching a *woman*! And you, you pitiable scrap of flotsam! You dare to preach to me! Who the hell do you think you are?"

Phoebe stared at him, shrinking from the ugly, twisted viciousness of his countenance. All civility, all grace, had been stripped away, and she knew she was seeing the real Brian. The Brian Meg had seen beneath the urbane surface. The Brian Olivia knew. And it was a terrifying sight. This was a man who knew no boundaries.

"You would ruin everything with your stupid childishness," Brian raged softly. "You think for one moment that you know better than I do? Do you?" He pushed his face close to hers, spittle flying with each word.

Phoebe could find nothing to say. She felt sick. She told

herself that they were in the middle of the stable yard, surrounded by grooms and troopers. Brian might look as if he would hurt her, but he couldn't do so, not here, not now.

"I cannot do it," she repeated, keeping her voice steady even as she took a step back from him. "Deceit is no way to gain someone's trust. You must surely see that."

"You ninny! You utter fool!" he said again, but he was regaining control of himself, and biting scorn replaced the savagery of before. "I offered you a golden opportunity. . . . I should have guessed you wouldn't have the courage or the intelligence to take it." He spun on his heel and stalked away.

Phoebe was shaking. Maybe she'd been a little tactless but nothing she'd said warranted such a violent response.

She found she was stroking Sorrel's neck and discovered that she was gaining some steadying comfort from the animal's placid nuzzling. Brian Morse had had a lot more invested in his nasty little plan than he'd let on; that much was clear. So just what was it that he'd hoped to achieve with her cooperation? Cato would definitely be interested.

"Have I kept you waiting, Phoebe?" Olivia came hurrying across the cobbles. "I was saying goodbye to Meg. She says she's going home today."

"Yes, I know," Phoebe said, sounding distracted. "I tried to persuade her to stay longer, but she wouldn't."

"So, why are we going into Witney?" Olivia turned to mount her own pony, held by a groom.

Phoebe didn't reply immediately as she concentrated on mounting Sorrel with at least an air of confidence. She took up the reins, trying to remember Cato's instructions.

"I need to pawn my rings again," she said when the groom had moved away.

"Are you going to buy more c-clothes?"

"No, I need money for a journey."

Olivia's eyes widened. "Where are you going?"

Phoebe put a finger to her lips as their escort trotted across the yard towards them.

"Are you ready, Lady Granville?"

"Yes, indeed. Ride ahead of us if you please."

"Two in front and two behind, m'lady," the sergeant said. "Those are our orders. There's no knowing what we might meet on the roads."

Phoebe remembered the ambush on the Eynsham road and made no demur. The troopers fell into place and she urged Sorrel into a walk.

Olivia brought her pony alongside. "So, where are you going?" she prompted quietly.

"To Harwich, with Cato."

"But why do you need money?"

"Because he doesn't know I'm going to go with him," Phoebe returned, a sparkle in her eyes. "And I wish to be independent for once."

Olivia could understand this but she looked dubious nevertheless. "You're going to surprise him again?"

"Yes," Phoebe said firmly. "I'm going to give him the surprise of his life."

*C*ato looked up at the sound of a soft tap on the open door of his study. "Good day, Mistress Meg." He half rose from his chair, gesturing that she should come in.

"I'll not keep you above a minute, Lord Granville." Meg came towards him with brisk step. "I wish to thank you for your hospitality. I'm sure it's not what you would have chosen to offer." Her eyes had a twinkle that took any potential sting out of the words. "Phoebe has some of the characteristics of an avalanche on occasion."

"Pray be seated, mistress." Cato indicated the chair. "You're quite recovered?"

"Oh, yes, quite, I thank you."

Cato leaned back in his chair, turning his quill in his hand, regarding the woman keenly. "How do you think you'll be received in the village?"

"There'll be fences to mend," Meg replied. "But as I told Phoebe, you don't fight superstition by running from it. They're ignorant folk but perhaps I can teach them something."

"You're a brave woman."

Meg smiled at that. "Hardly, when I have the might of Lord Granville behind me as a protection. They'll not touch me again."

Cato could detect irony in both smile and tone, but he wasn't sure how to answer it. "Then should I say you're a forgiving woman?"

Meg inclined her head. "Maybe." She rose from her chair. "I'll be leaving now, my lord."

"Just one minute." Cato rose too. He pulled at his chin for a minute while Meg, politely patient, waited for him to gather his thoughts.

Finally he said, "I have to go on a journey. Probably of some months. Would you keep an eye on Phoebe while I'm gone? She trusts and respects you. I can think of no one else who might be able to steer her clear of pitfalls."

Meg regarded him steadily. "Phoebe is her own woman, Lord Granville. If you'll take my advice, you'll give her more credit than you do. She doesn't lack for sense."

"I worry about her," Cato said with a hint of desperation.

Meg paused. "I will have a care for my friend, you may rest assured."

"I thank you," Cato said to her retreating back. Strangely, he felt comforted. The woman had a power about her.

He pulled the bellrope and sat down again, reaching for the small knife he used to sharpen his pens.

"My lord?" Bisset bowed in the doorway.

"Ask Mr. Morse to come to me, if he's in the house." Cato didn't look up from his task.

"I believe he's abovestairs, my lord." Bisset left with stately tread to deliver the summons.

Brian was pacing his bedchamber, trying to calm himself

after that explosion of rage. It had been a grave error, had revealed far too much to Phoebe, and somehow he had to control the damage. His plans were in ruins, and with Cato going away, time was desperately short to come up with an alternative.

Bisset's summons was too soon. The blood was still pounding in his head and he wasn't sure he could show a calm exterior to Cato, but he had no choice but to obey the call. He walked casually downstairs, breathing slowly and deeply, and outside the closed study door he paused, took one more steadying breath, and knocked and opened the door.

"You wished to see me, Lord Granville?"

"Yes, come in, Brian." Cato laid down both quill and knife. Brian looked rather pale, he thought.

"There've been some new developments and I'm going away for several months."

"So I heard, my lord. May I ask where you're going?" Brian gave a slightly self-deprecating smile. "Or is it a state secret?"

"No. I'm going to Italy."

"On a mission for Parliament, I presume."

"You presume correctly." Cato gave him an agreeable nod. There was no reason for Brian to disbelieve this destination. Parliament's agents were spread all over the continent.

"If you've a mind to," Cato continued gravely, "I have a mission for you too."

"Anything I can do to prove myself," Brian said with eager boyish enthusiasm.

"We need someone to go to London, to spend time in the taverns and clubs. We need to gather the temper of the people. With the king on his way to Scotland, it's imperative that we discover what attitude London will take towards a Presbyterian covenant. We need someone who can assess and judge what he hears. I believe you could do that better than anyone."

Brian bowed low. "I'm honored by your trust, sir. I'll go and pack up my traps. I'll be on my way within the hour."

He hastened from the room, his expression now hard, his eyes calculating. He was not going to London. Wherever Cato was going, Brian was going too. One plan was in ruins, but he was adaptable. Another opportunity would turn up if he was ready for it.

19

"*I think someone's followin' us, m'lord.*" Giles eased his mount closer to Cato's on the lane. Frowning, he glanced over his shoulder.

"I've 'ad the feelin' like fer the last five miles. A pricklin' up me back."

"You haven't seen anything?"

"Nah." Giles shook his head. "It's jest a feelin' like."

Cato nodded. "Let's get around that corner and wait for them, shall we?"

"Aye." Giles looked happier, his frown lifting. "Mebbe nothin, but we might as well 'ave a look-see." He dropped back to give instructions to the six troopers accompanying them.

So, why would someone be following them? Cato wondered. If it was someone interested in his movements, they would surely be a little more secretive.

The eight men rounded the corner and Cato drew rein, turning his horse in the middle of the lane. Behind him Giles and the six troopers formed a crescent.

"Hands on your weapons, but no need to draw them," Cato instructed quietly. "We don't want to frighten an innocent party."

He sat his horse, the picture of relaxation, one hand holding the reins resting lightly on the pommel, the other, his whip hand, resting on his thigh. Curiously he waited to see what would appear around the bend.

Phoebe and Sorrel trotted into view. Sorrel whickered nervously at the blockade in front of her and began to dance backwards. Phoebe clung on, pressing her knees into the saddle and praying she wouldn't tumble ignominiously into the mud in front of this astounded audience.

Somehow she managed to bring Sorrel to a halt; either that or Sorrel of her own accord decided to stop. Phoebe was not sure which. But to her unspeakable relief, they were finally still on the lane.

"You stopped," Phoebe said with a touch of indignation. "I didn't expect you to stop until dinnertime."

Cato found his tongue. "What are you doing? Or is that a stupid question?"

"There was something I had to discuss with you," Phoebe said. "So I thought I'd ride after you. I stayed quite close, only just out of sight, in case of trouble," she added, as if this would ease any fear he might have had for her safety.

"How reassuring," Cato murmured. "But what were you intending to do if the mare bolted with you? As I recall, it's a habit horses have had in the past."

"There was no question of that," Phoebe said righteously. "I said I would be able to ride properly in two days, my lord, and I can."

Cato shook his head. "No," he said consideringly. "I wouldn't dignify your seat on the back of that mare with such a description. You look like a particularly uncomfortable sack of potatoes."

"That's unjust!" Phoebe fired back. "Two days ago I could never have stayed on for all these miles. And she *would* have run away with me. But she hasn't shown the slightest inclination to do so."

"She has a particularly amiable disposition," Cato returned. "That was why I bought her."

"Well, it must have had *something* to do with me," Phoebe said, aggrieved. "I've been thrown off horses with backs like tables and the placidity of a half-dead cow before now."

Giles Crampton coughed. Cato glanced over his shoulder and met the open grins of the men behind him.

"Anyway," Phoebe continued, "since I've come this far, I thought perhaps I would come the rest of the way. There's something most particular I have to discuss with you, sir."

Cato understood that he had been finessed. He could send her back with one of his men, but he realized that he had not the slightest desire to do so. Head on one side, she was regarding him with an appealing air that he could only describe as coquettish. It was a new side of Phoebe, and it entranced him. It was impossible to believe that he'd ever considered her a dull nonentity.

"We've ridden ten miles this morning. I intend to reach Aylesbury by noon—that's another thirteen miles—and ride another ten miles after dinner. We will cover the same distance tomorrow and the next day." His voice was uncompromising, revealing none of his thoughts.

Phoebe blanched. Ten miles had already left their mark. But she had made up her mind and she would not be defeated. "Do you think I can't keep up, sir?"

"That was rather the point of my remarks," he agreed with a cool nod.

"Well, I can," Phoebe declared.

Cato examined her for an unnerving few minutes. She met his scrutiny steadily, and finally with a slight twitch of his lips he said, "Your friend described you as an avalanche. A remarkably accurate description.

"Gentlemen, let us continue." Cato leaned back, took Sorrel's bit at the bridle and drew her up beside his mount, observing almost casually, "It's astonishing to me that in all your nineteen years, you've never learned to take no for an answer."

"I really do have something very important to tell you," Phoebe said.

"Well, it can wait until this evening." He trotted his horse to the front of the troop, bringing Sorrel with him. "There's no time for idle chatter now."

Phoebe bit back a retort. He still thought he was humoring her by allowing her to come with him. It didn't occur to him that she might have something really important and interesting to disclose. He was being an indulgent husband who, judging by the speculative gleam in his eye of a minute before, expected his indulgence to afford him some pleasure in return.

The day's ride was a nightmare. For someone who'd never spent more than an hour on horseback, the next six hours were unrelenting torture. But Phoebe said not a word, clinging numbly to Sorrel's reins, jouncing in the saddle when they broke out of a walk, closing her mind to the bruising soreness of her thighs and backside, and the dreadful deep ache in the small of her back.

Cato offered her neither sympathy nor an I-told-you-so exasperation. He helped her back into the saddle after the dinner break without comment, even though she was hard pressed to keep from crying out as her abused muscles were forced once again into screamingly unnatural positions.

But Cato knew exactly what she was going through. However, it was for Phoebe to say when she'd had enough; when she did, he'd arrange for her to return home with two of the troopers as escort. The journey took them through many small towns where it would be possible to acquire a gig or trap, and she could go back to Woodstock in easy stages.

He waited all afternoon for her to throw in the sponge, but she never did, merely sat in white-faced, tight-lipped endurance. He couldn't help admiring her stubborn fortitude even though he deplored it. It was ridiculous for her to suffer like this. But when they stopped for the night, she would see reason, he was certain of it.

Phoebe fell into his arms when, just before dusk, he helped her to dismount in the stable yard of a small inn in the village of Aston Clinton. But she refused his arm and walked stiffly into the inn although every muscle shrieked in rebellion.

"I've a private chamber over the washroom, m'lord, if that'll do ye," the landlord offered. "Otherwise, it's jest the loft above the stables. We don't get much call for gentryfolk wantin' beds fer the night."

In any other circumstances the loft would have suited Cato as well as it suited his men, but Phoebe's presence altered matters.

"I don't mind where it is!" Phoebe declared, speaking for the first time in hours, in a tone ringing with desperate frustration. "Just show me to it."

The landlord bowed and hastened down the passage, through the kitchen, and up a narrow wooden staircase at the rear. The small chamber was thick with the smell of lye soap from the great cauldrons boiling below, but it had a good-sized bed with a mattress stuffed with horsehair. Phoebe dismissed her escort with an inarticulate wave before falling facedown on the bed, smothering her groans in the patchwork quilt.

She had no idea how much time had passed before she heard the door open and Cato's unmistakable steady tread on the creaking floorboards.

"I'm not asleep," she mumbled. "I'm ready to come down for supper."

"We'll see about that in a minute," he said easily. Something clinked as he set it on the floor.

Phoebe turned her head, forcing herself to open leaden eyes as she attempted to struggle upright. A hand between her shoulder blades pushed her down again.

"Lie still, Phoebe. I'm no leech and can't emulate your friend's physician skills, but I've a trick or two for easing certain ills." His voice was light, a little amused, perhaps, but Phoebe found it as soothing as a dock leaf on a nettle sting.

He pulled off her boots as she lay across the bed, then tossed up the skirts of her riding dress and expertly reached beneath her for the buttons of her britches at her waist. He peeled them down and tossed them to the floor.

Phoebe gave a soft sigh of relief as the cool air laved her sore and burning flesh.

"Dear God!" Cato exclaimed softly as he surveyed the damage. "Why didn't you say something?"

"There wasn't any need to say anything," Phoebe insisted. "I was perfectly all right."

He shook his head in disbelief as he dipped a towel in the steaming water in the pail he'd brought up with him. He wrung it out and laid it across the small of her back.

"Oh," Phoebe mumbled in almost disbelieving relief as the heat from the towel began to unlock the tight ache.

Cato uncorked a small leather vial of witch hazel and gently smoothed it across her buttocks and down her thighs, before applying more hot towels.

"Oh, that feels wonderful." Phoebe stretched her arms over her head, relaxing as the heat seeped into the soreness.

"Tomorrow you can rest here and then the next day Adam and Garth will escort you home. I'll purchase a gig so—"

"No!" Phoebe turned over, scattering hot towels as she sat up. "No, I will not go home, Cato. You said I could accompany you to Harwich and I *will*. I'm just a little sore. It'll go away when my muscles become accustomed. And I'm perfectly capable of keeping up tomorrow."

Cato wrung out another hot towel. "Don't be ridiculous, Phoebe. Lie down again. You're one big bruise from the small of your back to your knees. You can't possibly ride another yard."

"I can and I will," she stated flatly. "It's not for you to say what I can manage and what I can't."

"Oh, isn't it?" Cato raised an eyebrow. "Since this is a military mission, it most certainly is for me to say. Let's have no more foolishness, Phoebe. You had your way for a day, but that's enough now."

Phoebe climbed gingerly off the bed, shaking down her skirts. "Brian Morse says he has a document from the king that gives conclusive evidence that the king has no intention of agreeing to the Scots' demands," she stated. "That's what I came to tell you."

Cato stood with the towel still in his hands. "You've talked with Brian about this?"

"Yes. And also about why Cromwell and some others doubt your commitment . . . and . . ." she went on in a rush, seeing him about to interrupt. "And why you won't defend yourself against those charges. Perhaps they're sending you on this mission to get rid of you. Perhaps they don't want you ever to come back."

"How dare you discuss me and my concerns with Brian . . . or indeed with anyone!"

"I didn't discuss them with Brian, he discussed them with me." Phoebe met his gaze steadily.

Cato regarded her in frowning silence, then the anger in his eyes faded, to be replaced by something hard and bright that Phoebe thought was even more menacing than anger. He dropped the towel into the bucket and went to the door. He bellowed down the stairs, "Landlord, bring me up a pint of canary sack and two cups."

He turned back to Phoebe. "All right. Now you may tell me exactly what went on between you and Brian. Every word, every gesture. You will leave nothing out."

His voice and that stony light in his eyes chilled her. Carefully Phoebe sat down on the bed. "Where shall I begin?"

"At the beginning."

Phoebe was searching for the right point when the landlord labored up the stairs with a jug of sack and two pewter cups.

"Ye'll be wantin' supper, sir?" Puffing, he set the jug and cups down on a rickety stool in the corner of the chamber. "The wife's done a nice jugged hare, an' there's a good morsel o' tripe."

He wiped his brow with a soiled neckerchief. "Quite warm 'tis fer April."

"Aye," Cato agreed shortly. "We'll sup anon."

"Right y'are, sir." The man bent his corpulent frame in the semblance of a bow and backed out.

Cato went to latch the door, then he poured sack into two cups, handed one to Phoebe, and ordered curtly, "Begin."

Phoebe left nothing out, except for how close she had nearly come to agreeing to help with Brian's plan. Just thinking about it brought a cold sweat to her brow. She certainly didn't want Cato to know of it.

Cato listened for the most part in silence, occasionally interjecting a question. But Phoebe was relieved to see his demeanor change, and she sensed he was no longer angry with her.

When she'd fallen silent, he nodded thoughtfully. "So, it's as I suspected all along."

"What is?"

Instead of answering, Cato asked with a slightly quizzical smile, "Why did you wait until now to tell me this? You could have told me anytime in the last two days, before I left, could you not?"

"It didn't suit me to do so," Phoebe said frankly.

Cato shook his head but there was a laugh in his voice. "What a devious ragged robin I've taken to wife."

"Well, when you won't include me or confide in me, then I have to take matters into my own hands," Phoebe responded, and now there was a distinctly martial light in her eye.

Cato frowned at this. "I give you much more rein than most wives have, Phoebe. You must know that."

"I don't want rein," Phoebe flashed. "I'm not a horse. I want to be a wife in every respect. Not just in bed, or arranging your household, or—"

"I hadn't noticed you did too much of that," Cato interrupted dryly.

He had her there. Phoebe conceded ruefully, "Mistress

Bisset is better at it than I am. And besides, I have other important things to do."

"Yes, like being taken up for a witch and meddling in my affairs with my snake of a stepson!"

"Oh, that's so unjust!" she fired.

He caught her chin on his palm, lifting her face so she had to meet his eye. "I do my best to accommodate your eccentricities, Phoebe. But there are areas of my life that I have no wish to share . . . with you or with anyone. You have to understand that."

"I don't wish to intrude," Phoebe said in a low voice. "But I love you." She hadn't meant to say it but it was done now.

Cato regarded her, an arrested look in his eye. *A woman bound in love . . .* Love. Such a wild, unruly passion.

Something hovered on the periphery of his mind. Something amorphous and warm and unnameable. "You're very precious to me, my sweet," he said, and kissed her. "Now, why don't I have them heat the water in the washhouse and you can have a long soak in a tub. Then you get into bed and I'll have a maid bring up your supper."

Phoebe moved away from him, averting her eyes so he wouldn't see the sheen of tears. Of course Cato wouldn't pretend to something he didn't feel. "A bath would help," she said. "Then I'll be ready for tomorrow."

"Phoebe, you can't seriously intend—"

"I am coming," she stated. "Could you please ask someone to bring up the valise I had strapped to Sorrel's saddle? It has a few necessities."

Cato shrugged. Her obstinacy carried its own penalty. "Very well. But don't expect any concessions."

"I don't!" she said with such ferocity he was taken aback. "I thought I'd made that clear, my lord."

She was exhausted, Cato reminded himself. He turned to the door, saying over his shoulder, "You were right. I needed to know about Brian. But you have no need to worry. I have matters well in hand."

Phoebe made no response to this confidence, and after a second, Cato left her.

*W*hen Cato came to bed some considerable time later, Phoebe seemed to be sleeping soundly. He undressed, snuffed the candle, and climbed in beside her.

With a sleepy little murmur she rolled over and reached for him as she always did when he joined her in bed.

"I see you've been raiding my kit," Cato observed with some amusement. Phoebe was enfolded in one of his own crisp cambric shirts.

"My shift was sweaty and I wanted to stay fresh after my bath," she murmured, pressing her lips to the hollow of his throat. "I wished to be fresh for you."

"You always are," he said with perfect truth. Fresh, surprising, beautiful. Infuriating, eccentric, stubborn . . . delightful.

He drew her beneath him.

*T*he next morning Phoebe emerged from the inn just after daybreak, her expression that of one about to face the torture chamber.

Cato was already mounted and talking with Giles Crampton and one of the troopers. Sorrel was standing at a mounting block, her rein held by one of the inn's grooms.

Phoebe set her teeth and climbed into the saddle. It wasn't at first too bad. Witch hazel, the hot bath, and a good night's rest had had some benefit. She nudged the mare into a walk and came up with Cato.

"Ah, there you are." Cato gave her a slightly distracted smile. "I thought to let you have your sleep out, so didn't wake you when I rose myself. Did you break your fast?"

"The goodwife made me some porridge," Phoebe answered. "How far will we ride today?"

"As far as Bishop's Stortford." He regarded her closely.

"The landlord here has a gig that he's prepared to sell me. Tom has to return to headquarters, and he and Adam will escort you back to Woodstock."

Phoebe shook her head. "I'm all right, my lord."

Cato contented himself with a raised eyebrow, before he turned back to Tom. "Very well, Tom, then you may make all speed. Make sure the dispatch goes directly to either Cromwell or Lord Fairfax."

"Aye, sir." The trooper patted the breast of his jerkin, where he held the document for Parliament's headquarters detailing Brian Morse's latest conduct. Cato had recommended that Brian should be traced and held until Cato returned from his mission and could interrogate him himself.

Cato gave the troop the signal to move out, and Phoebe, her lips set, encouraged Sorrel into a trot to keep up.

At the end of an hour Phoebe had drifted into a trance where her physical miseries seemed inseparable from herself and from each other. She could no longer distinguish between the deep muscle aches and the raw soreness of her flesh. If she allowed herself to think of the hours stretching ahead, she knew she would weep, so she let her mind drift into a realm of soft green valleys and heather-strewn hillsides, dappled streams, and the sweet scent of new-mown hay.

When Cato drew rein, she didn't notice. Sorrel would have trotted on without signal from her rider if Cato hadn't reached over and taken the mare's bridle, bringing her to a halt.

The cessation of motion shocked Phoebe out of her trance. She came back to the real world and the reality of pain with a moan.

"Come, I can't bear to see you like this," Cato said brusquely. "I'm going to lift you up. Help me by putting your arms around my neck."

For a moment Phoebe looked up at him in a bewilderment that was not eased by his contradictory expression. His mouth was impatient, and yet his dark eyes were filled with concern.

"Phoebe, did you hear me?" He leaned down from his saddle. "Take your feet out of the stirrups and put your arms around my neck."

Obediently she did so, raising her arms to clasp his neck. He lifted her bodily from the saddle and onto his own in front of him. "Sit back now and take the weight off your backside. Giles, lead the mare."

Giles had already taken Sorrel's bridle, and the cavalcade moved forward again.

Phoebe leaned back against Cato's broad chest. "I'm sorry," she said. "I really didn't want to give up."

He looked down at her and a slight smile touched his mouth. "You did better than I expected."

"I'll ride tomorrow."

He nodded. "For an hour or so. It takes time to build up endurance, particularly," he added with pointed emphasis, "when you have such an appalling seat."

Phoebe didn't protest this truth. She sat sideways on the saddle, taking the weight off her bruised flesh, and began to enjoy the scenery from a perch that was as comfortable as it was secure.

"It seems to me I have the best of both worlds this way, anyway," she observed after a while.

"How so?" He brushed away a lock of her hair that was tickling his chin.

"I can enjoy the ride from the best possible place — as close to you as it's possible to be. I can even hear your heart beat," she returned with a serene smile. "Oh . . . and I won't be tired when we stop for the night, so we'll be able to play much more than we could last night."

"You are incorrigible," Cato said, but he was grinning. His encircling arm tightened for a minute. His hand brushed the swell of her breast beneath her cloak and he could feel her heart beat against his palm.

Giles, riding in silence a little to one side of them, didn't hear the exchange, but he saw the grin and marveled at it. In all the years he'd served him, the marquis of Granville had never grinned. He smiled, he laughed even, but *grinned*? Unheard of. And to include the woman in his expedition! That was astounding. Lord Granville never allowed anything or anyone to interfere with his military concerns . . . or never had done before, Giles amended dourly.

There was just no accounting for it.

*W*hen Brian Morse discovered after a little rooting around and the disbursement of a few coins that Cato was heading for Harwich, he was immediately intrigued. Why would one journey to Italy from Harwich? It would make much better sense to take ship from one of the southern ports, Portsmouth or Southampton.

Obviously Cato had been less than frank with him. Not that that surprised Brian in the least. It was a fair guess that Lord Granville was heading for Holland from Harwich. Most of the shipping from that port went to the Low Countries. And that raised a great many interesting possibilities. If he was intending to make contact with Walter Strickland, then it was Brian's bounden duty to prevent it.

The king's own agents in Rotterdam had managed to do away with two of Parliament's envoys before they'd met up with Strickland. But they had been men of no real importance. The marquis of Granville, on the other hand, was one of the most influential members of Parliament's high command. To get rid of him while he was on this mission would be a coup indeed.

It was a coup Brian was going to engineer. It was a gift from the devil and Brian was not about to turn it down. And to make matters even simpler, Cato was apparently not intending to take any of his own men to Holland with him, not even Giles Crampton. It was almost too good to be true.

There was something deeply pleasing about the prospect of killing two birds with one stone. By assassinating Cato,

Brian would achieve kudos among his own leaders. And he himself would then inherit the Granville title and estates. He would then bring the wealth and influence of the Granville name to the king's side, a loss that Parliament could ill afford.

If he played his cards right, there would be a dukedom in it for Brian, once the king was restored to his throne.

And Brian would play his cards right. The only possible flaw was Phoebe. If she was breeding, he would have to get rid of her. And that, he thought, would be rather a shame. True, she'd made him lose his temper with her prissy refusal to cooperate, but he'd recovered from that now. Now he could see the possibilities. The new marquis of Granville would need a wife. Why not the present marchioness? He could knock her into shape, he was sure. And there were distinct possibilities in that voluptuous form.

Brian set off for Harwich a couple of hours after Cato. He took a different route, however, having no desire to run into his quarry. He reached Harwich on the afternoon of the third day, put up at the Pelican on the harbor, and set out on foot to discover whether Cato and his cavalcade had arrived at another of the town's numerous inns.

A man traveling with eight troopers couldn't arrive inconspicuously in this small port, and Brian was confident he'd run them to ground quickly.

He was in the taproom of the Ship, drinking ale and casually making inquiries, when he heard Giles Crampton's rough Yorkshire burr in the hallway.

"Eh, goodwife, we've need of a decent privy chamber fer Lord Granville. The rest of us'll settle neat enou' in the loft, or above the stables."

"I don't know as 'ow I've got a privy chamber," the goodwife was saying as Brian slipped unobtrusively into the vast inglenook. "If'n 'is lordship wouldn't mind sharin' though, there's a nice big chamber at the front. I let it out to three gentlemen at a time. Most don't mind bundlin'."

"Well, my wife and I do mind." Cato's authoritative tones chimed into the goodwife's speech. "I'll take that chamber and pay you well for it, mistress."

There was a chink of coin and the goodwife said with some satisfaction, "Well, I daresay I'll be able to move the other gentlemen, then, sir. Will 'er ladyship be wantin' a maid to 'elp 'er?"

"No, I don't believe so," Cato said. "But we're sharp set and looking forward to our supper."

"Oh, I'll be puttin' a goodly supper on the table fer ye, m'lord. Tripe an' onions, an' a nice piece of brawn."

"I don't suppose you have a roast chicken? We had tripe yesterday."

Brian listened to Phoebe's wistful tones in astonishment. What on earth was she doing here? Cato couldn't be intending to take her to Holland with him.

He moved further back into the inglenook. Phoebe's presence would make no difference. Once he discovered where Cato was going, he intended to take passage on the next ship going to the same port.

When he returned from Holland, it would be with Cato's blood on his knife.

A smile flickered over Brian's thin mouth.

20

Phoebe stood on the harbor at Harwich, drawing the hood of her cloak closer around her face against the freshening evening breeze. It was close to seven o'clock and the sky was already darkening.

The scene on the quay was hectic as ships prepared to leave on the evening tide and light spilled from the open doors and unshuttered windows of the taverns opening onto the cobbled, fishy-smelling landing stage.

Phoebe could see no sign of Cato. He'd supped with her earlier, made gentle love to her in farewell, and had then left her at the Ship inn, saying he was going to share a final pot of ale with Giles and his men at a tavern on the quay before boarding the *White Lady* en route for Italy.

Phoebe jumped out of the way as a pair of stevedores jogged past her, laboring under their load of flour sacks piled upon their backs. The lights of the ships riding at anchor further out in the harbor cast a pale glow over the dark water.

Phoebe felt bereft and utterly alone in this purposeful bustle. She had come on impulse, wanting—no, needing—to see Cato's ship finally depart, so that she could say one final farewell. She looked forlornly towards the taverns where Cato was presumably laughing and jesting with his men, having put aside all thoughts of the wife he'd left behind in safety in the inn. The wife who was to return with Giles Crampton to Woodstock on the morrow and await her husband's return as patiently as any Penelope.

She looked around and saw him. Brian Morse. He was deep in discussion with two men some twenty yards away, standing at the gangway of a small sloop. She stared at him, for a moment unable to believe her eyes. What could Brian possibly be doing here? As she gazed across at him, something changed hands, then Brian moved away from the two men. He raised his head and for one dreadful instant his eyes met Phoebe's across the distance that separated them.

Phoebe's stomach seemed to plunge into her boots. Had he recognized her? A cold wave of nameless panic crept up the back of her neck, shivered her scalp, brought a light dew of icy perspiration to her forehead. She felt the same terror she'd felt in the stable yard, when she'd had a glimpse of his true character beneath the urbane facade. Now she could almost fancy she could see the aura of malevolence emanating from him. It was fanciful, Phoebe knew, but she had a deep and absolute conviction of evil. Meg was always right.

Her hand instinctively went into the pocket of her cloak, closing comfortingly over the leather purse that lay heavily against her thigh. Without conscious intention she swung around to the gangway behind her leading onto the *White Lady*. It was for the moment deserted.

Phoebe darted up it, aware only of the overpowering need to get away from Brian before he saw her, if he hadn't already done so. She told herself he couldn't have recognized her, huddled in her cloak as she was. It wasn't as if he could have been expecting to see her.

Once she had felt that he was within an inch of hurting her; had felt that he was absolutely capable of cold, ruthless hurting if it suited him. And just then she'd seen that same look in his eyes, despite the distance between them. Maybe he hadn't seen her. Maybe it it wasn't directed at her. But it terrified her nevertheless.

She reached the deck and plunged into the shadow of the deck rail. Her heart was beating far too fast, her palms clammy.

"Eh, an' jest who might you be?"

Phoebe spun around at the voice at her elbow and found

herself face to face with a fresh-faced lad of about her own age. He stared at her curiously.

"What's it to you?" Phoebe demanded, unconsciously lifting her chin, her voice taking on the slight chill of hauteur.

"I'm a sailor," the lad said proudly. "An' I works the *White Lady*. An' it's my business to watch who comes on an' who goes off in port, see."

Phoebe regarded him closely. "You don't look much like a sailor to me," she said, gesturing to his ragged britches fastened at the waist with string, his bare feet, and the threadbare shirt. "You look more like a vagabond than a sailor."

The lad's grimy face took on a slightly crestfallen expression. "I'm the cabin boy," he stated. "An' it's my business to watch the gangplank in port."

Phoebe considered this. Once again her hand closed over the purse in her pocket. Something was taking shape in the back of her mind, something so audacious, so exciting, she hardly dared admit it to full consciousness.

Slowly she said, "I'm Lady Granville. Lord Granville has taken passage on this ship."

The lad's eyes sharpened. He said, "Aye, that 'e has. But nobody's said nothin' about a Lady Granville."

"No," Phoebe said. "I don't imagine they have." She drew out the purse, hefting it thoughtfully in her hand. "Lord Granville isn't exactly expecting me, but I'll give you a guinea if you'll show me to his cabin so I can leave a letter for him when he comes on board."

"A guinea?" The cabin boy stared at her in wide-eyed astonishment. "An 'ole guinea."

Phoebe nodded and loosened the purse strings. She extracted a coin and held it up so that the light from the stern lamps caught the gleam of gold. "Show me to Lord Granville's cabin and don't tell a soul before he comes on board, and I'll give you this."

The boy gazed at the coin. He licked his lips. It was more money than he'd ever seen, let alone possessed. "This a-way." He jerked his head towards the companionway and darted forward.

Phoebe followed him in the grip of a compulsion that made her shiver even as it enthralled her. She climbed down the narrow companionway in the wake of the lad and along a short, dark passage.

"In 'ere." The lad opened a door halfway down the passage, adding helpfully, "Mind the step."

Phoebe stepped over the high threshold into a small, cramped space. An oil lamp hung from a hook in the ceiling, throwing a shadowy light over the two narrow bunks set one atop the other in the bulwark, and illuminating the table and stool that were bolted to the floor beneath a round porthole. Cato's portmanteau stood on the floor beneath the table.

Phoebe put the coin into the lad's eager palm. "Just a minute," she said, laying a hand on his scrawny arm as he made for the door again. "There'll be another one, if you don't say a word of this to anyone until we're . . . we're . . ."

She considered for an instant, then said determinedly, "Until we're in the middle of the sea." Phoebe had but a hazy notion of what the middle of the sea might be like, but it sounded suitably far away for her purposes.

"I thought you said you was jest goin' to leave 'is lordship a letter." The cabin boy frowned at her even as he clutched the coin tightly in his palm.

"Well, I've just changed my mind. I'm going to stay," Phoebe said. "How long does it take to get to Italy?"

The lad shrugged. " 'Ow should I know, never been there . . . don't 'spect I ever will."

"But the ship is going there now," Phoebe said, bewildered.

He laughed raucously, as if at some trick of a fairground freak. "We're goin' to Rotterdam, in 'Olland, ye daft 'apoth!" He doubled over with a gust of exaggerated mirth.

Phoebe, however, was too incensed at this piece of information to take immediate exception to his mockery. Cato had *lied* to her. An out-and-out lie.

"The *White Lady* always goes to the Low Countries from 'ere," the cabin boy continued with a most infuriating air of superiority. "We got to cross the North Sea. Can't get to no Italy from there."

Phoebe was silent. Geography had never been her strong suit. But *why* had Cato lied to her? He had lied to everyone, except, presumably, Giles Crampton, she thought bitterly. It was yet another example of his refusal to trust his wife, to take her into his confidence. Did he think she'd betray his secrets if he asked her to keep them? Oh, he was impossible! Infuriating! She'd done nothing to deserve such lack of confidence.

Well, that was about to change. She repeated decidedly, "Another guinea if you don't say anything about me being here until we're in the middle of the sea."

The boy looked a little doubtful. "Aye," he said slowly. "That's all very well. But if the bosun gets to 'ear of it, I'll get the rope's end, I will."

Phoebe said persuasively, "If anyone asks, I'll say I came on board while you were looking the other way, and found my own way to my husband's cabin."

The boy gazed down at the coin winking in the lamplight on his palm. He put it to his mouth and bit it. The gold was hard and metallic tasting. He examined it carefully. It was round and smooth, no sign of clipped edges.

"Another one?" He raised his eyes to Phoebe's

She nodded. "Just like that one."

"Lord love a duck," he muttered. It was riches beyond imagining, worth even a painful session with the rope's end. It wasn't as if he was letting on board a gang of ruffians. It was only his lordship's wife, after all. No great crime. Not one to bring down drastic punishment.

"But you mustn't say a word," Phoebe insisted again. "Not one single word to *anyone*. You understand."

"All right," he said after a minute, his fingers closing over the coin. "I'd best be off now."

He ducked out of the cabin, leaving Phoebe to look around her surroundings and wonder whether she was quite mad. When she'd left the inn, she hadn't intended doing anything so unimaginable.

Or had she?

She looked at the purse in her hand. Why had she brought it with her if she hadn't had some idea that it might prove useful? Why had she pawned the rings in the first place if she hadn't envisaged doing something outside Cato's jurisdiction?

A tremor of excitement slid down her spine. Whether she'd intended it or not, it seemed she was now set on this adventure.

Phoebe frowned around the cabin again. She had to hide herself somewhere. Cato mustn't find her until it was too late to turn back to port. Did the two bunks mean he was sharing the cabin? That could prove a nuisance. But the cabin boy hadn't said anything about another passenger. Either way, there wasn't anywhere in the cramped functional space for a fugitive.

She opened the door and peered down the passage again. The only light came from the open companionway at the end. Voices mingled with running feet on the decks above her. She thought she could detect a heightened degree of urgency, as if preparations were growing close to fruition. If so, Cato would come on board within a short while. She had to find somewhere to hide.

Phoebe ventured into the corridor, closing the door gently behind her. A very narrow door in the wall opposite caught her eye. She opened it and peered into a tiny space occupied by several thick coils of rope, a bucket, and a mop. It smelled of fish and tar, with undercurrents of a more noxious odor. However, it would have to do.

She slipped inside, pulling the door to behind her. Immediately she felt as if she couldn't breathe; the rank stench filling her nostrils made her gag. She opened the door again a crack and sat down on the coils of rope, drawing her legs beneath her, holding the door almost closed, leaving just the tiniest crack for a reassuring breath of reasonably fresh air.

Phoebe lost track of time. Above her head the sounds of impending departure continued. She listened for the sound of Cato's voice but it never reached her. Once she had a moment of panic, imagining what would happen if he'd decided at the last minute not to board the *White Lady* and she'd be heading off for Holland all alone. But no one came down to the cabin opposite to retrieve his portmanteau.

A great rattling sound from immediately below her startled her so that she jumped and banged her head on the cupboard's low ceiling. A rattling, creaking, banging racket that set her perch shivering. And now the thudding feet above her took on a new urgency interspersed with voices raised in command. The ship began to move in what to Phoebe seemed a cumbersome swinging motion.

$\mathcal{A}$bove, Cato stood with the captain on the quarterdeck, watching as the ship's boats with their long sweeps of oars towed the *White Lady* to the mouth of the harbor. All around them ships riding the high tide were following the same course.

"What kind of a crossing are you expecting, Captain?" Cato inquired with an assumption of only mild curiosity, although his peace of mind, not to mention stomach, rested on the answer.

"Oh, quiet enough, sir," the captain replied, gazing upward into the deep blue sky now thickly studded with stars. "We should pick up a brisk wind come morning for the North Sea passage, but it's set fair for the moment."

Cato muttered a response and turned to look up into the rigging where sailors were moving purposefully, preparing for the moment when they'd pass the harbor bar and the oarsmen would return on board, their boats winched after them, and the *White Lady* would hit the open sea. He grimaced in anticipation.

"Grog, Lord Granville?" the captain inquired as a sailor ran up the gangway to the quarterdeck bearing two steaming pitch tankards. Captain Allan had no other passengers for this crossing; his cargo was tin from the Cornish mines for the Flemish market. Lucrative enough but not as much as the delicate Delftware, Brussels lace, and Flemish wool that he hoped to bring back to the quality English markets.

Cato took the tankard with a nod of thanks. The grog had a good spicy aroma, and its steam curled into the now chill air. He drew his cloak more securely over his shoulders, determined to remain on deck most of the night. Fresh air was the best antidote to seasickness.

They had reached the harbor bar and the oarsmen shipped their sweeps and swarmed up the rope ladders back on board the *White Lady* while the boats were winched up and secured on deck. Sipping his grog, Cato looked up at the masts as the sails were run up, bellying in the fresh cold wind. Phoebe would be asleep by now, snug beneath the feather quilt in the big four-poster at the Ship.

Cato sighed. He had hated to leave her, and the shadow of her absence was getting in the way of his clearheaded appraisal of the mission that lay ahead of him.

To be absent from thy heart is torment . . .

Mother of God, why couldn't he rid himself of that damned scene? The lines kept popping into his head completely unbidden. At least he thought they were unbidden. But supposing there was something over which he had no control. . . .

The captain said something and Cato banished introspection. "I beg your pardon, Captain . . . ?"

*P*hoebe remained in her cupboard until she felt the motion of the ship change and its slow steady progress seemed to quicken, to rise and fall beneath her. She found she rather liked the motion, although when she stood up, she tottered and had to grab at the cupboard door to steady herself.

She edged out of her hiding place and stood in the passage listening. Voices still called orders from above, feet still raced across the decks, but it was an orderly sound, as if the activity had settled down into an accustomed pattern.

Phoebe opened the door to the cabin and slipped inside, closing it at her back. No one had come down during her stay in the cupboard, and everything was just as she'd left it, the oil lamp throwing a swaying glow over the sparse furnishings. The ship lurched abruptly and she nearly fell against the bulkhead.

Righting herself, she looked around with rather more attention than hitherto. To her relief, she saw a commode in the far corner. She'd been puzzling about necessary arrangements on board ship, remembering the inadequate facilities at the Cotswold farmhouse. It seemed Cato had a degree of privacy in his cabin.

She took off her cloak, boots, riding habit, and britches, laying them neatly over the stool, then climbed the ladder into the top bunk. The ceiling was so low it seemed to press down upon her as she wriggled beneath the thin blanket and lay very still, feeling her body settle into the motion of the ship.

The scratchy sheet of rough calico covered a straw-filled pallet that rustled at the slightest movement. The sound of water flowing against the bulkhead and the gentle motion of the ship had a soporific effect, so that within a very few minutes, Phoebe felt her eyes growing heavy. She wasn't sure whether they were yet in the middle of the sea, but surely they were too far from shore now for the ship to put back to harbor. Cato was stuck with her now . . . on this journey to Holland.

How could he have told her he was going to Italy? He might never have come back to her, and she would never

have known where he'd died. Sometimes she couldn't begin
to understand why she loved him to such distraction.

It was gone midnight when Cato decided to go below. It
was too cold to sleep on deck, and the sea seemed calm
enough for the most susceptible stomach. The captain had
long left the quarterdeck to the quartermaster, who stood at
the helm, whistling softly between his teeth as he steered by
the North Star.

Cato bade him a courteous good night and descended the
companionway. He entered the cabin, yawning deeply, to
find it in darkness, the oil lamp out of fuel. By the faint moonlight coming through the small porthole, he struck flint on
tinder and lit the candle that stood on the table.

His foot caught the stool beside the table and he glanced
down. At first what he saw merely bemused him. A heap of
clothes that were not his own had no place in his cabin. But
there was something familiar about these garments. Something familiar . . .

With a creeping sense of inevitability Cato turned slowly
towards the bulkhead, raising the candle high.

The golden light fell upon a tangled glowing mass of light
brown hair, a pale cheek pillowed on the curve of her forearm, the crescent shadow of her eyelashes, the soft full
mouth, lips slightly parted in sleep.

Cato regarded his sleeping wife in disbelief.

Grimly he picked up a copper jug that stood beside the
commode and went back up on deck to the scuttlebutt. He
filled the jug and returned to his cabin.

Phoebe slept on.

Cato dipped a towel into the jug, wrung it out perfuncto-
rily, and approached the bunks.

Phoebe came to in a spluttering shower of cold water,
arms flailing, incoherent protest on her lips. Her eyes shot

open and she found herself looking up into her husband's flinty black eyes.

"Oh," she said inadequately, trying to dry her drenched face with the back of her hand. A complaint about his method of waking her died stillborn as she absorbed his furious countenance.

"How *dare* you!" Cato demanded.

Phoebe wiped her face on the scratchy sheet, trying to think of something to say. Unfortunately she was still half asleep and words seemed to have deserted her.

"Come down here," Cato commanded, tossing the soaked cloth into the jug.

Phoebe sat up properly and looked doubtful. It didn't seem like a wise move in the light of Cato's expression. "There's not a lot of room. I'm sure we could have a more comfortable conversation if I stayed up here," she suggested tentatively.

"Phoebe, get down here!" The softness of his voice did nothing to detract from its ferocity.

There seemed nothing for it. She pushed aside the thin blanket and wriggled around so that she could come down the ladder backwards. She tugged at the hem of her chemise, aware that it only reached mid-thigh and was riding up as she descended the ladder. It did nothing for her sense of vulnerability.

"I saw Brian on the quay. That's why I came on board . . . to tell you that," she declared in a rush, glancing hopefully over her shoulder to see the effect of her explanation.

Cato took her by the waist and swung her down the last two rungs of the ladder, setting her on her feet with a jarring thump. "*What?*" he demanded.

"Brian." Phoebe tugged again at her chemise. "On the quay. He was talking with two men. I thought you'd wish to know."

Cato stared at her. "Are you telling me you crept on

board, hid in my cabin, waited until the ship was well out of port, just to inform me that my stepson has found his way to Harwich?"

"Isn't it something you would wish to know?"

"That's beside the point." Cato dismissed the question with an impatient gesture. "And don't be disingenuous. If you wished to tell me something, just why did you wait until now to do so?"

"I was asleep," Phoebe offered.

Cato drew in a sharp breath.

Phoebe, regretting her flippancy, went on the attack. She said hastily, "You told me you were going to Italy, and you're not. Why did you lie to me? You could have been killed and I'd never have known where you died . . . always supposing someone bothered to tell me you were dead," she added with undisguised bitterness.

"My destination had to be a secret." To his astonishment Cato found himself on the defensive. "For safety reasons as much as anything."

"But why wouldn't you tell *me*?" Phoebe demanded. "I wouldn't jeopardize your safety . . . or did you think I might?"

"That has nothing to do with it. A secret mission is just that. *No one* can know of it."

"I'll lay odds Giles Crampton knows," Phoebe stated.

"That is different," Cato said firmly. "Giles is my lieutenant."

"And more important than your wife," Phoebe retorted.

"In some matters, yes. But none of this is to the point. I cannot believe you . . . *even you* . . . would have the brass-faced nerve to do this, Phoebe. Do you have any idea what's at stake? What you have put in jeopardy by your blind and utterly thoughtless impulses?"

"I saw Brian Morse on the quay and thought you ought to know of it," Phoebe reiterated. "Does he know where you're really going?"

"He didn't. I daresay he does now," Cato observed. "But that has nothing to do with you."

"It does! Everything that concerns you is to do with me," Phoebe said. "But you won't understand that. You're always telling me to sit at home and ply my needle—"

"I never said that!" Cato interrupted, thrown off course by this image. "I'd never say anything so ridiculous. Just the very idea of you plying a needle is an absurdity."

"Well, you didn't say that exactly," Phoebe conceded. "But you told me my place is at home."

"Which it is."

"No!" she cried. "No, it's not. My place is with you. You're where my home is . . . it's beside you." Impassioned, she jabbed at his chest to illustrate her point.

Cato caught her wrist. He looked down into her flushed face, her fiery eyes. She was impossible to ignore, impossible to manage, utterly determined, and so very, very loving. There was absolutely no point in being angry. It was a complete waste of time and effort. All his legitimate fury simply washed off her like rain on an oiled hide. She was so absolutely sure of herself, of what she believed was right.

A deep sigh, almost a groan, of resignation escaped him. "Whatever did I do to deserve you?" he muttered, his fingers still clamped around her wrist.

Phoebe put her head on one side, her bright eyes regarding him just like the ragged robin he so often called her. "A very good deed once that you've probably forgotten," she suggested with a smile that while tentative was also mischievous.

Cato put his hands lightly around her throat, pushing up her chin with his thumbs. "For two pins, Phoebe—"

The cabin floor suddenly shifted beneath his feet as the ship rolled violently. It seemed to hang in midair, then it pitched forward. The jug of water slid across the table, then back again as the ship pulled itself up and out of the trough.

Cato's hands dropped from Phoebe and with an incoherent mutter he turned and half ran from the cabin.

Puzzled Phoebe stood with one hand unconsciously at her throat where she could still feel the warmth of his fingers. The ship rolled sideways again and she allowed herself to move with it, realizing instinctively that fighting the motion would only unbalance her.

Where had Cato gone in such a hurry?

She scrambled into her clothes and left the cabin, grabbing onto the doorjamb as the pitch and roll intensified. She made her way towards the companionway, holding on to the passage wall for balance, and climbed up onto the deck.

It was a brilliant, star-filled night but the wind was strong and cold. Phoebe pulled the hood of her cloak tightly over her ears and looked around for Cato. She couldn't see any sign of him at first and watched for a minute as sailors swarmed the creaking rigging, taking a reef in the sails. No one seemed perturbed by the wind or the swell of the sea; indeed the men were chattering and laughing as they worked, clinging to the rigging as the ship rode the waves, as she plunged into deep troughs and hauled herself back up again.

Phoebe found it exhilarating as she stood braced against the wind and the motion, her feet planted well apart on the spray-soaked decking. A few curious glances came her way, but everyone seemed too busy to take much notice of this unknown passenger. Phoebe, assuming that Cato would have to negotiate passage for her with the captain once the bustle of present activity was over, looked around again for her husband.

She saw him eventually on the lee side of the ship, peering over the rail. She made her way towards him, holding on to the rail for safety.

"Isn't this exhilarating?" she called enthusiastically as she approached him. "Do you think you should explain to the captain that I'm here?"

Cato didn't respond. He remained hanging over the rail.

"Oh," Phoebe said as she reached him. "You're sick. I remember you said the sea made you so."

Cato straightened as the wrenching paroxysms ceased for a minute. He wiped his mouth on the handkerchief he clutched in his hand and regarded Phoebe, radiating rude health, with considerable disfavor. "Just go below and leave me alone," he said, then with a groan swung back to the rail, vomiting helplessly.

"But can't I do anything?" Phoebe touched his back in anxious concern. "There must be something."

"Just go away!" he directed when he could draw breath again. "I can't worry about you at the moment, so get below and stay out of the way!"

"You don't have to worry about me," Phoebe said in hopeful reassurance. "Indeed you don't. I am worried about *you*. There must be something I can get you." She put an arm around his shoulders, trying to support him through the violent retching.

"Brandy," Cato gasped after long minutes. "In my portmanteau there's a flagon of brandy. Sometimes it helps." He hung over the rail again.

Phoebe flew belowdecks. Tossing neatly folded shirts aside, she rummaged for the flagon and found it at the bottom of the portmanteau. Then she flew on deck again, uncorking the flask as she went.

Cato staggered upright, supporting himself on the rail. He reached for the flagon and tipped it to his mouth. Sometimes it steadied his stomach and eventually it could bring merciful sleep.

"How dreadful for you," Phoebe said sympathetically. "It's strange, but I don't feel in the least unwell."

"How fortunate for you," Cato muttered dryly, leaning back against the rail, holding the neck of the flask loosely between finger and thumb while the fiery liquid burned down his gullet and settled in his aching stomach.

"In fact," Phoebe said with devastating candor, "I seem to find myself very hungry. Perhaps it's the sea air."

"Repellent brat!" Cato declared with some force, before turning with a groan to lose the brandy to the waves.

"I beg your pardon, I didn't mean to make matters worse," Phoebe apologized.

"Just go *away!*"

Phoebe thought that perhaps she should. There didn't seem to be anything she could do to help him in his misery. And she *was* famished. She moved away from the deck rail, wondering where food might be found on a ship, and was swiftly accosted by the cabin boy.

"Eh, you owes me another guinea," he announced, grabbing her arm. "I 'aven't told nobody."

"Oh, yes." Phoebe reached for her purse, then had a thought. "You shall have the guinea as soon as you bring me something to eat in the cabin. Can you do that?"

"Watcha want?" He looked at her speculatively. "Might be able to lay me 'ands on a mite o' bread 'n' cheese."

"Perfect. And milk. Do you have any milk?"

"Nah!" The lad shook his head in unconcealed scorn. "Milk on a ship! Lor! You dunno much, do ya?"

"Not about ships," Phoebe agreed rather loftily, shaking the purse so that the coins clinked.

"There's ale," the lad suggested at the music of money. "Reckon I could bring ye ale."

"Thank you. That will do very well." Phoebe nodded at him and made her way belowdecks.

Seasickness was a really wretched ailment, Phoebe thought, as she headed for her cabin, her mouth watering at the prospect of bread and cheese.

21

"*Oh, I think we've landed.*" *Phoebe sat up on her bunk,* keeping her head bent. Experience in the last week had taught her the danger of incautious movements in the upper bunk. It was early morning, judging by the pinkish light coming through the porthole, and the ship was no longer moving. The rattling release of the anchor chain, together with the changed bustle on the decks above, had woken her. There was more running, more shouting than there had been in the days at sea.

"Cato?" she said when there was no response from the bottom bunk. Leaning over, she peered over the edge of her own into the narrow space below. It was empty.

Phoebe wriggled out of her bunk and climbed down the ladder, unaware that her mouth was pursed in a little moue of disappointment. Cato, once he'd finally acquired his sea legs on the second day of the voyage, usually awoke her himself in ways that made her blood sing. But not so this morning.

She went to the porthole and gazed out. They were docked at a quayside thronged with sailors, stevedores, carriers' wagons. Even at this early hour, the activity was frenetic, although her view was limited to a smallish stretch of cobbled quay and a red-brick, rather crooked building a few yards away.

At the sound of the cabin door opening behind her, she spun around. "We're here."

"A reasonable deduction," Cato agreed with a slight smile. But behind the smile, Phoebe could detect something else, something that made her a little uneasy.

He closed the door and said calmly, "Sit down, Phoebe. There's something we need to discuss."

Phoebe looked at him uncertainly. "What kind of thing?"

"Sit down." He put his hands on her shoulders and pushed her down firmly onto the stool, then leaned back against the closed door, his arms folded, his dark eyes, sharp and watchful, resting on her countenance.

He was dressed casually in shirt and britches, his doublet open, his dark brown hair ruffled by the wind. A streak of early sunlight coming through the small porthole caught the flicker of gold in the darker depths. Phoebe gazed at the pulse beating at the base of the strong column of his throat, and her belly jolted with familiar desire. She forgot the tingle of apprehension and made a move to stand up, but he spoke again and the gravity of his tone kept her seated.

"I'm going to ask you a question and I want you to consider very carefully before you make answer."

Phoebe swallowed, disliking the tenor of this discussion.

"Will you give me your word of honor that when I leave the ship you will make no attempt to follow me?" Cato put the question in his usual cool fashion, but his eyes never left her face.

"Where are you going?"

It was a mark of how far he'd progressed along the road to understanding his wife that Cato answered without hesitation. "I have to go into the town to look for someone."

"For Brian Morse?"

"No, no, indeed not." Cato shook his head.

"But do you think he's here?"

Cato shrugged. "Maybe. It matters not, but—"

"He's a bad man," Phoebe interrupted with some passion.

Cato frowned. "Misguided, untrustworthy, with an overweening ambition, certainly."

"He's *evil*," Phoebe declared. "I know it and Meg knows it . . . and Olivia."

Cato's question seemed to have become lost. He was

about to reiterate it when Phoebe said suddenly, "Could you not unadopt him? Disinherit him?"

Cato's frown deepened. The question touched on an issue he'd considered too delicate to bring up. He said gently, "I had never considered it. I had assumed it wouldn't be necessary."

Phoebe flushed to the roots of her hair. She had somehow forgotten, as she posed the question, her own part in the situation.

As he saw her distress Cato regretted his observation. He was enlightened enough to know that it wasn't Phoebe's fault that she was barren; it was just one of those wretched quirks of fate. "Let us not talk about this now, Phoebe. Brian is the least of my concerns at present."

"Yes," said Phoebe in a low voice.

"So. Will you give me your word of honor you will remain on the ship until I return?" His voice was once more cool and brisk.

"When will you return?"

Cato controlled his impatience. It never did any good with Phoebe, whose thought processes followed their own road. "I don't know exactly. I have to find this man . . . or discover what has happened to him. I may get news at the Black Tulip today, or it may take a week or so. Now, do I have your word?"

Phoebe stared down at her hands in her lap. She twisted her wedding ring, noticing absently that the circle of skin beneath was paler than the rest of her hand. Five days in the sun and sea air had given her a suntan.

Cato waited. Phoebe said nothing.

"Well, I commend your honesty," Cato said dryly into the silence. "But I'm afraid it leaves me no option."

He left his position by the door and reached for his swordbelt, which was hanging on a hook set into the bulkhead. He buckled the heavy studded belt at his narrow waist and settled the sword comfortably on his hip. He took his pair of pistols and thrust them into his belt and slipped a poignard into his boot.

Phoebe watched these preparations with sinking heart. She'd seen him dress for war before, but it never failed to fill her with dread. "Are you going to be fighting, then?"

"I'd be a fool not to be prepared," he returned, swinging his short black cloak around his shoulders. He looked down at Phoebe, still on her stool, and said, conscious of its inadequacy, "There's no need to be afeared, Phoebe."

"Isn't there?" Her eyes were bleak.

"I'll send a message this evening if I don't intend to return tonight," he said, turning back to the cabin door.

He opened it and then paused, his hand on the doorjamb. "Phoebe, I'll ask you once more. Will you give me your word you'll not attempt to leave the ship without my permission?"

An agreement trembled on her lips, but it was an agreement she knew she would never keep. Phoebe remained silent. Proving herself untrustworthy was no route to gaining her husband's trust, as she'd concluded long before.

Cato sighed. "So be it, then." He left, closing the door quietly behind him. Phoebe heard the key grate in the lock.

She jumped to her feet and went to the porthole, her eyes fixed to the small piece of quay visible. Cato appeared in a very few minutes, striding briskly. She watched until he'd disappeared from view.

Phoebe remained at the porthole, her forehead pressed against the glass, staring out as if she might somehow will him back. Her eyes grew somewhat unfocused as the scene ebbed and flowed in and around her telescoped view, and when Brian Morse first appeared across the glass, she barely noticed. Then, with an exclamation, she blinked as if to clear cobwebs from her mind and eyes, and stared fixedly.

Was it truly him? But he was unmistakable. Dressed as elegantly as ever in a dark green coat and britches, lace at throat and wrist, sword at his hip, he was crossing her line of vision and going towards the crooked red-brick building at the rear of the quay. A door stood open at the front of the building. Brian paused, glanced around, then entered the building with the air of one who knew exactly what he was doing.

Phoebe's heart begun to thud. He had followed Cato. And whatever Cato might say, Brian Morse had not come to Rotterdam with his stepfather's best interests at heart. Cato was out there in the town somewhere, and Brian was on his heels. The sense of Brian's malevolence chilled her anew. Cato might dismiss him as a threat, but Phoebe knew better.

She turned almost wildly back to the cabin. The Black Tulip. What was it? Where was it? It sounded like a tavern of some kind. She dressed, fingers fumbling in her haste, then paced the confined space between door and porthole, racking her brains for a means of escape.

She was staring desperately out of the porthole when the key turned in the lock and the door opened behind her.

" 'Ere's yer breakfast." The cabin boy entered with a tray. "Captain says as 'ow Lord Granville says y'are to stay in 'ere." He regarded her curiously as he set the tray down on the table.

Phoebe thought rapidly. Here was her only chance. The boy had helped her before; maybe the same inducements would work again. "D'you know what the Black Tulip is?" she asked.

"A tavern . . . in the town . . . up from the quay."

"Good. Now, listen, there's no time to lose," Phoebe said urgently. "If you leave the door unlocked when you go, I'll give you two more guineas."

The boy's jaw dropped. "I dursn't," he breathed.

"No one will blame you." Phoebe reached under her straw mattress for her purse. She shook out two guineas and laid them on the table beside the tray. "All you have to do is leave, pretend to lock the door, and go on your way."

The coins winked in the sunlight. The boy couldn't take his eyes off them. "I dursn't," he repeated in a whisper.

"I assure you that if Lord Granville's angry, his wrath will fall on my back, not on yours," Phoebe said with perfect truth. "He'll not blame you, I promise."

"But the captain . . ."

"The captain will only blame you if Lord Granville complains," she pointed out, trying to keep the desperation from her voice. Time was wasting. "He's not going to complain about *you*." She pushed the coins a little closer to the edge of the table.

The lad hesitated, thinking. It was true that there had been no unpleasant consequences after he'd let Lady Granville on board. The captain had offered no objections, no one had suspected his own involvement, and Lord Granville and his wife had seemed in perfect accord during the voyage.

And four guineas was unimaginable riches. Beyond the dreams of avarice. "I dunno . . ."

"Lend me your cap and your jerkin," Phoebe said, reaching into the purse for a sovereign, which she laid beside the guineas. "I'll return them to you as soon as I come back. I have to find my husband because there's something I have to tell him. It'll be disastrous if I don't."

The intense conviction in her clear blue eyes was utterly sincere and enough to persuade the already persuadable cabin boy.

He shrugged out of his jerkin and tossed his cap on the table. "You really wants 'em?"

"Yes, they'll make all the difference." Phoebe scooped up the coins and held them out to him. "Here."

He pocketed them and headed for the door. "I'll jest turn the key 'alfway. All you 'ave to do is give it a push."

"Let me try it before you go."

The lad pulled the door shut and turned the key a fraction. "Now," he whispered through the door.

Phoebe gave it a hearty shove. It resisted for a moment,

then flew open with a crack. "That's splendid," she declared. "Now you can say you locked the door without really lying."

"Aye," he agreed a mite doubtfully. "Still be best if nobody knows though."

"They won't," Phoebe assured, pulling the door closed again, listening for the turn of the key. Once she heard it, she resisted the urge to test again that it could be broken open, and turned back to the cabin.

She threw off the skirt, shirt, and jacket of her riding habit and rummaged through Cato's portmanteau for one of his shirts. Her fingers shook in her desperate haste.

Her close-fitting riding britches were not in the least like conventional men's britches, but they would have to do. Cato's shirt came down to mid-thigh and covered a multitude of sins. The cabin boy's ragged, grimy jerkin over the shirt disguised its pristine laundering and the ruffled front. She rolled up the sleeves to hide the ruffled wristbands and tied one of Cato's kerchief's at what she hoped was a jaunty angle into the open collar.

Instead of strapping the britches beneath her boots, she pulled her boots on over them, and then braided her hair tightly. She pinned the braids on top of her head and crammed the boy's greasy cap over them. Without a mirror, she had no idea whether she'd created an image that would pass muster in the streets of Rotterdam, but Phoebe was fairly certain no one would mistake her for Lady Granville, whatever else she might look like.

She felt both sick and hungry and as an afterthought swallowed a few spoonsful of breakfast porridge, hoping to settle her stomach. The she tackled the cabin door. It flew open with a shove from her shoulder, and she stepped out into the passage.

She had to find Brian and follow him. It seemed the most sensible course, rather than heading off blindly in search of the Black Tulip, where she might miss Cato. If she kept Brian in her sights, she was certain he would lead her to

Cato. Surely then there would be an opportunity to warn Cato before Brian sprang any unwelcome surprises.

Phoebe climbed the companionway and emerged on deck trying to maintain the air of one who had every right to be where she was and who knew exactly what she was doing. But she needn't have worried. No one had time to notice her. The deck was abustle as the cargo was unloaded from the hold onto wagons waiting on the quay, patient horses in the traces blowing steamy breaths in the early morning air. It was warming up quickly, though, as the sun climbed higher, promising a lovely spring day.

She glanced up at the quarterdeck, but there was no sign of the captain or the quartermaster, although the bosun was directing operations from the shore.

There was a secondary gangplank at the rear of the ship, and Phoebe headed to the far side of the ship, intending to approach the gangplank from the back. Two sailors on their knees were scrubbing the decking with the great holystones they called bibles. Phoebe slipped past them, and they didn't so much as look up as the unremarkable pair of boots stepped delicately over their newly cleaned decking.

Phoebe jumped down the gangplank to the harbor and felt immediately more secure. No one would stop her now. Purposefully she approached the red-brick building. All around her she heard a harsh guttural tongue that increased her sense of unreality. Did Brian speak Flemish? Did Cato? Curiously the question had never occurred to her before.

The door that Brian had entered was ajar. Was he still inside? She hadn't been able to keep the building under observation the whole time, so he could have left already. In which case she'd just have to find the Black Tulip.

Phoebe hesitated for only a second before she edged through the half-open door and into a dim square room lined with bales and crates. It was a warehouse of sorts, lit only by a couple of small unglazed windows high up on the walls.

She pressed herself against the stone wall and listened, ears straining to catch the slightest sound. Then she heard it. The low murmur of voices from the far side of the warehouse.

She couldn't distinguish any words at this distance and cautiously slid around the wall until she could dart behind a pile of bales. It was like being in a maze, she discovered. She could thread her way across the floor, concealed by bales and cartons, using the sound of voices as a compass.

The voices became more distinct and now she could distinguish Brian Morse's nasal tones. He seemed to be arguing about something. But he was speaking in English.

Phoebe stopped when she was as close as she dared, and quivered behind a bale of striped cotton ticking, barely daring to breathe. A mouse skittered across the straw-strewn floor at her feet, and she barely suppressed a startled cry.

"I want four men onto it," Brian said. "I know this man, I tell you."

"We got t'other agents with Johannes and Karl," his interlocutor said, his voice thickly accented. "They're good."

"But not good enough to get Strickland as well," Brian snapped. "This time we get Strickland as well as the agent. And there'll be no mistakes."

The other man only grunted and Brian continued in clipped and decisive tones, "You don't know our quarry, my friend. Granville is as wily as they come. Get Pieter and you join us yourself."

"Let's see the color of your money."

"There'll be ten guilders for you, I told you!" Brian's voice rose a notch. "You pay the men what you want and keep the rest for yourself. I'll be asking no questions."

"Let's see your purse" was the implacable response.

"It's on the ship. You don't think I'd be fool enough to go on such an errand with that kind of money on my person?" Brian demanded angrily.

"Fifteen guilders, and half now, half when we're done," the other man said after a minute. "You fetch the money and I'll send for the others."

Phoebe could hear Brian's noisy breathing as he wrestled with this expanded demand.

"Twelve," he said finally. "Six now, six later."

There was a short silence, then the other man grunted again and said, "Be back here in an hour."

Brian turned on his heel, his boot grating on the stone floor, and strode from the building.

Phoebe settled down to wait.

Brian cursed as he returned to the sloop that had brought him in pursuit of his stepfather, but the vile mutter was more for form's sake then from genuine annoyance. Twelve guilders was more money than he'd intended to pay, but it was worth it to achieve such a coup. The ever troublesome Walter Strickland eliminated; Cato dead, his stepson's inheritance secured; the certain accolades of the king . . . Oh, yes, it would be worth it.

He glanced at the *White Lady* as he hurried up the gangplank of his own vessel. Where was Phoebe? He'd watched her dart on board at Harwich. Had she stayed? Was she even now below decks on the graceful three-masted schooner?

He'd find out later, once he had Cato spitted on the point of a sword. It would be done before nightfall. It was as certain as the sunset.

His hard little eyes narrowed as he counted coins out of his purse and dropped them into his britches pocket.

No, all in all, for twelve guilders the job was not overpriced. He hurried back to the warehouse.

Phoebe was still crouched behind the bale of ticking when Brian returned. In his absence three other men had arrived, but they were talking incomprehensibly in Flemish. From the tone it seemed as if the discussion was on occasion acrimonious, but the language was so harsh and strange that she couldn't be sure whether she was interpreting the tone correctly.

"Is everyone here?" Brian spoke as he crossed the floor towards the group. "Good." He shook hands with the newcomers before saying brusquely, "Granville will have gone first to the Black Tulip to try to get news of Strickland . . ."

"Strickland's there already," one of the men said.

Brian spun around on him. "How do you know, Pieter? The man hasn't been seen in three months."

Pieter shrugged. "He's come out of hiding, then. He's shown himself at the Black Tulip, according to my source."

"Who's reliable?" Brian snapped the question. It was received in sardonic silence that carried its own answer.

Brian controlled his anger. His companions were hired assassins who operated according to their own rules. If they decided they didn't like him, or the job, they'd drop both without compunction. And he needed them. He needed to be able to trust them to watch his back. Their loyalty was given in direct proportion to its financial worth, and he considered he'd paid over the odds for it, but he still couldn't risk antagonizing them.

"So presumably Strickland has some information to impart," Brian mused as if the previous awkwardness had not occurred. "Important enough to let himself be seen by anyone on the watch for him."

"It's his way," one of the others responded. "He goes underground for weeks until he's acquired something of interest, then he pops up like a rabbit, just shows his head. That's how we've managed to grab the last two agents. Strickland comes up for air, they move towards him, we snap 'em up."

"This time we get both of them," Brian declared, then he couldn't help adding, "What I don't understand is why, when you all know so much about Strickland's habits, he's constantly eluded you. The bounty for his head would be tempting enough, I would have thought."

"The man's slippery as an eel," Heinrich growled. "We've followed him often enough, then he goes to ground just as we're within an inch of catching him."

"Aye, but I'll lay odds he's not sent any dispatches off in a while," the first man declared. "We've made it too hot for him."

"A matter for congratulation," Brian muttered, then recollected himself. "We'll start at the Tulip. If Strickland's not there, Granville will be trying to track him down."

The five men left the warehouse, and Phoebe, after she forced herself to wait a few minutes until they were clear of the building, ducked out of hiding and sped to the door in their wake.

She stood blinking in the sunshine, looking around the quay, but there was no sign of Brian or of a group of likely-looking assassins. She went over to a carrier supervising the unloading of his cart.

"The Black Tulip?"

He frowned as if he didn't understand her, but when she repeated the words, he nodded and jerked a thumb towards a narrow alley leading off the harbor.

Phoebe thanked him and ran for the alley. It was shadowed by the overarching roofs of the houses on each side, and the kennel was thick with refuse, the cobbles on either side slimy so that she nearly slipped in her haste.

The steep alley turned a corner and she saw her quarry way up ahead, the five men striding easily, purposefully. They had the air of men on a mission and were clearly unconcerned that any of the town's inhabitants might take exception to their rule of law.

*C*ato leaned against the counter in the taproom, one hand circling his pot of ale as his deceptively idle gaze roamed around the dark room. The low rafters were blackened with smoke, and blue rings of pipe smoke wreathed heavily above the heads of the taproom's occupants. This early morning it was a dour, generally silent crowd, but Cato was aware that he was under observation by more than one man.

A tavern wench threaded her way through the room, hefting her tray of tankards aloft, deftly sidestepping the streams of tobacco spittle that arched through the air to clot in the sawdust scattered over the floor. Boiling cabbage, smoking tallow, and stale beer mingled in a noxious mélange.

Cato waited. He knew he'd been noticed and he hoped that someone in contact with Walter Strickland would pass on the news of his presence. Of course, there was another side to the coin. Not just friends, but enemies also would be aware of the Englishman's arrival in town. But to catch Strickland's attention, he had to make himself generally visible.

It was to be hoped Strickland would find him first, Cato reflected aridly as he called for a refill, his right hand tightening instinctively over his sword hilt.

The tavern keeper, a red-faced man with a sour and harried expression, refilled Cato's tankard at the keg. "There's a lad just come, sir," he murmured. "Says yer 'onor might want a word with 'im."

Cato raised an eyebrow. "Might I?"

The tavern keeper shrugged. "That's fer Yer Worship to decide."

Cato drank his ale. He glanced casually around and caught sight of a small boy in the doorway. Cato set his empty tankard on the counter, tossed a silver coin beside it, and strolled to the door. He walked past the boy and went out into the alley.

The boy darted after him and kept pace, trotting at his heels. Neither of them spoke but when they reached a side turning, the boy tugged Cato's cloak, gesturing that he should take the turning.

Wondering whether he was walking blithely into a trap, Cato followed the child. He could see no alternative to taking the risk. They were in the street of the cobblers, and shoemakers sat in doorways plying their trade. Several glanced up as the elegant gentleman passed, and a few exchanged looks.

At a house at the very end of the street, the lad stopped. He stood in the doorway regarding Cato with hopeful eyes.

Cato dug into his pocket and gave him a coin, wryly trusting that he was not paying an assassin's lure. The boy grabbed it and took to his heels with an alacrity that increased Cato's unease.

He glanced up and down the street. People seemed to be minding their own business, goodwives bustling with baskets and brooms, shaking mats from upper windows, calling to each other in a cheerful stream of incomprehensible chatter.

After a tiny hesitation Cato stepped through the doorway into the darkness beyond. It took a minute for his eyes to become accustomed to the gloom after the sunshine outside. He was in a long, narrow passage with a door at the far end. A staircase rose to his right. It was very quiet and yet he knew he was not alone.

He glanced at the door behind him, half expecting to see his retreat cut off, but there was no one there, just a puddle of sunshine on the threshold. With another mental shrug, he headed for the stairs, climbing rapidly on the smooth wooden steps worn down over the years by the procession of countless feet.

The stairs emerged onto a small landing at the head. There were two doors, one of which stood slightly ajar. Cato pushed it open. The chamber appeared to be deserted. The grate was empty and the small window was unshuttered. He stood in the doorway listening intently. Then quietly he closed the door at his back and dropped the heavy bar across it, locking himself in. If there was danger, it was not going to come up behind him.

"A wise move," a voice murmured.

Cato spun round, his sword already in his hand, and found

himself facing a broad-shouldered man in rough homespuns who also held a naked blade in one hand and a dagger in the other.

Cato realized the man had stepped out of the fireplace. "Strickland?" he inquired calmly, sheathing his sword.

"Who wants him?"

"Cato, Marquis of Granville." Cato held out his hand.

"Well, I'm honored indeed." Walter Strickland sheathed his own sword and took Cato's hand in a brief clasp. "It's been the devil's own job just staying alive in the last weeks." He gave a short laugh and thrust his dagger into the sheath at his hip.

"We assumed so. All the agents we sent have disappeared." Cato walked to the window and looked down onto the street. "Is this house secure?"

"No. I know of no such place," Strickland responded. "I move constantly. You were lucky to catch me today. I'm heading for The Hague this evening. I thought to try to send my dispatches from there, since Rotterdam's become so chancy."

"You've heard that the king has gone to join the Scots?" Cato left the window and came into the middle of the room.

"No." Strickland shook his head. "But that'll set the cat among the king of Orange's pigeons." He went to a tall cupboard and opened it, taking out a bottle of some clear liquid.

"Genever," he said, uncorking the bottle. "The Dutch distill it out of juniper berries." He poured a measure into two cups. "Crude stuff but I've seen it put courage into many a craven heart." He handed Cato one of the cups.

Cato drank it and grimaced. "Foul," he pronounced.

Strickland grinned. "It's an acquired taste." He refilled his own cup and drained it in one. "So the king's gone for a Scot, eh?"

Cato nodded, setting his cup down with another grimace. "And I'm sent to bring you back. Your work here is done and there's a feeling that you've much you can tell us . . . the kind of fine details and opinions that don't find space in a dispatch."

"Aye, I reckon so," Strickland agreed. "And I'll not be sorry to see the green fields of home again." He gave another short laugh. "Or do I mean the bloody fields of home."

Cato's expression was somber. "There's been much of that, but we're nearing the end."

"Unless the Scots throw their weight behind the king?"

"All things are possible," Cato said.

"But not probable?" Strickland heard the cynical note.

"The king's never been a trustworthy ally. But we shall see." Cato walked to the window again. He was feeling uneasy, superstitiously uncomfortable at the handy speed with which he'd accomplished his mission.

Something in the street below caught his eye. A figure in the most bizarre array of garments had darted into the doorway of the house opposite. It wasn't the oddity of the boy's clothing that caused Cato to knit his brow, however. It was the sense of something all too familiar about him.

22

*P*hoebe had followed Brian and his cohorts to the Black Tulip. She had lingered outside, kicking pebbles, whistling casually between her teeth, trying to look inconspicuous while she kept the door under observation.

It was a new role for her, this one of spy, and she felt self-conscious, wondering if her disguise would pass muster, wondering if she looked convincingly idle, indifferent to her surroundings. Reassuringly, no one seemed to cast her a second glance, and she was beginning to relax into the part when one of Brian's associates reappeared in the doorway of the tavern.

He was a heavily bearded man, stocky, with powerful biceps and very large hands. He glanced up and down the street, then put his fingers to his lips and whistled, a piercing sound that seemed to spin away, shivering into the clear air.

Phoebe slid around a convenient corner from where she could watch unobserved. Presently a ragged child came running up the alley from the quay. He came to a full stop in front of the burly man who still stood in the doorway of the inn.

Phoebe could hear the man's voice raised and hectoring. The child cowered as if expecting a blow. It didn't come but the boy still shrank back as he poured forth a voluble stream of words to which the burly man appeared to be paying considerable attention.

Brian stepped into the doorway as the child fell silent. He spoke to the burly man. Phoebe couldn't hear what was said but it seemed to satisfy Brian, who tossed a groat to the cobbles at the boy's feet and turned back to the inn.

The child grabbed up his meager payment and flew down the street. The burly man spat onto the cobbles and drew a knife from a sheath at his hip. He held the blade up to the sun, then whetted it against the stone lintel of the door above his head.

The gesture was so redolent of menace that Phoebe's skin prickled.

Brian and the three other men joined the burly man in the street. There was a short colloquy and then they strode off towards the town.

Phoebe followed at a safe distance, ducking into doorways, sliding around corners, always trying to vary her progress so that her pursuit wouldn't be too obvious should any one of them chance to look behind. But they seemed blithely oblivious of everyone around them as they turned onto the street of the cobblers.

They walked without subterfuge, as if their errand had no sinister intent, and Phoebe found this more menacing than anything else. She knew in her gut that they had mischief in mind, and the idea that they didn't give a damn who knew it was terrifying. It seemed to imply that murderous mayhem in broad daylight would draw no remark on the streets of Rotterdam.

Halfway down the street of the cobblers they stopped. Phoebe dropped back, wishing she could get close enough to hear what they were saying. The burly man gestured to the end of the lane. After a few words the five men continued, but now they left the center of the lane and moved to the right, keeping close against the lime-washed half-timbered walls of the row houses so that they were shielded from view from above.

Phoebe crept along on the opposite side of the street, keeping just behind them, moving from doorway to doorway. She drew a few curious glances now, and she responded with a vacant slack-mouthed smile that she hoped would label her as rather less than mentally alert. She had absolutely no idea what she was going to do, only that she needed to do something.

Brian and his accomplices stopped just to the right of the house at the very end of the lane. It looked an unremarkable building, with a narrow door, a window on the ground floor, and another above, beneath a sloping red-tiled roof.

Brian and the burly man were conferring, their backs to the street. Phoebe darted into the doorway of the house directly opposite where they were standing. She looked up at the window of the house and her heart did a swallow dive. Cato stood there. He was looking down but he wouldn't see Brian and his fellows, who were pressed against the wall to either side of the door.

Would he see her if she gestured? No, how could he? Phoebe chewed her lip, conscious of her helplessness, and yet every muscle strained to seize whatever opportunity arose.

The door behind her was closed. A flowerpot bursting with geraniums stood on the windowsill beside the door. Phoebe reached around and took possession of the flowerpot. They were very pretty geraniums, pink and white striped.

She held the pot between her hands, took a deep breath, and hurled it up and across the narrow street. It fell short of the window but smashed against the stone in a discordant clatter, with shards of earthenware, black earth, and striped flowers cascading to the ground.

For a moment there was confusion. Brian and his men jumped instinctively as if they were under fire. Cato disappeared from the window. Phoebe hurled herself out of the doorway and dived under a bush at the side of the building.

"Sounds like trouble," Walter Strickland observed in the tone of one accustomed to such inconveniences. He moved to the fireplace. "There's a way out here."

"No," said Cato, making for the door.

"Man, don't be foolhardy! What if there's an ambush on the street?" Strickland protested.

"Maybe there is," Cato agreed grimly. "But that's not all that's down there." He drew his pistols from his belt. "Are you with me?"

Strickland looked at him in puzzlement for a moment, then shrugged. "Of course." He drew his sword and headed for the stairs. "I'm accustomed to rather more clandestine operations," he observed cheerfully at the head of the stairs. "I suppose you don't care to tell me what we're facing?"

"Apart from my wife, I can only guess, my friend," Cato said and jumped ahead of him onto the stairs. "But at least we've been warned."

Strickland shook his head in even greater puzzlement. Granville seemed to be talking in riddles. He followed, however, raising his sword. Scraps didn't come in an agent's way too often, but he was not averse once in a while.

They broke into the sunlit morning. Cato's eyes met Brian's. Cold and hard over a leveled pistol. Cato read murder in his stepson's clear gaze and he knew that he had underestimated him. There was much more to Brian's ambitions than politics. He and he alone was Brian's target on this Rotterdam street. The shot came in the very instant Cato understood his stepson's intent. Cato whirled sideways with battlefield instinct, and the ball whistled over his shoulder, embedding itself into the soft wood of the doorjamb at his back.

Cato himself had hesitated to fire. His finger was on the trigger, his aim steady as he'd looked down the barrel of Brian's weapon, and yet against every soldier's instinct, some deep sense of moral obligation had held his hand. But Brian had shot to kill. And now Cato was aware only of a cold determination to overcome an enemy. And there were five of them. Of Phoebe there was no sign, for which he offered a prayer of thanks. He had to hope that wherever she was now, she would have the sense to stay there.

He swung sideways and fired both pistols at the two men who were grappling with Strickland. One of them went down with a shriek of pain, and Strickland shook himself free of the other rather like a dog ridding himself of water and jumped sideways, sword slashing.

One down. Four against two. Cato was aware of the odds even as he forced himself to forget that his adopted son and heir was intending to kill him. He cast aside his now useless pistols and drew his sword.

Phoebe was still crouched beneath the bush. She had realized belatedly that it was a hawthorn bush, and her back felt like a porcupine's as the wicked thorns pricked with every shallow breath she took. The jarring slam and crash of steel on steel assailed her ears, but she could see little of what was happening. However, she knew the odds had to be against Cato. A boot she knew was not Cato's pranced within her grasp. She lunged and grabbed it with both hands. Its owner went down with a yell of astounded outrage.

Emboldened, Phoebe wormed her way out of the shelter of the bush. She had lost the cabin boy's cap in her first dive beneath the thorns, and her braids were uncoiling onto her shoulders, but her appearance was the least of her concerns now. Her anxious gaze sought Cato.

There was blood on the lane, which was now empty of all but the seven men and Phoebe. The inhabitants of the street of the cobblers had made themselves scarce at the first pistol shot.

The man Phoebe had pulled down scrambled to his feet and saw her. He leaped for her. Phoebe jumped sideways. Cato's sword slashed, catching the man's forearm. Phoebe saw Cato's eyes, dark, brilliant, utterly intimidating as they seemed to look straight through her. She ducked and raced for the far side of the alley.

A hand grabbed her, dragged her back hurtfully, yanking her arm up behind her back so that she bit back a scream of pain.

And then everything stopped.

Cato dropped his swordpoint. Walter Strickland remained where he was, his own swordpoint poised.

Brian Morse hauled Phoebe closer against him, and her bent arm shrieked in agony. She closed her lips and stared at the ground, fighting the welling tears.

"Well, well," Brian murmured, his free hand twisting into her loosened braids. This wasn't what he would have chosen, but a man accepted opportunities as they arose. There were other women as enticing as the ramshackle Phoebe. Plenty of them, ready and willing to lie down for the new marquis of Granville.

He gave a short laugh. "Talk about where angels fear to tread! Really, Phoebe, one can't help but pity your husband."

He raised his eyes and looked with naked triumph at Cato "Drop your sword, my lord." His voice was soft and smooth as he brought up his dagger, laying its edge against Phoebe's throat. "And yours, Mr. Strickland." He smiled at the agent. "I'm certain Lord Granville will accede to my request."

Walter Strickland glanced at Cato. Lord Granville's expression was carved in ice. Strickland's glance asked a question, but it received no answer and the agent remained with his swordpoint raised.

"Come, sir," Brian cajoled as the edge of his dagger pressed against Phoebe's throat. "Lay down your weapons or she dies . . . right now." He turned the dagger slightly so that she could feel the cutting edge rasp against the tender underside of her chin.

Phoebe raised her eyes and met Cato's bleak gaze. Fear shivered down her spine, crawled over her scalp. The knife at her throat pressed harder and she knew with chill, despairing certainty that she was going to die . . . that Cato was not going to save her. She had forced herself into the middle of his mission, and Cato would permit nothing and no one to come between himself and his duty. She had always known it.

Brian repeated, "Lay down your arms, my lord."

Cato regarded Phoebe with a blank stare. It seemed he was looking right through her.

"You're more of a fool than I thought you, Brian," Cato said harshly. "I've no time for sentiment. I hadn't with your mother. Why should I have with this meddlesome chit?" He spun around, his sword catching the light as it cut, breaking the momentary spell of inaction.

The movement was so sudden, the sentiment so harshly surprising that Brian's attention wavered for an instant. Phoebe kicked up and back at the same moment she drove her free elbow into the pit of Brian's belly. As he bent forward, gasping with the nauseating pain wrenching his groin and stomach, she sank her teeth into the hand that now wavered at her throat.

His hold slackened and she spun away from him, delivering an almighty kick to his thigh as she went.

Cato caught her, threw her sideways out of the fray, and went for Brian. He was filled with a cold fury that had only one target. There was no room in Cato's soul now for compassion, for remorse, for family ties. He would kill the man who had come within a breath of killing Phoebe.

Phoebe had been thrown to her knees by the side of the lane. She dragged herself to her feet, her eyes taking in the scene. Cato was fighting Brian. Cato's friend was hard pressed by the others. A knife lay in the gutter. Phoebe picked it up, closed her eyes, and plunged it downward in the general direction of one of Walter Strickland's assailants. It met the resistance of clothing and the flesh beneath, before penetrating the man's shoulder.

He dropped his sword to the cobbles with a vile curse and Phoebe jumped back, leaving the knife sticking up from his back. She bent and picked up the dropped sword, holding the heavy blade effortfully with two hands clasped around the hilt. She had no idea whether she could wield it to any purpose, but she felt more useful holding it. Behind her she could hear the clash of swords as Cato's advance inexorably forced Brian back towards the wall of the house.

Cato was a better swordsman than Brian, and on an even field the younger man had not a chance. Brian knew it. His eyes grew wild as he searched for an advantage that would overcome his stepfather's greater skill. Only his accomplices could give it to him, but his bellows for assistance fell on deaf ears. He saw Cato's eyes. Black as agate. Pitiless as they'd never been before. And Brian knew he was lost.

When Cato's sword slid beneath his arm as easily as a knife through butter, Brian sighed almost with relief that it was over. He fell to one knee and then slowly dropped in a fetal curl to the ground.

The two men left standing took one glance and then with an almost comical gesture of resignation backed off and melted into the passage alongside the house, leaving their wounded comrades to fend for themselves. Unseen eyes from every window along the street watched the battleground.

Cato, his gaze unreadable, stood looking down at Brian Morse.

"Is he dead?" Phoebe asked, breathless, still hefting the great sword between both hands.

"Not quite." Cato sheathed his bloody sword. He looked her over, a swift appraising glance. He tilted her chin and examined the skin where Brian's knife had pressed, then he nodded as if satisfied.

"Give me that." He took the weapon from her and walked over to the other wounded men. He regarded them unspeaking for a moment, then turned to Strickland, who was sheathing his own sword. "All well?"

"Aye," Strickland said. "But I didn't fancy the odds, I have to say." He looked curiously at Phoebe, who still stood beside Brian, unsure what to say or do next. A faint grin quirked

Strickland's firm mouth. "Although they seemed to even up a little," he added.

Cato offered no comment. "Let's get out of here," he said. "We'll have the entire town around our ears soon." He crooked a commanding finger in Phoebe's direction. "Come."

Phoebe came slowly. "Will you leave Brian?"

"I'll not kill him if I haven't already done so," Cato replied. "Now come."

The curt tone was not reassuring but Phoebe could not imagine ever being reassured by Cato again. She glanced once more at the wounded men. The street was still deserted. She could see no one but she could sense many eyes upon them.

Cato put a hand in the small of her back, urging her forward, and Phoebe, bewildered and unhappy, obeyed the pressure because she could see no alternative.

"So, who's this?" Walter Strickland inquired, wiping his dagger on the side of his thigh. He regarded Phoebe with a degree of fascination.

"Would you believe—my wife?" Cato inquired, removing a thorn sticking out from the back of Phoebe's jerkin.

"No," Strickland said frankly. He examined her closely and Phoebe felt her color mount.

"Then believe it, my friend." Cato took a fold of the jerkin between finger and thumb. "This is the most disgusting article. Where did you get it?"

"I have to give it back," Phoebe said dully. "I only gave him a sovereign for it. And I seem to have lost the cap."

"That wasn't an answer to my question," Cato commented aridly, "but I suppose I'll make sense of it all at some point." He shook his head with an air of mock dismay. "Is that one of my shirts you're wearing under that revolting jerkin?"

Phoebe was too confused by this sudden change of tone to reply. He sounded amused, the curtness of a moment ago vanished. She could detect no anger in his expression, but no gratitude for her intervention either. She could make no sense of anything except the simple fact of Cato's safety; it was all that mattered.

And yet in the aftermath of that burst of intense physical and emotional activity came a deep trough of depression. She couldn't lose the memory of his eyes: cold, bleak, utterly rejecting. He had turned from her. He'd told Brian only his duty mattered. She had saved herself. Cato had done nothing to save her. *He'd turned from her.*

"Your *wife*, Granville?" Walter Strickland was finally shaken out of his customary composure.

"Lady Granville . . . Walter Strickland," Cato said with a ceremonious gesture.

"I'm very pleased to meet you, sir," Phoebe responded numbly. Then a flicker of spirit came to her aid. She added with a lift of her chin, "But you shouldn't judge by appearances."

"Oh, believe me, Strickland, in this case you should," Cato declared.

"I'm delighted to make your acquaintance, Lady Granville." Walter Strickland offered a bow, an amused gleam in his eye as he responded to the odd formality of the introduction. "You've done us good service this morning."

Phoebe waited for some acknowledgment from Cato, but all he said, in a voice as dry as sere leaves, was "My wife is a woman of many parts. All of them as eccentric as her present disreputable costume."

They had reached the quay where the decks of the *White Lady* were now quiet, the unloading over, the crew taking liberty in the town under the warm rays of the noon sun. Phoebe felt tears pricking behind her eyes. Cato was making fun of her. First he abandoned her, then he made mock of her. Maybe he was punishing her; maybe he thought she deserved it; it was unjust and unkind.

She took a step away from him, towards the gangway to the ship, longing for the privacy of the little cabin.

"You'll want to negotiate your passage with Captain

Allan, Strickland," Cato said putting a firm hand on Phoebe's shoulder, wordlessly bringing her back beside him. "I imagine you'll find him in the Seagull. He told me this morning he'd be spending most of the day there."

Strickland looked over at the tavern in question, then cast a sidelong glance at Phoebe, who stood stiff and silent under Cato's hand. "Reckon I'll find him, then. I daresay it's safe to show my face about town now. Unless there are more bands of mischief makers after my blood." He gave an easy chuckle as if the idea were absurd, and loped off to the Seagull.

"I wish to go to the cabin," Phoebe said, trying once more to move away from Cato's restraining hand.

"That is precisely where we're going," Cato responded imperturbably. "We have a great deal to discuss, you and I." His hand slid to her arm and he urged her forward onto the *White Lady*.

"I wish to go to the cabin alone," Phoebe protested. "I don't feel very well."

"That's perhaps not surprising after such an adventure," he returned with a calm nod and without releasing his hold. "Let us see what we can do to improve matters."

It seemed she had no choice. He was going to accompany her whether she wished it or not.

"Just who does that vile jerkin belong to?" he asked when they had reached the privacy of the cabin. He closed the door and stood against it, his hands resting on his hips, an unmistakable glimmer of amusement in his eye.

"The cabin boy," Phoebe said, shrugging out of the garment with a jerky movement. She was beginning to feel angry now. His mockery was the last straw, and she welcomed this clean emotion spurting through the mire of her wretched confusion. "I gave him a sovereign, but now I've lost his cap, so I'll have to pay him more for it."

"You enlisted the help of this cabin boy to get off the ship?"

Phoebe glared at him. "He helped me to get on it at Harwich."

Cato whistled softly. "I never did ask how you managed that. How stupidly remiss of me. If I'd known, I daresay I could have prevented this morning's little escapade. What inducements did you use to persuade this hapless boy?"

"Guineas," Phoebe snapped. "Four of them in all."

Cato was astounded. "Where in hell did you get such a sum, Phoebe?"

She turned her back to him as she unbuttoned his shirt. "The pawnbroker in Witney."

There was silence. Then Cato said in conversational tones, "Forgive me, but I thought I had forbidden you to visit the pawnbroker again. Alas, my imperfect memory."

Phoebe closed her lips firmly and cast aside his shirt. She reached for her own, which still lay across the stool.

"Of course," Cato continued in the same affable tone, "that was in the days when I was still laboring under the delusion that I had some husbandly authority over your actions. I can't imagine how I could have been so foolishly mistaken."

Anger took hold, burning away the last wretched vestige of self-pity. Phoebe turned on him, holding the shirt in her hands, her eyes blazing in her now pale face.

"Must you mock me as well? What difference does it make to you what I do so long as I keep out of your way?" she cried bitterly. "I know full well how I stand with you, my lord."

Cato was taken aback. The amusement died out of his eyes. "What are you talking about, Phoebe?" His voice was suddenly very quiet.

"You needn't worry," she said in the same low bitter tone. "I'll not step between you and your work again. I know my place, sir. It's taken me a long time, I admit, but I'm obviously rather slow-witted. It took a hammer to knock it into my thick skull, but believe me, I have finally taken the point."

She raised a hand as if to ward him off as she fumbled with the sleeves of her shirt, which somehow seemed to have turned themselves inside out.

Cato twisted the garment from her grasp and threw it onto the bunk. He took her by the shoulders, his fingers sliding beneath the thin straps of her chemise to close warmly on the bare skin beneath.

"I'm not certain what you're talking about, Phoebe, but I think you had better make it crystal clear to me without delay."

Tears of anger, disappointment, the deepest hurt stood out in the speedwell blue eyes as she met his gaze. "Isn't it obvious?" she demanded, her voice thick but steady. "I know I've never been more than a convenience to you . . . or rather, most of the time an *inconvenience*," she added caustically.

"I tried to show you that I could be more to you than that, that I was worthy of your confidence, that I could take part in your work, in everything that concerns you, but you won't see it, you won't listen . . . you just won't open your mind!"

She dashed a hand across her eyes, but the flood of angry words continued. "And now I really know what I'm worth! *Nothing!* Isn't that so?"

"Hey . . . hey!" Cato shook her in an attempt to stop the raging, tear-drenched tirade. "What in hell's teeth are you talking about, woman! I realize you've had a nasty experience, but you can't hold me responsible for that! You've made it clear countless times that you'll plow your own furrow, Phoebe, and the consequences of your own decisions are yours to bear."

"Yes," Phoebe said, her voice now dull. "That's true. But I didn't think I meant so little to you that you'd . . . you'd . . ." Her voice faltered. Somehow she couldn't say it.

"That I would what?" Cato inquired in a tone suddenly as soft as silk.

"That you would have abandoned me," Phoebe said. "If

I hadn't saved myself, you would have left me to Brian's knife."

Cato stared, unable to believe what he was hearing. "You think I would have done *what*?"

Phoebe tried to shrug out of his hold. "It doesn't matter," she said. "I should have known. You've always made it clear that your duty comes first. I got in the way. Of course you couldn't sacrifice your mission because of my stupid mistake."

Slowly Cato began to understand what she was talking about. But it was incomprehensible. Impossible that she should imagine him capable of such a barbarity. "Let me understand this. Because I really want to be sure I have this right."

His fingers curled into her shoulders with bruising pressure. "You're accusing me of being ready to leave you to Brian? Is that really what you're saying, Phoebe?"

Phoebe felt the bright glaze of her righteous conviction dim somewhat. "But you did," she said. "You told him you didn't care about me. You turned away. I don't know how you could do that, but you did."

"Dear God! How could you even *imagine* such a thing? What the devil have I ever done that you would believe such a thing of me?" Cato demanded.

"You said it."

"And what happened when I said it?" he inquired, a muscle twitching at the corner of his mouth.

There was something dangerous about that muscle. Phoebe thought back, looking for the right answer. She could still feel the knife at her throat. She could still see Cato's eyes, so black, so blank, looking straight through her. She made no reply, but her hand went unconsciously to her throat.

"Brian was thrown off balance by the unexpected." Cato answered his own question. "If you hadn't been quick enough to take advantage of his momentary surprise, I would have done so myself."

Had she been mistaken? Had she in the rush of hurt and uncertainty drawn the wrong conclusion?

"Come!" he commanded, clicking finger and thumb imperatively. Phoebe could see in the hard set of his mouth, the dark blaze in his eyes how he struggled to contain his own anger. "You owe me an explanation for such an accusation. And I would hear it *now*."

Why had he suddenly managed to put her in the wrong? It was so unfair. All the months of frustrated hopes came rushing to the fore, and she faced him now with a wild outpouring of her deepest emotion, the truth tumbling from her lips in a passionate cascade.

"You don't love me. I love you so much and you don't feel anything much for me. Oh, I'm an amusing toy, sometimes. Good for bedsport. You said once you liked me, and I daresay you do, most of the time, except when I get in the way. I know I'm not important to you, not truly important. You've made that clear many times. Your own world is the only thing that matters to you, so why would you make such a sacrifice for me?"

She turned her eyes from him, unable to look at him as she poured out her heart. "Don't you understand? I *need* you to love me. I've loved you for so long; you're my life. I need to be *your* life. But I know you can't love me, and since I don't mean anything really important to you, it's hardly surprising I should take your words at face value."

"Dear God, Phoebe!" Cato caught her face with hard hands, forcing her to look at him.

"How can you say such things! Oh, I agree that you have come close to driving me to insanity on occasion. So close that sometimes I have been on the brink of losing all vestige of civilized control. I don't know what to do with you. I can't manage you. But dear God, girl!"

He stopped, looking down at her intense countenance, at the wide, generous mouth, the rounded chin, the snub nose. He looked deep into her passion-filled eyes. And it was as if he was seeing her for the first time. He saw her uncertainty, her vulnerability, the trust with which she had given him her heart. And he saw the deep well of love and passion, saw into the very depths of her soul . . . and finally Cato understood his own. Unwieldy, troublesome emotion though it was, love held him in thrall. He'd denied it because it frightened him. To lose control was his ultimate fear. He never admitted anger, and he never admitted love. But Phoebe had driven him to fury, as she had enwrapped him in love.

He ran his hands through his hair in a gesture of resigned defeat. "I couldn't imagine taking a daily breath without knowing that you were beside me," he said, making no attempt to conceal his surprise at the revelation.

"It's taking me a long time to understand you, but God help me, that's part of your fascination. I am in thrall to you. I cannot do without you."

Phoebe, dumbstruck, just stared up at him. In her wildest imaginings she had never expected to hear such a declaration of love. It was not tender, not sweet, not loving. It was positively outraged. And yet she had never heard such music.

"I didn't know," she said eventually. "How could I have known?"

"You could have used the sense God gave you," Cato snapped. "At this moment I don't know whether I'm closer to making love to you or wringing your neck. Both options have a distinct appeal."

"Could I choose?" Phoebe slipped her arms around his neck. She smiled at him. It was a tremulous smile and yet beneath lurked the suddenly acquired power of a woman who finally knew her self. And knew that she was loved.

Cato read that knowledge in the narrowed, seductive gaze as surely as if it had been written on vellum. "Dear God," he muttered. "What have I unleashed?"

"Anything you wish, sir," Phoebe responded. "I can be anything . . . and everything . . . you wish."

He pushed his hands through her hair, smoothing it back, outlining her skull, leaving her face clear and open.

"Believe me, my ragged robin, you are."

Phoebe was not fooled by the resignation in his voice. How could she be when his eyes glowed with such a powerful marriage of love and lust?

When finally all was right with the world.

"I love you," she whispered and felt his love flow into her with his soft breath as he brought his mouth to hers.

Epilogue

"*See how fat I am, Olivia!*" There was no lamentation in Phoebe's voice, rather a note of smug satisfaction, as she stood sideways to the mirror, cupping her round belly in both hands.

Olivia looked up from the letter she was reading. "You're not fat. If anything, your face is thinner than before."

"Do you think so?" Phoebe pinched the skin beneath her chin, examining her countenance closely. "Yes, I think you're right. I can see my cheekbones. I look quite elegant, don't you think?" She chuckled at this absurdity and walked to the window.

"Portia says they might be able to c-come for Christmas . . . at least she and the children. Rufus has to be in London again." Olivia refolded the letter.

"Oh, how splendid," Phoebe said with satisfaction. "Then they can all take part in my pageant on Twelfth Night." She wandered over to the window where a bare branch scratched the pane under a brisk early November wind.

"Actually, now I'm quite glad we couldn't put it on in midsummer. There was so much excitement with the Scots giving the king to Parliament, and then Cato couldn't be here. People couldn't concentrate properly. But it'll be much better as part of the Christmas festivities, don't you think?"

"Very," Olivia agreed. "Everyone will be much more inclined for revelry. When should we start rehearsals? And we should be thinking about—"

"Oh, here's Cato!" Phoebe interrupted her without ceremony. A party of horsemen had just ridden up the drive, Lord Granville at their head. Phoebe gathered up her skirts and hurried to the door, saying delightedly, "I didn't think he'd be back for days."

She hastened from the parlor and ran down the stairs to the door that Bisset had already opened. She ran past the butler and down the shallow steps to the gravel sweep where Cato had just dismounted.

"You're almost a week before you said to expect you!" Phoebe's eyes glowed as she came towards him.

"Well, my business was conducted sooner than I'd expected," Cato said. He took her hands and drew her against him, heedless of their audience. "And in truth, sweet, I was impatient to get back to you. Are you well?" He clasped the back of her neck, running his fingers into the loose coil of hair on her nape.

"Oh, wonderfully well," Phoebe assured him, standing on tiptoe to kiss the corner of his mouth. "I don't think I've ever felt better."

Cato laughed softly. If pregnancy ever suited any woman, it suited Phoebe. Everything about her radiated a lush, sensual richness that was accentuated by her own delight in her condition. She carried herself with a pride and intrinsic elegance of spirit that transcended the haphazard pinning and buttoning and hemming of her various garments. Even with dirt on her hands and smudges on her face, she was radiant.

"Will you be home long this time?" She tucked her hand into his as they went into the house.

"No . . . but when I leave, we will all leave."

"Oh." Phoebe frowned. "Do we go far?"

"To Hampton Court, where the king is in residence during negotiations with Parliament. I'll be negotiating with his advisors throughout Christmas, so we may as well make a family party of it."

"Oh, then I'll have to put on my pageant in the palace." Phoebe frowned as she stopped in the doorway to his study.

"I'm going to stage it for Twelfth Night. Do you think that's a good idea?"

Cato had a rather conspiratorial smile on his face. "An excellent idea, but you can hardly play Gloriana with a swollen belly."

"No, but Portia is coming to visit and she can play it. I'm sure they'll be welcome at Hampton Court too."

"Decatur has already been asked by Parliament to mediate. He'll be at Hampton Court," Cato informed her. "But who then do you have in mind to play Dudley to Portia's queen?" He raised a quizzical eyebrow. "Not I, I trust?"

"No, of course not," Phoebe said vigorously. "I wrote the part for you, but only for you to play it opposite me. Maybe Rufus would take it . . . but he's so . . . so plain and uncompromising, not at all like Robert Dudley."

Cato's secretive smile seemed to deepen. "I have a present for you. And in the circumstances, it seems a remarkably appropriate one."

"Oh?" Phoebe's eyes widened in anticipation. "What could it be?"

"Well, if you'd step inside instead of blocking the doorway, I might be able to show you." He propelled her forward into his study as he spoke.

Phoebe gazed at him raptly as he reached inside his black velvet doublet and drew out a slim package wrapped in oiled parchment.

He handed it to her, still smiling.

"Whatever is it?" Phoebe exclaimed, turning it around in her hands.

"There's a simple way to find out."

Phoebe tore at the wrappings and then stared, her mouth open. She held a leather-bound book, gold lettering on the spine and cover. It was her name. She opened the book and with an expression of awe turned the delicate vellum pages.

"It's my pageant," she said in wonderment, slowly raising

her eyes to Cato's face. "All printed up. How did it get into a book?"

"A printer in London," he replied.

"But . . . but how could he have had it? Where did it come from?"

"My sweet, I gave it to him," Cato explained patiently, amused and delighted by her reaction.

"But how could you have? It's in the parlor abovestairs."

She looked at him in bemusement.

"I confess to some help," he said. "Olivia secretly made a copy of it. Fortunately she's able to read your writing . . . I doubt the printer could have made it out," he added with a chuckle.

"All this time you've been planning this and you never said a word!" Phoebe cried. "You never said anything about my work. I assumed you weren't interested in it."

"Once upon a time, that may have been true." He brushed a straying lock of hair from her forehead. "But it's been many months since that was the case. And you are a most accomplished poet. I've taken the liberty of showing this and some other examples of your poetry to several people, all of whom are looking forward to meeting you when we go to London."

"Poets?"

"Some. Most notably, John Suckling and Mr. Milton."

"They *liked* my work?" Phoebe stared in total disbelief now.

"Reluctantly, at least on the part of Mr. Milton. He doesn't consider it possible for a mere female to aspire to his own realm, but he was heard to mutter that there were some interesting stanzas . . . some lyrical speeches, even." Cato grinned.

"When can we go?" Phoebe demanded, turning the book around in her hands with the same air of disbelieving wonder.

"Soon, since we must be established well before the babe is due."

"I must have Meg to midwife," Phoebe said, her attention at last distracted from the wonderful thing she held in her hands. Reluctantly she laid it down on a table. "I cannot have anyone else."

"Then if Meg is willing, she must come with us."

"And cat," Phoebe stated.

"Yes, indeed. And anyone else necessary to your comfort," he responded with quiet conviction.

"Don't you think I'm wonderfully round?" Phoebe said, giving him her profile. "See what a big bump. I wonder if it could be two boys. What do you think?" She raised her eyes to his face, feeling the connection between them as strong and powerful as any lodestone.

"I'll settle for one," Cato said, once again smoothing the tumbled hair from her forehead. "But if truth be told, my sweet, you are all and everything to me, and I would not lose you for an entire tribe of sons."

Phoebe came into his arms. "You won't," she promised. "I am made to give you sons, my lord." She leaned back against his encircling arm and smiled up at him with a mischievous glint in her eye. "As you are made to give them to me," she murmured, touching his mouth with a fingertip. "One cannot have sons without love . . . or loving," she added.

"Then I foresee a large nursery," Cato responded, but the fierce passion in his eye belied the light words. He leaned back against the table, moving his hands to her waist as he repeated softly, "You are all and everything to me, my love."

Phoebe leaned into him with her hard belly. The child kicked and she saw Cato's swift recognition as he felt the movement against his own body. Her bright gaze held his and read in the dark intensity of his look the knowledge that she had sought for so long.

His life, his soul, his heart belonged to her, as hers belonged to him.

About the Author

JANE FEATHER is the nationally bestselling, award-winning author of *The Emerald Swan*, *The Silver Rose*, *The Diamond Slipper*, *Vanity*, *Vice*, *Violet*, and many more historical romances. She was born in Cairo, Egypt, and grew up in the New Forest, in the south of England. She began her writing career after she and her family moved to Washington, D.C., in 1981. She now has over two million books in print.